CLOUD CUCKOO LAND

'Ambitious and complex ... [Doerr] weaves it all together beautifully'
Washington Post

'Packed with lush details and a gripping narrative'
Vanity Fair

'A fascinatingly ambitious tale that's worth the seven-year wait'
Stylist

'Doerr builds a community of readers and nature lovers that transcends the boundaries of time and space ... As the pieces of this magical literary puzzle snap together, a flicker of hope is sparked for our benighted world'
Kirkus

'A seamless tapestry ... Ultimately, Doerr seeks to remind us of the many ways we are tied to the natural world'
Los Angeles Times

'Anthony Doerr's talent for deftly weaving the crisscrossed stories of adults and children will tug at your heartstrings and remind you of the power of resilience and hope'
Country Living

'Sweeping and atmospheric'
Time

'A magical (and hopeful) tale of humanity'
People

'As intimate as a bedtime story, a love letter to libraries and bibliophiles'
Oprah Daily

CLOUD CUCKOO LAND

ALSO BY ANTHONY DOERR

All the Light We Cannot See
Memory Wall
Four Seasons in Rome
About Grace
The Shell Collector

CLOUD CUCKOO LAND

ANTHONY DOERR

4th ESTATE • London

4th Estate
An imprint of HarperCollins*Publishers*
1 London Bridge Street
London SE1 9GF

www.4thEstate.co.uk

HarperCollins*Publishers*
1st Floor, Watermarque Building, Ringsend Road
Dublin 4, Ireland

First published in Great Britain in 2021 by 4th Estate
First published in the United States by Scribner, an imprint of
Simon & Schuster, Inc., in 2021
This 4th Estate paperback edition published in 2022

1

A catalogue record for this book is
available from the British Library

ISBN 978-0-00-847867-4

Set in Minion Pro
Printed and bound in the UK using 100%
renewable electricity at CPI Group (UK) Ltd

For the librarians
then, now, and in the years to come

Chorus Leader: To work, men. How do you propose to name our
city?

Peisetairos: How about Sparta? That's a grand old name with a fine
pretentious ring.

Euelpides: Great Hercules, call my city Sparta? I wouldn't even
insult my mattress by giving it a name like Sparta.

Peisetairos: Well, what do you suggest instead?

Chorus Leader: Something big, smacking of the clouds. A pinch of
fluff and rare air, a swollen sound.

Peisetairos: I've got it! Listen—Cloud Cuckoo Land!

—Aristophanes, *The Birds*, 414 B.C.E.

CLOUD CUCKOO LAND

PROLOGUE

TO MY DEAREST NIECE WITH HOPE
THAT THIS BRINGS YOU HEALTH
AND LIGHT

THE ARGOS

MISSION YEAR 65

DAY 307 INSIDE VAULT ONE

Konstance

A fourteen-year-old girl sits cross-legged on the floor of a circular vault. A mass of curls haloes her head; her socks are full of holes. This is Konstance.

Behind her, inside a translucent cylinder that rises sixteen feet from floor to ceiling, hangs a machine composed of trillions of golden threads, none thicker than a human hair. Each filament twines around thousands of others in entanglements of astonishing intricacy. Occasionally a bundle somewhere along the surface of the machine pulses with light: now here, now there. This is Sybil.

Elsewhere in the room there's an inflatable cot, a recycling toilet, a food printer, eleven sacks of Nourish powder, and a multidirectional treadmill the size and shape of an automobile tire called a Perambulator. Light comes from a ring of diodes in the ceiling; there is no visible exit.

Arranged in a grid on the floor lie almost one hundred rectangular scraps Konstance has torn from empty Nourish powder sacks and written on with homemade ink. Some are dense with her handwriting; others accommodate a single word. One, for example, contains the twenty-four letters of the ancient Greek alphabet. Another reads:

> In the millennium leading up to 1453, the city of
> Constantinople was besieged twenty-three times, but no
> army ever breached its land walls.

She leans forward and lifts three scraps from the puzzle in front of her. The machine behind her flickers.

It is late, Konstance, and you have not eaten all day.

"I'm not hungry."

How about some nice risotto? Or roast lamb with mashed pota-
toes? There are still many combinations you have not tried.

"No thank you, Sybil." She looks down at the first scrap and reads:

> The lost Greek prose tale *Cloud Cuckoo Land*, by the
> writer Antonius Diogenes, relating a shepherd's journey
> to a utopian city in the sky, was probably written around
> the end of the first century C.E.

The second:

> We know from a ninth-century Byzantine summary of
> the book that it opened with a short prologue in which
> Diogenes addressed an ailing niece and declared that he
> had not invented the comical story which followed, but
> instead discovered it in a tomb in the ancient city of Tyre.

The third:

> The tomb, Diogenes wrote to his niece, was marked
> *Aethon: Lived 80 Years a Man, 1 Year a Donkey, 1 Year*
> *a Sea Bass, 1 Year a Crow*. Inside, Diogenes claimed to
> have discovered a wooden chest bearing the inscription,
> *Stranger, whoever you are, open this to learn what will*
> *amaze you*. When he opened the chest, he found twenty-
> four cypress-wood tablets upon which were written
> Aethon's story.

Konstance shuts her eyes, sees the writer descend into the dark
of the tombs. Sees him study the strange chest in the torchlight. The
diodes in the ceiling dim and the walls soften from white to amber
and Sybil says, *It will be NoLight soon, Konstance.*

She picks her way through the scraps on the floor and retrieves what's left of an empty sack from beneath her cot. Using her teeth and fingers, she tears away a blank rectangle. She places a little scoop of Nourish powder into the food printer, pushes buttons, and the device spits an ounce of dark liquid into its bowl. Then she takes a length of polyethylene tubing, the tip of which she has carved into a nib, dips her makeshift pen into the makeshift ink, leans over the blank scrap, and draws a cloud.

She dips again.

Atop the cloud she draws the towers of a city, then little dots of birds soaring around the turrets. The room darkens further. Sybil flickers. *Konstance, I must insist that you eat.*

"I'm not hungry, thank you, Sybil."

She picks up a rectangle inscribed with a date—*February 20, 2020*—and sets it beside another that reads, *Folio A*. Then she places her drawing of a cloud city on the left. For a breath, in the dying light, the three scraps seem almost to rise up and glow.

Konstance sits back on her heels. She has not left this room for almost a year.

ONE

STRANGER, WHOEVER YOU ARE,

OPEN THIS TO LEARN WHAT

WILL AMAZE YOU

Cloud Cuckoo Land by Antonius Diogenes, Folio A

The Diogenes codex measures 30 cm x 22 cm. Holed by worms and significantly effaced by mold, only twenty-four folios, labeled here from A to Ω, were recovered. All were damaged to some degree. The hand is tidy and leftward sloping. From the 2020 translation by Zeno Ninis.

. . . how long had those tablets moldered inside that chest, waiting for eyes to read them? While I'm sure you will doubt the truth of the outlandish events they relate, my dear niece, in my transcription, I do not leave out a word. Maybe in the old days men did walk the earth as beasts, and a city of birds floated in the heavens between the realms of men and gods. Or maybe, like all lunatics, the shepherd made his own truth, and so for him, true it was. But let us turn to his story now, and decide his sanity for ourselves.

THE LAKEPORT
PUBLIC LIBRARY

FEBRUARY 20, 2020

4:30 P.M.

Zeno

He escorts five fifth graders from the elementary school to the public library through curtains of falling snow. He is an octogenarian in a canvas coat; his boots are fastened with Velcro; cartoon penguins skate across his necktie. All day, joy has steadily inflated inside his chest, and now, this afternoon, at 4:30 p.m. on a Thursday in February, watching the children run ahead down the sidewalk— Alex Hess wearing his papier-mâché donkey head, Rachel Wilson carrying a plastic torch, Natalie Hernandez lugging a portable speaker—the feeling threatens to capsize him.

They pass the police station, the Parks Department, Eden's Gate Realty. The Lakeport Public Library is a high-gabled two-story gingerbread Victorian on the corner of Lake and Park that was donated to the town after the First World War. Its chimney leans; its gutters sag; packing tape holds together cracks in three of the four front-facing windows. Several inches of snow have already settled on the junipers flanking the walk and atop the book drop box on the corner, which has been painted to look like an owl.

The kids charge up the front walk, bound onto the porch, and high-five Sharif, the children's librarian, who has stepped outside to help Zeno navigate the stairs. Sharif has lime-green earbuds in his ears and craft glitter twinkles in the hair on his arms. His T-shirt says, *I LIKE BIG BOOKS AND I CANNOT LIE.*

Inside, Zeno wipes fog from his eyeglasses. Construction paper hearts are taped to the front of the welcome desk; a framed needlepoint on the wall behind it reads, *Questions Answered Here.*

On the computer table, on all three monitors, screen-saver spirals twist in synchrony. Between the audiobook shelf and two shabby armchairs, a radiator leak seeps through the ceiling tiles and drips into a seven-gallon trash can.

Plip. Plop. Plip.

The kids scatter snow everywhere as they stampede upstairs, heading for the Children's Section, and Zeno and Sharif share a smile as they listen to their footfalls reach the top of the staircase and stop.

"Whoa," says the voice of Olivia Ott.

"Holy magoley," says the voice of Christopher Dee.

Sharif takes Zeno's elbow as they ascend. The entrance to the second story has been blocked with a plywood wall spray-painted gold, and in its center, over a small arched door, Zeno has written:

Ὦ ξένε, ὅστις εἶ, ἄνοιξον, ἵνα μάθῃς ἃ θαυμάζεις

The fifth graders cluster against the plywood and snow melts on their jackets and backpacks and everyone looks at Zeno and Zeno waits for his breath to catch up with the rest of him.

"Does everyone remember what it says?"

"Of course," says Rachel.

"Duh," says Christopher.

On her tiptoes, Natalie runs a finger beneath each word. "*Stranger, whoever you are, open this to learn what will amaze you.*"

"Oh my flipping gosh," says Alex, his donkey head under his arm. "It's like we're about to walk *into* the book."

Sharif switches off the stairwell light and the children crowd around the little door in the red glow of the *EXIT* sign. "Ready?" calls Zeno, and from the other side of the plywood, Marian, the library director, calls, "Ready."

One by one the fifth graders pass through the little arched doorway into the Children's Section. The shelves, tables, and beanbags that normally fill the space have been pushed against the walls and in their places stand thirty folding chairs. Above the chairs, dozens of cardboard clouds, coated with glitter, hang from the rafters by threads. In front of the chairs is a small stage, and behind the stage, on a canvas sheet hung across the entire rear wall, Marian has painted a city in the clouds.

Golden towers, cut by hundreds of little windows and crowned by pennants, rise in clusters. Around their spires whirl dense flights of birds—little brown buntings and big silver eagles, birds with long curving tails and others with long curving bills, birds of the world and birds of the imagination. Marian has shut off the overhead lights, and in the beam of a single karaoke light on a stand, the clouds sparkle and the flocks shimmer and the towers seem illuminated from within.

"It's—" says Olivia.

"—better than I—" says Christopher.

"Cloud Cuckoo Land," whispers Rachel.

Natalie sets down her speaker and Alex leaps onstage and Marian calls, "Careful, some of the paint may still be wet."

Zeno lowers himself into a chair in the front row. Every time he blinks, a memory ripples across the undersides of his eyelids: his father pratfalls into a snowbank; a librarian slides open the drawer of a card catalogue; a man in a prison camp scratches Greek characters into the dust.

Sharif shows the kids the backstage area that he has created behind three bookshelves, packed with props and costumes, and Olivia pulls a latex cap over her hair to make herself look bald and Christopher drags a microwave box painted to look like a marble sarcophagus to the center of the stage and Alex reaches to touch a tower of the painted city and Natalie slides a laptop from her backpack.

Marian's phone buzzes. "Pizzas are ready," she says into Zeno's good ear. "I'll walk over and pick them up. Be back in a jiff."

"Mr. Ninis?" Rachel is tapping Zeno's shoulder. Her red hair is pulled back in braided pigtails and snow has melted to droplets on her shoulders and her eyes are wide and bright. "You built all this? For us?"

Seymour

One block away, inside a Pontiac Grand Am mantled in three inches of snow, a gray-eyed seventeen-year-old named Seymour Stuhlman drowses with a backpack in his lap. The backpack is an oversize dark green JanSport and contains two Presto pressure cookers, each of which is packed with roofing nails, ball bearings, an igniter, and nineteen ounces of a high explosive called Composition B. Twin wires run from the body of each cooker to the lid, where they plug into the circuit board of a cellular phone.

In a dream Seymour walks beneath trees toward a cluster of white tents, but every time he takes a step forward, the trail twists and the tents recede, and a terrible confusion presses down on him. He wakes with a start.

The dashboard clock says 4:42 p.m. How long did he sleep? Fifteen minutes. Twenty at most. Stupid. Careless. He has been in the car for more than four hours and his toes are numb and he has to pee.

With a sleeve he clears vapor from the inside of the windshield. He risks the wipers once and they brush a slab of snow off the glass. No cars parked in front of the library. No one on the sidewalk. The only car in the gravel parking lot to the west is Marian the Librarian's Subaru, humped with snow.

4:43 p.m.

Six inches before dark, says the radio, *twelve to fourteen overnight.*

Inhale for four, hold for four, exhale for four. Recall things you know. Owls have three eyelids. Their eyeballs are not spheres but elongated tubes. A group of owls is called a parliament.

All he needs to do is stroll in, hide the backpack in the southeast

16

corner of the library, as close as possible to the Eden's Gate Realty office, and stroll out. Drive north, wait until the library closes at 6 p.m., dial the numbers. Wait five rings.

Boom.

Easy.

At 4:51, a figure in a cherry-red parka exits the library, pulls up her hood, and pushes a snow shovel up and down the front walk. Marian.

Seymour shuts off the car radio and slips lower in his seat. In a memory he is seven or eight years old, in Adult Nonfiction, somewhere in the 598s, and Marian retrieves a field guide to owls from a high shelf. Her cheeks are a sandstorm of freckles; she smells like cinnamon gum; she sits beside him on a rolling stool. On the pages she shows him, owls stand outside burrows, owls sit on branches, owls soar over fields.

He pushes the memory aside. What does Bishop say? *A warrior, truly engaged, does not experience guilt, fear, or remorse. A warrior, truly engaged, becomes something more than human.*

Marian runs the shovel up the wheelchair ramp, scatters some salt, walks down Park Street, and is swallowed by the snow.

4:54.

All afternoon Seymour has waited for the library to be empty and now it is. He unzips the backpack, switches on the cell phones taped to the lids of the pressure cookers, removes a pair of rifle-range ear defenders, and rezips the backpack. In the right pocket of his windbreaker is a Beretta 92 semiautomatic pistol he found in his great-uncle's toolshed. In the left: a cell phone with three phone numbers written on the back.

Stroll in, hide the backpack, stroll out. Drive north, wait until the library closes, dial the top two numbers. Wait five rings. Boom.

4:55.

A plow scrapes through the intersection, lights flashing. A gray pickup passes, *King Construction* on the door. The *OPEN* sign glows in the library's first-floor window. Marian is probably running an errand; she won't be gone long.

Go. Get out of the car.

4:56.

Each crystal that strikes the windshield makes a barely audible tap, yet the sound seems to penetrate all the way to the roots of his molars. Tap tap tap tap tap tap tap tap tap. Owls have three eyelids. Their eyeballs are not spheres but elongated tubes. A group of owls is called a parliament.

He clamps the ear defenders over his ears. Pulls up his hood. Sets a hand on the door handle.

4:57.

A warrior, truly engaged, becomes something more than human.

He gets out of the car.

Zeno

Christopher arranges Styrofoam tombstones around the stage and angles the microwave-box-turned-sarcophagus so the audience can read its epitaph: *Aethon: Lived 80 Years a Man, 1 Year a Donkey, 1 Year a Sea Bass, 1 Year a Crow.* Rachel picks up her plastic torch and Olivia emerges from behind the bookshelves with a laurel wreath crammed over her latex cap and Alex laughs.

Zeno claps once. "A dress rehearsal is a practice we pretend is real, remember? Tomorrow night, your grandma in the audience might sneeze, or someone's baby might cry, or one of you might forget a line, but whatever happens, we'll keep the story going, right?"

"Right, Mr. Ninis."

"Places, please. Natalie, the music."

Natalie pokes her laptop and her speaker plays a spooky organ fugue. Behind the organ, gates creak, crows caw, owls hoot. Christopher unrolls a few yards of white satin across the front of the stage and kneels at one end, and Natalie kneels at the other, and they wave the satin up and down.

Rachel strides into the center of the stage in her rubber boots. "It's a foggy night on the island kingdom of Tyre"—she glances down at her script, then back up—"and the writer Antonius Diogenes is leaving the archives. Look, here he comes now, tired and troubled, fretting over his dying niece, but wait until I show him the strange thing I have discovered among the tombs." The satin billows, the organ plays, Rachel's torch flickers, and Olivia marches into the light.

Seymour

Snow crystals catch in his eyelashes and he blinks them away. The backpack on his shoulder is a boulder, a continent. The big yellow owl eyes painted on the book drop box seem to track him as he passes.

Hood up, ear defenders on, Seymour ascends the five granite steps to the library's porch. Taped to the inside of the glass on the entry door, in a child's handwriting, a sign reads:

TOMORROW
ONE NITE ONLY
CLOUD CUCKOO LAND

There's no one behind the welcome desk, no one at the chessboard. No one at the computer table, no one browsing magazines. The storm must be keeping everyone away.

The framed needlepoint behind the desk says, *Questions Answered Here.* The clock says one minute past five. On the computer monitors, three screen-saver spirals bore ever deeper.

Seymour walks to the southeast corner and kneels in the aisle between Languages and Linguistics. From a bottom shelf he removes *English Made Easy* and *501 English Verbs* and *Get Started in Dutch*, wedges the backpack into the dusty space behind, and replaces the books.

When he stands, purple streaks cascade down his vision. His heart thuds in his ears, his knees tremble, his bladder aches, he can't feel his feet, and he has tracked snow all the way down the row. But he has done it.

Now stroll out.

As he travels back through Nonfiction, everything seems to tilt uphill. His sneakers feel leaden, his muscles unwilling. Titles tumble past, *Lost Languages* and *Empires of the Word* and *7 Steps to Raising a Bilingual Child*; he makes it past Social Sciences, Religion, the dictionaries; he's reaching for the door when he feels a tap on his shoulder.

Don't. Don't stop. Don't turn around.

But he does. A slim man with green earbuds in his ears stands in front of the welcome desk. His eyebrows are great thatches of black and his eyes are curious and the visible part of his T-shirt says *I LIKE BIG* and in his arms he cradles Seymour's JanSport.

The man says something, but the earmuffs make him sound a thousand feet away, and Seymour's heart is a sheet of paper crumpling, uncrumpling, crumpling again. The backpack cannot be here. The backpack needs to stay hidden in the southeast corner, as close as possible to Eden's Gate Realty.

The man with the eyebrows glances down, into the backpack, the main compartment of which has become partially unzipped. When he looks back up, he's frowning.

A thousand tiny black spots open in Seymour's field of vision. A roar rises inside his ears. He sticks his right hand into the right pocket of his windbreaker and his finger finds the trigger of the pistol.

Zeno

Rachel pretends to strain as she lifts away the sarcophagus lid. Olivia reaches into the cardboard tomb and withdraws a smaller box tied shut with yarn.

Rachel says, "A chest?"

"There's an inscription on top."

"What does it say?"

"It reads, *Stranger, whoever you are, open this to learn what will amaze you.*"

"Think, Master Diogenes," says Rachel, "of the years this chest has survived inside this tomb. The centuries it has endured! Earthquakes, floods, fires, generations living and dying! And now you hold it in your hands!"

Christopher and Natalie, arms tiring, continue to wave the satin fog, and the organ music plays, and snow bats the windows, and the boiler in the basement groans like a stranded whale, and Rachel looks at Olivia and Olivia unravels the yarn. From inside she lifts an outdated encyclopedia that Sharif found in the basement and spray-painted gold.

"It's a book."

She blows pretend-dust off its cover and in the front row Zeno smiles.

"And does this book explain," Rachel says, "how someone could be a man for eighty years, a donkey for one, a sea bass for another, and a crow for a third?"

"Let's find out." Olivia opens the encyclopedia and sets it on a lectern up against the backdrop, and Natalie and Christopher drop the satin and Rachel clears the tombstones and Olivia clears the sarcophagus, and Alex Hess, four and a half feet tall, with a lion's mane of golden hair, carrying a shepherd's crook and wearing a beige bathrobe over his gym shorts, takes center stage.

Zeno leans forward in his chair. His aching hip, the tinnitus in his left ear, the eighty-six years he has lived on earth, the near-infinity of decisions that have led him to this moment—all of it fades. Alex stands alone in the karaoke light and looks out over the empty chairs as though he gazes not into the second story of a dilapidated public library in a little town in central Idaho but into the green hills surrounding the ancient kingdom of Tyre.

"I," he says in his high and gentle voice, "am Aethon, a simple shepherd from Arkadia, and the tale I have to tell is so ludicrous, so incredible, that you'll never believe a word of it—and yet, it's true. For I, the one they called birdbrain and nincompoop—yes, I, dull-witted muttonheaded lamebrained Aethon—once traveled all the way to the edge of the earth and beyond, to the glimmering gates of Cloud Cuckoo Land, where no one wants for anything and a book containing all knowledge—"

From downstairs comes the bang of what sounds to Zeno very much like a gunshot. Rachel drops a tombstone; Olivia flinches; Christopher ducks.

The music plays, the clouds twist on their threads, Natalie's hand hovers over her laptop, a second bang reverberates up through the floor, and fear, like a long dark finger, reaches across the room and touches Zeno where he sits.

In the spotlight, Alex bites his lower lip and glances at Zeno. One heartbeat. Two. Your grandma in the audience might sneeze. Someone's baby might cry. One of you might forget a line. Whatever happens, we'll keep the story going.

"But first," Alex continues, returning his gaze to the space above the empty chairs, "I should start at the beginning," and Natalie changes the music and Christopher changes the light from white to green and Rachel steps onstage carrying three cardboard sheep.

TWO

AETHON HAS A VISION

———————

Cloud Cuckoo Land by Antonius Diogenes, Folio β

Though the intended order of the twenty-four recovered folios has been debated, scholars are unanimous that the episode in which drunken Aethon sees actors performing Aristophanes's comedy The Birds *and mistakes Cloud Cuckoo Land for an actual place falls at the beginning of his journey. Translation by Zeno Ninis.*

. . . tired of being wet, of the mud, and of the forever bleating of the sheep, tired of being called a dull-witted muttonheaded lamebrain, I left my flock in the field and stumbled into town.

In the square, everyone was on their benches. In front of them, a crow, a jackdaw, and a hoopoe as big as a man were dancing, and I was afraid. But they proved to be mild-mannered birds, and two old fellows among them spoke of the wonders of a city they would build in the clouds between earth and heaven, far from the troubles of men and accessible only to those with wings, where no one ever suffered and everyone was wise. Into my mind leapt a vision of a palace of golden towers stacked on clouds, ringed by falcons, redshanks, quails, moorhens, and cuckoos, where rivers of broth gushed from spigots, and tortoises circulated with honeycakes balanced on their backs, and wine ran in channels down both sides of the streets.

Seeing all this with my own two eyes, I stood and said, "Why stay here when I could be there?" I let fall my wine jug and set straightaway on the road to Thessaly, a land, as everyone knows, notorious for sorcery, to see if I might find a witch who could transform me . . .

CONSTANTINOPLE

1439–1452

Anna

On the Fourth Hill of the city we call Constantinople, but which the inhabitants at the time simply called the City, across the street from the convent of Saint Theophano the Empress, in the once-great embroidery house of Nicholas Kalaphates, lives an orphan named Anna. She does not speak until she's three. Then it's all questions all the time.

"Why do we breathe, Maria?"

"Why don't horses have fingers?"

"If I eat a raven's egg will my hair turn black?"

"Does the moon fit inside the sun, Maria, or is it the other way around?"

The nuns at Saint Theophano call her Monkey because she's always climbing their fruit trees, and the Fourth Hill boys call her Mosquito because she won't leave them alone, and the Head Embroideress, Widow Theodora, says she ought to be called Hopeless because she's the only child she has ever known who can learn a stitch one hour and completely forget it the next.

Anna and her older sister, Maria, sleep in a one-window cell barely large enough for a horsehair pallet. Between them they own four copper coins, three ivory buttons, a patched wool blanket, and an icon of Saint Koralia that may or may not have belonged to their mother. Anna has never tasted sweet cream, never eaten an orange, and never set foot outside the city walls. Before she turns fourteen, every person she knows will be either enslaved or dead.

• • •

Dawn. Rain falls on the city. Twenty embroideresses climb the stairs to the workroom and find their benches and Widow Theodora moves from window to window opening shutters. She says, "Blessed One, protect us from idleness," and the needleworkers say, "For we have committed sins without number," and Widow Theodora unlocks the thread cabinet and weighs the gold and silver wire and the little boxes of seed pearls and records the weights on a wax tablet and as soon as the room is bright enough to tell a black thread from a white one, they begin.

The oldest, at seventy, is Thekla. The youngest, at seven, is Anna. She perches beside her sister and watches Maria unroll a half-completed priest's stole across the table. Down the borders, in neat roundels, vines twist around larks, peacocks, and doves. "Now that we've outlined John the Baptizer," Maria says, "we'll add his features." She threads a needle with matching strands of dyed cotton, fastens an embroidery frame to the center of the stole, and executes a hail of stitches. "We turn the needle and bring the point up through the center of the last stitch, splitting the fibers like so, see?"

Anna does not see. Who wants a life like this, bent all day over needle and thread, sewing saints and stars and griffins and grapevines into the vestments of hierarchs? Eudokia sings a hymn about the three holy children and Agata sings one about the trials of Job, and Widow Theodora steps through the workroom like a heron stalking minnows. Anna tries to follow Maria's needle—backstitch, chain stitch—but directly in front of their table a little brown stonechat alights on the sill, shakes water off its back, sings *wheet-chak-chak-chak*, and in an eye-blink Anna has daydreamed herself into the bird. She flutters off the sill, dodges raindrops, and rises south over the neighborhood, over the ruins of the basilica of Saint Polyeuktus. Gulls wheel around the dome of the Hagia Sophia like prayers gyring around the head of God, and wind rakes the broad strait of the Bosporus into whitecaps, and a merchant's galley rounds the promontory, its sails full of wind, but Anna flies higher still, until the city is a fretwork of rooftops and gardens far below, until she's in the clouds, until—

"Anna," hisses Maria. "Which floss here?"

From across the workroom, Widow Theodora's attention flickers to them.

"Crimson? Wrapped around wire?"

"No." Maria sighs. "Not crimson. And no wire."

All day she fetches thread, fetches linen, fetches water, fetches the needleworkers their midday meal of beans and oil. In the afternoon they hear the clatter of a donkey and the greeting of the porter and the tread of Master Kalaphates upon the stairs. Every woman sits a little straighter, sews a little faster. Anna crawls beneath the tables, collecting every scrap of thread she can find, whispering to herself, "I am small, I am invisible, he cannot see me."

With his overlong arms, wine-stained mouth, and bellicose hunch, Kalaphates looks as much like a vulture as any man she has seen. He emits little clucks of disapproval as he hobbles between the benches, eventually choosing a needleworker to stop behind, Eugenia today, and he pontificates about how slowly she works, how in his father's day an incompetent like her would never be allowed near a bale of silk, and do these women not understand that more provinces are lost to the Saracens every day, that the city is a last island of Christ in a sea of infidels, that if not for the defensive walls they'd all be for sale in a slave market in some godforsaken hinterland?

Kalaphates is working himself into a froth when the porter rings the bell to signal the arrival of a patron. He mops his forehead and settles his gilt cross over the placket of his shirt and flaps downstairs and everyone exhales. Eugenia sets down her scissors; Agata rubs her temples; Anna crawls out from beneath a bench. Maria keeps sewing.

Flies draw loops between the tables. From downstairs comes the laughter of men.

• • •

An hour before dark, Widow Theodora summons her. "Lord will-ing, child, it's not too late in the day for caper buds. They'll ease the pain in Agata's wrists and help Thekla's cough too. Look for ones just about to bloom. Be back before the vesper bell, cover your hair, and watch for rogues and wretches."

Anna can hardly keep her feet on the ground.

"And don't run. Your wombs will fall out."

She forces herself to go slowly down the steps, slowly through the courtyard, slowly past the watchman—then she flies. Through the gates of Saint Theophano, around the huge granite pieces of a fallen column, between two rows of monks plodding up the street in their black habits like flightless crows. Puddles glimmer in the lanes; three goats graze in the shell of a fallen chapel and raise their heads to her at the exact same instant.

Probably twenty thousand caper bushes grow closer to the house of Kalaphates, but Anna runs the full mile to the city walls. Here, in a nettle-choked orchard, at the base of the great inner wall, is a pos-tern, older than anyone's memory. She clambers over a pile of fallen brick, squeezes through a gap, and scales a winding staircase. Six turns to the top, through a gauntlet of cobwebs, and she enters a little archer's turret illuminated by two arrow slits on opposite sides. Rub-ble lies everywhere; sand sifts through cracks in the floor beneath her feet in audible streams; a frightened swallow wings away.

Breathless, she waits for her eyes to adjust. Centuries ago, someone—perhaps a lonely bowman, bored with his watch—made a fresco on the southern wall. Time and weather have flaked away much of the plaster, but the image remains clear.

At the left edge, a donkey with sad eyes stands on the shore of a sea. The water is blue and cut with geometric waves and at the right edge, afloat on a raft of clouds, higher than Anna can reach, shines a city of silver and bronze towers.

A half-dozen times she has stared at this painting, and each time something stirs inside her, some inarticulable sense of the pull of distant places, of the immensity of the world and her own smallness inside it. The style is entirely different from the work done by the needleworkers in Kalaphates's workshop, the perspective stranger, the colors more elemental. Who is the donkey and why do his eyes look so forlorn? And what is the city? Zion, paradise, the city of God? She strains on her tiptoes; between cracks in the plaster she can make out pillars, archways, windows, tiny doves flocking around towers.

In the orchards below, nightingales are beginning to call. The light ebbs and the floor creaks and the turret seems to tip closer toward oblivion, and Anna squeezes out the west-facing window onto the parapet where caper bushes in a line hold their leaves to the setting sun.

She collects buds, dropping them into her pocket as she goes. Still, the larger world pulls at her attention. Past the outer wall, past the algae-choked moat, it waits: olive groves, goat trails, the tiny figure of a driver leading two camels past a graveyard. The stones release the day's heat; the sun sinks out of sight. By the time the vesper bells are ringing, her pocket is only a quarter full. She will be late; Maria will be worried; Widow Theodora will be angry.

Anna slips back into the turret and pauses again beneath the painting. One more breath. In the twilight the waves seem to churn, the city to shimmer; the donkey paces the shore, desperate to cross the sea.

A WOODCUTTERS' VILLAGE IN THE RHODOPE MOUNTAINS OF BULGARIA

THOSE SAME YEARS

Omeir

Two hundred miles northwest of Constantinople, in a little wood-cutters' village beside a quick, violent river, a boy is born almost whole. He has wet eyes, pink cheeks, and plenty of spring in his legs. But on the left side of his mouth, a split divides his upper lip from his gum all the way to the base of his nose.

The midwife backs away. The child's mother slips a finger into his mouth: the gap extends deep into his palate. As though his maker grew impatient and quit work a moment too soon. The sweat on her body turns cold; dread eclipses joy. Pregnant four times and she has not yet lost a baby, even believed herself, perhaps, blessed in that way. And now this?

The infant shrieks; an icy rain batters the roof. She tries bracing him upright with her thighs while squeezing a breast with both hands, but she can't get his lips to form a seal. His mouth gulps; his throat trembles; he loses far more milk than he gets.

Amani, the eldest daughter, left hours ago to summon the men down from the trees; they'll be hurrying the team home by now. The two younger daughters glance from their mother to the newborn and back again as though trying to understand if such a face is permissible. The midwife sends one to the river for water and the other to bury the afterbirth and it's fully dark and the child is still howling when they hear the dogs, then the bells of Leaf and Needle, their oxen, as they stop outside the byre.

Grandfather and Amani come through the door aglitter in ice, their eyes wild. "He fell, the horse—" Amani says, but when she sees the baby's face, she stops. From behind her Grandfather says, "Your husband went ahead, but the horse must have slipped in the dark, and the river, and—"

Terror fills the cottage. The newborn wails; the midwife edges toward the door, a dark and primeval fear warping her expression.

The farrier's wife warned them that revenants had been making mischief on the mountain all winter, slipping through locked doors, sickening pregnant women and suffocating infants. The farrier's wife said they should leave a goat tied to a tree as an offering, and pour a pot of honey in a creek for good measure, but her husband said they could not spare the goat, and she did not want to give up the honey.

Pride.

Every time she shifts, a little stroke of lightning discharges in her abdomen. With every passing heartbeat, she can sense the midwife hurrying the story from house to house. A demon born. His father dead.

Grandfather takes the crying child and unwraps him on the floor and places a knuckle between his lips and the boy falls quiet. With his other hand he nudges apart the cleft in the infant's upper lip.

"Years ago, on the far side of the mountain, there was a man who had a split under his nose like this. A good horseman, once you forgot how ugly he was."

He hands him back and brings the goat and cow in from the weather, then goes back into the night to unyoke the oxen, and the eyes of the animals reflect the glow of the hearth, and the daughters crowd their mother.

"Is it a jinn?"

"A fiend?"

"How will it breathe?"

"How will it eat?"

"Will Grandfather put it on the mountain to die?"

The child blinks up at them with dark, memorizing eyes.

The sleet turns to snow and she sends a prayer through the roof that if her son has some role to play in this world could he please be spared. But in the last hours before dawn she wakes to find Grandfather standing over her. Shrouded in his oxhide cape with snow on his shoulders he looks like a phantom from a woodcutter's song, a monster accustomed to doing terrible things, and though she tells herself that by morning the boy will join her husband on thrones in a garden of bliss, where milk pours from stones and honey runs in streams and winter never comes, the feeling of handing him over is a feeling like handing over one of her lungs.

Cocks crow, wheel rims crunch snow, the cottage brightens, and horror strikes her anew. Her husband drowned, the horse with him. The girls wash and pray and milk Beauty the cow and bring fodder to Leaf and Needle and cut pine twigs for the goat to chew and morning turns to afternoon but still she cannot summon the energy to rise. Frost in the blood, frost in the mind. Her son crosses the river of death now. Or now. Or now.

Before dusk, the dogs growl. She rises and limps to the doorway. A gust of wind, high on the mountain, lifts a cloud of glitter from the trees. The pressure in her breasts nears intolerable.

For a long moment nothing else happens. Then Grandfather comes down the river road on the mare with something bundled across the saddle. The dogs explode; Grandfather dismounts; her arms reach to take what he carries even as her mind says she should not.

The child is alive. His lips are gray and his cheeks are ashen but not even his tiny fingers are blackened with frost.

"I took him to the high grove." Grandfather heaps wood onto the fire, blows the embers into flames; his hands tremble. "I set him down."

She sits as close to the fire as she dares and this time braces the infant's chin and jaw with her right hand, and with her left expresses jets of milk down the back of his throat. Milk leaks from the baby's nose and from the gap in his palate, but he swallows. The girls slip through the doorway, boiling with the mystery of it, and the flames rise, and Grandfather shivers. "I got back on the horse. He was so quiet. He just looked up into the trees. A little shape in the snow."

The child gasps, swallows again. The dogs whine outside the door. Grandfather looks at his shaking hands. How long before the rest of the village learns of this?

"I could not leave him."

Before midnight they are driven out with hayforks and torches. The child caused the death of his father, bewitched his grandfather into carrying him back from the trees. He harbors a demon inside, and the flaw in his face is proof.

They leave behind the byre and hayfield and root cellar and seven wicker beehives and the cottage that Grandfather's father built six decades before. Dawn finds them cold and frightened several miles upriver. Grandfather tramps beside the oxen through the slush, and the oxen pull the dray, atop which the girls clutch hens and earthenware. Beauty the cow trails behind, balking at every shadow, and in the rear the boy's mother rides the mare, the baby blinking up from his bundle, watching the sky.

By nightfall they are in a trackless ravine nine miles from the village. A creek winds between ice-capped boulders, and wayward clouds, as big as gods, drag through the crowns of the trees, whistling strangely, and spook the cattle. They camp beneath a limestone overhang inside which hominids painted cave bears and aurochs and flightless birds eons ago. The girls crowd their mother and Grandfather builds a fire and the goat whimpers and the dogs tremble and the baby's eyes catch the firelight.

"Omeir," says his mother. "We will call him Omeir. One who lives long."

Anna

She is eight and returning from the vintner's with three jugs of Kalaphates's dark, head-splitting wine, when she pauses to rest outside a rooming house. From a shuttered window she hears, in accented Greek:

> Meanwhile Ulysses at the palace waits,
> There stops, and anxious with his soul debates,
> Fix'd in amaze before the royal gates.
> The front appear'd with radiant splendors gay,
> Bright as the lamp of night, or orb of day,
> The walls were massy brass: the cornice high
> Blue metals crown'd in colors of the sky,
> Rich plates of gold the folding doors incase;
> The pillars silver, on a brazen base;
> Silver the lintels deep-projecting o'er,
> And gold the ringlets that command the door.
> Two rows of stately dogs, on either hand,
> In sculptured gold and labor'd silver stand
> These Vulcan form'd with art divine, to wait
> Immortal guardians at Alcinous's gate . . .

Anna forgets the handcart, the wine, the hour—everything. The accent is strange but the voice is deep and liquid, and the meter catches hold of her like a rider galloping past. Now come the voices of boys, repeating the verses, and the first voice resumes:

> Close to the gates a spacious garden lies,
> From storms defended and inclement skies.
> Four acres was the allotted space of ground,
> Fenced with a green enclosure all around.
> Tall thriving trees confess'd the fruitful mold:
> The reddening apple ripens here to gold.
> Here the blue fig with luscious juice o'erflows,
> With deeper red the full pomegranate glows;
> The branch here bends beneath the weighty pear,
> And verdant olives flourish round the year,
> The balmy spirit of the western gale
> Eternal breathes on fruits, unthought to fail:
> Each dropping pear a following pear supplies,
> On apples apples, figs on figs arise . . .

What palace is this, where the doors gleam with gold and the pillars are silver and the trees never stop fruiting? As though hypnotized, she advances to the rooming house wall and scales the gate and peers through the shutter. Inside, four boys in doublets sit around an old man with a goiter ballooning from his throat. The boys repeat the verses in a bloodless monotone, and the man manipulates what looks like leaves of parchment in his lap, and Anna leans as close as she dares.

She has seen books only twice before: a leather-bound Bible, winking with gems, conducted up the central aisle by elders at Saint Theophano; and a medical catalogue in the market that the herb seller snapped shut when Anna tried to peer inside. This one looks older and grimier: letters are packed onto its parchment like the tracks of a hundred shorebirds.

The tutor resumes the verse, in which a goddess disguises the traveler in mist so that he can sneak inside the shining palace, and Anna bumps the shutter, and the boys look up. In a heartbeat a wide-shouldered housekeeper is waving Anna back through the gate as though chasing a bird off fruit.

She retreats to her handcart and pushes it against the wall, but wagons rumble past and raindrops begin to strike the rooftops, and she can no longer hear. Who is Ulysses and who is the goddess who cloaks him in magical mist? Is the kingdom of brave Alcinous the same one that's painted inside the archer's turret? The gate opens and the boys hurry past, scowling at her as they skirt puddles. Not long after, the old teacher comes out leaning on a stick and she blocks his path.

"Your song. Was it inside those pages?"

The tutor can hardly turn his head; it is as though a gourd has been implanted beneath his chin.

"Will you teach me? I know some signs already; I know the one that's like two pillars with a rod between, and the one that's like a gallows, and the one that's like an ox head upside down."

With an index finger in the mud at his feet she draws an *A*. The man raises his gaze to the rain. Where his eyeballs should be white, they are yellow.

"Girls don't go to tutors. And you don't have any money."

She lifts a jug from the cart. "I have wine."

He comes alert. One arm reaches for the jug.

"First," she says, "a lesson."

"You'll never learn it."

She does not budge. The old teacher groans. With the end of his stick in the wet dirt he writes:

Ὠκεανός

"*Ōkeanos*, Ocean, eldest son of Sky and Earth." He draws a circle around it and pokes its center. "Here the known." Then he pokes the outside. "Here the unknown. Now the wine."

She passes it to him and he drinks with both hands. She crouches on her heels. Ὠκεανός. Seven marks in the mud. And yet they contain the lonely traveler and the brass-walled palace with its golden watchdogs and the goddess with her mist?

• • •

For returning late, Widow Theodora beats the sole of Anna's left foot with the bastinado. For returning with one of the jugs half-empty, she beats the right. Ten strokes on each. Anna hardly cries. Half the night she inscribes letters across the surfaces of her mind, and all the following day, as she hobbles up and down the stairs, as she carries water, as she fetches eels for Chryse the cook, she sees the island kingdom of Alcinous, wreathed with clouds and blessed by the west wind, teeming with apples, pears, and olives, blue figs and red pomegranates, boys of gold on shining pedestals with burning torches in their hands.

Two weeks later she is coming back from the market, going out of her way to pass the rooming house, when she spies the goitrous tutor sitting in the sun like a potted plant. She sets down her basket of onions and with a finger in the dust writes,

Ὠκεανός

Around it she draws a circle.

"Eldest son of Sky and Earth. Here the known. Here the unknown."

The man strains his head to one side and swivels his gaze to her, as though seeing her for the first time, and the wet in his eyes catches the light.

His name is Licinius. Before his misfortunes, he says, he served as tutor to a wealthy family in a city to the west, and he owned six books and an iron box to hold them: two lives of the saints, a book of orations by Horace, a testament of the miracles of Saint Elisabeth, a primer on Greek grammar, and Homer's *Odyssey*. But then the Saracens captured his town, and he fled to the capital with nothing, and thank the angels in heaven for the city walls, whose foundation stones were laid by the Mother of God Herself.

From inside his coat Licinius produces three mottled bundles of parchment. Ulysses, he says, was once a general in the greatest army ever assembled, whose legions came from Hyrmine, from Dulichium, from the walled cities of Cnossos and Gortyn, from the farthest reaches of the sea, and they crossed the ocean in a thousand black ships to sack the fabled city of Troy, and from each ship spilled a thousand warriors, as innumerable, Licinius says, as the leaves in the trees, or as the flies that swarm over buckets of warm milk in shepherds' stalls. For ten years they sieged Troy, and after they finally took it, the weary legions sailed home, and all arrived safely except Ulysses. The entire song of his journey home, Licinius explains, consisted of twenty-four books, one for each letter of the alphabet, and took several days to recite, but all Licinius has left are these three quires, each containing a half-dozen pages, relating the sections where Ulysses leaves the cave of Calypso, is broken by a storm, and washes up naked on the island of Scheria, home of brave Alcinous, lord of the Phaeacians.

There was a time, he continues, when every child in the empire knew every player in Ulysses's story. But long before Anna was born, Latin Crusaders from the west burned the city, killing thousands, and stripped away much of its wealth. Then plagues halved the population, and halved it again, and the empress at the time had to sell her crown to Venice to pay her garrisons, and the current emperor wears a crown made of glass and can hardly afford the plates he eats from, and now the city limps through a long twilight, waiting for the second coming of Christ, and no one has time for the old stories anymore.

Anna's attention remains fixed on the leaves in front of her. So many words! It would take seven lifetimes to learn them all.

Every time Chryse the cook sends Anna to the market, the girl finds a reason to visit Licinius. She brings him crusts of bread, a smoked fish, half a hoop of thrushes; twice she manages to steal a jug of Kalaphates's wine.

In return, he teaches. A is ἄλφα is alpha; B is βῆτα is beta; Ω is ὦ μέγα is omega. As she sweeps the workroom floor, as she lugs another roll of fabric or another bucket of charcoal, as she sits in the workroom beside Maria, fingers numb, breath pluming over the silk, she practices her letters on the thousand blank pages of her mind. Each sign signifies a sound, and to link sounds is to form words, and to link words is to construct worlds. Weary Ulysses sets forth upon his raft from the cave of Calypso; the spray of the ocean wets his face; the shadow of the sea-god, kelp streaming from his blue hair, flashes beneath the surface.

"You fill your head with useless things," whispers Maria. But knotted chain stitches, cable chain stitches, petal chain stitches— Anna will never learn it. Her most consistent skill with a needle seems to be accidentally pricking a fingertip and bleeding onto the cloth. Her sister says she should imagine the holy men who will perform the divine mysteries wearing the vestments she helped decorate, but Anna's mind is constantly veering off to islands on the fringe of the sea where sweet springs run and goddesses streak down from the clouds upon a beam of light.

"Saints help me," says Widow Theodora, "will you ever learn?" Anna is old enough to understand the precariousness of their situation: she and Maria have no family, no money; they belong to no one and maintain their place in the house of Kalaphates only because of Maria's talent with a needle. The best life either of them can hope for is to sit at one of these tables embroidering crosses and angels and foliage into copes and chalice veils and chasubles from dawn until dusk until their spines are humped and their eyes give out.

Monkey. Mosquito. Hopeless. Yet she cannot stop.

"One word at a time."

Once more she studies the muddle of marks on the parchment.

πολλῶν δ᾽ ἀνθρώπων ἴδεν ἄστεα καὶ νόον ἔγνω

"I can't."

"You can."

Ἄστεα are cities; νόον is mind; ἔγνω is learned.

She says, "He saw the cities of many men and learned their ways."

The mass on Licinius's neck quakes as his mouth curls into a smile.

"That's it. That's it exactly."

Almost overnight, the streets glow with meaning. She reads inscriptions on coins, on cornerstones and tombstones, on lead seals and buttress piers and marble plaques embedded into the defensive walls—each twisting lane of the city a great battered manuscript in its own right.

Words glow on the chipped rim of a plate Chryse the cook keeps beside the hearth: *Zoe the Most Pious*. Over the entrance to a little forgotten chapel: *Peace be to thee whoever enterest with gentle heart*. Her favorite is chiseled into the lintel above the watchman's door beside the Saint Theophano gate and takes her half of a Sunday to puzzle out:

> *Stop, ye thieves, robbers, murderers, horsemen and soldiers,*
> *in all humility, for we have tasted the rosy blood of Jesus.*

The last time Anna sees Licinius, a cold wind is blowing, and his complexion is the color of a rainstorm. His eyes leak, the bread she has brought him remains untouched, and the goiter on his neck seems a more sinister creature entirely, inflamed and florid, as though tonight it will devour his face at last.

Today, he says, they will work on μῦθος, *mýthos*, which means a conversation or something said, but also a tale or a story, a legend from the time of the old gods, and he is explaining how it's a delicate, mutable word, that it can suggest something false and true at the same time, when his attention frays.

The wind lifts one of the quires from his fingers and Anna chases it down and brushes it off and returns it to his lap. Licinius rests his eyelids a long time. "Repository," he finally says, "you know this word? A resting place. A text—a book—is a resting place for the memories of people who have lived before. A way for the memory to stay fixed after the soul has traveled on."

His eyes open very widely then, as though he peers into a great darkness.

"But books, like people, die. They die in fires or floods or in the mouths of worms or at the whims of tyrants. If they are not safe-guarded, they go out of the world. And when a book goes out of the world, the memory dies a second death."

He winces, and his breathing comes slow and ragged. Leaves scrape down the lane and bright clouds stream above the rooftops and several packhorses pass, their riders bundled against the cold, and she shivers. Should she fetch the housekeeper? The bloodletter?

Licinius's arm rises; in the claw of his hand are the three battered quires.

"No, Teacher," says Anna. "Those are yours."

But he pushes them into her hands. She glances down the lane: the rooming house, the wall, the rattling trees. She says a prayer and tucks the leaves of parchment inside her dress.

Omeir

The oldest daughter dies of worms, fever takes the middle one, but the boy grows. At three, he can hold himself upright on the sledge as Leaf and Needle clear, then plow a hayfield. At four, he can fill the kettle at the creek and lug it through the boulders to the one-room stone house Grandfather has built. Twice his mother pays the farrier's wife to travel nine miles upriver from the village to stitch together the gap in the boy's lip with a needle and twine and twice the project fails. The cleft, which extends through his upper mandible into his nose, does not close. But though his inner ears sometimes burn, and his jaw sometimes aches, and broth regularly escapes his mouth and dribbles onto his clothes, he is sturdy, quiet, and never ill.

His earliest memories are three:

1. Standing in the creek between Leaf and Needle as they drink, watching drops fall from their huge round chins and catch the light.

2. His sister Nida grimacing over him as she prepares to jab a stick into his upper lip.

3. Grandfather unbuckling the bright pink body of a pheasant from its feathers, as though undressing it, and spitting it over the hearth.

The few children he manages to meet make him play the monsters when they act out the adventures of Bulukiya and ask him if it's true that his face can cause mares to miscarry and wrens to drop from the sky mid-flight. But they also show him how to find quail eggs and which holes in the river hold the largest trout, and they point out a half-hollow black yew growing from a karst bluff high above the ravine which they say harbors evil spirits and can never die.

Many of the woodcutters and their wives won't come near him. More than once a merchant, traveling along the river, spurs his horse up through the trees rather than risk passing Omeir on the road. If a stranger has ever looked at him without fear or suspicion, he cannot remember it.

His favorite days come in summer, when the trees dance in the wind and the moss glows emerald green on the boulders and swallows chase each other through the ravine. Nida sings as she takes the goats to graze, and their mother lies on a stone above the creek, her mouth open, as though inhaling the light, and Grandfather takes his nets and pots of birdlime and leads Omeir high on the mountain to trap birds.

Though his spine is hunched and he's missing two toes, Grandfather moves quickly, and Omeir has to take two strides for every one of his. As they climb, Grandfather proselytizes about the superiority of oxen: how they're calmer and steadier than horses, how they don't need oats, how their dung doesn't scorch barley like horse dung does, how they can be eaten when they're old, how they mourn each other when one dies, how if they lie on their left side it means fair weather is coming but if they lie on their right it means rain. The beech forests give way to pine, and the pines give way to gentians and primrose, and by evening Grandfather has caught a dozen grouse with his snares.

At dusk they stop for the night in a boulder-strewn glade, and the dogs swirl around them, testing the air for wolves, and Omeir starts a fire and Grandfather dresses and roasts four of the grouse, and the ridges of the mountains below fall away in a cascade of deepening blues. They eat, the fire burns to embers, Grandfather drinks from a gourd of plum brandy, and with the purest happiness the boy waits, feels it trundling toward him like a lamplit cart, full of cakes and honey, about to round a bend in the road.

"Have I ever told you," Grandfather will say, "about the time I climbed on the back of a giant beetle and visited the moon?"

Or: "Have I ever told you about my journey to the island made of rubies?"

He tells Omeir about a glass city, far to the north, where everyone speaks in whispers so they don't break anything; he says he once turned into an earthworm and tunneled his way to the underworld. The tales always end with Grandfather's safe return to the mountain, having survived another terrifying and wondrous adventure, and the embers burn to ash, and Grandfather begins to snore, and Omeir looks up into the night and wonders what worlds drift among the faraway lights of the stars.

When he asks his mother if beetles can fly all the way to the moon or if Grandfather ever spent an entire year inside a sea monster, she smiles and says that as far as she knows, Grandfather has never left the mountain, and now could Omeir please concentrate on helping her render the beeswax?

Still the boy often wanders alone up the trail to the half-hollow yew on the bluff, climbs into its branches, peers down at the river where it disappears around the bend, and imagines the adventures that might lie beyond: forests where trees walk; deserts where men with horse-bodies run as fast as swifts fly; a realm at the top of the earth where the seasons end and sea dragons swim between mountains of ice and a race of blue giants lives forever.

He's ten when Beauty, the family's swaybacked old cow, goes into labor for the final time. For most of an afternoon, two little hooves, dripping with mucus and steaming in the cold, stick out beneath the raised arch of her tail, and Beauty grazes as though nothing in the world has ever changed, and eventually she gives a spasm and a mud-brown calf slides the rest of the way out.

Omeir takes a step forward but Grandfather tugs him back, a question on his face. Beauty licks her calf, its little body rocking beneath the weight of her tongue, and Grandfather whispers a prayer, and a gentle rain falls, and the calf does not stand.

Then he sees what Grandfather saw. A second pair of hooves has appeared beneath Beauty's tail. A snout with a little pink tongue stuck between its jaws soon joins the hooves, followed by a single eye, and finally a second calf—this one gray—is born.

Twins. Both males.

Almost as soon as the gray calf touches the ground, he stands and begins to nurse. The brown one keeps its chin planted. "Something wrong with that one," whispers Grandfather, and curses the breeder who charged him for the services of his bull, but Omeir decides the calf is just taking his time. Trying to solve this strange new mix of gravity and bones.

The gray one suckles on its bent-twig legs; the firstborn remains wet and folded in the ferns. Grandfather sighs, but just then the first calf stands, and takes a step toward them as if to say, "Which of you doubted me?" and Grandfather and Omeir laugh, and the family's wealth is doubled.

Grandfather warns that it will be a challenge for Beauty to produce enough milk for two, but she proves up to the task, grazing nonstop in the lengthening daylight, and the calves grow swiftly and without pause. They name the brown one Tree, the gray one Moonlight.

Tree likes to keep his hooves clean, bleats if his mother dips out of sight, and will stand patiently for half a morning while Omeir picks burrs out of his coat. Moonlight, on the other hand, is always trotting somewhere to investigate moths, toadstools, or stumps; he nibbles ropes and chains, eats sawdust, wades in mud up to his knees, gets a horn stuck in a dead tree and bawls for help. What the two calves share from the start is an adoration for the boy, who feeds them by hand, who strokes their muzzles, who often wakes in the byre outside the cottage with their big, warm bodies wrapped around his. They play hide-and-seek and race-to-Beauty with him; they stomp through spring puddles together amid glittering clouds of flies; they seem to accept Omeir as a brother.

Before their first full moon, Grandfather fits them to a yoke. Omeir loads the dray with stones, picks up a goad stick, and begins to work them. Step in, step out, *gee* means right, *haw* means left, *whoa* means stop—at first the calves pay the boy no mind. Tree refuses to back up and be hitched to the load; Moonlight tries to dislodge the yoke on every available tree. The dray tips, the stones roll off, the calves go to their knees, bawling, and old Leaf and Needle look up from their grazing and shake their grizzled heads as though amused.

"What creature," laughs Nida, "would trust someone with a face like that?"

"Show them that you can meet all of their needs," says Grandfather.

Omeir starts again. He taps them on the knees with the goad; he clucks and whistles; he whispers in their ears. That summer the mountain turns as green as anyone can remember, and the grasses shoot high, and his mother's hives grow heavy with honey, and for the first time since being driven from the village, the family has plenty to eat.

The horns of Moonlight and Tree spread, their rumps thicken, their chests broaden; by the time they are castrated, they are bigger than their mother, and make Leaf and Needle look slight. Grandfather says that if you listen hard enough you can hear them growing, and although Omeir is pretty sure that Grandfather is joking, when no one is looking, he presses an ear to Moonlight's huge rib and shuts his eyes.

In autumn word filters up the valley that the ghazi sultan, Murad the Second, Guardian of the World, has died, and his eighteen-year-old son (bless and keep him forever) has ascended to power. The traders who buy the family's honey declare that the young sultan is ushering in a new golden age, and in the little ravine it seems true. The road stays clear and dry, and Grandfather and Omeir thresh their largest-ever crop of barley and Nida and her mother toss the seeds into baskets, and a bright clean wind carries away the chaff.

One evening, just before the first snows, a traveler on a glossy mare rides up the track from the river, his servant riding a nag behind. Grandfather sends Omeir and Nida into the byre and they watch through the gaps in the logs. The traveler wears a grass-green turban and a riding coat lined with lambswool and his beard looks so tidy that Nida speculates whether sprites must trim it at night. Grandfather shows them the ancient pictographs in the cavern, and afterward the traveler walks through the little homestead admiring the terraces and crops, and when he sees the two young bullocks his jaw drops.

"Do you feed them the blood of giants?"

"It is a rare blessing," Grandfather says, "to have twins to share the same yoke."

At dusk Mother, her face covered, feeds the guests butter and greens, then the last melons of the year, drizzled with honey, and Nida and Omeir creep around the back of the cottage to listen, and Omeir prays they'll overhear tales of cities the visitor has seen in the lands beyond the mountain. The traveler asks how they have come to live all alone in a ravine miles from the nearest village and Grandfather says they live here by choice, that the sultan, may he have peace always, has provided everything the family needs. The traveler murmurs something they cannot hear, and his servant stands and clears his throat and says, "Master, they're concealing a demon in the byre."

Silence. Grandfather sets a log on the fire.

"A ghoul or a mage, pretending to be a child."

"I apologize," says the traveler. "My attendant has forgotten his place."

"He has the face of a hare and when he speaks the beasts do his bidding. This is why they live alone, miles from the nearest village. Why their bullocks are so large."

The traveler rises. "Is this true?"

"He is only a boy," says Grandfather, though Omeir hears a sharpness creep into his voice.

The servant edges toward the door. "You think that now," he says, "but his true nature will show in time."

Anna

Outside the city walls, old resentments stir. The sultan of the Saracens has died, the women in the workroom say, and the new one, barely out of boyhood, spends every waking breath planning to capture the city. He studies war, they say, like the monks study scripture. Already his masons are constructing brick-baking kilns a half day's walk up the Bosporus Strait, where, at the narrowest point of the channel, he intends to construct a monstrous fortress that will be able to capture any ship which tries to deliver armor, wheat, or wine to the city from outposts along the Black Sea.

As winter comes on, Master Kalaphates sees portents in every shadow. A pitcher cracks, a bucket leaks, a flame goes out: the new sultan is to blame. Kalaphates complains that orders have stopped arriving from the provinces; the needleworkers do not work hard enough, or they have used too much gold thread, or they have not used enough, or their faith is impure. Agata is too slow, Thekla is too old, Elyse's designs are too dull. A single fruit fly in his wine can send a black thread twisting through his mood that lingers for days.

Widow Theodora says that Kalaphates needs compassion, that the remedy to every woe is prayer, and after dark Maria kneels in their cell in front of the icon of Saint Koralia, her lips moving silently, sending devotions up past the beams. Only in the latest hours, long after Compline, does Anna risk crawling out from beside her sleeping sister, taking a tallow candle from the scullery cupboard, and removing Licinius's quires from their hiding place beneath the pallet.

If Maria notices, she says nothing, and Anna is too absorbed to care. The candlelight flickers over the leaves: words become verses, verses become color and light, and lonesome Ulysses drifts into the storm. His raft capsizes; he gulps saltwater; the sea-god roars past on his sea-green steeds. But there, in the turquoise distance, past the booming surf, glimmers the magical kingdom of Scheria.

It's like constructing a little paradise, bronze and shining, aglow with fruit and wine, inside their cell. Light a taper and read a line and the west wind begins to blow: a handmaid brings one ewer of water and another of wine, Ulysses sits at the royal table to eat, and the king's favorite bard begins to sing.

One winter night Anna is coming down the corridor from the scullery when she hears, through the half-open door of their cell, the voice of Kalaphates.

"What witchcraft is this?"

Ice tumbles through every channel in her body. She creeps to the threshold: Maria is kneeling on the floor, bleeding from her mouth, and Kalaphates is stooped under the low beams, the sockets of his eyes lost in shadow. In the long fingers of his left hand are the leaves of Licinius's quires.

"It was you? All along? Who helps yourself to candles? Who causes our misfortunes?" Anna wants to open her mouth, to confess, to wipe all this away, but the fear is such that it has stopped her ability to speak. Maria is praying without moving her mouth, praying behind her eyes, retreating to some private sanctum at the very center of her mind, and her silence only infuriates Kalaphates more.

"They said, 'Only a saint would bring children who are not his own into the house of his father. Who knows what evils they'll bring?' But did I listen? I said, 'They're only candles. Whoever steals them only does so to illuminate her nightly devotions.' And now I see this? This poison? This sorcery?" He seizes Maria by the hair and something inside Anna screams. Tell him. You are the thief; you are the misfortune. Speak. But Kalaphates is dragging Maria by her hair into the hall, right past Anna as though she were not there, and

Maria is trying to scramble to her feet and Kalaphates is twice their size and Anna's courage is nowhere.

He hauls Maria past the cells where other needleworkers crouch behind their doors. For a moment she manages to get a foot under her, but stumbles, a great fistful of hair tearing away in Kalaphates's fist, and the side of Maria's head strikes the stone step leading to the scullery.

The sound is that of a hammer passing through a gourd. Chryse the cook watches from her wash pot; Anna stays in the corridor; Maria bleeds on the floor. No one speaks as Kalaphates grabs her dress and drags her limp body to the hearth and pitches the pieces of parchment into the fire and holds Maria's unseeing eyes to the flames while the quires burn to ash one two three.

Omeir

Twelve-year-old Omeir is sitting on a limb of the half-hollow yew, gazing down at the bend in the river, when Grandfather's smallest dog appears on the road below, running hard for home with its tail between its legs. Moonlight and Tree—resplendent two-year-olds, heavy through the neck and shoulders, cords of muscle rippling across their chests—lift their chins in tandem from where they're grazing among the last of the foxgloves. They sniff the air, then raise their eyes to him as though awaiting instructions.

The light turns platinum. The evening becomes so still that he can hear the dog pounding toward the cottage, and his mother say, "What's got into that one?"

Four breaths five breaths six. Down on the road, heralds with mud-spattered banners come round the bend three abreast. Behind them come more riders, some carrying what look like trumpets, others with spears, a dozen at first, and behind them still more: donkeys pulling carts, soldiers on foot—more men and beasts than he has ever seen.

He leaps down from the tree and sprints the trail home, Moonlight and Tree trotting behind, still chewing their cud, pushing through the tall grass like the prows of ships. By the time Omeir reaches the byre, Grandfather is already limping out of the house, looking grim, as though some unpleasant reckoning he has delayed a long time has finally arrived. He hushes the dogs and sends Nida into the root cellar and stands with his spine rigid and his fists at his sides as the first riders come up the track from the river.

They ride tasseled ponies with painted bridles, and wear red bonnets, and carry halberds or iron rods or have compound bows strapped to their saddles. Little powder horns dangle from their necks; their hair is strangely cut. A royal emissary with boots to his knees and his sleeves bunched in ruffles at his wrists dismounts and picks his way between the boulders and stops with his right hand resting on the pommel of his dagger.

"Blessings on you," says Grandfather.

"And on you."

A first few raindrops fall. Farther back along the procession Omeir can see more men turn off the road, a few with skinny mountain oxen hitched to carts, others on foot with quivers of arrows on their backs or swords in their hands. The gaze of one of the heralds stops on Omeir's face and his expression twists in disgust, and the boy gets a flicker of what he and this place together must present: a rude dwelling carved into a hollow, home to a gash-faced boy, hermitage of the deformed.

"Night is coming," says Grandfather, "and rain with it. You must be weary. We have fodder for your animals, and shelter for you to rest out of the weather. Come, you are welcome here." He ushers a half-dozen heralds into the cottage with stiff formality and perhaps does so genuinely, though Omeir can see that he brings his hands to his beard over and over, plucking at hairs with a thumb and forefinger as he does whenever he is anxious.

By nightfall rain falls steadily, and forty men and almost as many animals shelter beneath the limestone overhang around a pair of smoky fires. Omeir brings firewood, then oats and hay, hurrying about in the wet dark between the byre and cavern, keeping his face hidden inside his hood. Every time he stops, tendrils of panic clutch his windpipe: Why are they here and where are they going and when will they leave? What his mother and sister distribute among the men—the honey and preserves, the pickled cabbage, the trout, the sheep's cheese, the dried venison—comprises almost all of their food for the winter.

Many of the men wear cloaks and mantles like woodsmen but others dress in coats of fox fur or camel hide and at least one wears ermine with the teeth still attached. Most have daggers attached to girdles around their waists and everyone speaks of the spoils they are going to win from a great city to the south.

It's after midnight when Omeir finds Grandfather at his bench in the byre working in the light of the oil lamp—an expense Omeir has rarely seen him be so reckless with before—fashioning what looks like a new yoke beam. The sultan, may God keep him, Grandfather says, is gathering men and animals in his capital at Edirne. He requires fighters, herders, cooks, farriers, smiths, porters. Everyone who goes will be rewarded, in this life or in the next.

Little whorls of sawdust rise through the lamplight and melt back into shadow. "When they saw your oxen," he says, "their heads nearly fell off their necks," but he does not laugh and does not look up from his work.

Omeir sits against the wall. A particular combination of dung and smoke and straw and wood shavings make a familiar warm tang in the back of his throat and he bites back tears. Each morning comes along and you assume it will be similar enough to the previous one—that you will be safe, that your family will be alive, that you will be together, that life will remain mostly as it was. Then a moment arrives and everything changes.

Images of the city to the south speed through his consciousness, but he has seen neither a city nor a likeness of one and does not know what to imagine, and his visions intermingle with Grandfather's tales of talking foxes and moon-spiders, of towers made of glass and bridges between stars.

Out in the night a donkey brays. Omeir says, "They're going to take Tree and Moonlight."

"And a teamster to drive them." Grandfather lifts the beam, studies it, sets it back down. "The animals won't follow anyone else."

An axe falls through Omeir. All his life he has wondered what adventures await beyond the shadow of the mountain, but now he wants only to crouch here against the logs of the byre until the seasons have turned and these visitors are a memory and everything has gone back to the way it was.

"I won't go."

"Once," Grandfather says, finally looking at him, "the people of an entire city, from beggars to butchers to the king, refused the call of God and were turned to stone. A whole city, every woman, every child, turned to stone. There is no refusing this."

Against the opposite wall, Tree and Moonlight sleep, their ribs rising and falling in tandem.

"You will gain glory," Grandfather says, "and then you will return."

THREE

THE CRONE'S WARNING

Cloud Cuckoo Land by Antonius Diogenes, Folio Γ

. . . as I left the village gate, I passed a foul crone seated on a stump. She said, "Where to, dimwit? It'll soon be dark and this is no time to be on the road." I said, "All my life I have longed to see more, to fill my eyes with new things, to get beyond this muddy, stinking town, these forever bleating sheep. I am traveling to Thessaly, the Land of Magic, to find a sorcerer who will transform me into a bird, a fierce eagle or a bright strong owl."

She laughed and said, "Aethon, you dolt, everyone knows you cannot count to five yet you believe you can count the waves of the sea. You will never fill your eyes with anything more than your own nose."

"Quiet, hag," I said, "for I have heard of a city in the clouds where thrushes fly into your mouth fully cooked and wine runs in channels in the streets and warm breezes always blow. As soon as I become a brave eagle or a bright strong owl, it is there I intend to fly."

"You always think the barley is more plentiful in another man's field, but it's no better out there, Aethon, I promise you," said the crone. "Bandits wait around every corner to bash your skull and ghouls lurk in the shadows, hoping to drink your blood. Here you have cheese, wine, your friends, and your flock. What you already have is better than what you so desperately seek."

But as a bee hurries to and fro, visiting every flower without pause, so my restlessness . . .

LAKEPORT, IDAHO

1941–1950

Zeno

He's seven when his father is hired to install a new sash saw at the Ansley Tie and Lumber Company. It's January when they arrive and the only snowflakes Zeno has seen before are asbestos fibers a druggist in Northern California sprinkled over a Christmas display. The boy touches the frozen surface of a puddle on the train platform, then yanks back his fingers as though burned. Papa pratfalls into a snowbank, smears snow over his coat, and staggers toward him. "Looks! Looks at mes! I big snowman!"

Zeno bursts into tears.

The company leases them an under-insulated two-room cabin a mile from town on the edge of a blinding-white plain that the boy will only later understand is the icebound lake. At dusk Papa opens a two-pound can of Armour & Company spaghetti and meatballs and sets it on the wood stove. The bottom half burns Zeno's tongue; the top half is slush.

"This be terrific homes, yes, lamb chop? Tremendous, yes?"

All night cold seeps through a thousand chinks in the walls and the boy cannot get warm. Navigating the canyon of shoveled snow to the privy an hour before dawn is a horror so grim he prays he will never have to pee again. At daybreak Papa walks him a mile to the general store and spends four dollars on eight pairs of Utah Woolen Mills socks, the best they have, and they sit on the floor beside the register and Papa pulls two socks over each of Zeno's feet.

"You remembers, boy," he says, "there is no bad weathers, only bad clothes."

Half the children in the schoolhouse are Finns and the rest are Swedes, but Zeno has dark eyelashes, nut-brown irises, skin the color of milk tea, and that name. Olivepicker, Sheep Shagger, Wop, Zero— even when he doesn't understand the epithets, their message is plain: don't stink, don't breathe, stop shivering, stop being different. After school he wanders the labyrinth of plowed snow that is downtown Lakeport, five feet atop the service station, six feet on the roof of M. S. Morris Hardware. Inside Cadwell's Confectionery, older boys chew bubble gum and talk of lamebrains and fairies and flivvers; they go quiet when they notice him; they say, "Don't be a spook."

Eight days after arriving in Lakeport, he pauses in front of a light-blue two-story Victorian on the corner of Lake and Park. Icicles fang the eaves; the sign, half-submerged in snow, says:

Public Library

He's peering through a window when the door opens and two identical-looking women in high-collared housedresses beckon him in.

"Why," says one, "you don't look warm at all."

"Where," says the other, "is your mother?"

Goose-necked lamps illuminate reading tables; a needlepoint on the wall says *Questions Answered Here.*

"Mama," he says, "lives in the Celestial City now. Where everyone is untouched by sorrow and no one wants for anything."

The librarians incline their heads at the exact same angle. One seats him in a spindle-back chair in front of the fireplace while the other disappears into the shelves and returns with a clothbound book in a lemon-yellow jacket.

"Ah," says the first sister, "fine choice," and they sit on either side of him and the one who fetched the book says, "On a day like this, when it's chilly and damp, and you can't get warm, sometimes all you need are the Greeks"—she shows him a page, dense with verse—"to fly you all the way around the world to somewhere hot and stony and bright."

The fire flickers, and the brass pulls on the card catalogue drawers glimmer, and Zeno tucks his hands beneath his thighs as the second sister begins to read. In the story a lonely sailor, the loneliest man in the world, rides a raft for eighteen days before he is caught in a terrible storm. His raft is smashed, and he washes naked onto the rocks of an island. But a goddess named Athena disguises herself as a little girl carrying a pitcher of water and escorts him into an enchanted city.

The chief with wonder sees the extended streets, she reads,

> The spreading harbors, and the riding fleets;
> He next their princes' lofty domes admires,
> In separate islands, crown'd with rising spires;
> And deep entrenchments, and high walls of stone,
> That gird the city like a marble zone.

Zeno sits rapt. He hears the waves crash on the rocks, smells the salt of the sea, sees the lofty domes shine in the sun. Is the island of the Phaeacians the same thing as the Celestial City and did his mother also have to float alone beneath the stars for eighteen days to get there?

The goddess tells the lonely sailor not to be afraid, that it is better to be brave in all things, and he enters a palace that gleams like the rays of moonlight, and the king and queen give him honey-hearted wine, and seat him in a silver chair, and ask him to tell the stories of his travails, and Zeno is eager to hear more, but the heat of the fire and the smell of old paper and the cadence of the librarian's voice join together to cast a spell over him, and he falls asleep.

Papa promises insulation, indoor plumbing, and a brand-new electric Thermador space heater ordered direct from Montgomery Ward but most nights he comes home from the mill too tired to unlace his boots. He sets a can of beef and noodles on the stove, smokes a cigarette, and falls asleep at the kitchen table, a puddle of snowmelt around his feet, as though he thaws a little in his sleep before heading back out the door at dawn to turn solid once more.

Every day after school Zeno stops at the library, and the librarians—both named Miss Cunningham—read him the rest of *The Odyssey*, then *The Golden Fleece and the Heroes Who Lived Before Achilles*, touring him through Ogygia and Erytheia, Hesperia and Hyperborea, places the sisters call mythical lands, which means that they aren't real places, that Zeno can travel to them only in his imagination, though at other times the librarians say that the old myths can be more true than truths, so maybe they are real places after all? The days lengthen and the library roof drips and the big ponderosas standing over the cabin unload snow with great whumps that sound to the boy like Hermes plunging in his golden sandals down from Olympus on another errand from the gods.

In April Papa brings home a piebald collie from the mill yard, and though she smells like a swamp and regularly defecates behind the stove, when she climbs onto Zeno's blanket at night and presses her body against his, letting off periodic sighs of great contentment, his eyes water with happiness. He names her Athena, and every afternoon when he leaves school, the dog is there, wagging her tail in the slush outside the split-rail fence, and the two of them walk to the library, and the Cunningham sisters let Athena sleep on the rug in front of the fireplace while they read to Zeno about Hector and Cassandra and the hundred children of King Priam, and May becomes June, and the lake turns sapphire blue, and saws echo through the forests, and log decks as big as cities rise beside the mills, and Papa buys Zeno a pair of overalls three sizes too big with a lightning bolt sewn on the pocket.

In July he is passing a house on the corner of Mission and Forest with a brick chimney, a second story, and a light-blue 1933 Buick

Model 57 in the driveway, when a woman steps out of the front door and beckons him to the porch.

"I won't bite," she says. "But leave the dog."

Inside, mulberry curtains block the light. Her name, she says, is Mrs. Boydstun, and her husband died in a mill accident a few years earlier. She has yellow hair, blue eyes, and moles on her throat that look like beetles paralyzed mid-crawl. On a platter in the dining room stands a pyramid of star-shaped cookies, their backs glistening with icing.

"Go ahead." She lights a cigarette. On the wall behind her a foot-tall Jesus glowers down from his cross. "I'll just throw them away."

Zeno takes one: sugar, butter, delicious.

On shelves running round the circumference of the room stand hundreds of pink-cheeked porcelain children in red caps and red dresses, some in clogs and some with pitchforks and some kissing and some peering into wishing wells.

"I've seen you," she says. "Wandering around town. Talking with those witches at the library."

He does not know how to answer and the ceramic children make him uneasy and his mouth is full besides.

"Have another."

The second is even better than the first. Who would bake a plate of cookies only to throw them away?

"Your father is the new one, isn't he? At the mill? With the shoulders."

He manages a nod. Jesus stares down unblinking. Mrs. Boydstun takes a long inhalation of smoke. Her manner is casual but her attention is ferocious and he thinks of Argus Panoptes, the watchman of Hera, who had eyeballs all over his head and even on the tips of his fingers, so many eyes that when he closed fifty of them to sleep he held fifty more open to keep watch.

He takes a third cookie.

"And your mother? Is she in the picture?"

Zeno shakes his head, and suddenly it feels airless in the house, and the cookies are turning to clay in his gut, and Athena whines on the porch, and waves of guilt and confusion break over Zeno with such force that he backs away from the table and hurries outside without saying thanks.

The following weekend he and Papa attend a Sunday service with Mrs. Boydstun where a pastor with wet underarms warns that dark forces are gathering. Afterward the three of them walk back to Mrs. Boydstun's house, and she pours something called Old Forester into matching blue tumblers, and Papa switches on her Zenith tabletop wireless, sending big band music through the dark, heavy rooms, and Mrs. Boydstun laughs a big tooth-filled laugh and touches Papa's forearm with her fingernails. Zeno is hoping she will put out another plate of cookies when Papa says, "You plays outside now, boy."

He and Athena walk the block to the lake and he builds a miniature kingdom of the Phaeacians in the sand, replete with high walls and twig orchards and a fleet of pine cone ships, and Athena fetches sticks from up and down the beach and carries them to Zeno so he can throw them into the water. Two months ago he would have been ecstatic to spend time in a real house with a real fireplace and a Buick Model 57 in the driveway, but right now all he wants to do is walk home to the little cabin with Papa so they can heat canned noodles on the stove.

Athena keeps bringing him larger and larger sticks until she is dragging whole uprooted saplings through the sand, and the sunlight glitters on the lake and the great ponderosas quake and shimmy and send needles down onto his kingdom, and Zeno shuts his eyes and feels himself grow very small, small enough to enter the royal palace at the center of his sand island, where attendants dress him in a warm gown and lead him down torchlit corridors, and everyone is overjoyed to welcome him, and in the throne room he joins Ulysses and his mother and handsome, mighty Alcinous and they pour libations to Zeus the Thunderlord, who guides wanderers on their way.

Eventually he shuffles back to Mrs. Boydstun's and calls for Papa, and Papa calls from the back room, "Three minutes more, lamb chops!" and Zeno and Athena sit on the porch in a halo of mosquitoes.

September closes around August like the pincers of a claw, and in October snow dusts the shoulders of the mountains, and they spend every Sunday with Mrs. Boydstun, and plenty of evenings in between, and by November Papa still has not installed an indoor toilet, and there is no brand-new electric Thermador heater ordered direct from Montgomery Ward. On the first Sunday in December they walk back from church to Mrs. Boydstun's house and Papa switches on her wireless and the broadcaster says that 353 Japanese airplanes have bombed an American naval base somewhere called Oahu.

In the kitchen Mrs. Boydstun drops a bag of flour. Zeno says, "What's 'all auxiliary personnel'?" No one answers. Athena barks on the porch and the broadcaster speculates that thousands of sailors may be dead and a vein throbs visibly on the left side of Papa's forehead.

Outside, along Mission Street, the snowbanks are already as tall as Zeno. Athena digs a tunnel in the snow and no cars come by and no airplanes pass overhead and no children come out of the other houses. The whole world seems to have been struck silent. When, hours later, he comes back inside, his father is walking laps around the radio, cracking the knuckles of his right hand with the fingers of his left, and Mrs. Boydstun is standing at the window with a glass of Old Forester, and no one has cleaned up the flour.

On the wireless a woman says, "Good evening, ladies and gentlemen," and clears her throat. "I am speaking to you tonight at a very serious moment in our history."

Papa holds up a finger. "It is wife of president."

Athena whines at the door.

"For months now," says the president's wife, "the knowledge that something of this kind might happen has been hanging over our heads and yet it seemed impossible to believe."

Athena barks. Mrs. Boydstun says, "Can you please shut that beast up?"

Zeno says, "Can we go home now, Papa?"

"Whatever is asked of us," the president's wife continues, "I am sure we can accomplish it."

Papa shakes his head. "These boys have their faces blown off at breakfasts. They burns alives."

Athena barks again and Mrs. Boydstun clenches her forehead with trembling hands and the hundreds of porcelain children on their shelves—holding hands, jumping rope, carrying pails—seem suddenly charged with a terrible power.

"Now," says the radio, "we will go back to the program we had arranged for the night."

Papa says, "We will shows these Jap fuck-fuckers. Boys oh boys we will shows them."

Five days later he and four other men from the sawmill ride to Boise to have their teeth counted and their chests measured. And on the day after Christmas Papa is on his way to something called boot camp somewhere called Massachusetts and Zeno is living with Mrs. Boydstun.

LAKEPORT, IDAHO

2002–2011

Seymour

As a newborn, he screeches, howls, bawls. As a toddler, he will eat only circles: Cheerios, freezer waffles, and plain M&M's from a 1.69-ounce package. No Fun Size, no Sharing Size, God help Bunny if she offers him Peanut. She can touch his arms and legs but not his feet or hands. Never his ears. Shampooing is a nightmare. Haircuts = impossible.

Home is a weekly motel in Lewiston called the Golden Oak; she pays for her one room by cleaning the other sixteen. Boyfriends roll through like storms: there's Jed, there's Mike Gawtry, there's a guy Bunny calls Turkey Leg. Lighters flick; ice machines grumble; logging trucks rattle the windows. On the worst nights they sleep in the Pontiac.

At three, Seymour decides he cannot abide the tags on any of his underwear, nor the rustling certain breakfast cereals make against the interiors of their plastic bags. At four, he shrieks if the straw in a juice box rubs the wrong way against the foil it has been struck through. If she sneezes too loudly, he trembles for half an hour. Men say, "What's wrong with him?" They say, "Can't you shut him up?"

He's six when Bunny learns that her great-uncle Pawpaw, a man she has not seen in twenty years, has died and left her his manufactured double-wide in Lakeport. She closes her flip phone, drops her rubber gloves in the tub of Room 14, abandons her cleaning cart in the half-open doorway, loads the Grand Am with the toaster oven, the Magnavox DVD all-in-one, and two trash bags of clothes, and drives Seymour three hours south without stopping once.

The house sits on an acre of weeds a mile from town at the dead end of a gravel road called Arcady Lane. One window is shattered, the siding has *I DONT CALL 911* spray-painted on it, and the roof curls upward at one end as though a giant has tried to peel it off. As soon as the lawyer drives away, Bunny kneels in the driveway and sobs with a persistence that frightens them both.

Pine forest wraps the acre on three sides. Thousands of white butterflies drift between the heads of the thistles in the yard. Seymour sits beside her.

"Oh, Possum." Bunny wipes her eyes. "It's just been a long fucking time."

The trees rising above the back of the property shimmer; the butterflies float.

"Since what, Mom?"

"Since hope."

A strand of spiderweb, sailing through the air, catches the light. "Yeah," he says. "It's been a long fucking time since hope." And is startled when his mother bursts into laughter.

Bunny nails plywood over the broken window and wipes rodent turds out of the kitchen cabinets and drags Pawpaw's chipmunk-chewed mattress to the road and finances two new ones at nineteen-percent-no-money-down. At the thrift store she finds an orange love seat and douses it with half a can of Glade Hawaiian Breeze before she and Seymour drag it inside. At sunset they sit side by side on the front step and eat two waffles each. An osprey passes high above, heading for the lake. A doe and two fawns materialize beside the toolshed and twitch their ears. The sky turns purple.

"*Seed's a-growing*," sings Bunny, "*and the meadow's a-blooming, and the wood's a-coming into leaf now . . .*"

Seymour shuts his eyes. The breeze feels as soft as the blue blankets at the Golden Oak, maybe softer, and the thistles are pumping off a smell like warm Christmas trees, and through the wall directly behind them is his very own room with stains on the ceiling that look like clouds or cougars or maybe sea sponges, and his mother sounds so happy that when she gets to the part in her song about the ewe bleating, and the bullock prancing, and the billy goat farting, he can't keep himself from laughing.

First grade at Lakeport Elementary = twenty-six six-year-olds in a twenty-four-by-forty-foot portable presided over by a seasoned ironist named Mrs. Onegin. The navy-blue desk she assigns to Seymour is hateful: its frame is warped and its bolts are rusted and its feet make squeaks against the floor that feel like needles perforating the backs of his eyeballs.

Mrs. Onegin says, "Seymour, do you see any other children sitting on the floor?"

She says, "Seymour, are you waiting for a specially engraved invitation?"

She says, "Seymour, if you don't sit—"

On the principal's desk, a mug says, *SMILING IS MY FAVORITE*. Cartoon roadrunners jog across his belt. Bunny is wearing her brand-new Wagon Wheel Custodial Services polo, cost to be deducted from her first paycheck. She says, "He's pretty sensitive," and Principal Jenkins says, "Is there a father figure?" and glances for a third time at her breasts, and later, in the car, Bunny pulls onto the shoulder of Mission Street and dry-swallows three Excedrin.

"Possum, are you listening? Touch your ears if you're listening."

Four trucks whizz past: two blue, two black. He touches his ears.

"What are we?"

"A team."

"And what does a team do?"

"Helps each other."

A red car passes. Then a white truck.

"Can you look at me?"

He looks. The magnetized name-tag clipped to her shirt says, *HOUSEKEEPING ATTENDANT BUNNY*. Her name is smaller than her job. Two more trucks rock the Grand Am as they pass but he cannot hear what color they are.

"I can't leave work in the middle of a shift because you don't like your desk. They'll fire me. And I can't get fired. I need you to try. Will you try?"

He tries. When Carmen Hormaechea touches him with her poison ivy arm, he tries not to scream. When Tony Molinari's Aerobie hits him in the side of the head, he tries not to cry. But nine days into September, a wildfire in the Seven Devils chokes the whole valley with smoke, and Mrs. Onegin says the air quality is too low for outside recess, and they'll need to keep the windows closed because of Rodrigo's asthma, and within minutes the portable reeks like Pawpaw's microwave when Bunny defrosts a freezer fajita.

Seymour makes it through Group Math, through Lunch, through Fluency Tubs. But by Reflection Time, his endurance is fracturing. Mrs. Onegin sends everyone to their desks to color their North Americas, and Seymour tries to draw faint green circles in the Gulf of Mexico, tries to move only his hand and wrist, not shifting so the desk frame doesn't go *screek screek*, not breathing so he doesn't smell any smells, but sweat is trickling down his ribs, and Wesley Ohman keeps opening and closing the Velcro on his left shoe, and Tony Molinari's lips are going *poppoppop*, and Mrs. Onegin is writing a huge, terrible A-M-E-R-I-C- on the whiteboard, the marker tip rasping and squeaking, the classroom clock tickticticking, and all these sounds race into his head like hornets into a nest.

The roar: all his life it has rumbled in the distance. Now it rises. It obliterates the mountains, the lake, downtown Lakeport; it smashes across the school parking lot, tossing cars everywhere; it growls outside the portable and rattles the door. Black pinholes open in his vision. He clamps his hands over his ears but the roar eats the light.

Miss Slattery the school counselor says it could be sensory processing disorder or attention deficit disorder or hyperactivity disorder or some combination thereof. The boy is too young for her to know for sure. And she's not a diagnostician. But his screaming frightened the other children and Principal Jenkins has suspended Seymour for Friday and Bunny should make an appointment with an occupational therapist as soon as possible.

Bunny pinches the bridge of her nose. "Is that, like, included?"

Manager Steve at the Wagon Wheel says, you bet, Bunny, bring your kid to work, so long as you want to get fired, so on Friday morning she plucks the knobs off the stove burners, sets a box of Cheerios on the counter, and puts the *Starboy* DVD on repeat.

"Possum?"

On the Magnavox Starboy drops from the night in his bright-shining suit.

"Touch your ears if you're listening."

Starboy finds a family of armadillos trapped in a net. Seymour touches his ears.

"When the microwave timer says zero zero zero, I'll be home to check on you. All right?"

Starboy needs help. Time to call Trustyfriend.

"You'll sit tight?"

He nods; the Pontiac rattles down Arcady Lane. Trustyfriend the Owl soars out of the cartoon night. Starboy lights the way while Trustyfriend tears through the net with his bill. The armadillos squirm free; Trustyfriend announces that friends who help friends are the best friends of all. Then something that sounds like a giant scorpion starts scratching on the roof of the double-wide.

Seymour listens in his room. He listens at the front door. At the sliding door off the kitchen. The sound goes: *tap scratch scratch*.

On the Magnavox a big yellow sun is coming up. Time for Trustyfriend to fly back to his roost. Time for Starboy to fly back to the Firmament. *Best friends best friends*, Starboy sings,

> *We're never apart,*
> *I'm in the sky,*
> *And you're in my heart.*

When Seymour opens the sliding door, a magpie sails off the roof and lands on an egg-shaped boulder in the backyard. It dips its tail and calls *wock wock wock*.

A bird. Not a scorpion at all.

An overnight storm has cleared the smoke and the morning is bright. The thistles nod their purple crowns and tiny insects sail everywhere. The thousands of pines stacked against the back of the property, rising toward a ridge, seem to breathe as they sway. In out in out. It's nineteen paces through waist-high weeds to the egg-shaped boulder and by the time Seymour climbs on top, the magpie has flapped to a branch at the edge of the forest. Splotches of lichen—pink, olive, flame orange—decorate the boulder. It's amazing out here. Big. Alive. Ongoing.

Twenty paces past the boulder, Seymour reaches a single strand of barbed wire sagging between posts. Behind him is the sliding door, the kitchen, Pawpaw's microwave; ahead are three thousand acres of forest owned by a family in Texas no one in Lakeport has ever met.

Wock wock-a-wock, calls the magpie.

It's easy to duck under the wire.

Beneath the trees, the light changes entirely: another world. Pennants of lichen sway from branches; snippets of sky glow overhead. Here's an ant mound half as tall as he is; here's a granite rib the size of a minivan; here's a sheet of bark that fits around his midsection like the chest plate of Starboy's armor.

Halfway up the hill behind the house, Seymour comes to a clearing ringed by Douglas firs with a big dead ponderosa in the center like the many-fingered arm of a skeleton-giant thrust up from the underworld. Parachuting through the air around him, blown out of the firs, are hundreds of pine needles bundled in twos. He catches one, imagines it as a little man with a truncated torso and long slender legs. The NeedleMan ventures across the clearing on his pointy feet.

At the foot of the dead tree, Seymour constructs a house for the NeedleMan from bark and twigs. He is installing a lichen mattress inside when a ghost shrieks ten feet above his head.

Ee-ee? Ee-ee-eet?

Every hair on Seymour's arms stands up straight. The owl is so well camouflaged that it vocalizes three more times before the boy sets eyes on it, and when he does he gasps.

It blinks three times, four. In the shadow against the bark, with its eyelids closed, the owl vanishes. Then the eyes open again and the creature rematerializes.

It is the size of Tony Molinari. Its eyes are the color of tennis balls. It is looking right at him.

From his spot at the base of the big dead tree, Seymour gazes up and the owl gazes down and the forest breathes and something happens: the unease mumbling at the margins of his every waking moment—the roar—falls quiet.

There is magic in this place, the owl seems to say. *You just have to sit and breathe and wait and it will find you.*

He sits and breathes and waits and the Earth travels another thousand kilometers along its orbit. Lifelong knots deep inside the boy loosen.

When Bunny finds him there's bark in her hair and snot on her Wagon Wheel polo and she yanks him to his feet and Seymour could not say if a minute or a month or a decade has passed. The owl vanishes like smoke. He twists to see where it might have gone, but it's nowhere, sucked deeper into the woods, and Bunny is touching his hair, she's sobbing, "—about to call the cops, why didn't you stay put?—" she's swearing, pulling him home through the trees, ripping her jeans on the barbed wire; the microwave timer in the kitchen is going *boopboopboopboop*, Bunny is talking on her phone, she's getting fired by Manager Steve, she's throwing her phone at the love seat, she's squeezing Seymour's shoulders so he can't squirm away, she's saying, "I thought we were doing this together," she's saying, "I thought we were a team."

• • •

After bedtime he crawls to his window, slides it open, thrusts his head into the dark. The night exudes a wild, oniony smell. Something barks, something goes *chee chee chee*. The forest is right there, just past the barbed wire.

"Trustyfriend," he says. "I name you Trustyfriend."

Zeno

Downstairs adults clomp through Mrs. Boydstun's living room in their heavy shoes. Five Playwood Plastic soldiers climb out of their tin box. Soldier 401 creeps toward the headboard with his rifle; 410 drags his anti-tank gun over a furrow of quilt; 413 gets too close to the radiator and his face melts.

Pastor White labors up the stairs with a plate of ham and crackers and sits on the little brass bed breathing hard. He picks up Soldier 404, the one with the rifle held over his head, and says he's not supposed to tell Zeno this, but he heard that on the day Zeno's Papa died, he sent four Japs to hell all by himself.

At the bottom of the stairwell someone says, "Guadalcanal, now, that's where?" and someone else says, "It's all the same to me," and snowflakes float past the bedroom window. For a split second Zeno's mother sails down from the sky in a golden boat and while everyone watches, stupefied, he and Athena climb aboard and she sails them to the Celestial City, where a turquoise sea breaks against black cliffs and lemons, warm with sunlight, hang from every tree.

Then he's back on the brass bed and Pastor White is frog-walking Soldier 404 around the bedspread, reeking of hair tonic, and Papa is never coming back.

"Bona fide honest-to-God hero," the pastor says. "What your daddy was."

Later Zeno sneaks down the staircase with the plate and slips out the back door. Athena limps out of the junipers, stiff with cold, and he feeds her the ham and crackers and she gives him a look of pure gratitude.

The snow falls in big conglomerated flakes. A voice inside his head whispers, You are alone and it's probably your fault, and the daylight wanes. In something like a trance he leaves Mrs. Boydstun's yard and walks Mission Street to the intersection with Lake Street and clambers over the plowed berm and punches through the drifts, snow gushing into his funeral shoes, until he reaches the lake's edge.

It's the tail end of March and out in the center of the lake, a half mile away, the first dark patches of melt have begun to show. The ponderosas along the shore to his left form a vast, flickering wall.

As Zeno steps onto the ice, the snowpack gets thinner, freeze-dried and blown flat by wind. With each step away from shore, his sense of the great dark basin of water beneath his shoes deepens. Thirty paces, forty. When he turns, he cannot see the mills or town or even the trees along the shore. His own tracks are being erased by wind and snow; he is suspended in a universe of white.

Six paces farther. Seven eight stop.

Nothingness in every direction: an all-white jigsaw puzzle with the pieces thrown into the air. He feels himself teetering at the edge of something. Behind is Lakeport: the drafty schoolhouse, the slushy streets, the library, Mrs. Boydstun with her kerosene breath and her ceramic children. Back there he is Olivepicker, Sheep Shagger, Zero: an undersized orphan with foreigner's blood and a weirdo name. Ahead is what?

An almost subsonic crack, muffled by the snow, rifles out into the white. Flickering behind the flakes does he see the royal house of the Phaeacians? The bronze walls and silver pillars, the vineyards and pear orchards and springs? He tries to get his eyes to work, but somehow their seeing-power has been reversed; it is as though they look inward, into a white, swirling cavity inside his head. *Whatever is asked of us*, said the president's wife, *I am sure we can accomplish it*. But what is he being asked and how is he supposed to accomplish it without Papa?

Just a little farther. He slides one shoe another half pace forward and a second crack croaks through the lake ice, seeming to begin in the center of the lake and pass directly between his legs before shooting toward town. Then he feels a tug at the back of his trousers, as though he has reached the end of a tether and now a cord is pulling him home, and he turns and Athena has a hold of his belt in her teeth.

Only now does fear fill his body, a thousand snakes slithering beneath his skin. He stumbles, holds his breath, tries to make himself as light as possible, as the collie leads him, track by track, back across the ice to town. He reaches shore, staggers through the drifts, and crosses Lake Street. Heartbeats gallop through his ears. He shivers at the end of the lane and Athena licks his hand and inside the lit windows of Mrs. Boydstun's house adults stand in the living room, their mouths moving like the mouths of nutcracker dolls.

Teenagers from church shovel the walk. The butcher gives them ends and bones for free. The Cunningham sisters move him to the Greek comedies, aiming for lighter fare, a playwright called Aristophanes who, they say, invented some of the best worlds of all. They read *The Clouds*, then *Assemblywomen*, then *The Birds*, about two old guys, sick of earthly corruption, who go to live with the birds in a city in the sky only to find that their troubles follow them there, and Athena drowses in front of the dictionary stand. In the evenings Mrs. Boydstun drinks Old Forester and chain-smokes Camels and they play cribbage, working the pegs around the board. Zeno sits upright with his cards neatly fanned in one hand, thinking, I'm still in this world, but there's another one, right out there.

Fourth grade, fifth grade, the end of the war. Vacationers trickle up from lower elevations to sail across the lake in boats that seem to Zeno full of happy families: moms, dads, kids. The city puts Papa's name on a downtown memorial and someone hands Zeno a flag and someone else says heroes this, heroes that, and afterward, at supper,

Pastor White sits at the head of Mrs. Boydstun's table and waves a turkey leg.

"Alma, Alma, what do you call a queer boxer?"

Mrs. Boydstun stops mid-chew, parsley flecking her teeth.

"Fruit punch!"

She cackles; Pastor White grins into the mouth of his drink. On the shelves around them two hundred plump porcelain children watch Zeno with wide-open eyes.

He's twelve when the Cunningham twins call him to the circulation desk and hand across a book: *The Mermen of Atlantis*, eighty-eight four-color pages. "Ordered this with you in mind," the first sister says and the skin around her eyes crinkles, and the second sister stamps the due date in the back and Zeno carries the book home and sits on the little brass bed. On page one a princess is abducted off a beach by strange men in bronze armor. When she wakes, she finds herself imprisoned in an underwater city beneath a great glass dome. Under their bronze armor the men of the city are web-toed creatures in golden armbands with pointy ears and gill slits on their throats, and they have thick triceps and powerful legs and bulges at the intersections of their thighs that start a buzzing in Zeno's gut.

The strange, beautiful men breathe underwater; they are deeply industrious; their city sports delicate towers made of crystal and high-arched bridges and long lustrous submarines. Bubbles rise past shafts of golden, watery light. By page ten, a war has begun between the underwater men and the clumsy above-water men, who have come to reclaim their princess, and the above-water men fight with harpoons and muskets while the underwater men fight with tridents, and their muscles are long and fine, and Zeno, heat spreading through his body, cannot keep his eyes off the little red slashes of gill slits in their throats and their long, muscular limbs. In the final pages the battle increases in ferocity, and just as cracks appear in the dome over the city, endangering everyone, the book says, *To Be Continued*.

For three days he keeps *The Mermen of Atlantis* in a drawer, where it glows like something dangerous, pulsing in his mind even when he is at school: radioactive, illegal. Only when he's sure Mrs. Boydstun is asleep and the house is utterly quiet does he risk further study: the angry sailors beat against the protective dome with their harpoons; the elegant underwater warriors swim about in their burgundy robes with their tridents and ropy thighs. In dreams they tap at his bedroom window, but when he opens his mouth to speak, water rushes in, and he wakes with a feeling like he has fallen through the lake ice.

Ordered this with you in mind.

On the fourth night, hands shaking, Zeno carries *The Mermen of Atlantis* down the creaking stairs, past the mulberry curtains and lace runners and the kettle of potpourri pumping out its nauseating perfume, slides open the fireplace screen, and shoves the book in.

Shame, fragility, fear—he's the opposite of his father. He seldom ventures downtown, takes pains to avoid walking past the library. If he glimpses one of the Cunningham sisters by the lake or in a store, he about-faces, ducks, hides. They know he has not returned the book, that he has destroyed public property: they will guess why.

In the mirror his legs are too short, his chin too weak; his feet embarrass him. Maybe in some distant, glittering city, he would belong. Maybe in one of those places, he could emerge, bright and new, as the man he wishes he could become.

Some days, walking to school, or simply rising from bed, he is knocked off-balance by a sudden, stomach-churning sense of spectators ringed around him, their shirts soaked in blood and accusation on their faces. Pansy, they say, and level their outstretched fingers at him. Sissy. Fruit Punch.

Zeno is sixteen and apprenticing part-time in the machine shop at Ansley Tie and Lumber when seventy-five thousand soldiers in the North Korean People's Army cross the 38th parallel and start the Korean War. By August the churchmen who gather around Mrs.

Boydstun's table on Sunday afternoons are complaining about the shortcomings of the new generation of American soldiers, how they've become pampered, made weak by an overindulgent culture, infected with give-up-itis, and the lit ends of their cigarettes draw orange circles above the chicken.

"Not brave like your daddy," Pastor White says, and makes a show of slapping Zeno's shoulder, and somewhere in the distance Zeno hears a door slide open.

Korea: a small green thumb on the schoolhouse globe. It looks about as far from Idaho as a person can get.

Every evening, after his shift at the mill, he runs partway around the lake. Three miles to the turn at West Side Road, three miles back, splashing through the rain, Athena—white-muzzled now, lion-hearted—limping behind. Some nights, the sleek and shining warriors of Atlantis keep pace beside him as though drawn along hot wires, and he runs harder, trying to leave them behind.

The day he turns seventeen, he asks Mrs. Boydstun to let him drive the old Buick to Boise. She lights a new cigarette from her old one. The cuckoo clock ticks; her throngs of children stand on their shelves; three different Jesuses stare down from three different crosses. Over her shoulder, out the kitchen window, Athena curls up beneath the hedges. A mile away mice drowse inside the cabin where he and Papa spent their first Lakeport winter. The heart heals but never completely.

On the switchbacks down the canyon he gets carsick twice. At the recruitment office, a medic presses the cold cup of a stethoscope to his sternum, licks the tip of a pencil, and checks every box on the form. Fifteen minutes later he's Private E-1 Zeno Ninis.

Seymour

Bunny owns the double-wide free and clear, but Pawpaw still had a loan on the acre: $558 a month. Then there's V-1 Propane + Idaho Power + Lakeport Utilities + trash + Blue River Bank for the mattress loan + insurance on the Pontiac + flip phone + snowplowing so she can get the car out of the driveway + $2,652.31 past due on the Visa + health insurance, ha ha, just kidding, she'll never afford health insurance.

She finds at-will employment cleaning rooms at the Aspen Leaf Lodge—$10.65 an hour—and picks up dinner shifts at the Pig N' Pancake—$3.45 an hour plus tips. If no one is ordering pancakes, Mr. Burkett makes her clean the walk-in, and no one tips you for cleaning the walk-in.

Every weekday six-year-old Seymour gets off the school bus by himself, walks down Arcady Lane by himself, opens the front door by himself. Eat a waffle and watch a Starboy and do not leave the house. Are you listening, Possum? Can you touch your ears? Can you cross your heart?

He touches his ears. Crosses his heart.

Nonetheless, as soon as he gets home, no matter the weather, no matter how deep the snow, he drops his backpack, goes out the sliding door, ducks under the wire, and climbs through the forest to the big dead ponderosa in the clearing halfway up the hill.

Some days he only senses a presence, a tingling at the base of his neck. Some days he hears low, booming *whooo*s riding through the forest. Some days there's nothing. But on the best days Trustyfriend is right there, drowsing at the same guano-spattered intersection of trunk and limb where Seymour first saw him, ten feet off the ground.

"Hello."

The owl gazes down at Seymour; the wind ruffles the feathers of his face; in the whirlpool of his attention spins an understanding as old as time.

Seymour says, "It's not just the desk either, it's the smell of Mia's pickle stickers, the way it gets after recess when Duncan and Wesley are all sweaty, and . . ."

He says, "They say I'm weird. They say I'm scary."

The owl blinks into the fading light. His head is the size of a volleyball. He looks like the souls of ten thousand trees distilled into a single form.

One afternoon in November, Seymour is asking Trustyfriend whether loud noises startle him too, whether sometimes it feels as though he hears too much—and does he ever wish the whole world were as quiet as this clearing is right now, where a million tiny silver snowflakes are flying silently through the air?—when the owl drops from its branch, glides across the clearing, and lands in a tree at the far side.

Seymour follows. The owl slips silently down through the trees, back toward the double-wide, calling now and then as though inviting him along. When Seymour reaches the backyard, the owl is perched on top of the house. It sends a big, deep *hoo* into the falling snow, then twists its gaze to Pawpaw's old toolshed. Back to Seymour. Back to the toolshed.

"You want me to go in there?"

In the overstuffed gloom of the shed the boy finds a dead spider, a Soviet gas mask, rusty tool boxes, and on a hook above the workbench, a pair of rifle-range ear defenders. When he puts them on, the din of the world fades.

Seymour claps his hands, shakes a coffee can full of bearings, bangs a hammer: all muted, all better. He goes back into the snow and looks up at the owl standing on the gable of the roof. "These? Are these what you meant?"

Mrs. Onegin allows him to wear the muffs at Recess, during Snack, and at Reflection Time. After five consecutive school days without reprimand, she agrees to let him switch desks.

Miss Slattery the counselor awards him a donut. Bunny buys him a new Starboy DVD.

Better.

Whenever the world becomes too loud, too clamorous, too sharp at the edges, whenever he feels that the roar is creeping too close, he shuts his eyes, clamps the muffs over his ears, and dreams himself into the clearing in the woods. Five hundred Douglas firs sway; NeedleMen parachute through the air; the dead ponderosa stands bone-white beneath the stars.

There is magic in this place.

You just have to sit and breathe and wait.

Seymour makes it through the Thanksgiving Pageant, through the Christmas Music Spectacular, through the pandemonium that is Valentine's Day. He accepts toaster strudel, Cinnamon Toast Crunch, and croutons into his diet. He consents to a bribe-free shampoo every other Thursday. He is working on not flinching when Bunny's fingernails tat-a-tat-a-tat-a-tat on the steering wheel.

One bright spring day Mrs. Onegin leads the first graders through puddles of snowmelt to a light-blue house with a crooked porch on the corner of Lake and Park. The other kids swarm upstairs; a librarian with freckles all over her face finds Seymour alone in Adult Nonfiction. He has to lift one of the cups of his ear defenders to hear her.

"How big did you say he is? Does he sort of look like he's wearing a bow tie?"

She brings down a field guide from a high shelf. On the very first page she shows him, there's Trustyfriend, hovering with a mouse clamped in his left foot. In the next photo, there he is again: standing in a snag overlooking a snowy meadow.

Seymour's heart catapults.

"*Great grey owl*," she reads. "*World's largest species of owl by length. Also called sooty owl, bearded owl, spectral owl, Phantom of the North.*" She smiles at him from inside her sandstorm of freckles. "Says here that their wingspans can exceed five feet. They can hear the heartbeats of voles under six feet of snowpack. Their big facial disk helps them by collecting sounds, like cupping your hands to your ears."

She sets her palms beside her ears. Seymour takes off his muffs and does the same.

Every day that summer, as soon as Bunny leaves for the Aspen Leaf, Seymour pours Cheerios into a baggie, heads out the sliding door, passes the egg-shaped boulder, and slips under the wire.

He makes Frisbees from plates of bark, pole-vaults over puddles, rolls rocks down slopes, befriends a pileated woodpecker. There's a living ponderosa in those woods as big as a school bus stood on end with an osprey nest at the very top, and an aspen grove whose leaves sound like rain on water. And every second or third day, Trustyfriend is there, on his branch in his skeleton tree, blinking out at his dominion like a benevolent god, listening as hard as any creature has ever listened.

Inside the pellets the owl coughs into the needles the boy discovers squirrel mandibles and mouse vertebrae and astonishing quantities of vole skulls. A section of plastic twine. Greenish pieces of eggshell. Once: the foot of a duck. On the workbench in Pawpaw's shed he assembles chimerical skeletons: three-headed zombie voles, eight-legged spider-chipmunks.

Bunny finds ticks on his T-shirts, mud on the carpet, burrs in his hair; she fills the tub and says, "Someone is going to have me arrested," and Seymour pours water from one Pepsi bottle into another and Bunny sings a Woody Guthrie song before falling asleep on the bathmat in her Pig N' Pancake shirt and big black Reeboks.

. . .

Second grade. He walks from school to the library, settles his ear defenders around his neck, and sits at the little table beside Audiobooks. Owl puzzles, owl coloring books, owl games on the computer. When the freckled librarian, whose name is Marian, has a free minute, she reads to him, explaining things along the way.

Nonfiction 598.27:

Ideal habitats for great greys are forests bordered by open areas with high vantage points and large populations of voles.

Journal of Contemporary Ornithology:

Great greys are so elusive and easily spooked that we still know very little about them. We are learning, though, that they serve as threads in a meshwork of relationships between rodents, trees, grasses, and even fungal spores that is so intricate and multidimensional that researchers are only beginning to comprehend a fraction of it.

Nonfiction 598.95:

Only about one in fifteen great grey eggs hatch and make it to adulthood. Hatchlings get eaten by ravens, martens, black bears, and great horned owls; nestlings often starve. Because they require such extensive hunting grounds, great greys are particularly vulnerable to habitat loss: cattle trample meadows, decimating prey numbers; wildfires incinerate nesting areas; the owls eat rodents that have eaten poison, die in vehicle collisions, and fly into utility wires.

"Let's see, this site estimates the current number of great greys in the U.S. at eleven thousand one hundred." Marian retrieves her big desk calculator. "Say, three hundred million Americans, give or take. Hit the three, now eight zeroes; good, Seymour. Remember the division sign? One, one, one. There you go."

27,027.

Both of them stare at the number, absorbing it. For every 27,027 Americans, one great grey owl. For every 27,027 Seymours, one Trustyfriend.

At the table beside Audiobooks he tries to draw it. An oval with two eyes in the center—that's Trustyfriend. Now to make 27,027 dots in rings around it—the people. He makes it to somewhere around seven hundred before his hand is throbbing and his pencil is dull and it's time to go.

Third grade. He gets a ninety-three percent on a decimals assignment. He accepts Slim Jims, saltines, and macaroni-and-cheese into his diet. Marian gives him one of her Diet Cokes. Bunny says, "You're doing so well, Possum," and the moisture in her eyes reflects the lights of the Magnavox.

Walking home one October afternoon, ear defenders on, Seymour turns right onto Arcady Lane. Where this morning there was nothing, now stands a double-posted four-by-five-foot oval sign. *EDEN'S GATE*, it reads,

COMING SOON
CUSTOM TOWNHOMES AND COTTAGES
PREMIER HOMESITES AVAILABLE

In the illustration, a ten-point buck drinks from a misty pool. Beyond the sign, the road home looks the same: a dusty strip of potholes flanked on both sides by huckleberry bushes, their leaves flaring autumn red.

A woodpecker dips across the road in a low parabola and disappears. A pine marten chatters somewhere. The tamaracks sway. He looks at the sign. Back at the road. Inside his chest rises a first black tendril of panic.

FOUR

THESSALY, LAND OF MAGIC

Cloud Cuckoo Land by Antonius Diogenes, Folio Δ

*Tales of a comic hero who travels to a distant place seeking magic show up in virtu-
ally every folklore in virtually every culture. Though several folios of the manuscript
that may have narrated Aethon's journey to Thessaly are lost, it's evident that by
Folio Δ, he has arrived. Translation by Zeno Ninis.*

. . . eager to find evidence of sorcery, I headed straight for the town
square. Were the doves on that awning wizards in feathered disguise?
Would centaurs stride between the market stalls and deliver speeches?
I stopped three maids carrying baskets and asked where I might find a
powerful witch who could turn me into a bird: a brave eagle, possibly, or
a bright strong owl.

One said, "Well, Canidia here, she can extract sunbeams from melons,
turn stones into boars, and pluck stars from the sky, but she can't make
you an owl." The other two tittered.

She continued, "And, Meroë here, she can stop rivers from running,
turn mountains to dust, and rip the gods from their thrones, but she
can't make you an eagle either," and all three of their bodies split with
laughter.

Undeterred, I went to the inn. After dark, Palaestra, the innkeeper's
maid, called me into the kitchen. She whispered that the wife of the
innkeeper kept a bedchamber at the top of the house stocked with all
sorts of equipment for the practice of magic, bird claws and fish hearts
and even bits of corpse flesh. "At midnight," she said, "if you crouch
at the keyhole outside the door of that room, you might find what you
seek . . ."

THE ARGOS

MISSION YEARS 55–58

Konstance

She's four. Inside Compartment 17, an arm's reach away, Mother walks on her Perambulator, the gold band of her Vizer sealed over her eyes.

"Mother."

Konstance taps Mother's knee. Tugs the fabric of her worksuit. No response.

A tiny black creature, no longer than Konstance's pinkie nail, is climbing the wall. Its antennae wave; its leg joints extend, bend, extend again; the jagged tips of its mandibles would frighten her if they weren't so small. She sets a finger in the creature's path and it climbs aboard. It crosses her palm, proceeds to the back of her hand; the intricate complexity of its movements dazzles.

"Mother, look."

The Perambulator whirs and pivots. Her mother, absorbed in another world, pirouettes, then extends her arms as though soaring.

Konstance presses her hand to the wall: the animal climbs off and continues along its original path, ascending past Father's berth, until it disappears through the joint where wall meets ceiling.

Konstance stares. Behind her Mother flaps her arms.

An ant. On the *Argos*. Impossible. All the grown-ups agree. *Don't worry*, Sybil tells Mother. *It takes children years to learn the difference between fantasy and reality. Some longer than others.*

• • •

She's five. The ten-and-unders sit in a circle around the classroom Portal. Mrs. Chen says, "Sybil, please display Beta Oph2," and a black-and-green sphere, ten feet in diameter, materializes in front of them. "These brown patches here, children, are silica deserts at the equator, and we believe that these are bands of deciduous forest in the higher latitudes. We expect that the oceans at the poles, here and here, will freeze over seasonally . . ."

Several of the children reach to touch the image as it rotates past, but Konstance keeps her hands pinned beneath her thighs. The green patches are beautiful, but the black ones—blank and serrated at the edges—frighten her. Mrs. Chen has explained that these are simply regions of Beta Oph2 that have not yet been mapped, that the planet is still too far away, that as they draw closer Sybil will take more detailed images, but to Konstance they look like chasms a person could fall into and from which a person could never escape.

Mrs. Chen says, "Planetary mass?"

"One-point-two-six Earth masses," recite the children.

Jessi Ko pokes Konstance's knee.

"Nitrogen in the atmosphere?"

"Seventy-six percent."

Jessi Ko pokes Konstance's thigh.

"Oxygen?"

"Konstance," whispers Jessi, "what's round, on fire, and covered with trash?"

"Twenty percent, Mrs. Chen."

"Very good."

Jessi leans halfway into Konstance's lap. Into her ear she hisses, "Earth!"

Mrs. Chen glares in their direction and Jessi straightens and Konstance feels heat rush to her cheeks. The image of Beta Oph2 rotates above the Portal: black, green, black, green. The children sing:

You can be one,
Or you can be one hundred and two,
It takes everyone together,
Everyone together,
to get to Beta Oph2.

The *Argos* is an interstellar generation ship shaped like a disk. No windows, no stairs, no ramps, no elevators. Eighty-six people live inside. Sixty were born on board. Twenty-three of the others, including Konstance's father, are old enough to remember Earth. New socks are issued every two mission years, new worksuits every four. Six two-kilo bags of flour come out of the provision vaults on the first of every month.

We are the lucky ones, the grown-ups say. We have clean water; we grow fresh food; we are never ill; we have Sybil; we have hope. If we allocate carefully, everything we have with us is everything we will ever need. Anything we cannot solve for ourselves, Sybil will solve for us.

Most of all, the grown-ups say, we must mind the walls. Beyond the walls waits oblivion: cosmic radiation, zero gravity, 2.73 Kelvin. In three seconds outside the walls, your hands and feet would double in size. The moisture on your tongue and eyeballs would boil away, and the nitrogen molecules in your blood would clump together. You'd suffocate. Then you'd freeze solid.

Konstance is six and a half when Mrs. Chen brings her, Ramón, and Jessi Ko to see Sybil in person for the first time. They arc down corridors, past the Biology Labs, past the doors to Compartments 24, 23, and 22, curling inward toward the center of the ship, and step through a door marked *Vault One.*

"It's very important that we don't bring in anything that might affect her," says Mrs. Chen, "so the vestibule will clean us. Shut your eyes, please."

Outer door sealed, announces Sybil. *Beginning decontamination.*

From somewhere deep inside the walls comes a sound like fans accumulating speed. Chilled air whooshes through Konstance's worksuit and a bright light pulses three times on the other side of her eyelids and an inner door sighs open.

They step into a cylindrical vault fourteen feet across and sixteen feet high. At the center, Sybil hangs suspended inside her tube.

"So tall," whispers Jessi Ko.

"Like a gatrillion golden hairs," whispers Ramón.

"This vault," says Mrs. Chen, "has autonomous thermal, mechanical, and filtration processes, independent of the rest of the *Argos*."

Welcome, says Sybil, and pinpricks of amber go fluttering down her tendrils.

"You're looking lovely today," says Mrs. Chen.

I adore visitors, says Sybil.

"Inside there, children, is the collective wisdom of our species. Every map ever drawn, every census ever taken, every book ever published, every football match, every symphony, every edition of every newspaper, the genomic maps of over one million species—everything we can imagine and everything we might ever need. Sybil is our guardian, our pilot, our caretaker: she keeps us on course, she keeps us healthy, and she safeguards the heritage of all humanity against erasure and destruction."

Ramón breathes on the glass, puts a finger to the vapor, and draws an *R*.

Jessi Ko says, "When I'm old enough to go to the Library, I'm going straight to the Games Section to fly around Flower-Fruit Mountain."

"I'm going to play Swords of Silverman," says Ramón. "Zeke says it goes on for twenty thousand levels."

Konstance, Sybil asks, *what will you do when you get to the Library?*

Konstance glances over her shoulder. The door they entered through has sealed so tightly behind them that it is indistinguishable from the wall. She says, "What's 'erasure and destruction'?"

• • •

Night terrors come next. After Third Meal is cleaned up, after the other families retire to their compartments, after Father heads back to his plants in Farm 4, Mother and Konstance walk back to Compartment 17 and tidy the various worksuits waiting their turn at Mother's sewing machine—here the bin for malfunctioning zippers, here the bin of scraps, here the loose threads, nothing wasted, nothing lost. They powder their teeth and brush their hair and Mother takes a SleepDrop and kisses Konstance on the forehead and they climb into their respective berths, Mother on the bottom and Konstance on the top.

The walls dim from purple to gray to black. She tries to breathe, tries to hold her eyes open.

Still they come. Beasts with glittering razor-teeth. Slavering devils with horns. Eyeless white larvae swarming inside her mattress. The worst are the ogres with skeleton limbs that come scuttling down the corridor; they tear open the compartment door, climb the walls, and chew through the ceiling. Konstance clings to her berth as her mother is sucked out into the void; she tries to blink but her eyes are boiling; she tries to scream but her tongue has turned to ice.

"Where," Mother asks Sybil, "does she get it? I thought we were selected for higher cognitive reasoning? I thought we were supposed to have suppressed imaginative faculties."

Sybil says, *Sometimes genetics surprise us.*

Father says, "Thank goodness for that."

Sybil says, *She'll outgrow it.*

She's seven and three-quarters. DayLight dims and Mother takes her SleepDrop and Konstance climbs into her berth. She holds her eyes open with her fingertips. Counts from zero to one hundred. Back to zero again.

"Mother?"

No response.

She slips down the ladder, past her sleeping mother, and out the door, blanket trailing behind. In the Commissary two grown-ups walk on Perambulators, Vizers over their eyes, tomorrow's schedule flickering in the air behind them—*DayLight 110 Tai Chi in Library Atrium, DayLight 130 Bioengineering Meeting*. She whispers down the corridor in her socks, past Lavatories 2 and 3, past the closed doors of a half-dozen compartments, and stops outside the door with the glowing edges marked *Farm 4*.

Inside, the air smells of herbs and chlorophyll. Grow lights blaze at thirty different levels on a hundred different racks, and plants fill the room all the way to the ceiling: rice here, kale there, bok choi growing next to arugula, parsley above watercress above potatoes. She waits for her eyes to adjust to the glare, then spots her father on his stepladder fifteen feet away, entwined in drip tubes, his head in the lettuces.

Konstance is old enough to understand that Father's farm is unlike the other three: those spaces are tidy and systematic, while Farm 4 is a tangle of wires and sensors, grow-racks skewed at every angle, individual trays crowded with different species, creeping thyme beside radishes beside carrots. Long white hairs sprout from Father's ears; he's at least two decades older than the other children's fathers; he's always growing inedible flowers just to see what they look like and muttering in his funny accent about compost tea. He claims he can taste whether a lettuce has lived a happy life; he says one sniff of a properly grown chickpea can whisk him three zillion kilometers back to the fields he grew up in Scheria.

She picks her way to him and pokes his foot. He raises his eyeshade and smiles. "Hi, kid."

Bits of soil show against the silver of his beard; there are leaves in his hair. He descends his ladder and wraps her blanket around her shoulders and guides her to where the steel handles of thirty refrigerated drawers protrude from the far wall.

"Now," he says, "what's a seed?"

"A seed is a little sleeping plant, a container to protect the little sleeping plant, and a meal for the little sleeping plant when it wakes up."

"Very good, Konstance. Who would you like to wake up tonight?"

She looks, thinks, takes her time. Eventually she chooses a handle four from the left and pulls. Vapor sighs out of the drawer; inside wait hundreds of ice-cold foil envelopes. She chooses one in the third row.

"Ah," he says, reading the envelope. "*Pinus heldreichii*. Bosnian pine. Good choice. Now hold your breath."

She takes a big inhalation and holds it and he tears open the envelope and onto his palm slides a little quarter-inch seed clasped by a pale brown wing. "A mature Bosnian pine," he whispers, "can grow thirty meters high and produce tens of thousands of cones a year. They can withstand ice and snow, high winds, pollution. Folded inside that seed is a whole wilderness."

He brings the seed close to her lips and grins.

"Not yet."

The seed almost seems to tremble in anticipation.

"Now."

She exhales; the seed takes flight. Father and daughter watch it sail above the crowded racks. She loses track as it flutters toward the front of the room, then spies it as it settles among the cucumbers.

Konstance pinches it between two fingers, and unclips the seed from its wing. He helps her poke a hole in the gel membrane of an empty tray; she presses the seed in.

"It's like we're putting it to sleep," she says, "but really we're waking it up."

Beneath his big white eyebrows Father's eyes shine. He bundles her beneath an aeroponic table, crawls in beside her, and asks Sybil to dim the lights (plants eat light, Father says, but even plants can overeat). She pulls her blanket to her chin, and presses her head against her father's chest as shadows fall over the room, and listens to his heart thrum inside his worksuit, and to conduits hum inside the walls, and to water drip from the long white threads of thousands of rootlets, down through the tiers of plants, into channels beneath the floor where it is collected to be resprayed once more, and the *Argos* hurtles another ten thousand kilometers through the emptiness.

"Will you tell some more of the story, Father?"

"It's late, Zucchini."

"Just the part when the witch changes herself into an owl. Please?"

"All right. But only that."

"Also the part where Aethon turns into a donkey."

"Fine. But then sleep."

"Then sleep."

"And you won't tell Mother."

"And I won't tell Mother. I promise."

Father and daughter smile, playing their familiar game, and Konstance wriggles inside her blanket, anticipation rolling through her, and the roots drip, and it is as if they drowse together inside the digestive system of a huge and gentle beast.

She says, "Aethon had just arrived in Thessaly, Land of Magic."

"Right."

"But he didn't see any statues come to life or witches flying over rooftops."

"But the maid at the inn where he was staying," Father says, "told Aethon that that very night, if he knelt at the door to the room at the top of the house, and peeked through the keyhole, he might see some magic. So Aethon crept to the door and watched the mistress of the house light a lamp, bend over a chest full of hundreds of tiny glass jars, and select one. Then she took off her clothes and rubbed whatever was inside the jar all over her body, head to toe. She took three lumps of incense, dropped them into the lamp, said the magic words—"

"What were they?"

"She said, 'goobletook' and 'dynacrack' and 'jimjimsee.'"

Konstance laughs. "Last time you said it was 'fliggleboom' and 'cracklepack.'"

"Oh, those too. The lamp grew very bright, then—poof!—went out. And though it was hard to see, in the moonlight that spilled through the open window, Aethon watched feathers sprout from the mistress's back, from her neck, and from the tips of her fingers. Her nose grew hard and turned downward, her feet curled into yellow talons, her arms became big beautiful brown wings, and her eyes—"

"—they grew three times as large and turned the color of liquid honey."

"That's right. And then?"

"Then," says Konstance, "she spread her wings and flew right out the window, over the garden, and into the night."

FIVE

THE ASS

Cloud Cuckoo Land by Antonius Diogenes, Folio E

Tales of a man unwittingly transformed into a donkey, such as Apuleius's well-known picaresque The Golden Ass, *proliferated in western antiquity. Diogenes unabashedly borrows from them here; whether he improved any of them remains up for debate. Translation by Zeno Ninis.*

As soon as the owl flew out the window, I crashed through the door. The maid opened the strongbox and rummaged among the witch's jars while I removed every stitch of clothing. I rubbed myself head to toe with the ointment she chose, took three pinches of frankincense, just as I had seen the witch do, and dropped them into the lamp. I repeated the magic words and the lamp flared, just as before, then went out. I closed my eyes and waited. Soon my luck was going to change. Soon I would feel my arms transform into wings! Soon I would leap from the ground like the horses of Helios and soar among the constellations, on my way to the city in the sky where wine runs in the streets and tortoises circulate with honeycakes on their backs! Where no one wants for anything and the west wind always blows and everyone is wise!

From the bottoms of my feet, I felt the transformation begin. My toes and fingers bunched and fused. My ears stretched and my nostrils grew huge. I could feel my face elongating, and what I prayed were feathers growing out of my . . .

THE LAKEPORT
PUBLIC LIBRARY

FEBRUARY 20, 2020

5:08 P.M.

Seymour

His first shot buried itself somewhere in the romance novels. His second hit the man with the eyebrows in the left shoulder and spun him. The man lowered himself to one knee, set the backpack on the carpet as though it were a large and fragile egg, and began crawling away from it.

Move, says a voice in Seymour's head. Run. But his legs refuse. Snow flows past the windows. An ejected bullet casing smokes by the dictionary stand. Minerals of panic glitter in the air. Jean Jacques Rousseau, in a green-spined hardcover that's right over there, one shelf away, JC179.R, said: *You are lost, if you forget that the fruits of the earth belong equally to us all, and the earth itself to nobody!*

Go. Now.

He has shot two holes in his windbreaker, the nylon melted around the edges. He has ruined the jacket; Bunny will be disappointed. The man with the eyebrows is dragging himself by one set of fingertips down the aisle between Fiction and Nonfiction. The JanSport waits on the carpet, the main compartment half-zipped.

In the space inside his ear defenders, Seymour waits for the roar. He watches the leak seep through the stained ceiling tile and fall into the half-full trash can. Plip. Plop. Plip.

Zeno

Gunshots? In the Lakeport Public Library? Impossible to unfasten the question marks from such statements. Maybe Sharif dropped a stack of books, or a century-old truss in the floor finally snapped, or a prankster set off a firecracker in the bathroom. Maybe Marian slammed the microwave door. Twice.

No, Marian walked over to Crusty's to pick up the pizzas, *back in a jiff*.

Were other patrons on the first floor when he and the children came in? At the chess table or in the armchairs or using the computers? He can't remember.

Except for Marian's Subaru, the parking lot was empty.

Wasn't it?

To Zeno's right, Christopher is managing the karaoke light perfectly, spotlighting only Rachel-who-is-the-innkeeper's-maid, while Alex-who-is-Aethon delivers his lines from the darkness in his bright, clear voice: "What's happening to me? This hair growing out of my legs—why, these aren't feathers! My mouth—it doesn't feel like a beak! And these aren't wings—they're hooves! Oh, I haven't become a bright strong owl, I've become a big dumb donkey!"

When Christopher brings the lights back up, Alex is wearing his papier-mâché donkey head, and Rachel is trying to stifle a laugh as Alex staggers about, and owls are hooting from Natalie's portable speaker, and Olivia-the-bandit is offstage with her ski mask and foil-covered sword, ready for her cue. Creating this play with these children is the best thing that has happened to Zeno in his life, the best thing he has ever done—and yet something isn't right, those two question marks riding the conduits of his brain, slithering past whatever barricades he tries to set in front of them.

Those weren't dropped books. That wasn't the microwave door.

He glances over his shoulder. The wall they've built across the entrance to the Children's Section is unpainted on this side, bare plywood nailed to two-by-fours, and here and there dried drips of gold paint catch the light and glimmer. The little door in the center is closed.

"Oh dear," says Rachel-the-maid, still laughing, "I must have mixed up the witch's jars! But don't worry, Aethon, I know all the witch's antidotes. You go wait in the stable, and I'll bring you some fresh roses. As soon as you eat them, the spell will be undone, and you'll transform from a donkey back to a man as quick as a swish of your tail."

From Natalie's speaker comes the sound of crickets rubbing their forewings at night. A shiver runs through Zeno.

"What a nightmare!" cries Alex-the-donkey. "I try to speak, but all that comes out of my mouth are bleats and brays! Will my luck ever change?"

In the shadows offstage, Christopher joins Olivia and pulls on his own ski mask. Zeno rubs his hands. Why is he cold? It's a summer evening, isn't it? No, no, it's February, he's wearing a coat and two pairs of wool socks—it's only summer in the children's play, summer in Thessaly, Land of Magic, and bandits are about to rob the inn and load Aethon-who-has-become-a-donkey with saddlebags full of stolen goods and hurry him out of town.

There's a benign explanation for those two bangs; of course there is. But he should go downstairs. Just to be sure.

"Oh, I never should have dabbled in this witchery," says Alex. "I do hope the maid hurries up with those roses."

Seymour

Beyond the library windows, beyond the storm, the horizon eats the sun. The wounded man with the eyebrows has dragged himself to the base of the staircase and curled up against the bottom stair. Blood is filling the upper corner of his T-shirt, blotting out the *BIG* in *I LIKE BIG BOOKS*, turning his neck and shoulder a vivid crimson: it frightens Seymour that the body contains such an extravagant color.

He only wanted to take a bite out of the Eden's Gate Realty office on the other side of the library wall. Make a statement. Wake people up. Be a warrior. Now what has he done?

The wounded man flexes his right hand, and the radiator to Seymour's left hisses, and his paralysis finally breaks. He lifts the backpack, hurries it into the same corner of Nonfiction, hides it on a higher shelf than before, then trots to the front door and peers past the sign taped to the glass:

TOMORROW
ONE NITE ONLY
CLOUD CUCKOO LAND

Through the falling snow, down the line of junipers, as though trapped inside a snow globe, he can see the book drop box, the empty sidewalk, and, beyond that, the shape of the Pontiac under half a foot of snow. Across the intersection, approaching the library, a figure in a cherry-red parka emerges carrying a stack of pizza boxes.

Marian.

He throws the deadbolt, kills the lights, scurries past the Reference section, skirting the wounded man, and makes for the fire exit at the back of the library. *EMERGENCY EXIT*, says the door. *ALARM WILL SOUND.*

He hesitates. When he lifts his ear defenders, sounds come rushing in. The moaning boiler, the plip-plopping leak, a distant, incongruous sound like the chirping of crickets, and what sounds like police sirens: blocks away but approaching fast.

Sirens?

He replaces the muffs and puts both hands on the push-bar. The electronic alarm shrieks as he sticks his head into the snow. A set of blue and red lights is careering into the alley.

He pulls his head back inside and the door closes and the alarm ceases. By the time he has rushed back to the front door, a police SUV, emergency lights whirling, is rolling halfway onto the sidewalk, nearly hitting the book drop box. Its driver's door flies open and a figure rushes out and Marian drops the pizzas.

A spotlight hits the front of the library.

Seymour sinks to the floor. They will storm in here and shoot him and it will be over. He scurries behind the welcome desk and drives it across the entry mat and barricades the front door. Next he seizes the shelf of audiobooks, cassettes and CDs falling everywhere, and drags it across the front window. Then he crouches with his back to it and tries to recover his breath.

How did they get here so quickly? Who called the police? Is it possible that the sounds of two gunshots could be heard five blocks away at the police station?

He has shot a man; he hasn't detonated his bombs; Eden's Gate is untouched. He has botched everything. The eyes of the wounded man at the base of the stairwell track his every movement. Even in the dusky, snow-veiled light, Seymour can see that the patch of blood on his shirt is larger. The lime-green wireless earbuds in each of his ears: they must be connected to a phone.

Zeno

Christopher and Olivia, wearing their ski masks, pile treasure into saddlebags on the back of Aethon-the-conveniently-located-donkey. Alex says, "Ow, that's heavy, stop, please, this is a misunderstanding, I'm not a beast, I'm a man, a simple shepherd from Arkadia," and Christopher-who-is-Bandit-Number-One says, "Why is this donkey making so much danged noise?" and Olivia-who-is-Bandit-Number-Two says, "If it doesn't shut up, we'll be caught," and she whacks Alex with her foil-covered sword, and the exit alarm downstairs blares, then stops.

All five children glance at Zeno where he sits in the front row, apparently decide that this, too, must be a test, and the masked bandits continue ransacking the inn.

A familiar jolt of pain rides through Zeno's hip as he rises. He gives his actors a thumbs-up, hobbles to the back of the room, and eases open the little arched door. The stairwell lights are off.

From the first floor comes the jumbled thuds of what sounds like a shelf being pushed over. Then it's quiet again.

There's only the red glow of the *EXIT* sign at the top of the stairs, transforming the gold paint on the plywood wall into a frightening, poisonous green, and the far-off keen of a siren, and a red-blue-red-blue light licking along the edges of the stairs.

Memories sweep through the dark: Korea, a shattered windshield, the silhouettes of soldiers swarming down a snow-covered slope. He finds the handrail, eases down two steps, then realizes that a figure is curled at the bottom of the stairwell.

Sharif looks up, his face drawn. On the left shoulder of his T-shirt is a shadow or a spatter or something worse. With his left hand, he puts an index finger to his lips.

Zeno hesitates.

Go back, waves Sharif.

He turns, tries to make his boots quiet on the stairs; the golden wall looms above him—

Ὦ ξένε, ὅστις εἶ, ἄνοιξον, ἵνα μάθῃς ἃ θαυμάζεις

—the severity of the old Greek striking him suddenly as alien and chilling. For an instant Zeno feels as though, like Antonius Diogenes studying the inscription on a centuries-old chest, he is a stranger from the future, about to enter some unknowable and deeply foreign past. *Stranger, whoever you are . . .* To pretend he knows anything about what those words signify is absurd.

He ducks back through the arched doorway and fastens the door behind him. Onstage the bandits are driving Aethon-the-donkey down the stony road out of Thessaly. Christopher says, "Well, this has to be the most worthless donkey I've ever seen! It complains with every step," and Olivia says, "As soon as we get back to our hide-out and unload this loot, let's cut its throat and throw it off a cliff," and Alex pushes his donkey head up over his nose and scratches his forehead.

"Mr. Ninis?"

The karaoke light is blinding. Zeno leans on a folding chair to keep his balance.

Through his ski mask Christopher says, "I'm sorry I messed up my line before."

"No, no," Zeno says, trying to keep his voice quiet. "You're doing wonderfully. All of you. It's very funny. It's brilliant. Everyone is going to love it." The cicadas and crickets drone from the speaker. The cardboard clouds twist on their threads. All five kids watch him. What is he supposed to do?

"So," Olivia-the-bandit says, and twirls her plastic sword, "should we keep the story going?"

SIX

THE BANDITS' HIDEOUT

Cloud Cuckoo Land by Antonius Diogenes, Folio Z

. . . through my big nostrils I could smell roses growing in the last gardens at the edge of town. Oh, what sweet, melancholy perfume! But each time I veered to investigate, the cruel robbers beat me with their sticks and swords. My load poked my ribs through the saddlebags, and my unshod hooves ached, and the road wound higher into parched, stony mountains in the north of Thessaly, and again I cursed my luck. Each time I opened my mouth to sob, what came out was a loud, pathetic bray, and the knaves only whacked me harder.

The stars sank away and the sun rose hot and white, and they drove me higher into the mountains, until hardly anything grew at all. Flies hounded me, my back roasted, and there were only rocks and cliffs for as far as I could see. When we stopped, I was left to nibble spiky nettles that stung my tender lips, while my saddlebags were loaded with everything they had stolen from the inn, not only the jeweled bracelets and headdresses of the innkeeper's wife, but soft white loaves and salted meats and sheep's cheeses.

At nightfall, high on a rocky pass, we reached the mouth of a cave. More thieves came out to embrace the thieves who brought me here, and they prodded me through room after room twinkling with stolen gold and silver, and left me in a miserable unlit cavern. All I had to eat was fusty straw, and all I had to drink from was a little seep bubbling through the rock, and all night I could hear the echoes of the marauders laughing as they feasted. I wept at my . . .

CONSTANTINOPLE

AUTUMN 1452

Anna

She turns twelve, though no one marks the day. She no longer runs through ruins, playing at being Ulysses as he steals into the palace of brave Alcinous: it's as if, when Kalaphates pitched Licinius's parchment into the flames, the kingdom of the Phaeacians went to ashes too.

Maria's hair has grown back where Kalaphates tore it out and the bruises around her eyes have long since faded, but some deeper injury persists. She grimaces in sunlight, forgets the names of things, leaves phrases half-finished. Headaches send her scurrying for the dark. And one bright morning, before the noon bell, Maria drops her needle and scissors and claws at her eyes.

"Anna, I cannot see."

Widow Theodora frowns on her stool; the other embroideresses glance up, then back at their work. Kalaphates is just downstairs, entertaining some diocesan. Maria knocks things off her table as she sweeps her arms around. A spool of thread rolls past her feet, slowly unwinding.

"Is there smoke?"

"There's no smoke, sister. Come."

Anna leads her down the stone steps to their cell and prays, Saint Koralia, help me be better, help me learn the stitches, help me make this right, and it is another hour before Maria can see her hand in front of her face. At the evening meal the women attempt various diagnoses. Strangury? Quartan agues? Eudokia offers a talisman; Agata recommends tea of astragalus and betony. But what the needleworkers do not voice aloud is their belief that Licinius's old manuscript has worked some dark magic—that despite its destruction, it continues to blight the sisters with misfortune.

What witchcraft is this?

You fill your head with useless things.

After evening prayers Widow Theodora enters their cell with herbs smoldering in a brazier and sits beside Maria and folds her long legs beneath her. "A lifetime ago," she says, "I knew a lime-burner who would see the world one hour and nothing the next. Over time his world went as dark as the darks of hell, and none of the doctors, local or foreign, could do a thing. But his wife put her faith in the Lord, and scraped together every piece of silver she could, and took him out the God-protected gate of the Silivri to the shrine of the Virgin of the Source, where the sisters let him drink from the holy well. And when the lime-burner came back—"

Theodora draws a cross in the air, remembering it, and the smoke drifts from wall to wall.

"What?" whispers Anna. "What happened when the lime-burner came back?"

"He saw the gulls in the sky and the ships on the sea and the bees visiting the flowers. And every time people saw him, for the rest of his life, they spoke of this miracle."

Maria sits on the pallet, hands in her lap like broken sparrows.

Anna asks, "How much silver?"

A month later at dusk she stops in an alley beneath the wall of the convent of Saint Theophano. Look. Listen. Up she goes. At the top she squeezes through the iron grillwork. From there it's a short drop to the roof of the buttery, where she crouches a moment, listening.

Smoke rises from the kitchens; a low chant filters from the chapel. She thinks of Maria sitting on their pallet right now, squinting to unknot and remake a simple wreath Anna tried to embroider earlier today. In the gathering darkness she sees Kalaphates seize Maria's hair. He drags her down the hall, her head strikes the stair, and it is as though Anna's own head is being struck, sparks exploding across her field of vision.

She lowers herself off the roof, enters the laying house, and grabs a hen. It squawks once before she breaks its neck and shoves it into her dress. Then back onto the roof of the buttery, back through the iron pickets, down through the ivy.

Over the past weeks she has sold four stolen chickens in the market for six coppers—hardly enough to buy her sister a blessing at the shrine of the Virgin of the Source. As soon as her slippers touch the ground, she hurries down the alley, keeping the nunnery wall on her left, and reaches the street where a stream of men and beasts moves in both directions through the failing light. Head down, one arm folded over the hen, she makes her way into the market, invisible as a shadow. Then a hand falls on the back of her dress.

It's a boy, about her age. Bulge-eyed, huge-handed, barefoot, so skinny he seems all eyeballs—she knows him: a fisherman's nephew named Himerius, the kind of boy Chryse the cook would say is as bad as a tooth-pulling and as useless as singing psalms to a dead horse. A heavy shank of hair lies across his forehead and the handle of a knife shows above the waistband of his breeches and he smiles the smile of someone who has the upper hand.

"Stealing from the servants of God?"

Her heart booms so loudly that she is surprised passersby cannot hear it. The gate to Saint Theophano is within sight: he could drag her to it, denounce her, make her open her dress. She has seen thieves on gibbets before: last autumn three were dressed as harlots and seated backward on donkeys and driven to the gallows in the Amastrianum and the youngest of them could not have been much older than Anna is now.

Would they hang her for stealing fowl? The boy looks back up the alley at the wall she just descended, calculating. "Do you know the priory on the rock?"

She gives a wary nod. It's a ruin on the edge of the city, near the harbor of Sophia, a forbidding place surrounded on three sides by water. Centuries ago it might once have been a welcoming abbey but now it seems a frightening and desolate relic. The Fourth Hill boys have told her that soul-eating wraiths haunt it, that they carry their chamberlain from room to room on a throne of bones.

Two Castilians, wrapped in brocaded coats and doused liberally with perfume, pass on horses and the boy bows lightly as he steps out of their way. "I've heard," Himerius says, "that inside the priory are many things of great antiquity: ivory cups, gloves covered with sapphires, the skins of lions. I've heard the Patriarch kept shards of the Holy Spirit glowing inside golden jars." The bells of a dozen basilicas begin their slow toll and he looks over her head, blinking those huge eyes, as though seeing gemstones twinkle in the night. "There are foreigners in this city who will pay a great deal for old things. I row us to the priory, you climb up, fill a sack, and we sell whatever you find. Find me beneath the tower of Belisarius on the next night the sea smoke comes. Or I will tell the holy sisters about the fox who steals their chickens."

Sea smoke: he means fog. Every afternoon she checks the workshop windows, but the autumn days stay fine, the sky a crisp, heart-aching blue, the weather clear enough, Chryse says, to see into the bedroom of Jesus. From the narrow lanes, between houses, Anna sometimes glimpses the priory in the distance: a collapsed tower, soaring walls, windows blockaded with bricks. It's a ruin. Gloves sewn with sapphires, the skins of lions—Himerius is a fool and only a fool would believe his tales. Yet, beneath her apprehension, a thread of hope rises. As though some part of her wishes the fog would come.

One afternoon, it does: a swirling torrent of white pours off the Propontis at dusk, thick, cool, silent, and drowns the city. From the workshop window she watches the central dome of the Church of the Holy Apostles disappear, then the walls of Saint Theophano, then the courtyard below.

After dark, after prayers, she crawls from beneath the blanket she shares with Maria, and slips to the door.

"You're going out?"

"Only to the toilet. Rest, sister."

Down the corridor, through the side of the courtyard so as to skirt the watchman, and into the lattice of streets. The fog dissolves walls, reshuffles sounds, transforms figures to shades. She hurries, trying not to think of the nightly terrors she has been warned about: roving witches, airborne maladies, rogues and wretches, the dogs of night slinking through shadows. She slips past the houses of metal-workers, furriers, shoemakers: all settled in behind barred doors, all obeying their god. She descends the steep lanes to the base of the tower and waits and trembles. Moonlight pours into the fog like milk.

With a mixture of relief and disappointment, she decides that Himerius must have abandoned his scheme, but then he steps from the shadows. Over his right shoulder is a rope and in his left hand is a sack and he leads her without speaking through a fishermen's gate and across the cobbled beach past a dozen upturned boats to a skiff hauled up onto the gravel.

So covered with patches, so rotted in the boards, it hardly quali-fies as a boat. Himerius sets the rope and sack in the bow and drags the craft to the waterline and stands submerged to his shins.

"It will stay afloat?"

He looks offended. She climbs in, and he pushes the skiff off the gravel and swings his body neatly over the wale. He settles the oars into their locks and waits a moment and the blades of the oars drip drip drip and a cormorant passes overhead and both boy and girl watch it come out of the fog and disappear again.

She sinks her fingernails into the thwart as he rows them into the harbor. A carrack at anchor looms suddenly close, dirty and barnacled and huge, the railings impossibly high, black water suck-ing at its hull, at the weed-wrapped anchor chains. She had imag-ined boats were swift and majestic; up close they make her hair stand on end.

Every breath she waits for someone to stop them but no one does. They reach a breakwater and Himerius ships the oars and hangs two unbaited lines off the stern. "If anyone asks," he whispers, "we are fishing," and rattles one of the lines as though in evidence.

The skiff wobbles; the air reeks of shellfish; out beyond the breakwater, waves shatter onto rocks. This is as far from home as she has ever been.

Every now and then the boy leans forward and uses a wide-mouthed jug to bail water from between his bare feet. Behind them the great towers of the Portus Palatii are lost in the fog and there is only the faraway boom of surf against rocks and the knocking of the oars against the boat and her simultaneous terror and exhilaration.

When they reach a gap in the breakwater, the boy gestures with his chin toward the heaving blackness beyond. "When the tide is wrong, a current comes here that would sweep us straight out to sea." They keep on a while longer and he feathers the oars and hands her the sack and the rope. The fog is so thick that at first she does not see the wall and when she finally does it seems the oldest, weariest thing in the world.

The skiff rises and falls and somewhere inside the city, as though on the far edge of the world, bells toll once. From the catacombs of her mind leak horrors: blind wraiths, the demonic chamberlain on his throne of bones, his lips dark with the blood of children.

"Near the top," whispers Himerius, "can you see the drainage holes?"

She sees only a towering crumble of brick, encrusted with mussels where the wall rises out of the water, striated with weeds and discolorations, rising higher into the fog as though into infinity.

"Reach one of those and you should be able to crawl through."

"And then?"

In the dark his enormous eyeballs seem almost to glow.

"Fill the sack and lower it to me."

Himerius holds the bow as close as he can to the wall; Anna gazes upward and trembles.

"It's a good rope," he says, as though the quality of the rope were her objection. A single bat flies a figure eight over the skiff and departs. If not for her, Maria's vision would be clear. Maria could be Widow Theodora's most skilled embroideress; God would smile on her. It is Anna who cannot sit still, who cannot learn, who has made everything wrong. She watches the dark, glassy water and imagines it closing over her head. And would she not deserve it?

She hangs the rope and sack around her neck and scratches letters across the surface of her mind. A is ἄλφα is alpha; B is βῆτα is beta. Ἄστεα are cities; νόον is mind; ἔγνω is learned. When she stands, the boat wobbles dangerously. By pushing first one oar, then the other, Himerius holds the stern against the base of the wall, the skiff scraping as it falls, shuddering as it rises, and Anna grabs a hank of seaweed growing from a crevice with her right hand, finds a little shelf for her left, swings one foot off the boat, and brings her body to the wall, and the skiff falls away beneath her.

She clings to the brick as Himerius backs the skiff away. All that remains below her feet is black water flowing Saint Koralia knows how deep and Saint Koralia knows how cold and alive with Saint Koralia knows what terrors. The only way is up.

Masons and time have left the butt ends of bricks sticking out here and there, so finding holds isn't difficult, and despite the fear, the rhythm of climbing soon absorbs her. One handhold, two, one toehold, two; before long, the fog erases Himerius and the water below and she climbs as if ascending a ladder into the clouds. Too little fear and you don't pay enough attention; too much and you freeze. Reach, cling, push, ascend, reach. No room in the mind for anything else.

Rope and sack around her neck, Anna rises through a stratigraphy of rotting brick, from the first emperor to the last, and soon the holes Himerius spoke of are upon her: a series of ornamented scuppers shaped like the heads of lions, each as big as she is. She manages to pull herself up and through the open mouth of one. As soon as she has weight beneath her knees, she twists her shoulders, and crawls through a cradle of muck.

Damp and streaked with mud, she lowers herself into what, centuries ago, might have been a refectory. Somewhere ahead rats scrabble in the dark.

Stop. Listen. Much of the timbered ceiling has caved in, and in the fog-scattered moonlight she can see a debris-littered table as long as Kalaphates's workshop running through the center of the room with a garden of ferns growing on top. A rain-ruined tapestry hangs on one wall; when she touches the hem, invisible things behind it go flapping deeper into the shadows. On the wall her fingers find an iron bracket, perhaps for a torch, badly rusted. Could this be worth something? Himerius had conjured visions of forgotten treasures—she imagined the palace of brave Alcinous—but this is hardly a treasury; everything has been corroded by weather and time; it is an empire of rats, and whatever chamberlain once watched over this place must be three hundred years dead.

To Anna's right gapes what might be a sheer drop, but turns out to be a staircase. She feels her way along the wall, one step at a time; the stairs twist, branch, and branch again. She tries a third hall and finds cells like the cells of monks running down both sides of a corridor. Here's a pile of what might be bones, the rustle of dried leaves, a crevice in the floor waiting to swallow her.

She turns around, stumbles forward, and in the spectral quarterlight space and time muddle. How long has she been in here? Has Maria fallen asleep, or is she awake and frightened, still waiting for Anna to return from the toilet? Has Himerius waited for her, is his rope long enough, have he and his derelict skiff been swallowed by the sea?

Weariness crashes over her. She has risked everything for nothing; soon cocks will crow, matins will begin, and Widow Theodora will open her eyes. She'll reach for her rosary, lower her kneecaps onto the cold stone.

Anna manages to feel her way back to the staircase and climb to a small wooden door. She pushes through into a round room, partially open to the sky, that smells of mud and moss and time. And something else.

Parchment.

What ceiling remains is blank, smooth, and unadorned, as though she has climbed inside the braincase of a big, punctured skull, and on the walls of this little chamber, scarcely visible in the moonlit fog, doorless cupboards run from floor to ceiling. Some are filled with debris and moss. But others are full of books.

Her breath stops. Here a heap of rotting paper, here a crumbling scroll, here a stack of bound codices wet with rain. From her memory comes the voice of Licinius: *But books, like people, die.*

She fills the sack with a dozen manuscripts, as many as it will hold, and drags it back down the staircase, down the corridor, guessing at various turns. When she finds the great room with the tapestry, she ties the throat of the sack to one end of the rope and scrambles up a pile of rubble and crawls through the scupper, pushing the sack before her.

The taut rope makes a high, ratcheting whine as she lowers it down the wall. Just as she decides that he is gone, that he has left her here to die—Himerius and his skiff emerge next to the wall, wrapped in fog and much smaller than she expected them to look. The rope goes slack, the weight comes off, and she drops the end.

Now to climb down. To glance below her feet starts a feeling in her abdomen like she will be sick, so she looks only at her hands, then her toes, easing her way down through the ivy and capers and clumps of wild thyme, and in another minute her left foot touches the thwart, then her right, and she is in the boat.

Her fingertips are raw, her dress grimed, her nerves frayed. "You were gone too long," hisses Himerius. "Was there gold? What did you find?"

The hem of night is already pulling away as they come round the edge of the breakwater into the harbor. Himerius pulls so hard on the oars she worries the shafts will snap, and she removes a first manuscript from the sack. It is large and bloated and she tears the first leaf trying to turn it. The page appears to be full of little vertical scratches. The next is the same, column after column of tally marks. The whole book seems to be like this. Receipts? A register of something? She withdraws a second book, a smaller one, but this too appears to be full of columns with unvarying marks in them, though this one is water-stained and possibly charred as well.

Her heart drops.

The fog suffuses with a pale lavender light, and Himerius ships the oars a moment and takes the second codex from her and smells it and stares at her with his brows bunched.

"What is this?"

He expected leopard hides. Ivory wine cups inlaid with jewels. She searches her memory, finds Licinius there, his lips like pale worms inside the nest of his beard. "Even if what they contain is not valuable, the skins they are written on are. They can be scraped and reused—"

Himerius drops the codex back in the sack and jabs it with his toe, vexed, and continues rowing. The big carrack at anchor seems to float on a looking glass, and Himerius beaches the skiff and drags it above tideline and turns it over and coils the rope carefully over one shoulder and sets off with the sack over the other, Anna trailing behind, like some ogre and his slave from a nursemaid's rhyme.

They head through the Genoese quarter, where the houses grow fine and tall, many with windowglass and some with mosaics set into the facades and ornate sun balconies overlooking the sea walls fronting the Golden Horn. At the entrance to the Venetian quarter, men-at-arms stand yawning beneath an archway and let the children walk by with no more than a glance.

They pass a series of workshops and stop outside a gate. "If you speak," says Himerius, "call me Brother. But don't speak."

A servant with a clubfoot leads them into a courtyard where a lone fig tree struggles for light and they lean against a wall and cocks crow and dogs bark and Anna imagines the bell ringers climbing right now into the fog, reaching for ropes to wake the city, wool brokers raising shutters, pickpockets slinking home, monks submitting themselves to the first lash of the day, crabs drowsing beneath boats, terns diving for breakfast in the shallows, Chryse stirring the hearth-fire to life. Widow Theodora ascending the stone stairs to the workroom.

Blessed One, protect us from idleness.

For we have committed sins without number.

Five gray stones at the opposite end of the courtyard transform into geese that wake and flap and stretch and cluck at them. Soon the sky is the color of concrete and carts are moving out in the streets. Maria will tell Widow Theodora that Anna has a rheum or a fever. But how long can such a ruse last?

Eventually a door opens and a drowsy Italian in a velvet coat with half-length sleeves looks at Himerius long enough to decide he is insignificant and shuts the door again. Anna digs among the damp manuscripts in the burgeoning light. The leaves of the first she pulls out are so splotched with mold that she cannot make out a single character.

Licinius used to swoon about vellum—parchment made from the skin of a calf cut out of the womb of its mother before it was born. He said that to write on vellum was like hearing the finest music, but the membrane from which these books are made feels coarse and bristly and smells like rancid broth. Himerius is right: these will be worth nothing at all.

A maidservant comes past carrying a basin of milk, taking small steps so as not to spill it, and the hunger in Anna's gut is enough to make the courtyard swim. She has failed again. Widow Theodora will beat her with the bastinado, Himerius will denounce her for stealing chickens from the convent, Maria will never have enough silver for a blessing from the shrine of the Virgin of the Source, and when Anna's body swings from the gibbet the throngs will say alleluia.

How does a life get to be like this? Where she wears her sister's castoff underlinen and a thrice-patched dress while men like Kalaphates go about in silk and velvet with servants trotting behind? While foreigners like these have basins of milk and courtyards of geese and a different coat for every feast day? She feels a scream building inside her, a shriek to shatter glass, when Himerius hands her a small battered codex with clasps on the binding.

"What's this?"

She opens to a leaf in the middle. The old Greek Licinius taught her proceeds across the page line after systematic line. *India*, it reads,

> produces horses with one horn, they say, and the same
> country fosters asses with a single horn. And from these
> horns they make drinking-vessels, and if anyone puts
> deadly poison in them, and a man drinks, the plot will do
> him no harm.

On the next page:

> The Seal, I am told, vomits up the curdled milk from
> its stomach so that epileptics may not be cured thereby.
> Upon my word the Seal is indeed a malignant creature.

"This," she whispers, her pulse accelerating. "Show them this."

Himerius takes it back.

"Hold it the other way. Like so."

The boy kneads the great orbs of his eyeballs. The lettering is beautiful and practiced. Anna glimpses, *I have heard the people say that the Pigeon is of all birds the most temperate and restrained in its sexual relations*—is it a treatise about animals?—but now the club-footed servant calls to Himerius and he takes the book and sack and follows the servant into the house.

The geese watch her.

Himerius is not gone fifty heartbeats before he comes back out.

"What?"

"They want to speak to you."

Up two stone stairs, past a storeroom stacked with barrels, and into a room that smells of ink. Across three large tables are scattered tapers, quills, inkpots, nibs, awls, blades, sealing wax, reed pens, and little sandbags to hold down parchment. Charts line one wall, rolls of paper lean against another, and goose droppings are coiled here and there on the tiles, some of it stepped in and smeared about. Around the center table, three clean-shaven foreigners study the pages of the codex she has found and speak their rapid language like excited birds. The darkest and smallest of them looks at her with some incredulity. "The boy claims you can decipher this?"

"We are not as proficient in the old Greek as we would prefer," says the mid-sized one.

Her finger does not shake as she sets it to the parchment. "*Nature*," she reads,

> has made the Hedgehog prudent and experienced in
> providing for its own wants. Thus, since it needs food to
> last a whole year, and since every . . .

All three men resume trilling like sparrows. The smallest begs her to continue, and she muddles through another few lines, strange observations about the habits of anchovies, then of some creature called a clapperbill, and the tallest and best-dressed of them stops her and walks among the scrolls and homiliaries and writing implements and stands staring into a cupboard as though into a distant landscape.

Beneath a table, a melon rind foams with ants. Anna feels as if she has entered some slip of Homer's song about Ulysses, as if the gods are whispering to each other high on Olympus, then reaching down through the clouds to arrange her fate. In his splintery Greek the tall one asks: "Where did you get this?"

Himerius says, "A hidden place, very hard to get to."

"A monastery?" asks the tall man.

Himerius gives a tentative nod, and all three Italians look at each other, and Himerius nods some more, and soon everyone is nodding.

"Where in the monastery," says the smallest of them, removing the other manuscripts from the sack, "did you find it?"

"A chamber."

"A large chamber?"

"Small to average to large," says Himerius.

All three men start talking at once.

"And are there other manuscripts like this one?"

"How are they arranged?"

"On their backs?"

"Or stood up in stacks?"

"How many are there?"

"How is the room decorated?"

Himerius puts a fist to his chin, pretending to sift through his memory, and the three Italians watch him.

"The room is not large," Anna says. "I could not see any adornments. It was round and once had arches in its ceiling. But the roof is broken now. There were other books and scrolls stacked in recesses like cookware."

Excitement cascades through the three men. The tallest one rummages inside his fur-trimmed coat and takes out a bag of money and pours coins into his palm. Anna sees gold ducats and silver *stavrata* and morning light dances across the writing tables and she is suddenly dizzy.

"Our lord," says the tall Italian, "he puts a finger in every dish, you know this phrase? Shipping, trade, liturgical, soldiering. But his real interest, his love, so to speak, is locating manuscripts from the antique world. He believes all the best thinking was done a thousand years ago."

The man shrugs. Anna cannot take her eyes off the money.

"For the animal text," he says, and gives Himerius a dozen coins, and Himerius gapes, and the medium-sized man picks up a quill and trims its tip with a blade, and the smallest says, "Bring us more and we will pay you more."

As they leave the courtyard, the morning is glorious, the sky rosy, the fog burning away, and Anna follows Himerius's long strides as they wind their way through a row of tall, beautiful wooden houses—which seem taller and more beautiful now—joy cartwheeling through her, and at the first market they pass a vendor is already frying flatcakes stuffed with cheese and honey and bay leaves, and they buy four, and stuff them into their mouths, the grease hot on the back of her throat, and Himerius counts out her share of the money, and she buries the heavy, bright coins beneath the sash of her dress, and hurries through the shadow of the church of Saint Barbara, then through a second, larger market full of carts and fabrics, oil in wide-lipped jugs, a knife-sharpener setting up his wheel, a woman reaching to pull the cloth off a birdcage, a child carrying October roses in bunches, the avenue filling with horses and donkeys, Genoese and Georgians, Jews and Pisans, deacons and nuns, moneychangers, musicians and messengers, two gamblers already throwing oxhorn dice, a notary carrying documents, a nobleman pausing at a stall while a servant holds a parasol high above his head, and if Maria wants to buy angels, she can buy them now; they'll flutter around her head and batter her eyes with their wings.

THE ROAD TO EDIRNE

THAT SAME AUTUMN

Omeir

Nine miles from home they pass the village where he was born. The caravan halts in the road while heralds ride among the houses enlisting more men and animals. Rain falls steadily and Omeir shivers inside his oxhide cape and watches the river roar past, full of debris and foam, and remembers how Grandfather would say that the littlest streams, high on the mountain, small enough to dam with your hand, would eventually join the river, and that the river, though quick and violent, was but a drop in the eye of the great Ocean that encircles all the lands of the world, and contains every dream everyone has ever dreamed.

Daylight drains from the valley. How will his mother and Nida and Grandfather survive the winter? Practically all of their stores have disappeared into the mouths of the riders around him. Piled on the dray behind Tree and Moonlight is most of the family's seasoned wood, and half of their barley. They have Leaf and Needle and the goat. A last few pots of honey. They have hope that Omeir will return with spoils from war.

Moonlight and Tree stand patiently in their yoke, horns dripping, backs steaming, and the boy checks their hooves for stones and their shoulders for cuts and envies that they seem to live only in the moment, without dread for what is to come.

That first night the company camps in a field. Karst megaliths stand on ridge lines high above them like the watchtowers of races long since perished, and ravens go squawking up over the camp in great noisy legions. After dark the clouds tear away and the frayed banner of the Milky Way unfurls overhead. Around the fire nearest Omeir teamsters speak in myriad accents about the city they are traveling to conquer. The Queen of Cities, they call it, bridge between East and West, crossroads of the universe. In one version it is a seedbed of sin where heathens eat babies and copulate with their mothers; in the next it is a place of unthinkable prosperity, where even the paupers wear earrings of gold and the whores use pisspots encrusted with emeralds.

An old man says he has heard the city is protected by huge, impenetrable walls and everyone falls silent a moment until a young oxherd named Maher says, "But the women. Even a boy as ugly as him can wet his dick in that place." He points at Omeir and there is laughter.

Omeir drifts off into the dark and finds Moonlight and Tree grazing at the far end of the field. He rubs their flanks and tells them not to be afraid but it's not clear if he is trying to soothe the animals or himself.

In the morning the road drops into a gorge of dark limestone and the wagons bottleneck at a bridge. Riders dismount and drivers shout and strike animals with whips and switches, and both Tree and Moonlight defecate from fear.

A terrible lowing flows through the animals. Slowly Omeir talks the oxen forward. When they reach the bridge he sees that it has no curb or rail but consists only of skinned logs lashed together with chains. Sheer walls, studded here and there with spruce trees growing from impossibly steep perches, drop almost straight down, and far below the log-deck, the river roars fast and loud and white.

On the far side two mule carts make it across and Omeir turns and faces his oxen and steps backward out over the void. The logs are slick with manure and in the gaps between them, beneath his boots, he can see whitewater flashing over boulders.

Tree and Moonlight lumber out. The bridge is scarcely wider than the axle of the dray. They make it one revolution, two three four; then the wheel on Tree's side slips off. The cart lists and the oxen stop and multiple pieces of firewood go rolling off the back.

Moonlight spreads his legs, bearing most of the weight of the load by himself, waiting for his brother, but Tree has immobilized with fright. His eyes roll and all around them shouts and bellows echo off the rocks.

Omeir swallows. If the axle slips any farther, the weight of the cart will pull it off the bridge and drag the oxen with it.

"Pull, boys, pull." The bullocks do not move. Mist rises from the rapids below and little birds swoop from rock to rock and Tree pants as though trying to draw the entire scene up through his nostrils. Omeir runs his hands over Tree's muzzle and strokes his long brown face. His ear twitches, and his thick front legs tremble from strain or terror or both.

The boy can feel gravity pulling at their bodies, at the cart, at the bridge, at the water below. If he was never born, his father would still be alive. His mother would still live in the village. She could talk with other women, trade honey and gossip, share her life. His older sisters might still be alive.

Don't look down. Show the oxen that you can meet all of their needs. If you stay calm so will they. His heels hanging over the chasm, Omeir ducks Moonlight's horns, shimmies around his flank, and speaks directly into the bullock's ear. "Come, brother, pull. Pull for me, and your twin will follow." The ox tilts his horns to one side, as though considering the merits of the boy's request, the bridge and cliffs and sky reproduced in miniature in the dome of his huge, wet pupil, and just when Omeir is convinced that the matter is lost, Moonlight leans into the harness, veins rising visibly in his chest, and hauls the wheel of the dray back onto the bridge.

"Good boy, steady now, that's it."

Moonlight pushes forward, and Tree comes with him, placing one hoof in front of the next on the slick logs, and Omeir grabs the back of the dray as it passes, and in a few more heartbeats they are across.

From there the gorge opens, and the mountains turn into hills, and hills into rolling flatlands, and muddy bridleways into proper roads. Moonlight and Tree move easily along the wide surface, their big hipbones rising and falling, happy to be on sure ground. With every passing village, the heralds recruit more men and beasts. Always their pitch is the same: the sultan (God be pleased with him) calls you to the capital where he gathers forces to take the Queen of Cities. Its streets overflow with jewels, silks, and girls; you will have your pick.

Thirteen days after leaving home, Omeir and his oxen reach Edirne. Everywhere gleam mountains of peeled logs and the air smells of wet sawdust and children run the roadsides selling bread and skins of milk or just to gape at the caravan as it rumbles past, and after dark criers on ponies meet the heralds and sort the animals by torchlight.

Omeir, Tree, and Moonlight are directed with the largest and strongest of the cattle to a vast, treeless field on the outskirts of the capital. At one end glows a tent larger than any he has ever imagined—a whole forest could grow beneath it. Inside men work by torchlight, unloading wagons, cutting trenches, and excavating a casting pit like the grave bed for a giant. Inside the pit lie matching cylindrical molds made from clay, one nested in the other, each thirty feet long.

Every daylight hour Omeir and the oxen walk a mile to a charcoal pit and haul cartloads of charcoal back to the enormous tent. As more and more charcoal is brought in, the area inside the tent grows hotter, the animals balking at the heat as they approach, and the teamsters unload the carts while foundry men pitch the charcoal into furnaces, and groups of mullahs pray, and still more men work in teams of three at great bellows, soaked to their bones in sweat, pumping air into the furnaces. In lulls between the chanting, Omeir can hear the fires burn: a sound like something huge inside the tent chewing, chewing, chewing.

At night he approaches the drivers who will tolerate his face and asks what they have been brought here to help create. One says he has heard that the sultan is casting a propeller from iron but that he does not know what a propeller is. Another calls it a thunder cata-pult, another a torment, another the Destroyer of Cities.

"Inside that tent," explains a gray-bearded man with gold rings through his earlobes, "the sultan is making an apparatus that will change history forever."

"What does it do?"

"The apparatus," says the man, "is a way for a small thing to destroy a much larger thing."

New teams of oxen arrive carrying pallets of tin, trunks of iron, even church bells, the teamsters whisper, from sacked Christian cities, dragged here over hundreds of miles. The whole world, it seems, has sent tributes: copper coin, bronze coffin lids of noble-men centuries forgotten; the sultan, Omeir hears, has even brought the wealth of an entire nation he conquered in the east, enough to make five thousand men rich for five thousand lifetimes, and this too will be pitched in—the gold and silver becoming part of the apparatus too.

Back cold, front burning, the fabric of the tent swimming behind heat blurs, Omeir watches transfixed. The foundry men, their arms and hands wrapped in cowhide gloves, approach the blearing, wavering inferno and climb scaffolding and pitch raw pieces of brass into an enormous cauldron and skim away the dross. Some constantly check the melting metal for any sign of moisture, while others check the sky, while others pray prayers specifically bent on the weather—the slightest raindrop, a man beside Omeir whispers, could set the entire cauldron hissing and cracking with all the fires of hell.

When it is time to add tin to the molten brass, turbaned soldiers drive everyone out. During this delicate moment, they say, the metal cannot be looked at with impure eyes, and only the blessed may go in. The doors of the tent are drawn and tied, and Omeir wakes in the night to see a glow rising from the far end of the field, and it appears that the ground beneath the tent glows also, as though drawing some stupendous power up from the center of the earth.

Moonlight lies on his side and presses his ear against Omeir's shoulder, and the boy curls up in the damp grass, and Tree stands to the side, his back to the tents, still grazing, as though bored by the ridiculous fanaticisms of men.

Grandfather, Omeir thinks, already I have seen things I did not know how to dream.

For two more days the massive tent glows, sparks rising through its chimney holes, and the weather stays fair, and on the third day the foundry men release the molten alloy from the cauldron, directing it through channels until it disappears into the molds belowground. Men move up and down the lines of flowing bronze, knocking out bubbles with iron poles, while others throw shovels of wet sand upon the casting pit, and the tent is dismantled and teams of mullahs take turns praying beside the mounds as they cool.

At dawn they dig away the sand, break apart the molds, and send tunnelers beneath the apparatus to sling chains around its girth. These chains they tether to ropes and the lead teamsters gather oxen in five teams of ten each to try to drag the Destroyer of Cities out of the earth.

Tree and Moonlight are placed on the second team. The order is given and the animals are goaded. Ropes groan, yokes squeak, and the oxen march slowly in place, churning the soil to a sea of mud.

"Pull, boys, all your strength," Omeir calls. The entire team drives their hooves deeper into the clay. The teamsters add a sixth chain, a sixth rope, a sixth team of ten. By now it is nearly dusk and the bullocks stand heaving in the shafts. With a sharp cry, the air fills with "Ho!" and "Hai!" and sixty oxen begin to pull.

The animals lean forward, are hauled back as one by the incredible weight, then lean forward again, earning one step, another, drivers yelling, switching their animals, the bullocks bellowing in fear and confusion.

The immense load is a whale swimming out of the earth. They haul it maybe fifty yards before the order is given to stop. Vapor gushes from the bullocks' nostrils and Omeir checks Tree's and Moonlight's yoke and shoes, and already scrapers and polishers are scrambling over the apparatus where it smokes in the cold twilight, the bronze still warm.

Maher crosses his skinny arms. He says, to no one in particular, "They will need to invent an entirely different kind of cart."

To pull the apparatus the mile from the foundry to the sultan's testing ground takes three days. Three times the spokes on the wagon's wheels splinter and the rims fall out of round; wheelwrights rush around it, working day and night; the load is so heavy that every hour it sits on the cart it drives the wheels another inch into the ground.

In a field within sight of the sultan's new palace, a crane is used to hoist the huge hooped tube of the apparatus onto a wooden platform. An impromptu bazaar springs up: traders sell bulgur and butter, roasted thrushes and smoked ducks, sacks of dates and silver necklaces and wool bonnets. Fox fur is everywhere, as though every fox in the world has been slain and turned into a cape, and some men wear gowns of snow-white ermine, and others wear mantles of fine felt upon which raindrops bead up and skitter off, and Omeir cannot take his eyes off any of them.

At midday the crowd is parted to either side of the field. He and Maher climb a tree at the edge of the testing ground so they can see over the assembled heads. A parade of shorn sheep painted red and white and ornamented with rings are driven toward the platform, followed by a hundred riders riding bareback on black horses, followed by slaves reenacting salient episodes of the sultan's life. Maher whispers that somewhere at the end of the procession must be the sovereign himself, may God bless and greet him, but Omeir can see only attendants and banners and musicians with cymbals and a drum so large that it takes a boy on either side to strike it.

The bite of Grandfather's saw, the ever-present cud-chewing of the cattle, and the nickering of the goat and the panting of dogs and the burbling of the creek and the singing of starlings and the scurryings of mice—a month ago he would have said the ravine at home overflowed with sound. But all of that was silence compared to this: hammers, bells, shouts, trumpets, the groaning of ropes, the whinnying of horses—the noise is an assault.

In the afternoon buglers blow six bright notes and everyone looks to the great polished implement where it gleams on its platform. A man in a red cap crawls inside and disappears entirely and a second man crawls in behind with a sheet of sheepskin, and someone at the foot of the tree says that they must be packing powder into place, though what this means the boy cannot guess. The two men crawl out and next comes a huge piece of granite chiseled and polished into a sphere; a crew of nine rolls it to the front of the barrel and tips it inside.

The heavy, eerie rasp it makes as it rolls slowly down the inclined barrel carries all the way to Omeir over the gathered heads. An imam leads a prayer, and cymbals clash and trumpets blow, and along the top of the apparatus the first man, the one in the red cap, packs what looks like dried grass into a hole in the back, touches a lit taper to the grass, then leaps off the platform.

The onlookers go quiet. The sun swings imperceptibly lower, and a chill falls across the field. Once, Maher says, in his home village, a stranger appeared on a hilltop and claimed he would fly. All day a crowd gathered, he says, and every now and then the man would announce, "Soon I will fly," and would point out various places in the distance he would fly to, and he walked around stretching and shaking his arms. When the crowd had grown large, so large that not everyone could see, and the sun was nearly down, the man, not knowing what to do, pulled down his pants and showed everybody his ass.

Omeir smiles. Up on the rostrum men are scrambling around the apparatus again, and a few snow crystals sift down from the sky, and the crowd shifts, restless now, and the cymbals start up a third time, and at the head of the field, where the sultan may or may not be watching, a breeze lifts the hundreds of horsetails strung from his banners. Omeir leans against the bole of the tree, trying to stay warm, and the two men clamber over the bronze cylinder, the one in the red cap peering into its mouth, and just then the huge cannon fires.

It's as though the finger of God reaches down through the clouds and flicks the planet out of orbit. The thousand-pound stone ball moves too fast to see: there is only the roar of its passage lacerating the air as it screams over the field—but before the sound has even begun to register in Omeir's consciousness, a tree at the opposite end of the field shatters.

A second tree a quarter mile farther also vaporizes, seemingly simultaneously, and for a heartbeat he wonders if the ball will travel forever, beyond the horizon, smashing through tree after tree, wall after wall, until it flies off the edge of the world.

In the distance, what must be a mile away, rocks and mud spray in all directions, as though an invisible plow rakes a great furrow in the earth, and the report of the detonation reverberates in the marrow of his bones. The cheer that comes up from the gathered crowd is less a cheer of triumph than of stupefaction.

Up on its brace, the mouth of the apparatus leaks smoke. Of the two gunners, one stands with both hands to his ears looking down at what little is left of the man in the red cap.

Wind carries the smoke out over the platform. "Fear of the thing," Maher murmurs, more to himself than to Omeir, "will be more powerful than the thing itself."

Anna

She and Maria queue outside the Church of Saint Mary of the Spring with a dozen other penitents. Beneath their wimples the faces of the nuns of the order resemble dried thistles, colorless and brittle: none look younger than a century. One collects Anna's silver in a bowl and a second takes the bowl and tips it into a fold inside her tunic and a third waves them down a flight of stairs.

Here and there in candlelit reliquaries rest the finger- and toe-bones of saints. At the far end, deep beneath the church, they squeeze past a crude altar crusted a foot deep with candlewax and fumble their way into a grotto.

A well gurgles; the soles of Anna's and Maria's slippers slide on the wet stones. An abbess lowers a lead cup into a basin, draws it back up, pours in a significant measure of quicksilver, and gives it a swirl.

Anna holds the cup for her sister.

"How does it taste?"

"Cold."

Prayers echo in the damp.

"Did you drink it all?"

"Yes, sister."

Back aboveground, the world is all color and wind. Leaves blow everywhere, scraping through the churchyard, and the bands of limestone in the city walls catch the low-angled light and glow.

"Can you see the clouds?"

Maria turns her face to the sky. "I think so. I feel the world is brighter now."

"Can you see the banners flapping above the gate?"

"Yes. I see them."

Anna lofts prayers of thanks into the wind. Finally, she thinks, I have done something right.

For two days Maria is clear-minded and serene, threading her own needles, sewing dawn to dusk. But on the third day after drinking the holy mixture, her headache returns, invisible goblins chewing away once more at the peripheries of her vision. By afternoon her forehead shines with sweat and she cannot rise from her bench without help.

"I must have spilled some," she whispers as Anna helps her down the stairs. "Or I did not drink enough?"

At the evening meal everyone is preoccupied. "I hear," Eudokia says, "the sultan has brought in a thousand more masons to complete his fortress upstream of the city."

"I hear," Irene says, "that they have their heads cut off if they work too slowly."

"We can relate," Helena says, but no one laughs.

"Know what he's calling the fort? In the infidel language?" Chryse glances over her shoulder. Her eyes glow, a mix of relish and fear. "The Throat Cutter."

Widow Theodora says that this sort of talk will not improve anyone's needlework, that the city walls are impregnable, that their gates have turned back barbarians on elephants, and Persians with stone-hurling machines from China, and the armies of Krum the Bulgar, who used human skulls as wine cups. Five hundred years ago, she says, a barbarian fleet so large that it stretched to the horizon block-aded the city for five years, and all the citizens ate shoe leather until the day the emperor took the robe of the Virgin from the holy chapel at Blachernae, paraded it around the walls, then dipped it in the sea, and the Mother of God called up a storm and smashed the fleet on the rocks, and every single one of the godless barbarians drowned, and still the walls stood.

Faith, says Widow Theodora, will be our breastplate and piety our sword, and the women fall quiet. The ones with families head home while the others drift back to their cells, and Anna stands at the well filling the water jugs. Kalaphates's donkey nibbles at a thin pile of hay. Doves flutter beneath the eaves; the night turns cold. Maybe Maria is right; maybe she didn't drink enough of the holy mixture. Anna thinks of the eager Italians with their silk doublets and velvet coats and ink-stained hands.

And are there other manuscripts like this one?

How are they arranged?

On their backs? Or stood up in stacks?

As though she has willed it into existence, a tendril of fog comes trickling over the roofline.

Again she slips past the watchman and descends the twisting lanes to the harbor. She finds Himerius asleep beside his skiff and when she wakes him he frowns as if trying to resolve multiple girls into one. Finally he wipes a hand across his face and nods and urinates a long time onto the rocks before dragging the boat into the water.

She stows the sack and rope in the bow. Four gulls pass overhead, crying softly, and Himerius peers up at them, then rows to the priory on the rock. This time she is more determined. With each movement up the wall, her fear thins, and soon there is only the movement of her body and her memory of the holds, her fingers keeping her against the cold brick, her legs sending her up. She reaches the scupper, crawls through the mouth of the lion, and drops into the big refectory. Spirits, let me pass.

A three-quarter moon sends more light filtering through the fog. She finds the stairs, ascends, travels the long corridor, and steps through the door into the circular room.

It's a ghostland, brimming with dust, little ferns growing here and there from clumps of damp paper, everything moldering to pieces. Inside some of the cupboards are vast monastic records so big she can hardly lift them; in others she finds tomes whose pages have been conglutinated by moisture and mildew into a solid mass. She fills the sack as full as she can and drags it down the steps and lowers it to the skiff and walks one pace behind Himerius as he carries it through the misty lanes to the house of the Italians.

The clubfooted servant gives a jaw-cracking yawn as he waves them into the courtyard. Inside the workshop, the two smaller scribes are collapsed on chairs in the corner, sound asleep, but the tall one rubs his hands as though he has waited for them all night. "Come, come, let's see what the mudlarks have brought." He upends the sack onto the table between an array of lit tapers.

Himerius stands with his hands to the fire while Anna watches the foreigner go through the manuscripts. Charters, wills, transcriptions of orations; requests for requisitions; what appears to be a list of personages who attended some long-ago monastic gathering: the Grand Domestic; His Excellency the Vice-Treasurer; the Visiting Scholar from Thessalonica; the Grand Chancellor of the Imperial Wardrobe.

One by one he leafs through the mildewed codices, tipping his candelabra this way and that, and Anna notices things that she missed the first time: his hose are torn on one knee, and his coat is tarnished at the elbows, and ink is spattered up both of his sleeves. "Not this," he says, "not this," then murmurs in his own language. The room smells of oak gall ink and parchment and woodsmoke and red wine. A looking glass in the corner reflects the candle flames; someone has pinned a series of small butterflies to a linen board; someone else is copying what looks like a navigational chart on the corner table—the room overflows with curiosity and ardor.

"All useless," the Italian concludes, rather cheerfully, and stacks four silver coins on the table. He looks at her. "Do you know the story of Noah and his sons, child? How they filled their ship with everything to start the world anew? For a thousand years your city, this crumbling capital"—he waves a hand toward a window—"was like that ark. Only instead of two of every living creature, do you know what the good Lord stacked inside this ship?"

Beyond the shuttered window the first cocks crow. She can feel Himerius twitching beside the fire, all his attention on the silver.

"Books." The scribe smiles. "And in our tale of Noah and the ship of books, can you guess what is the flood?"

She shakes her head.

"Time. Day after day, year after year, time wipes the old books from the world. The manuscript you brought us before? That was written by Aelian, a learned man who lived at the time of the Caesars. For it to reach us in this room, in this hour, the lines within it had to survive a dozen centuries. A scribe had to copy it, and a second scribe, decades later, had to recopy that copy, transform it from a scroll to a codex, and long after the second scribe's bones were in the earth, a third came along and recopied it again, and all this time the book was being hunted. One bad-tempered abbot, one clumsy friar, one invading barbarian, an overturned candle, a hungry worm—and all those centuries are undone."

The flames of the tapers flicker; his eyes seem to gather all the light in the room.

"The things that look fixed in the world, child—mountains, wealth, empires—their permanence is only an illusion. We believe they will last, but that is only because of the brevity of our own lives. From the perspective of God, cities like this come and go like anthills. The young sultan is assembling an army, and he has new war engines that can bring down walls as though they were air."

Her gut lurches. Himerius inches toward the coins on the table.

"The ark has hit the rocks, child. And the tide is washing in."

Her life splits in two. There are her hours in the house of Kalaphates, a monotony of fatigue and dread: broom and pan, thread and wire, fetch water fetch charcoal fetch wine fetch another bale of linen. Seemingly every day a new story about the sultan filters into the workshop. He has trained himself not to sleep; he is leading teams of surveyors outside the city walls; his soldiers at the Throat Cutter have launched a ball that shattered a Venetian galley carrying food and armor from the Black Sea to the city.

For a second time Anna leads Maria to the shrine of the Virgin of the Source, where they buy a blessing from the stooped and withered nuns for eleven *stavrata*, and Maria swallows the mixture of water and mercury and feels better for a day before feeling worse. Her hands throb; she suffers from cramps; some nights she says she feels as though the claws of some devil have closed around her limbs and he is trying to tear her apart.

Then there's Anna's other life, when fog shrouds the city and she hurries through the echoing streets, and Himerius rows her around the breakwater to scale the wall of the priory. If asked, she would say she does it to make money to relieve her sister's suffering—but is there not another part of her that also wants to climb that wall? To bring another sack of mildewed books to the copyists in their ink-filled shop? Twice more she fills a sack with books and twice more it turns out to contain only moldy inventories. But the Italians ask her and Himerius to keep bringing whatever they find, that soon they may unearth something as precious as the Aelian or better—a lost tragedy from Athens or a series of orations by a Greek statesman or a *seismobrontologion* that reveals the secrets of the weather and the wind.

The Italians are not, she learns, from Venice, which they call a mink's den of mercenaries and greed, nor from Rome, which they say is a nest of parasites and whores. They're from a city called Urbino, where they say the granaries are always full and the oil presses overflow and the streets gleam with virtue. Inside the walls of Urbino, they say, even the poorest child, girl or boy, studies numbers and literature, and there is no season of killing malaria as there is in Rome nor a season of chilling fog, like in this city. The smallest of them shows her a collection of eight snuffboxes, on the lids of which are painted miniatures: a great domed church; a fountain in a town square; Justice holding her scales; Courage holding a marble column; Moderation diluting wine with water.

"Our master, the virtuous count and lord of Urbino, never loses," he says, "in battle or otherwise," and the mid-sized scribe adds, "He is magnanimous in all ways, and will listen to anyone who wishes to speak with him at any hour of the day," and the tall one says, "When His Magnificence dines, even when he is on the field of war, he asks that the old texts be read to him."

"He dreams," says the first, "of erecting a library to surpass the pope's, a library to contain every text ever written, a library to last until the end of time, and his books will be free to anyone who can read them." Their eyes glow like coals; their lips are stained with wine; they show her treasures that they have already procured for their master on their travels—a terra-cotta centaur made in the time of Isaac, an inkpot that they say was used by Marcus Aurelius, and a book from China they say was written not by a scribe with quill and ink but by a carpenter turning a wheel of movable bamboo blocks, and they say this machine can make ten copies of a text in the time it takes a scribe to make one.

It all leaves Anna breathless. All her life she has been led to believe that she is a child born at the end of things: the empire, the era, the reign of men on earth. But in the glow of the scribes' enthusiasm, she senses that in a city like Urbino, beyond the horizon, other possibilities might exist, and in daydreams she takes flight across the Aegean, ships and islands and storms passing far below, the wind streaming through her spread fingers, until she alights in a bright clean palace, full of Justice and Moderation, its rooms lined with books, free to anyone who can read them.

The front appear'd with radiant splendors gay, bright as the lamp of night, or orb of day.

The ark has hit the rocks, child.

You fill your head with useless things.

• • •

One night the scribes riffle through another sack of bloated, musty manuscripts and shake their heads. "What we seek," says the smallest one, slurring his Greek, "is nothing like these." Scattered among their parchment and penknives are plates of half-eaten turbot and dried grapes. "What our master seeks in particular are compendiums of marvels."

"We believe that the ancients traveled to distant places—"

"—all four corners of the world—"

"—lands known to them but as yet unknown to us."

Anna stands with her back to the fire and thinks of Licinius writing Ὠκεανός into the dust. Here the known. Here the unknown. Out of the corner of her eye she can see Himerius pilfering raisins. "Our master," says the tall scribe, "believes that somewhere, perhaps in this old city, slumbering beneath a ruin, is an account that contains the entire world."

The mid-sized one nods, eyes shining. "And the mysteries beyond."

Himerius looks up, his mouth full. "And if we were to find it?"

"Our master would be very pleased."

Anna blinks. A book containing the entire world and the mysteries beyond? Such a book would be enormous. She'd never be able to carry it.

SEVEN

THE MILLER AND THE CLIFF

Cloud Cuckoo Land by Antonius Diogenes, Folio H

. . . the bandits prodded me right to the cliff's edge and talked about what a worthless donkey I was. One argued they should drive me off the precipice to be split open on the rocks so the buzzards could pick my flesh, and a second suggested they put a sword in my side and a third, the worst of them, said, "Why not do both?" Put a sword in my side, then drive me off! I urinated all over my hooves as I looked over the edge at the terrible drop.

What a muddle I'd made for myself! I didn't belong here, high on a crag, among rocks and thorns; I belonged high in the blue, sailing through the clouds, heading to the city where there is no baking sun nor icy wind, where the zephyrs nourish every flower and the hills are always clad in green and no one wants for anything. What a fool I was. What was this hunger that drove me to seek more than what I already had?

Just then a potbellied miller and his potbellied son rounded the bend on their way north. The miller said, "What plans have you for this worn-out donkey?" The bandits replied, "He is feeble and gutless and never stops complaining, so we are going to pitch him off this cliff, but first we are debating whether to stick a sword in his ribs." The miller said, "My feet are smarting, and my son can hardly breathe, so we'll give you two coppers for him and let's see if he has a few more miles left in him."

The bandits were happy to be rid of me for two coppers, and I was elated not to be thrown off the cliff. The miller climbed on my back and his son too, and though my spine ached, my head filled with visions of a pretty little miller's cottage and a pretty little miller's wife and a garden chockablock with roses . . .

KOREA

1951

Zeno

Polish this, swab that, carry this, grin when they call you a pussy, sleep the sleep of the dead. For the first time in his memory Zeno is not the darkest-skinned person in the group. Halfway across the South Pacific someone nicknames him Z, and he likes being Z, the skinny Idaho kid slipping through the clanging darkness of the lower decks, male bodies everywhere he looks, young and crew-cut, torsos flowering up out of narrow belts, veins twining round forearms, men with trunks like inverted triangles, men with chins like cowcatchers at the fronts of trains. With each mile he puts between himself and Lakeport, his sense of possibility builds.

In Pyongyang, ice glazes the river. The quartermaster issues him a quilted field jacket, a knit cap, and a lightweight pair of cushion-sole cotton-blend socks; Zeno wears two pairs of Utah Woolen Mills socks instead. A motor transport officer assigns him and a freckled private from New Jersey named Blewitt to drive a Dodge M37 supply truck from the air base in the city to forward outposts. Most of the roads are unpaved, single-lane, and snow-packed, hardly roads at all, and in early March of 1951, eleven days after his arrival in Korea, Zeno and Blewitt are driving a load of rations and fresh produce around a hairpin turn, following a jeep up a steep grade, Blewitt behind the wheel, both of them singing

I'm forever blowing bubbles,
Pretty bubbles in the air,
They fly so high,
nearly reach the sky

when the jeep in front of them tears in half. Pieces of it cartwheel off the side of the road to their left, gun barrels flash to their right, and a figure materializes in front of them waving what looks like an old potato-masher grenade. Blewitt cuts the wheel. There's a blaze of light, followed by a strange booming, like a steel drum being pounded underwater. Then Zeno feels as though the delicate parts of his inner ears are yanked out of his head all at once.

The Dodge rolls twice and comes to rest on its side on an open slope half-covered with snow. He sprawls against the windshield, something hot trickling out of his forearm, a high whine clogging both ears.

Blewitt is no longer in the driver's seat. Through the shattered side window Zeno can see soldiers wearing the woolen green uniforms of the Chinese seething down the scree toward him. Multiple sacks of dehydrated eggs, ejected from the back of the truck, have been punctured, and clouds of egg powder hang in the air, and one soldier after another passes through, their bodies and faces streaked yellow.

He thinks: I knew it. All the way to the other side of the globe and I still couldn't outrun it. They'll come now, all my deficiencies promenading past: Athena dragging me off the ice, *The Mermen of Atlantis* shriveling to black. Once, Mr. McCormack, the Ansley machine shop manager, told him his fly was open, and when Zeno, blushing, went to button it, Mr. McCormack said, don't, he liked it like that.

Fruit, the older men called Mr. McCormack. Sissy. Swish.

Zeno tells himself to locate his M1, climb out of the truck, fight, do what his father would have done, but before he can convince his legs to move, a middle-aged Chinese soldier with small beige teeth drags him out of the passenger's door and into the snow. In another breath there are twenty men around him. Their mouths move but his hearing registers nothing. Some carry Russian burp guns; some have rifles that look four decades old; some wear only rice bags for shoes. Most are tearing open C rations they've taken out of the back of the Dodge. One holds a can printed *PINEAPPLE UPSIDE-DOWN CAKE* while another tries to saw it open with a bayonet; another stuffs his mouth with crackers; a fourth bites into a head of cabbage as though it were a giant apple.

Where is the rest of the convoy, where is Blewitt, where is their cover? Strangely, as he is prodded back up the slope, Zeno feels no panic, only a remoteness. The piece of metal sticking out of his forearm, and through the sleeve of his parka, is shaped like a willow leaf, but it does not hurt, not yet, and mostly he is conscious of the striking of his heart and the buzz of nothingness in his ears, as though a pillow is clamped around his head, as though he were back in the little brass bed at Mrs. Boydstun's house, and all this was an unpleasant dream.

He is directed across the road and through the icebound terraces of what might be a vegetable farm and pushed into an animal pen that already contains Blewitt, who is bleeding from the nose and ear, and who keeps miming that he needs a cigarette.

They huddle next to each other on frozen ground. All night they wait to be shot. At some point Zeno pulls the metal leaf out of his forearm and ties his sleeve over the injury and puts his field jacket back on.

At dawn they are marched across a jagged landscape, joining a few other rivulets of prisoners heading north: French, Turks, two Brits. Every day fewer aircraft come overhead. One man coughs incessantly, another has two broken arms, another cradles an eyeball still hanging from its socket. Gradually the hearing in Zeno's left ear returns. Blewitt suffers such intense tobacco withdrawal that, more than once, when a guard throws away a butt, he dives into the snow after it, though he never manages to recover one while it's still lit.

The water they are given smells of excrement. Once a day the Chinese set a pot of boiled whole-kernel corn down in the snow. A few shy away from eating the carbonized crust burned to the bottom of the pot but Zeno remembers the Armour & Company cans Papa used to heat on the wood stove in the cabin beside the lake and chokes it down.

Every time they stop, he unlaces his boots, peels off one pair of Utah Woolen Mills socks, tucks them inside his coat, up against his armpits, and puts on the warmer, drier pair, and this more than anything is what saves him.

In April they reach a permanent camp on the south bank of a river the color of creamed coffee. The prisoners are sorted into two companies, and Blewitt and Zeno are put with the healthier group. Past a series of wooden peasant huts stands a galley kitchen and storeroom; beyond that lies a ravine, the river, Manchuria. Spindly, windwracked conifers stoop here and there, their branches all sculpted by wind in the same direction. No guard dogs, no alarms, no barbed wire, no watchtowers. "The whole country's a damn ice-cold prison," whispers Blewitt, "where are we going to run?"

Their quarters are thatched huts that accommodate twenty licetortured men arrayed on the floor on straw mats. No officers, all enlisted men, all older than Zeno. In the dark they whisper about wives, girlfriends, the Yankees, a trip to New Orleans, Christmas dinners; the ones who have been here the longest report that during winter they lost multiple men every day, that their lot has improved since the Chinese took over the camps from the North Koreans, and he comes to learn that anyone who fixates—who talks nonstop about ham sandwiches, or a girl, or a certain memory of home—is usually the next to die.

Because he can walk without trouble, Zeno is assigned duty as a fireman: he spends most of every day gathering wood to heat black pots hung over the fireplaces in the prisoners' kitchen. Those first weeks they eat soybeans or dry field corn boiled to a paste. For dinner there might be wormy fish or potatoes, none larger than an acorn. Some days, with his wounded forearm, it's all Zeno can do to gather a single load of wood, bundle it, drag it into the galley, and lie down in the corner.

Panic attacks come on late at night: slow, constricting things in which Zeno cannot breathe for terrifying intervals and from which he worries he will never recover. In the mornings intelligence officers give speeches in broken English about the perils of fighting on behalf of warmongering capitalists. You are imperialist pawns, they say, your system is a failure, don't you know that half the people in New York are starving?

They pass around drawings of Uncle Sam with vampire teeth and dollar signs for eyes. Anybody want a hot shower and a T-bone steak? All you have to do is pose for some photos, sign a petition or two, sit in front of a microphone, and read some sentences condemning America. When they ask Zeno how many B-29s the U.S. Army keeps at Okinawa, he says, "Ninety thousand," probably more airplanes than there have ever been in the history of the world. When he explains to an interrogator that he lives near water, the interrogator makes Zeno draw the marina at Lakeport. Two days later he tells Zeno that they lost the map and makes him draw it again to see if he draws it the same way twice.

One day a guard summons Zeno and Blewitt from their barracks and leads them behind the camp headquarters to the rim of a ravine the prisoners call Rock Gully. With the barrel of his carbine he points at one of the four isolation boxes there, then walks away. The box looks like a big coffin made from mud, pebbles, and cornstalks, with a wooden lid latched over the top. Seven feet long and maybe four high, it's big enough that a man could lie down inside, and possibly kneel, but not stand up.

Loathsome, abhorrent, repugnant: the smell as they approach surpasses adjectives. Zeno holds his breath as he undoes the latches. Waves of flies rise out.

"Holy Christ," breathes Blewitt.

Inside, tucked against the far wall, is a corpse: small, anemic, pale blond. His uniform, or what's left of it, is the British battle-dress blouse with two huge chest pockets. One of the lenses of his eyeglasses is cracked and when he raises one hand to thumb them higher on his nose, Zeno and Blewitt jump.

"Easy," says Blewitt, and the man peers up as though encountering beings from another galaxy.

His fingernails are black and cracked and, beneath the seething flies, his face and throat are veined with filth. It's only when Zeno turns over the lid to set it down that he sees that, scratched into every available inch of its underside, are words. Half in English, half in something else.

ἔνθα δὲ δένδρεα μακρὰ πεφύκασι τηλεθόωντα, reads one line, the strange printing sagging to one side.

Therein grow trees, tall and luxuriant.

ὄγχναι καὶ ῥοιαὶ καὶ μηλέαι ἀγλαόκαρποι.

Pears and pomegranates and apple-trees with their bright fruit.

A throbbing starts in his chest. He knows this verse.

ἐν δὲ δύω κρῆναι ἡ μέν τ᾽ ἀνὰ κῆπον ἅπαντα.

And therein are two springs, one of which sends its water throughout all the garden.

"Kid? You gone deaf again?" Blewitt has climbed into the box and is trying to lift the man by his armpits, his face wrenched away from the odor, and the man is simply blinking through his broken glasses.

"Z? You planning to pick your nose all day?"

He gathers what information he can. The soldier is Lance Corporal Rex Browning, a grammar school teacher from East London who volunteered for the war, and he spent two weeks inside that box, sentenced to "attitude reorientation" for trying to escape, and was let out for only twenty minutes a day.

"A corner-turner," someone calls him. "Sectionable," another says, because, as everyone knows, successfully escaping from Camp Five is a fantasy. The prisoners are unshaven, they're feeble from malnutrition, and they're taller than the Koreans—instantly recognizable as Westerners. Anyone who managed to get past the guards would have to pass undetected through a hundred miles of mountains, slip around dozens of checkpoints, make his way over gorges and across rivers, and any Koreans who might take pity on him would almost certainly be denounced and shot.

And yet, Zeno learns, Rex Browning the grammar school teacher tried. He was found a few miles south of camp, fifteen feet up a pine tree. The Chinese cut down the tree, then dragged him behind a jeep all the way back.

A few weeks later Zeno is gathering firewood from a hillside, the nearest guard several hundred yards away, when he sees Rex Browning picking his way along the trail below. Though his frame is skeletal, he doesn't limp. He moves with efficiency, pausing now and then to pluck leaves from plants and stuff them into his shirt pockets.

Zeno shoulders his bundle and hurries down through the brush. "Hello?"

Thirty feet, twenty, ten. "Hello?"

Still the man doesn't stop. Zeno reaches the trail out of breath, and, praying the guards won't hear, calls, "*Such were the glorious gifts of the gods in the palace of brave Alcinous, king of the Phaeacians.*"

Rex turns then and nearly falls, and stands blinking his big eyes behind his broken glasses.

"Or something like that," says Zeno, blushing.

The other man laughs, a warm, irresistible laugh. The grime has been scrubbed out of the folds of his neck, his trousers mended with neat stitches: he is maybe thirty years old. His cornsilk hair, his flaxen eyebrows, his fine hands—in other circumstances, in another world, Zeno realizes, Rex Browning is handsome.

Rex says, "Zenodotus."

"What?"

"The first librarian at the library at Alexandria. He was named Zenodotus. Appointed by the Ptolemaic kings."

That accent: *library* becomes *lie-brury*. The trees vibrate in the wind and the firewood cuts into Zeno's shoulders and he sets down his load.

"It's just a name."

Rex looks at the sky as though awaiting instructions. The skin of his throat is drawn so thin that Zeno can almost see the blood ticking through his arteries. He seems too insubstantial for such a place, as though any moment he will blow away.

Abruptly he turns and starts down the trail again. Lesson over. Zeno picks up his bundle and follows. "The two librarians in my town read it to me. *The Odyssey*, I mean. Twice. Once after I moved there, again after my father died. Who knows why."

They keep on for a few more paces and Rex pauses to collect more leaves and Zeno leans over his knees and waits for the ground to stop spinning.

"It's like they say," says Rex. High above them the wind is shredding a vast sheet of cirrus. "Antiquity was invented to be the bread of librarians and schoolmasters."

He cuts his eyes to Zeno and smiles, so Zeno smiles back, though he does not understand the joke, and a guard at the top of the ridge shouts something down through the trees in Chinese and the two men continue along the trail.

"That was Greek, then? That you scratched into the wooden lid?"

"As a schoolboy, you know, I didn't care for it. Seemed so dusty and dead. The classics master made us choose four pages of Homer, memorize and translate them. I chose Book Seven. Torment, or so I thought at the time. I'd walk the lines into my memory, one word at a time. Out the door: *I could tell yet a longer tale of all the evils which I have endured by the will of the gods.* Down the stairs: *But as for me, suffer me now to eat, despite my grief.* To the loo: *For there is nothing more shameless than a hateful belly.* But during a fortnight alone in the dark"—he taps his temple—"you'd be surprised what you can find etched in the old brain box."

They walk several more minutes in silence, Rex slowing with each step, and soon they are at the edge of Camp Five.

Woodsmoke, a rumbling generator, the Chinese flag. The reek of the latrines. All around them the little hunched trees whisper. Zeno can see a darkness seize Rex, then slowly release him.

"I know why those librarians read the old stories to you," Rex says. "Because if it's told well enough, for as long as the story lasts, you get to slip the trap."

LAKEPORT, IDAHO

2014

Seymour

For months after the Eden's Gate sign appears on the shoulder of Arcady Lane, nothing changes. The osprey leaves her nest atop the tallest tree in the woods and heads for Mexico, and the first snows blow down from the mountains, and the county plow plows it into berms, and Lake Street fills with weekenders driving to the ski hill, and Bunny cleans their rooms at the Aspen Leaf Lodge.

Every day after school, eleven-year-old Seymour walks past the sign

COMING SOON
CUSTOM TOWNHOMES AND COTTAGES
PREMIER HOMESITES AVAILABLE

and drops his backpack on the love seat in the living room and postholes up through the snow to the big dead ponderosa, and every few days Trustyfriend is there, listening to the squeaks of voles, and the scratchings of mice, and the beating inside Seymour's chest.

But on the first warm morning in April, two dump trucks and a flatbed carrying a steamroller stop in front of the double-wide. Airbrakes moan and walkie-talkies squawk and trucks beep, and by Friday after school, Arcady Lane is paved.

Seymour crouches on the brand-new asphalt at the tail end of a spring rain. Everything smells of fresh tar. With two fingers he tweezers up a stranded earthworm, hardly more than a waterlogged pink string. This worm did not expect rain to wash it from its tunnels onto pavement, did it? To find itself on this strange new impenetrable surface?

Two clouds separate and sunlight spills onto the street, and

Seymour glances to his left, and the bodies of what might be fifty thousand earthworms catch the light. Worms, he realizes, cover the whole blacktop. Thousands upon thousands. He deposits the first at the base of a huckleberry bush, rescues a second, then a third. The pines drip; the asphalt steams; the worms thresh.

He rescues twenty-four twenty-five twenty-six. Clouds seal off the sun. A truck turns off Cross Road and approaches, crushing the bodies of how many? Faster. Pick up the pace. Forty-three worms forty-four forty-five. He expects the truck to stop, an adult to climb out, wave the boy over, offer an explanation. The truck keeps going.

Surveyors park white pickups at the end of the road and climb through the trees behind the house. They set up tripods, tie ribbons around trunks. By late April, chain saws are droning in the woods.

As he walks home from school, fear buzzes in Seymour's ears. He imagines looking down at the forest from above: there's the double-wide, the dwindling forest, the clearing at the center. There's Trusty-friend, sitting on his limb, an oval with two eyes surrounded by 27,027 dots in rings.

Bunny is at the kitchen table, lost behind a drift of bills. "Oh, Possum, it's not our property. They can do whatever they want with it."

"Why?"

"Because those are the rules."

He presses his forehead to the sliding door. She tears out a check, licks an envelope. "Know what? Those saws could mean good news for us. Remember Geoff-with-a-G from work? He says that lots at the top of Eden's Gate might go for two hundred thousand."

Darkness is falling. Bunny says the number a second time.

Trucks grumble past the double-wide loaded with logs; bulldozers punch through the end of Arcady Lane and cut a Z-shaped extension up the hillside. Every day, as soon as the last truck leaves, Seymour walks the new roadway with his earmuffs on.

Sewage pipes loll like fallen pillars in front of mounds of debris; great coils of cables lie here and there. The air smells of shattered wood, sawdust, and gasoline.

NeedleMen lie crushed in the mud. *Our legs are broken*, they murmur in their xylophone voices. *Our cities are ruined.* Halfway up the hill, Trustyfriend's clearing has become a tire-churned welter of roots and branches. For now the big dead ponderosa still stands. Seymour trawls his gaze along every limb, every branch, until his neck aches from looking.

Empty empty empty empty.

"Hello?"

Nothing.

"Can you hear me?"

He does not see Trustyfriend for four weeks. Five. Five and a half. Every day more light spills into what was, hours before, forest.

Realty signs sprout up and down the newly paved road, two with *SOLD* placards already attached. Seymour takes a flyer. *Live the Lakeport lifestyle*, it reads, *that you've always wanted.* There's a map of homesites, a drone photograph with the lake in the distance.

At the library Marian tells him that the Eden's Gate people jumped through all the planning and zoning hoops, hosted a public hearing, handed out some seriously delicious cupcakes with their logo in the frosting. She says they even purchased the crumbling old Victorian next to the library and plan to remodel it as a showroom.

"Development," she says, "has always been part of the story of this town." From a file cabinet in Local History she produces black-and-white prints from a century ago. Six lumbermen stand shoulder to shoulder on the stump of a felled cedar. Fishermen hold yard-long salmon up by their gills. Several hundred beaver pelts hang from a cabin wall.

Looking at the images starts the roar murmuring at the base of Seymour's spine. In a vision he imagines a hundred thousand NeedleMen rising from the ruins of the forest and marching on the contractors' trucks, a vast army, fearless despite the incredible odds, swinging tiny picks at tires, driving nails through men's boots. Plumbing vans go up in flames.

"A lot of folks in Lakeport," says Marian, "are excited about Eden's Gate."

"Why?"

She gives him a sad smile. "Well, you know what they say."

He chews his shirt collar. He doesn't know what they say.

"Money isn't everything. It's the only thing."

She looks as though she expects him to laugh, but he doesn't understand what's funny, and a woman wearing sunglasses jerks a thumb toward the back of the library and says, "I think your toilet is overflowing," and Marian hurries away.

Nonfiction 598.9:

Between 365 million and one billion birds die just from crashing into windows in the United States each year.

Digest of Avian Biology:

Multiple onlookers reported that after the crow died, a large number of fellow crows (well over one hundred individuals by some accounts) descended from the trees and walked circles around the deceased for fifteen minutes.

Nonfiction 598.27:

After its mate struck the utility wire, researchers witnessed the owl return to its roost, turn its face to the trunk, and stand motionless for several days until it died.

• • •

One day, halfway through June, Seymour comes home from the library, stares up into Eden's Gate, and sees that Trustyfriend's big dead tree has been cut down. Where this morning the snag stood on the hillside behind the double-wide, now there is only air.

A man unrolls an orange hose from a truck; a backhoe cuts galleries for culverts; someone yells, "Mike! Mike!" The view from the egg-shaped boulder now stretches up a bare drumlin of shredded forest all the way to the top.

He drops his books and runs. Down Arcady Lane, down Spring Street, south along the gravel shoulder of Route 55, traffic roaring past, running not so much in rage but in panic. All this must be undone.

It's the dinner hour and the Pig N' Pancake is packed. Seymour pants in front of the hostess stand and scans faces. The manager eyes him; people waiting for tables watch. Bunny comes through the kitchen door with platters stacked along both arms.

"Seymour? Are you hurt?"

Somehow still balancing five plates of patty melts and chicken-fried steaks on her arms, she crouches, and he lifts one cup of his ear defenders.

Smells: ground beef, maple syrup, French fries. Sounds: the grading of rocks, the driving of sledges, the back-up alarms of dump trucks. He's a mile and a half from Eden's Gate but somehow he can still hear it, as though it's a prison being built around him, as though he's a fly being wrapped and spun in a spiderweb.

Diners watch. The manager watches.

"Possum?"

Words stack up against the backs of his teeth. A busboy trundles past, pushing an empty high chair on wheels, the wheels going *thumpthwock* over the tiles. A woman laughs. Someone yells, "Order up!" The woods the tree the owl—through the soles of his feet he feels a chain saw bite into a trunk, feels Trustyfriend startle awake. No time to think: you drop like shadow into the daylight, as one more safe harbor is wrenched out of the world.

"Seymour, put your hand in my pocket. Do you feel the keys? The car is right outside. Go sit in there, where it's quiet, do your breathing exercise, and I'll be out as soon as I can."

He sits in the Pontiac as shadows trickle down through the pines. Inhale for four, hold for four, exhale for four. Bunny comes out in her apron and gets in the car and rubs her forehead with the heels of her hands. In a to-go box she has three pancakes with strawberries and cream.

"Use your fingers, honey, it's all right."

The fading light plays tricks; the parking lot stretches; trees become dream trees. A first star shows, then hides itself again. Best friends best friends, we're never apart.

Bunny tears off a piece of pancake and hands it to him.

"Okay if I take off your muffs?"

He nods.

"And touch your hair?"

He tries not to wince as her fingers catch in his snarls. A family leaves the restaurant, climbs into a truck, and drives away.

"Change is tough, kid, I know. Life is tough. But we still have the house. We still have our yard. We still have each other. Right?" He closes his eyes and sees Trustyfriend cruise over a wasteland of endless parking lots, nowhere to hunt, nowhere to land, nowhere to sleep.

"It won't be the worst thing to have neighbors close by. Maybe there will be kids your age."

An aproned teenager crashes out the back door and lobs a plump black bag into the dumpster. Seymour says, "They need big hunting ranges. They especially like high vantage points so they can hunt voles."

"What's a vole?"

"They're like mice."

She turns his earmuffs in her hands. "There are at least twenty places like that north of here your owl could fly to. Bigger forests, better forests. He could have his pick."

"There are?"

"Sure."

"With lots of voles?"

"Tons of voles. More voles than there are hairs on your head."

Seymour chews some pancake and Bunny looks at herself in the rearview mirror and sighs.

"You promise, Mom?"

"I promise."

THE ARGOS

MISSION YEAR 61

Konstance

It's the morning of her tenth birthday. Inside Compartment 17, NoLight brightens to DayLight, and she uses the toilet and brushes her hair and powders her teeth and when she pulls back the curtain, Mother and Father are standing there.

"Close your eyes and put out your hands," says Mother, and Konstance does. Even before she opens her eyes, she knows what her mother is setting onto her forearms: a new worksuit. The fabric is canary yellow and the cuffs and hems are tacked with little *x*'s of thread and Mother has embroidered a little Bosnian pine on the collar to match the two-and-a-half-year-old seedling growing inside Farm 4.

Konstance presses it to her nose; it smells of the rarest thing: newness.

"You'll grow into it," says Mother, and zips the suit to Konstance's throat. In the Commissary everyone is there—Jessi Ko and Ramón and Mrs. Chen and Tayvon Lee and Dr. Pori the ninety-nine-year-old mathematics teacher—and everyone sings the Library Day song and Sara Jane sets two big pancakes, made with real flour, one stacked atop the other, in front of her. Little cascades of syrup trickle off the edges.

Everyone watches, the teenaged boys especially, none of whom have eaten a pancake made with real flour since their own tenth birthdays. Konstance rolls up the first cake and eats it in four bites; she takes her time with the second. After she finishes, she raises the tray to her face and licks it, and there is applause.

Then Mother and Father walk her back to Compartment 17 to wait. Somehow she has gotten a blob of syrup on her sleeve, and she worries Mother will be upset, but Mother is too excited to notice, and Father only winks, licks a finger, and helps her blot it out.

"It'll be a lot to take in at first," Mother says, "but eventually you'll love it, you'll see, it's time for you to grow up a little, and this may help with some of your—" but before she can finish Mrs. Flowers arrives.

Mrs. Flowers's eyes are foggy with cataracts and her breath reeks of concentrated carrot paste and every day she seems smaller than the last. Father helps her set the Perambulator she's carrying on the floor beside Mother's sewing table.

From the pocket of her worksuit Mrs. Flowers produces a Vizer twinkling with golden lights. "It's secondhand, of course, belonged to Mrs. Alegawa, rest her soul. It may not look perfect, but it passed all the diagnostics."

Konstance steps onto the Perambulator and it thrums beneath her feet. Father squeezes her hand, looking sad and happy at the same time, and Mrs. Flowers says, "See you in there," and totters back out the door, heading for her own compartment six doors down. Konstance feels Mother fit the Vizer over the back of her head, feels it squeeze her occipital bones, extend past her ears, and seal across her eyes. She worried it would hurt, but it only feels as though someone has crept up behind her and pressed two cold hands over her face.

"We'll be right here," says Mother, and Father adds, "Next to you the whole time," and the walls of Compartment 17 disintegrate.

She stands in a vast atrium. Three tiers of bookshelves, each fifteen feet tall, served by hundreds of ladders, run for what appear to be miles down either side. Above the third tier, twin arcades of marble columns support a barrel-vaulted ceiling cut through its center by a rectangular aperture, above which puffy clouds float through a cobalt sky.

Here and there in front of her, figures stand at tables or sit in armchairs. On the tiers above, others peruse shelves or lean on railings or climb or descend the ladders. And through the air, for as far as she can see, books—some as small as her hand, some as big as the mattress on which she sleeps—are flying, lifting off shelves, returning to them, some flitting like songbirds, some lumbering along like big ungainly storks.

For a moment she simply stands and looks, speechless. Never has she stood in a space remotely this large. Dr. Pori the mathematics teacher—only his hair is rich and black, not silver, and looks wet and dry at the same time—slips down a ladder to her right, skipping every other rung like an athletic young man, and lands neatly on both feet. He winks at her; his teeth look milk white.

The yellow of Konstance's worksuit is even more vibrant than it was in Compartment 17. The spot of syrup is gone.

Mrs. Flowers marches toward her from a long way off, a little white dog trotting at her heels. She's a cleaner, younger, brighter Mrs. Flowers, with clear hazel eyes and mahogany hair cut in a professorial bob, and she wears a skirt and blazer that are the deep green of living spinach, and on one breast golden stitching reads, *Head Librarian*.

Konstance bends over the little dog: its whiskers twitch; its black eyes shine; its fur, when she puts her fingers in it, feels like fur. She almost laughs from the joy of it.

"Welcome," says Mrs. Flowers, "to the Library."

She and Konstance start down the length of the atrium. Various crew members glance up from tables and smile as they pass; a few conjure balloons that say *IT'S YOUR LIBRARY DAY* and Konstance watches them sail up through the aperture into the sky.

The spines of the books closest to them are teal and maroon and imperial purple and some look slender and delicate and others resemble great legless tabletops stacked on shelves. "Go on," says Mrs. Flowers, "you can't damage them," and Konstance touches the spine of a little one and it rises and opens in front of her. From its onionskin pages, three daisies grow, and in the center of each glow the same three letters, *M C V*.

"Some are quite bewildering," says Mrs. Flowers. She taps it and it closes and flits back to its place. Konstance gazes down the line of bookshelves to where the atrium fades into the distance.

"Does it go on—?"

Mrs. Flowers smiles. "Only Sybil could say for sure."

Three teenaged boys, the Lee brothers and Ramón—only it's a leaner, tidier version of Ramón—sprint and leap onto a ladder, and Mrs. Flowers calls, "Slowly, please," and Konstance tries to remind herself that she is still inside Compartment 17, wearing her new worksuit and a hand-me-down Vizer, walking on a Perambulator wedged beside Father's bunk and Mother's sewing table—that Mrs. Flowers and the Lee brothers and Ramón are in their own family compartments, walking on their own Perambulators, wearing their own Vizers, that they are all packed inside a disk hurtling through interstellar space, that the Library is just a swarm of data inside the flickering chandelier that is Sybil.

"History's on our right," Mrs. Flowers is saying, "to the left is Modern Art, then Languages; those boys are headed to the Games Section, very popular, of course." She stops at an unoccupied table with a chair on either side and gestures for Konstance to sit. Two little boxes rest on top: one of pencils, the other of rectangles of paper. Between them is a small brass slot and engraved onto its rim are the words *Questions Answered Here.*

"For a child's Library Day," says Mrs. Flowers, "when there is so much to absorb, I try to keep things simple. Four questions, a little scavenger hunt. Question number one. How far from Earth is our destination?"

Konstance blinks, unsure, and Mrs. Flowers's expression softens. "You needn't have it memorized, dear. That's what the Library is for." She points to the boxes.

Konstance picks up a pencil: it seems so real that she wants to sink her teeth into it. And the paper! It's so clean, so crisp: outside the Library, there is not a piece of paper this clean on the entire *Argos*. She writes *How far from Earth to Beta Oph2?* and looks at Mrs. Flowers and Mrs. Flowers nods and Konstance drops the slip through the slot.

The paper vanishes. Mrs. Flowers clears her throat and points, and behind Konstance, high on the third tier, a thick brown book slips off a shelf. It soars across the atrium, dodges a few other airborne books, hovers, then floats down and opens.

Across a double-fold inside spreads a chart titled *Confirmed List of Exoplanets in the Optimistic Habitable Zone, B-C.* In the first column, little worlds of every color rotate: some rocky, some swirling with gases, some ringed, some dragging tails of ice behind their atmospheres. Konstance runs a fingertip down the rows until she finds Beta Oph2.

"4.2399 light-years."

"Good. Question number two. How fast are we traveling?"

Konstance writes the question, drops it into the slot, and as the first volume rises away, a bundle of rolled charts arrives and unrolls across the tabletop. From its center a bright blue integer rises into the air.

"7,734,958 kilometers per hour."

"Right." Now three of Mrs. Flowers's fingers go up. "What is the lifespan of a genetically optimal human under mission conditions?" The question goes into the slot; a half-dozen documents of various sizes fly off shelves and flutter over.

114 years, reads one.

116 years, reads a second.

119 years, reads a third.

Mrs. Flowers bends to scratch the ears of the dog at her feet. All the while she watches Konstance. "Now you know the *Argos*'s velocity, the distance it needs to travel, and the expected lifespan of a traveler under these conditions. Last question. How long will our journey take?"

Konstance stares at the desk.

"Use the Library, dear." Again Mrs. Flowers taps the slot with one fingernail. Konstance writes the question on a sheet of paper and drops it in the slot, and as soon as it vanishes a single slip of paper emerges high in the barrel vault, drifting down, seesawing back and forth like a feather, and lands in front of her.

"216,078 Earth days."

Mrs. Flowers watches her, and Konstance gazes down the length of the vast atrium to where the shelves and ladders converge in the distance, and a glimmer of understanding rises, then sinks away again.

"How many years is that, Konstance?"

She looks up. A flock of digital birds passes above the barrel vault, and below that a hundred books and scrolls and documents crisscross the air at a hundred different altitudes, and she can feel the attention of others in the Library on her. She writes *216,078 Earth days in years?* and puts the paper in and a fresh slip flutters down.

592.

The pattern of woodgrain on the surface of the desk is churning now, or appears to be, and the marble floor tiles are swirling too, and something roils in her gut.

> *It takes everyone together,*
> *Everyone together . . .*

Five hundred and ninety-two years.

"We'll never—?"

"That's right, child. We know that Beta Oph2 has an atmosphere like Earth's, that it has liquid water like Earth does, that it probably has forests of some type. But we will never see them. None of us will. We are the bridge generations, the intermediaries, the ones who do the work so that our descendants will be ready."

Konstance presses her palms to the desk; she feels as though she might black out.

"The truth is a great deal to absorb, I know. That's why we wait to bring children to the Library. Until you are mature enough."

Mrs. Flowers lifts a slip of paper from the box and writes something. "Come, I want to show you one more thing." She tucks the paper into the slot and a tattered book, as wide and as tall as the entrance to Compartment 17, lurches off a second-floor shelf, gives a few inelegant flaps, and lands open in front of them. Its pages are profoundly black, as though a doorway has been opened on the rim of a bottomless pit.

"The Atlas," says Mrs. Flowers, "is a bit dated, I'm afraid. I introduce it to all the children on their Library Day, but after that they tend to prefer slicker, more immersive things. Go on."

Konstance pokes a finger into the page, pulls it back. Then a foot. Mrs. Flowers takes her hand and Konstance shuts her eyes and braces herself and they step through together.

They don't fall: they hang suspended in the black. In all directions, pinpricks of light perforate the dark. Over Konstance's shoulder floats the frame of the Atlas, a lit rectangle through which she can still glimpse shelves back inside the Library.

"Sybil," says Mrs. Flowers, "take us to Istanbul."

In the blackness far below a speck enlarges into a dot, then a blue-green sphere, growing larger; one blue hemisphere, aswirl with vapor, rotates through sunlight, while the other passes through an ultramarine darkness, latticed with electric light. "Is that—?" Konstance asks, but now they are dropping feet-first toward the sphere, or else it's hurtling toward them: it pivots, grows enormous, fills her entire field of vision. She holds her breath as a peninsula expands beneath them—jade-green mottled with beiges and reds, the richness of color overloading her eyes; what rushes toward her is more lavish, more complex, and more intricate than anything she has ever imagined or thought to imagine, a billion Farm 4s all in one place, and now she and Mrs. Flowers are falling through air that is somehow both transparent and aglow, descending over a dense circuitry of roads and rooftops, and finally her feet touch the Earth.

They're in an empty lot. The sky is jewel blue and cloudless. Huge white stones lie among weeds like the lost molars of giants. Off to their left, undulating alongside a crowded road for as far as she can see in both directions, runs a massive and derelict stone wall, tufted everywhere with grasses and punctuated every fifty meters or so by a broad, time-battered tower.

Konstance feels as though every neuron inside her head has been set on fire. They said Earth was a ruin.

"As you know," says Mrs. Flowers, "we're traveling too fast to receive any new data, so depending on when this imaging was done, this is Istanbul as it looked six or seven decades ago, before the *Argos* departed low Earth orbit."

The weeds! Weeds with leaves like the blades of Mother's sewing scissors, weeds with leaves shaped like Jessi Ko's eyes, weeds with tiny purple flowers on tiny green stems—how many times has Father reminisced about the glories of weeds? A stone beside her foot is mottled with black—is that lichen? Father is always talking about lichen! She reaches to touch it but her hand passes right through.

"All you can do is look," says Mrs. Flowers. "The only solid thing in the Atlas is the ground. As I said, once the children try the newer things, they hardly ever come back."

She leads Konstance toward the base of the wall. Everything is motionless. "Sooner or later, child," Mrs. Flowers says, "all living things die. You, me, your mother, your father, everyone and everything. Even the limestone blocks from which these walls were constructed consist predominantly of the skeletons of long-dead creatures, snails and corals. Come."

In the shadow of the nearest tower stand a few images of people: one looking up, another caught mid-climb along the stairs. Konstance can see a shirt with buttons, blue pants, a man's sandals, a woman's jacket, but the software has blurred their faces. "For privacy," explains Mrs. Flowers. She points to a staircase winding round the tower. "We go up."

"I thought you said the only solid thing is the ground."

Mrs. Flowers smiles. "Wander around in here long enough, dear, and you'll discover a secret or two."

With each step up, Konstance can see more of the modern city sprawled around both sides of the old wall: antennas, automobiles, tarps, a building with a thousand windows, everything frozen in time; she can hardly breathe trying to take it all in.

"For as long as we have been a species, whether with medicine or technology, by gathering power, by embarking on journeys, or by telling stories, we humans have tried to defeat death. None of us ever has."

They reach the top of the tower and Konstance gazes out, dizzy: the rust-red brick, the limestone made from the bodies of dead creatures, the green ivy flowing up the walls in waves—it's all too much.

"But some of the things we build," continues Mrs. Flowers, "do last. Around the year 410 of the Common Era, the emperor of this city, Theodosius the Second, began constructing these walls, four miles of them, to connect with the eight miles of sea walls the city already had. The Theodosian walls had an outer wall, two meters thick and nine high, and an inner one, five meters thick and twelve high—who can guess how many bodies were broken in their construction?"

A tiny insect has been captured crossing the railing directly in front of Konstance. Its carapace is blue-black and shiny, its legs incredible in their articulations: a beetle.

"For over a thousand years these walls warded off every attack," Mrs. Flowers says. "Books were confiscated at the ports and not returned until they had been copied, all by hand of course, and some believe that at various points the libraries inside the city contained more books than all the other libraries in the world combined. And all this time earthquakes and floods and armies came, and the people of the city worked together to fortify the walls even as weeds scrambled up their sides, and rain trickled down into fissures, until they could not remember a time when the walls didn't exist."

Konstance reaches to touch the beetle, but the railing frays into pixels and again her fingers pass through.

"You and I will never reach Beta Oph2, dear, and that is a painful truth. But in time you will come to believe that there is nobility in being a part of an enterprise that will outlast you."

The walls do not move; the people below do not breathe; the trees do not sway; the automobiles are still; the beetle is frozen in time. A thought, or a reconsidered memory, strikes her: of the ten-year-olds before her, like Mother, who were born on board, who woke up on their Library Days dreaming of the hour they'd set foot on Beta Oph2 and take a breath outside the *Argos*, the shelters they'd build, the mountains they'd climb, the life-forms they might discover— a second Earth!—and then they come out of their compartments after their Library Day looking different, valleys in their foreheads, shoulders drooped, lamps dimmed in their eyes. They stopped running down corridors, took SleepDrops at NoLight; sometimes she'd catch older children staring at their hands or the walls, or moving past the Commissary slumped and weary like they carried invisible backpacks made of stone.

You, me, your mother, your father, everyone and everything.

She says, "But I don't want to die."

Mrs. Flowers smiles. "I know, dear. You won't, not for a long time. You have an extraordinary journey to help complete. Come, it's time to go; time moves strangely in here and Third Meal is beginning." She takes Konstance's hand and they rise together up from the tower, the city falling away, a strait becoming visible, then seas, continents, the Earth dwindling until it's just a pinprick again, and they step back through the Atlas into the Library.

In the atrium the little dog wags its tail and paws at Konstance's leg and Mrs. Flowers looks at her kindly as the huge frayed Atlas closes, rises, and floats back to its shelf. The sky above the vault is lavender now. Fewer books fly through the air. Most of the crew members are gone.

Her palms are damp and her feet hurt. When she thinks of the younger children darting down the corridors right now, on their way to Third Meal, a long ache runs through her like a blade. Mrs. Flowers gestures at the measureless shelves. "Each of these books, child, is a door, a gateway to another place and time. You have your whole life in front of you, and for all of it, you'll have this. It will be enough, don't you think?"

EIGHT

ROUND AND ROUND

Cloud Cuckoo Land by Antonius Diogenes, Folio Θ

. . . north, north, for weeks the miller and his son rode me north. Cramps gnawed my muscles and cracks splintered my hooves, and I longed to rest and eat some bread, maybe a slice of lamb or two, some nice fish soup and a cup of wine, but no sooner had we arrived at their craggy, frozen farm than the miller brought me to the millhouse and harnessed me to the wheel.

I plodded in endless circles turning the stone, grinding wheat and barley for every farmer, it seemed, in the whole wretched, frigid country, and if I slowed for even a step, the miller's son was sure to take his stick from the corner and whack me on the hind legs. When at last they turned me out to pasture, ice rained from the sky and the wind blew with a frosty rage, and the horses were not pleased to share what little wisps of grass they had. Worse, they suspected me of seducing their wives, though I had no interest! There could be no roses here for months.

I watched birds flit overhead, on their way to greener places, and longing flared inside my ribs. Why were the gods so cruel? Had I not suffered enough for my curiosities? All I ever did in that brutish valley was grind the wheel, round and round, round and round, turn-sick and dizzy, until I felt I was drilling down to the underworld, and would soon stand to my belly in the boiling waters of Acheron, the river of pain, and look Hades in the face . . .

THE ROAD TO CONSTANTINOPLE

JANUARY–APRIL 1453

Omeir

I t is 140 miles from the testing ground in Edirne to the Queen of Cities and they bring the cannon there at a pace slower than a man can crawl. The train of oxen pulling it runs to thirty pairs, each harnessed to a jointed pole in the middle, a train so long and with so many potential points of failure that it comes to a halt dozens of times a day. Behind and in front of them, other oxen pull culverins and catapults and arquebuses, perhaps thirty artillery pieces in all, while still others pull wagons of powder or stone balls, some so large Omeir could not wrap his arms around them.

On both sides of the road, around the teams, men and beasts hurry past like a river flows around a boulder: mules loaded with saddlebags, camels with dozens of earthen jugs hung over their backs, carts laden with provisions and planks and ropes and cloth. How diverse the world is! Omeir sees fortune-tellers, dervishes, astrologers, scholars, bakers, munitions men, blacksmiths, mystics in tattered robes, chroniclers and healers and standard-bearers carrying banners of every color. Some wear leather armor, some have feathers tied to their caps, some are barefoot, some wear boots of shiny Damascene leather to their knees. He sees a group of slaves with three horizontal scars on their foreheads (one, Maher explains, for each of their masters who has died); he sees a man whose brow is so callused from prostrating himself in prayer that it seems he carries a great waxy fingernail on his head.

One afternoon: a mule driver wearing bearskin with a gap in his upper lip not at all unlike Omeir's, moving past the teams, head down. As he passes, their eyes meet, and the mule driver looks away, and Omeir never sees him again.

He oscillates between amazement and dejection. Going to bed beside a fire and waking beside the embers, frost sparkling on his clothes, sitting beside the other teamsters as the fire is stirred back to life, everyone eating cracked barley and herbs and bits of horsemeat from the same copper pot, he feels a sense of acceptance he has never come close to feeling before, of everyone participating in a massive and justified endeavor, an undertaking so worthy that it makes room even for a boy with a face like his—everyone moving east toward the great city as though called by a magical piper in one of Grandfather's stories. Each morning dawn arrives earlier, the hours of daylight expanding, flocks of migratory cranes, then ducks, then songbirds pouring overhead, as though the darkness is losing and victory is preordained.

But at other moments his enthusiasm plummets. Mud sticks in great clods to the hooves of Tree and Moonlight, and chains creak and ropes groan and whistles blow up and down the train, and the air seethes with the sounds of suffering animals. Many of the oxen are on fixed yokes, not sliding ones like the kind Grandfather builds, and few of them are used to such heavy loads on uneven ground, and cattle are injured by the hour.

For Omeir each day offers a new lesson in how careless men can be. Some don't bother to shoe their bullocks with two-piece shoes; others don't examine the yokes for cracks and the cracks abrade the backs of the steers; others don't let the animals recover by unyoking them as soon as they are done pulling; still others don't cap their horns to avoid them hooking one another. There is always blood, always groaning, always distress.

Teams of road-builders move ahead of the columns, shoring up crossings, laying boards over muddy ground, but eight days out from Edirne the train reaches an unbridged creek, the water high and turbid, the current in the deepest section rising in a great murky swill. Drivers in the front warn that slick cobbles lurk in the streambed, but the lead teamster says they must push on.

The train is about halfway across when the animal directly in front of Tree slips. The yoke attached to his mate holds him upright for a moment, then the leg of the bullock breaks so loudly that Omeir can feel the crack in his chest. The wounded bullock goes sideways with his partner roaring beside him, the whole train pulled to its left, and Omeir feels Tree and Moonlight brace to take the extra weight as the two cattle flail in the current. A driver hurries forward with a long spear and runs it through first one, then the other thrashing ox, and their blood flows into the water while smiths hack at the chains to break them free, and teamsters hurry up and down the line, ho'ing and settling their animals. Soon riders are hitching horses to each of the two dead bullocks to drag them out of the water so they can be butchered, and the blacksmiths set up a forge and bellows on the muddy bank to repair the chain, and Omeir leads Moonlight and Tree into the grass and wonders if they understand what they have seen.

As darkness falls he grooms first Tree and then Moonlight while they graze, and cleans their hooves, and tells himself he will not eat the slain animals out of respect, but later, after dark, when the smell fills the cold air and the bowls of meat are passed, he cannot help himself. He chews and feels the weight of the sky on him and with it a dark confusion.

With each passing sundown, more light drains out of his oxen. Once in a while Tree blinks his huge wet eyes at Omeir, as though in forgiveness, and in the mornings before he is yoked, Moonlight remains curious, watching butterflies or a rabbit or twitching his nostrils to parse different scents in the wind. But most of the time when they are unyoked they hang their heads and eat as though too weary to do anything more.

The boy stands beside them, ankle-deep in mud, hiding his face inside his hood, and watches the patient, mild way Moonlight's eyelashes glide up and down. His coat, which could look almost silver when he was young, full of little rainbows iridescing in the sun, now looks mouse gray. A cloud of flies floats over a suppurating wound on his shoulder—the first flies, Omeir realizes, of spring.

CONSTANTINOPLE

THOSE SAME MONTHS

Anna

The lead cup rises out of the trickling darkness, the water is mixed with quicksilver, and Maria drinks it down. On the walk home, sheets of snow sweep across the walls, erasing the road. Maria holds her shoulders back. "I can walk on my own," she says, "I feel excellent," but drifts into the path of a carter and is nearly crushed.

After dark she shivers in their cell. "I hear them whipping themselves in the street."

Anna listens. The whole city is still. The only sound is of snow blowing down onto the rooftops.

"Who, sister?"

"Their cries sound so beautiful."

Then come tremors. Anna swaddles her in every piece of clothing they own: linen undershirt, wool overskirt, cloak, scarf, blanket. She brings in coals in metal handwarmers, and still Maria shakes. All her life, her sister has been there. But for how much longer?

Above the city the skies remake themselves by the hour: purple, silver, gold, black. Graupel falls, then sleet, then hail. Widow Theodora peers out the shutters and murmurs verses from Matthew: *Then shall appear in heaven the sign of the Son of Man, and then shall all the tribes of the earth mourn*. In the scullery Chryse says that if the last days are upon them, they might as well finish all the wine.

The talk in the streets oscillates between the strange weather and numbers. The sultan, some say, is marching an army of twenty thousand from Edirne at this very moment. Others say his soldiers number closer to one hundred thousand. How many defenders can the dying city muster? Eight thousand? Others predict the number will be closer to four thousand, only three hundred of whom can properly use a crossbow.

Eight miles of sea walls, four miles of land walls, 192 total towers, and they're going to defend them all with four thousand men?

Arms are requisitioned by the emperor's guard for redistribution, but in the courtyard in front of the gates of Saint Theophano, Anna sees a soldier presiding over a sad pile of rusted blades. In one hour she hears that the young sultan is a wonder-worker who speaks seven languages and recites ancient poetry, that he is a diligent student of astronomy and geometry, a mild and merciful monarch, tolerant of all faiths. In the next hour he's a bloodthirsty fiend who ordered his baby brother drowned in his bath, then beheaded the man he sent to drown him.

In the workshop, Widow Theodora forbids the needleworkers from speaking of the looming threat: the only talk should be of needles, stitchwork, and the glory of God. Wrap the wire in dyed thread, group the wrapped wires in threes, place a stitch, turn the frame. One morning with great ceremony Widow Theodora rewards Maria for her diligence with the job of embroidering twelve birds, one for each apostle, into a green samite hood that will be attached to a bishop's cope. Maria, her fingers trembling, sets straight to work, murmuring a prayer as she locks the bright green silk in her hoop and twists floss through the eye of a needle. Anna watches and wonders: To what saints' days will bishops wear brocaded copes if the time of man on earth is ending?

Snow falls, freezes, melts, and an icy fog shrouds the city. Anna hurries through the courtyard and down to the harbor and finds Himerius shivering beside his skiff. Ice glazes the wales and oar shafts and glistens on the creases of his sleeves and on the chains of the few merchant ships still at anchor in the harbor. He sets a brazier in the bottom of the boat, lights a piece of charcoal, and runs out the fishing lines, and Anna takes a melancholic pleasure in watching sparks lift into the fog and melt away behind them. Himerius produces a string of dried figs from inside his coat, and the brazier glows at their feet like a warm and happy secret, a pot of honey hidden for some special night. The oars drip, and they eat, and Himerius sings a fisherman's song about a mermaid with breasts the size of lambs, and water laps against the hull, and his voice turns serious when he says that he has heard that Genoese captains will smuggle anybody who can pay enough across the sea to Genoa before the attack of the Saracens begins.

"You would flee?"

"They'll put me to oars. All day, all night, working the shafts belowdecks, wet to your waist in your own piss? While twenty Saracen ships try to ram you or set you afire?"

"But the walls," she says. "They have survived so many sieges before."

Himerius resumes rowing, the oarlocks creaking, the breakwater gliding past. "My uncle says that last summer a Hungarian foundry man visited our emperor. This man was renowned for making war engines that can turn stone walls to dust. But the Hungarian required ten times more bronze than we have in the whole city. And our emperor, Uncle says, cannot afford to hire one hundred bowmen from Thrace. He can hardly afford to keep himself out of the rain."

The sea laps against the breakwater. Himerius holds the oar blades in the air, his breath pluming.

"And?"

"The emperor couldn't pay. So the Hungarian went to find someone who could."

Anna looks at Himerius: his big eyeballs, his knobby knees, his duck-feet; he looks like an amalgam of seven different creatures. She hears the voice of the tall scribe: *The sultan has new war engines that can bring down walls as though they were air.*

"You mean the Hungarian does not care to what purposes his engines are put?"

"There are many people in this world," Himerius says, "who do not care to what purposes their engines are put. So long as they are paid."

They reach the wall; up she goes, a dancer; the world thins, and there is only the movement of her body, and the memory of finger- and footholds. Finally the crawl through the mouth of the lion, the relief of solidity beneath her feet.

In the ruined library she spends longer than usual pawing through the doorless cupboards from which she has already pillaged most everything of promise. She gathers some worm-eaten rolls of paper—bills of sale, she guesses—moving halfheartedly and without expectation through the gloom. In the back, behind several water-logged stacks of parchment, she finds a small stained brown codex, bound in what feels like goat leather, lifts it out, and tucks it into the sack.

The fog thickens and the quality of the moonlight dims. Pigeons coo somewhere above the broken roof. She whispers a prayer to Saint Koralia, ties the sack, hauls it down the stairs, crawls through the scupper, down-climbs the wall, and drops into the boat without a word. Gaunt and shivering, Himerius rows them back to the har-bor, and the charcoal in the brazier burns out, and the icy fog seems to cinch down around them like a trap. Beneath the archway into the Venetian quarter, there are no men-at-arms, and when they reach the house of the Italians, everything is dark. In the courtyard the fig tree stands glazed with ice, the geese nowhere to be seen. Boy and girl shiver against the wall and Anna wills the sun to rise.

Eventually Himerius tries the door and finds it unlatched. Inside the workshop, all the tables stand empty. The hearth is cold. Hime-rius pushes open the shutters and the room fills with flat, glacial light. The looking glass is gone, as is the terra-cotta centaur, and the board of pinned butterflies, the rolls of parchment, the scrapers and awls and penknives. The servants dismissed, the geese gone or cooked. A few chopped quills are scattered across the tiles; spills of ink stain the floor; the room is a vault stripped bare.

Himerius drops the sack. For a moment in the dawn light he looks hunched and gray, the old man he won't live long enough to become. Somewhere else in the quarter a man yells, "You know what I hate?" and a rooster crows and a woman starts to cry. The world in its final days. Anna remembers something Chryse once said: The houses of the rich burn quick as any other.

For all their talk of rescuing the voices of antiquity, of using the wisdom of the ancients to fertilize the seeds of a new future, were the scribes of Urbino any better than tomb robbers? They came and waited for what was left of the city to be split open so they could beetle in and scavenge whatever last treasures came spilling out. Then they ran for cover.

In the bottom of a bare cupboard something catches her eye: a little enameled snuffbox, one of the scribe's collection of eight. On its cracked lid, a rosy sky braces over the facade of a palace, flanked by twin turrets and tiered with three levels of balconies.

Himerius is gazing out the window, lost in disappointment, and Anna tucks the box into her dress. Somewhere above the fog, the sun comes up pale and faraway. She turns her face toward it but cannot feel any warmth at all.

She carries the sack of wet books to the house of Kalaphates and hides it in the cell she shares with Maria and no one bothers to ask where she has been or what she has done. All day the embroideresses, bent like winter grass, work in silence, blowing on their hands or putting them inside mittens to warm them, the tall, half-finished figures of monastic saints taking shape on the silk in front of them.

"Faith," says Widow Theodora as she walks between the tables, "offers passage through any affliction." Maria hunches over the samite hood, drawing her needle back and forth, the tip of her tongue clamped in her teeth, conjuring a nightingale from thread and patience. In the afternoon a wind howls off the sea and glues snow to the seaward sides of the dome of the Hagia Sophia, and the embroideresses say that this is a sign, and by nightfall the trees freeze again, the branches jacketed in ice, and the embroideresses say that this, too, is a sign.

The evening meal is broth and black bread. Some women say that the Christian nations to the west could save them if they wish, that Venice or Pisa or Genoa could send a flotilla of weapons and cavalry to crush the sultan, but others say that all the Italian republics care about are shipping lanes and trade routes, that they already have contracts in place with the sultan, that it would be better to die on the tips of Saracen arrows than let the pope come here and take credit for victory.

Parousia, the Second Coming, the end of time. At the monastery of Saint George, Agata says, the elders keep a grid made of tiles, twelve along one side and twelve along the other, and each time an emperor dies, his name is etched in the appropriate place. "In the whole grid there is but one blank tile left," she says, "and as soon as our emperor's name is written, the grid will be full, and the ring of history will be complete."

In the flames of the hearth Anna sees the shapes of soldiers hurrying past. She touches the snuffbox where it rests inside her dress, and helps Maria dip her spoon in her bowl, but Maria spills the broth before she can raise it to her mouth.

The following morning all twenty needleworkers are at their benches when the servant of Master Kalaphates scampers up the stairs—out of breath and red-faced with urgency—and rushes to the thread cabinet and shoves the gold and silver wire and the pearls and the spools of silk into a leather case, and scurries back downstairs without a word.

Widow Theodora follows him out. The needleworkers go to the windows to watch: down in the courtyard, the porter loads wrapped rolls of silk onto Kalaphates's donkey, his boots sliding in the mud, while Widow Theodora says things to the servant that they cannot hear. Eventually he hurries off, and Widow Theodora comes back up the stairs with rain on her face and mud on her dress and says for everyone to keep sewing, and tells Anna to pick up the pins the servant spilled on the floor, but it's plain to all of them that their master is deserting them.

At midday criers ride through the streets declaring that the gates of the city will be bolted at sundown. The boom, a chain as thick around as a man's waist and hung with floats, meant to prevent boats from sailing up the Golden Horn and attacking from the north, is drawn across the harbor and fixed to the walls of Galata across the mouth of the Bosporus. Anna imagines Kalaphates hunched on the deck of a Genoese ship, frantically checking his traveling trunks as the city dwindles behind him. She imagines Himerius standing barefoot among the fishermen as the city's admirals look them over. The cut of his hair, the leather-handled knife in his waistband—he tries so hard to give off an illusion of experience and daring, but really he is just a boy, tall and big-eyed, wearing his patched coat in the rain.

By mid-afternoon the embroideresses who are married and have children have abandoned their worktables. From out in the street come the clopping of hooves and the splashing of wheels and the cries of carters. Anna watches Maria squint over her silk hood. She hears the voice of the tall scribe: *The ark has hit the rocks, child. And the tide is washing in.*

Omeir

Everyone studies the weltering skies; everyone grows uneasy. Out loud the teamsters say that the sultan is patient and generous, that he recognizes what he has asked of them, that in his wisdom he understands that the bombard will arrive at the battlefield when it is most needed. But after so much exertion, Omeir senses an unspoken agitation running through the men. The weather lurches from storm to storm; whips crack; resentments simmer. Sometimes he can feel men staring with naked suspicion at his face, and he becomes used to rising from the fire and stepping into the shadows.

An uphill section of road can take all day, but the descents cause the most trouble. Brakes snap, axles bend, the cattle bawl in terror and misery; more than once a jointed section of pole splinters and drives an ox to its knees, and every few days another bullock is butchered. Omeir tells himself that what they're doing—all this exertion, all these lives put to the task of moving the cannon—is right. A necessary campaign, the will of God. But at unpredictable moments homesickness buries him: a sharp, smoky scent, the nickering of someone's horse in the night, and it's there again—the dripping of the trees, the burble of the creek. Mother rendering beeswax over the hearth. Nida singing among the ferns. Arthritic, eight-toed Grandfather limping to the byre in his wooden shoes.

"But how will he ever find a wife?" Nida asked once. "With that face of his?"

"It's not going to be his face that stops them," Grandfather said, "it'll be the odor of his toes," and grabbed one of Omeir's feet and brought it to his nose and took a big whiff, and everyone laughed, and Grandfather dragged the boy into a great embrace.

Eighteen days into their journey, several of the iron bands holding the monstrous cannon to the cart give way, and it rolls off. Everyone groans. The twenty-ton gun gleams in the clay like an instrument discarded by the gods.

As though on cue, it begins to rain. All afternoon they work to winch the cannon back onto the cart, and haul the cart back onto the road, and that night holy scholars move among the cookfires trying to raise morale. The people in the city, they say, cannot even raise horses properly and have to buy ours. They lie on plush couches all day; they train their miniature dogs to run about and lick each other's genitals. The siege will begin any day now, the scholars say, and the weapon that they pull will secure victory, click the wheels of fate in their favor. Because of their efforts, taking the city will be easier than peeling an egg. Easier than lifting a single hair from a cup of milk.

Smoke rises into the sky. As the men settle into sleep, Omeir feels a trickle of apprehension. He finds Moonlight just outside the fire-light, trailing his halter rope.

"What is it?"

Moonlight leads him to where his brother stands beneath a tree, alone, favoring a hind leg.

Though the sultan has willed it and God has ordained it, to move something so heavy so far is, in the end, on the farthest threshold of what is possible. In the last miles, for every step forward, the train of oxen seems also to take a step downward through the earth, as though it travels not a road toward the Queen of Cities but a decliv-ity into the underworld.

Despite Omeir's care, by the end of the journey Tree shows no interest in putting weight on his left hind leg, and Moonlight can hardly raise his head, the twins pulling, it seems, just to please Omeir, as though the only thing left that matters to them is to meet this one demand, no matter how incomprehensible, because the boy has wished it so.

He walks beside them with tears in his eyes.

They reach the fields outside the land walls of Constantinople during the second week of April. Trumpets blare, cheers rise, and men rush to get a glimpse of the great cannon. In daydreams Omeir imagined countless different iterations of the city: claw-toed fiends pacing atop towers, hellhounds dragging chains below, but when they come round a final bend and he sees it for the first time, he gasps. Ahead lies a great waste crowded with tents, equipment, animals, fires, and soldiers, pressed up against a moat as wide as a river. On the far side of the moat, past a low scarp, the walls ride the land for miles in either direction like a series of silent and insuperable cliffs.

In the strange, smoky light, beneath a low gray sky, the walls look endless and pale, as though they safeguard a city made of bones. Even with the cannon, how could they ever penetrate such a barrier? They will be fleas jumping at the eye of an elephant. Ants at the foot of a mountain.

Anna

S he is enlisted with several hundred other children to help shore up deteriorated sections of the walls. They haul paving stones, flagstones, even grave stones, and hand them up to bricklayers who mortar them into place. As though the whole city is being disassembled and rebuilt as an endless wall.

All day she lifts stones, carries buckets; among the masons working on scaffolding above her are a baker and two fishermen she recognizes. No one speaks the sultan's name aloud, as though saying it might cause his army to materialize inside the city. As the day wears on, a cold wind rises, the sun subsumed under swirls of cloud, and the spring afternoon feels like a winter night. Along the ramparts above them, barefoot monks carry a reliquary behind a crossbearer, chanting a low and somber song. Which, she wonders, will be more effective at keeping out invaders: mortar or prayer?

That night, the second of April, as the children drift back toward their homes, cold and hungry, Anna picks her way through the orchards near the Fifth Military Gate to the old archer's turret.

The postern is still there, full of debris. Six turns to the top. She yanks away a few creepers of ivy; the fresco of the silver and bronze city still floats among the clouds, gradually flaking away. On her tiptoes, Anna reaches to touch the donkey, eternally stuck on the wrong side of the sea, then climbs out the west-facing archer's loop.

What she sees, beyond the outer wall, beyond the fosse, turns her cold. Groves and orchards like the ones she and Maria passed through a month before on their way to Saint Mary of the Spring have been hacked down and in their place stretches a wasteland bordered by wooden posts, sharpened at their ends and rammed into the earth like the teeth of enormous combs. Beyond the spike walls and palisades, which extend as far as she can see in both directions, lies a second city haloed around the first.

Thousands of Saracen tents flap out in the wind. Fires, camels, horses, carts, a great distant whirling blur of dust and men, all in quantities so large she does not possess the numerals to count them. How was it that old Licinius described the armies of the Greeks as they assembled outside the walls of Troy?

> *But ne'er till now such numbers charged a field:*
> *Thick as autumnal leaves or driving sand,*
> *The moving squadrons blacken all the strand.*

The wind shifts and a thousand cookfires flare brighter, and a thousand banners flap on a thousand standards, and Anna's mouth goes dry. Even if a person were able to slip out a gate and try to flee, how would she ever pick her way through all that?

From a drawer in her memory comes something Widow Theodora once said: *We have provoked the Lord, child, and now he will open the ground beneath us.* She whispers a prayer to Saint Koralia that if there is any hope at all to send her a sign, and she watches and trembles, and the wind blows, and no stars show, and no sign comes.

The master has fled and the watchman is gone. The door to Widow Theodora's cell is barred. Anna takes a candle from the scullery cabinet—who do they belong to now?—and lights it in the hearth and lets herself into their cell, where Maria lies against the wall, thin as a needle. All her life she has been told to believe, tried to believe, wanted to believe, that if a person suffers long enough, works hard enough, then she—like Ulysses washing up on the shore of the kingdom of brave Alcinous—will ultimately reach a better place. That through suffering we are redeemed. That by dying we live again. And maybe in the end that's the easier thing. But Anna is tired of suffering. And she is not ready to die.

Little wooden Saint Koralia watches her from her niche, two fingers raised. In the sputtering candlelight, wrapped in her headscarf, Anna reaches beneath the pallet, draws out the sack she collected with Himerius days before, and removes the various wads of damp paper. Harvest records, taxation records. Finally the little stained codex bound in goatskin.

Water stains splotch the leather; the edges of the folios are speckled black. But her heart jolts when she sees the writing on the leaves: neat, inclined to the left, as though leaning into a wind. Something about a sick niece and men walking the earth as beasts.

On the next leaf:

> . . . a palace of golden towers stacked on clouds, ringed by
> falcons, redshanks, quails, moorhens, and cuckoos, where
> rivers of broth gushed from spigots, and . . .

She flips forward:

> . . . this hair growing out of my legs—why, these aren't
> feathers! My mouth—it doesn't feel like a beak! And these
> aren't wings—they're hooves!

A dozen leaves farther on:

> . . . I crossed mountain passes, rounded amber-bearing
> forests, staggered over mountains webbed with ice, to
> the frozen rim of the world, where on the solstice the
> people lost the sun for forty days, and they wept until

messengers on the mountaintops glimpsed the returning
light . . .

Maria moans in her sleep. Anna shakes, shocks of recognition
flashing through her. A city in the clouds. A donkey at the edge of
the sea. An account that contains the entire world. And the mysteries beyond.

NINE

AT THE FROZEN RIM
OF THE WORLD

Cloud Cuckoo Land by Antonius Diogenes, Folio I

Because of the loss of multiple folios, how Aethon escapes his post at the miller's wheel remains unclear. In some versions of the ass tale, the donkey is sold to a cult of traveling priests. Translation by Zeno Ninis.

. . . always farther north, the brutes drove me, until the land turned white. The houses were built from the bones of wild griffins, and it was so cold that when the hairy wildmen who lived there spoke, their words froze and their companions would have to wait for spring to hear what had been said.

My hooves, my skull, my very marrow stung with the chill, and I often thought of home, which in my memory no longer seemed a muddy backwater but a paradise, where bees hummed and cattle trotted happily in the fields and my fellow shepherds and I drank wine at sunset beneath the gaze of the evening star.

One night—for in that place the nights lasted forty days—the men built a great fire, and danced, working themselves into a trance, and I chewed free of my rope. I wandered alone through the starry darkness for weeks until I reached the place where nature came to an end.

The sky was black as the Stygian crypt, and on the Ocean great blue vessels of ice sailed to and fro, and I thought I could see slippery creatures with massive eyes swim back and forth through the sluggish water. I prayed to be transformed into a bird, a brave eagle or a bright strong owl, but the gods stayed silent. Hoof by hoof I paced the frozen shore, the cold moonlight on my back, and still I hoped . . .

KOREA

1952–1953

Zeno

In winter stalagmites of frozen urine reach up out of the latrines. The river freezes, the Chinese heat fewer bunkhouses, and the Americans and Brits are merged. Blewitt grumbles that they're already packed tighter than two coats of paint, but Zeno feels excitement as the British prisoners shuffle in. He and Rex meet each other's gaze, and soon their straw mats are next to each other, up against the wall, and every morning he wakes with the promise of finding Rex on the floor an arm's reach away, and the knowledge that there's nowhere else for either of them to go.

Each day, as they climb the frozen hills, cutting, collecting, and carrying brush for firewood, Rex produces a new lesson like a gift.

Γράφω, *gráphō*, to scratch, draw, scrape, or write: the root of calligraphy, geography, photography.

Φωνή, *phōnḗ*, sound, voice, language: the root of symphony, saxophone, microphone, megaphone, telephone.

Θεός, *theós*: a god.

"Boil the words you already know down to their bones," Rex says, "and usually you find the ancients sitting there at the bottom of the pot, staring back up."

Who says such things? And still Zeno steals glances: Rex's mouth, his hair, his hands; there is the same pleasure in gazing at this man as in gazing at a fire.

Dysentery comes for Zeno as it does for all of them. The minute he returns from the latrine, he has to beg permission to go back again. Blewitt says he'd carry Zeno to the camp hospital but the camp hospital is just a shed where so-called doctors cut open prisoners and put chicken livers inside their ribs to "cure them" and that he'd be better off dying right here so Blewitt can have his socks.

Soon he is too weak to even make it to the latrine. At his lowest point he curls on his mat, locked in a thiamine-deficiency paralysis, and believes he is eight years old again, at home, shivering atop the frozen lake in his funeral shoes, inching forward into the swirling white. Just ahead he glimpses a city studded with towers: it flickers and gutters. All he has to do is step forward and he'll reach its gates. But each time he tries, Athena tugs him back.

Sometimes he returns to awareness long enough to find Blewitt beside him, force-feeding him gruel and saying things like "Nuh-uh, no way, kid, you do not get to die, not without me." At other hours it's Rex who sits beside him, wiping Zeno's forehead, the frames of his eyeglasses held together with rusted wire. With a fingernail, into the frost on the wall, he scratches a verse in Greek, as though drawing mysterious glyphs to scare away thieves.

As soon as he can walk, Zeno is forced back into his duty as a fireman. Some days he is too weak to carry his meager bundle more than a few paces before setting it down again. Rex squats beside him and with a piece of charcoal writes Ἀλφάβητος on the trunk of a tree.

A is ἄλφα is alpha: the inverted head of an ox. B is βῆτα is beta: based on the floor plan of a house. Ω is ὦ μέγα is omega, the mega O: a great whale's mouth opening to swallow all the letters before it.

Zeno says, "Alphabet."

"Good. How about this?"

Rex writes, ὁ νόστος.

Zeno rummages in the compartments of his mind.

"Nostos."

"Nostos, yes. The act of homecoming, a safe arrival. Of course, mapping a single English word onto a Greek one is almost always slippery. A *nostos* also means a song about a homecoming."

Zeno rises, light-headed, and picks up his bundle.

Rex buttons his piece of charcoal into his pocket. "In a time," he says, "when disease, war, and famine haunted practically every hour, when so many died before their time, their bodies swallowed by the sea or earth, or simply lost over the horizon, never to return, their fates unknown . . ." He gazes across the frozen fields to the low, dark buildings of Camp Five. "Imagine how it felt to hear the old songs about heroes returning home. To believe that it was possible."

Out on the ice of the Yalu far below, the wind drives the snow in long, eddying swirls. Rex sinks deeper into his collar. "It's not so much the contents of the song. It's that the song was still being sung."

Singular and plural, noun stems and verb cases: Rex's enthusiasm for ancient Greek carries them through the worst hours. One February night, after dark, huddled around the fire in the kitchen shed, Rex uses his piece of charcoal to scratch two lines of Homer onto a board and passes it over.

τὸν δὲ θεοὶ μὲν τεῦξαν, ἐπεκλώσαντο δ᾽ ὄλεθρον
ἀνθρώποις, ἵνα ᾖσι καὶ ἐσσομένοισιν ἀοιδή

Through gaps in the shed walls, stars hang above the mountains. Zeno feels the cold at his back, the light pressure of Rex's frame against his own: they are hardly more than skeletons.

θεοὶ is the gods, nominative plural.

ἐπεκλώσαντο means they spun, aorist indicative.

ἀνθρώποις is for men, dative plural.

Zeno breathes, the fire sputters, the walls of the shed fall away, and in a crease of his mind, unreachable by the guards, hunger, or pain, the meaning of the verse ascends through the centuries.

"*That's what the gods do*," he says, "*they spin threads of ruin through the fabric of our lives, all to make a song for generations to come."*

Rex looks at the Greek on the board, at Zeno, back at the Greek. He shakes his head. "Well, that's just brilliant. Absolutely bloody brilliant."

LAKEPORT, IDAHO

2014

Seymour

Eleven-year-old Seymour is walking home from the library on the last Monday of August when he spies something brown on the shoulder of Cross Road just before the turn onto Arcady Lane. Twice before he has found roadkilled raccoons here. Once a smashed coyote.

It's a wing. The severed wing of a great grey owl, with downy coverts and brown-and-white primary flight feathers. A piece of clavicle still clings to the joint, a few sinews trailing out.

A Honda roars past. He scans the road, searches the weeds along the shoulder for the rest of the bird. In the ditch he finds an empty can that says *Übermonster Energy Brew*. Nothing else.

He walks the rest of the way home and stands in the driveway with his backpack on and the wing clamped against his chest. In the lots of Eden's Gate, a model townhome is nearly complete and four more are going up. A truss dangles from a crane while two carpenters move back and forth beneath. Clouds blow in and lightning flashes and for an instant he sees Earth from a million miles away, a mote hurtling through a barren and crushing vacuum, and then he's in the driveway again and there are no clouds, no lightning: it's a bright blue day, the carpenters are fixing the truss into place, their nail guns going pop-pop-pop.

Bunny is at work but has left the television on. On-screen an elderly couple pulls suitcases on wheels toward a cruise ship. They clink champagne glasses, play a slot machine. *Ha ha ha*, they say. *Ha ha ha ha ha ha*. Their smiles are excessively white.

The wing smells like an old pillow. The complexity of the brown, tan, and cream striping on the flight feathers is outrageous. For every 27,027 Americans, one great grey. For every 27,027 Seymours, one Trustyfriend.

The owl must have been hunting from one of the Douglas firs along the edge of Cross Road. Some prey, a mouse probably, crept to the edge of the pavement below, sniffing, twitching, its heartbeat flashing in Trustyfriend's preterhuman hearing like a buoy light.

The mouse started across the river of asphalt; the owl spread his wings and dropped. Meanwhile a car barreled west down the road, headlights cleaving the night, moving faster than any natural thing should move.

Trustyfriend: Who listened. Who had a pure bright beautiful voice. Who always came back.

On the Magnavox the cruise ship explodes.

Well after dark Seymour hears the Grand Am, hears Bunny's keys at the door. She comes into his room smelling of equal parts bleach and maple syrup. He watches her pick up the wing. "Oh, Possum. I'm sorry."

He says, "Somebody needs to pay."

She reaches to touch his forehead but he rolls against the wall.

"Somebody needs to go to jail."

She sets a hand on his back and his whole body stiffens. Through the closed window, through the walls, he can hear cars moving along Cross Road, the whole terrible unceasing human machine roaring on.

"Do you want me to stay home tomorrow? I could call in sick. We could make waffles?"

He hides his face in his pillow. Five months ago the hillside beyond the wire was home to red squirrels black finches pygmy shrews garter snakes downy woodpeckers swallowtail butterflies wolf lichen monkey flowers ten thousand voles five million ants. Now what is it?

"Seymour?"

She said there were twenty places north of here that Trustyfriend could fly to. Bigger forests. Better forests. Tons of voles, she said. More voles than there were hairs on Seymour's head. But that was just a story. Without raising his head, he reaches for his ear defenders and puts them on.

In the morning Bunny goes to work. Seymour buries the wing beside the egg-shaped boulder in the backyard and decorates the grave with pebbles.

Beneath the bench in Pawpaw's toolshed, beneath three crates of motor oil and a piece of plywood, is a tarp-lined recess Seymour found several years before. Inside are thirty yellowing flyers that say *IDAHO FREEDOM MILITIA*, two boxes of ammunition, one black Beretta pistol, and one rope-handled crate with *DELAY M67 25 GRENADE HAND FRAG* stenciled on the lid.

With his feet braced on either side of the hole, reaching down between his legs, he grasps one of the handles and heaves the crate up and out. He pops open the hasp with the blade of a screwdriver. Nestled inside, in a five-by-five grid, each in its own little cubby, are twenty-five olive-green hand grenades with their handles down and their pins in.

On a library computer a grizzled old-timer with a frighteningly inflamed nose explains the basics of the M67. Six-point-five ounces of high explosive. A four-to-five-second fuse. Lethal radius of five meters. "Once launched," the man says, "the internal spring pops the spoon and releases a striker, which strikes the primer. The primer will then initiate detonation . . ."

Marian walks past and smiles; Seymour hides the browser tab until she's out of sight.

The man stands behind a barricade, depresses the handle, pulls the pin, throws. On the far side of the barricade, dirt erupts into the sky.

Seymour hits replay. Watches again.

• • •

On Wednesdays Bunny works a double shift at the Pig N' Pancake and doesn't get home until after eleven. She leaves a tub of macaroni in the refrigerator. The note on top says, *It's all going to be okay.* All afternoon Seymour sits at the kitchen table with a forty-year-old fragmentation grenade in his lap.

The last truck leaves Eden's Gate around seven. Seymour puts on his ear defenders, crosses the backyard, slips through the new ranch-rail fence, and walks the empty lots with the grenade in his pocket. Sod, freshly laid in the backyard of the model townhome, glows a dark, malignant green. In the two framed units on either side of it, the front door has been installed, but there are only holes where the doorknob and deadbolt should go.

In front of each home stands a realty sign with its translucent box of flyers. *Live the Lakeport lifestyle that you've always wanted.* Seymour chooses the townhome on the left.

In what will become the kitchen, the shells of cabinets stand empty. From an upstairs window, still covered with stickers and plastic film, he can see out through the branches of a few remaining firs to the clearing where Trustyfriend's tree once stood.

No trucks anywhere. No voices, no music. In the darkening sky a single airplane contrail cuts past a quarter-moon.

He goes back downstairs and props open the front door with the butt end of a two-by-four and stands on the newly poured sidewalk in his shorts and sweatshirt with his ear defenders around his neck and the grenade in his hand.

It's not our property. They can do whatever they want with it.

Bigger forests, better forests. He could have his pick.

He keeps the spoon depressed, holds his breath, and loops his index finger through the safety ring. All he has to do is pull. He sees himself underhand the bomb into the house: the front of the structure splinters, the front door blows off its hinges, windows shatter, the concussion travels through Lakeport, over the mountains, until it reaches the ears of Trustyfriend in whatever mystic snag the one-winged ghosts of great grey owls stand in, blinking out at eternity.

Pull the pin.

His knees shake, his heart bellows, but his finger won't budge. He remembers the video: the whump, the dirt fountaining into the air. Five six seven eight. Pull the pin.

He can't. He can hardly keep his feet. His finger slides out of the safety ring. The moon is still there in the sky but it might fall at any moment.

THE ARGOS

MISSION YEAR 64

Konstance

The twelve- and thirteen-year-olds are giving presentations. Ramón describes which biosignature gases have been identified in the atmosphere of Beta Oph2, and Jessi Ko speculates about microclimates in temperate grasslands on Beta Oph2, and Konstance goes last. A book flies toward her from the second tier of the Library and opens flat on the floor and from its pages grows a six-foot-tall stem with a down-facing flower.

The other children groan.

"This," she says, "is a snowdrop. Snowdrops are tiny flowers that bloom on Earth in cold weather. In the Atlas I have found two places where you can see so many of them that they turn a whole field white." She waves her arms as though summoning carpets of snowdrops from the corners of the Library.

"On Earth, each individual snowdrop would produce hundreds of tiny seeds, and each seed had a little fatty drop stuck to it called an elaiosome, and ants loved—"

"Konstance," says Mrs. Chen, "your presentation is supposed to be about biogeographical indicators on Beta Oph2."

"Not dead flowers ten kajillion miles away," adds Ramón, and everyone laughs.

"Ants," continues Konstance, "would carry the seeds into their middens and lick off the elaiosomes, leaving the seed clean. So the snowdrops gave the ants a treat at a time of year when food was hard to find, and the ants planted more snowdrops, and this was called mutualism, a cycle that—"

Mrs. Chen steps forward and claps her hands and the flower vanishes and the book flaps away.

"That's enough, Konstance, thank you."

Second Meal is printed beefsteak with Farm 2 chives. Mother's expression puckers with worry. "First you're climbing inside that dusty Atlas all the time, and now ants again? I don't like it, Konstance, our mandate is to look forward, do you want to end up like—"

Konstance sighs, bracing for it, the great warning story of Crazy Elliot Fischenbacher, who, after his Library Day, would not get off his Perambulator day or night, ignoring his studies and violating every protocol in order to trek alone inside the Atlas until the soles of his feet cracked, and then, according to Mother, his sanity cracked too. Sybil restricted his Library access, and the grown-ups took away his Vizer, but Elliot Fischenbacher unbolted a support from a shelf in the galley and over a series of nights tried to chop through an outer wall, right through the skin of the *Argos* itself, imperiling everyone and everything. Thankfully, Mother always says, before he could get through the outermost layer, Elliot Fischenbacher was subdued and confined to his family compartment, but in his confinement he squirreled away SleepDrops until he had enough for a lethal dose, and when he died his body was sent out the airlock without so much as a song. More than once Mother has pointed out the titanium patch in the corridor between Lavatories 2 and 3 where Crazy Elliot Fischenbacher tried to hack his way out and kill everyone on board.

But Konstance has stopped listening. At the opposite end of the table Ezekiel Lee, a gentle teenager not much older than she is, is groaning and driving his knuckles into his eye sockets. His meal is untouched. His pallor is sickly white.

Dr. Pori the mathematics teacher, seated on Ezekiel's left, touches him on the shoulder. "Zeke?"

"He's just tired from his studies," says Ezekiel's mother, but to Konstance Ezekiel looks worse than tired.

Father comes into the Commissary with bits of compost stuck in his eyebrows. "You missed the conference with Mrs. Chen," says Mother. "And you have dirt on your face."

"Apologies," says Father. He tugs a leaf from his beard and pops it in his mouth and winks at Konstance.

"How's our little pine tree today, Father?" asks Konstance.

"On track to punch through the ceiling before you're twenty."

They chew their beefsteaks, and Mother embarks on a more inspiring tack, how Konstance ought to feel more pride to be part of this enterprise, that the crew of the *Argos* represents the future of the species, they exemplify hope and discovery, courage and endurance, they're widening the window of possibility, shepherding the cumulative wisdom of humanity into a new dawn, and in the meantime why not spend more time with her in the Games Section? How about Rainforest Run, where you tap floating coins with a glowing wand, or Corvi's Paradox, excellent for the reflexes—but now Ezekiel Lee is grinding his forehead into the table.

"Sybil," asks Mrs. Lee, rising from her seat, "what's wrong with Ezekiel?" and the boy rears back, moans, and falls off his stool.

There are gasps. Someone says, "What's happening?" Mother calls out to Sybil again while Mrs. Lee lifts Ezekiel's head and sets it in her lap and Father shouts for Dr. Cha, and that's when Ezekiel retches black vomit all over his mother.

Mother shrieks. Father drags Konstance away from the table. The vomit is on Mrs. Lee's throat and in her hair, it's on the legs of Dr. Pori's worksuit, and everyone in the Commissary is backing away from their meals, astonished, and Father is rushing Konstance into the corridor as Sybil says, *Initiating Quarantine Level One, all nonessential personnel to their compartments immediately.*

Inside Compartment 17, Mother makes Konstance sanitize her arms to her armpits. Four times she asks Sybil to check their vital signs.

Pulse and respiration rates stable, says Sybil. *Blood pressure normal.*

Mother climbs on her Perambulator and touches her Vizer and within seconds she's speed-whispering to people in the Library: "—how do we know it's not infectious—" and "—hope Sara Jane sterilized everything—" and "—aside from births, what has Dr. Cha seen, really? A few burns, a broken arm, some deaths from old age?"

Father squeezes Konstance's shoulder. "It'll be all right. Go to the Library and finish your school day." He slips out the door and Konstance sits with her back against the wall and Mother paces, chin jutted, forehead creased, and Konstance goes to the door and presses it.

"Sybil, why won't the door open?"

Only essential personnel are allowed to circulate right now, Konstance.

She sees Ezekiel wince at the lights, fall off his stool. Is it safe for Father to be out there? Is it safe in here?

She steps onto her own Perambulator, beside her mother's, and touches her Vizer.

In the Library grown-ups gesticulate around tables while cyclones of documents whirl above them. Mrs. Chen herds the teenagers up a ladder to a table on the second tier and sets an orange volume in the center. Ramón and Jessi Ko and Omicron Philips and Ezekiel's little brother Tayvon watch as a foot-tall woman in a light-blue worksuit with the word *ILIUM* stitched on the breast emerges from the book. *If at some point during your long voyage,* she says, *it becomes necessary to quarantine in your compartments, be sure to stick to your routines. Exercise daily, seek out fellow crew members in the Library, and . . .*

Ramón says, "You hear about people vomiting but to actually *see* it?" and Jessi Ko says, "I hear Quarantine One lasts seven days no matter what," and Omicron says, "I hear Quarantine Two lasts two months," and Konstance says, "I hope your brother feels better soon, Tayvon," and Tayvon bunches his eyebrows like he does when he's concentrating on a mathematics problem.

Below them Mrs. Chen crosses the atrium and joins grown-ups around a table, images of cells and bacteria and viruses rotating in the space between them. Ramón says, "Let's go play Ninefold Darkness," and the four of them scamper up a ladder toward the Games Section, and Konstance watches the flying books a moment longer, then takes a slip of paper from the box in the center of the table, writes *Atlas*, and drops it into the slot.

"Thessaly," she says, and drops through the Earth's atmosphere and floats over the olive-and-rust-colored mountainscape of central Greece. Roadways emerge below, the terrain cut into polygons by fences, hedgerows, and walls, a familiar village coming into view now—cinderblock privacy walls, slate rooftops beneath cliff faces—and she's walking the cracked pavement of a rural road in the Pindus Mountains.

Side streets split left and right, little dirt thoroughfares branching off those, drawing an elaborate tracery higher into the hills. She climbs past a row of houses built right up to the roadside, a disemboweled car in front of one, a face-blurred man in a plastic chair in front of the next. A houseplant wilts in a window; a sign with a skull on it has been mounted on a pole out front.

She turns right, following a route she knows well. Mrs. Flowers was right: the other kids find the Atlas hilariously obsolete. There's no jumping or tunneling like in the more sophisticated games in the Games Section: all you do is walk. You can't fly or build or fight or collaborate; you don't feel mud grab your boots or raindrops prick your face; you can't hear explosions or waterfalls; you can hardly leave the roads. And inside the Atlas everything besides the roads is as immaterial as air: walls, trees, people. The only solid thing is the ground.

Yet it fascinates Konstance; she cannot get enough of it. To drop feet-first into Taipei or the ruins of Bangladesh, a sand road on a little island off Cuba, to see the images of face-blurred people frozen here and there in their old-fashioned outfits, the pageants of traffic circles and piazzas and tent-cities, pigeons and raindrops and buses and soldiers in helmets frozen mid-gesture; the graffiti murals, the hulks of carbon-capture plants, the rusted army tanks, the water trucks—it's all there, an entire planet on a server. Gardens are her favorite: mango trees on a median reaching toward the sun in Colombia; wisteria heaped on a café pergola in Serbia; ivy swarming up an orchard wall in Syracuse.

Just ahead an old woman in black stockings and a gray dress has been captured by the cameras halfway up a steep hill, her back hunched in the heat, wearing a white respirator mask and pushing a baby stroller full of what look like glass bottles. Konstance shuts her eyes as she walks through her.

A high fence, a low wall, and the road thins to a track switchbacking up through mixed vegetation. A silver sky plays overhead. Strange bulges and shadows lurk behind trees where the software pixelates, and as the trail climbs it continues to thin, the landscape growing more desolate and windswept, until she reaches a place where the Atlas cameras went no farther, and the trail peters out at a massive Bosnian pine, probably twenty-five meters high, twisting up toward the sky, like the great-great-grandfather of her sapling in Farm 4.

She stops, inhales: a dozen times she has visited this tree, seeking something. Through the gnarled old branches the cameras have caught a great cavalcade of clouds, and the tree clings to the mountainside as though it has grown there since the beginning of time.

She pants, sweating on her Perambulator inside Compartment 17, and leans as far forward as she can to touch its trunk, her fingertips passing through, the interface breaking down into a grainy smudge, a girl alone with a centuries-old pine tree in the sunbaked mountains of Thessaly, land of magic.

Before NoLight Father comes through the door of Compartment 17 wearing an oxygen hood with a clear visor and a cyclopic headlamp. "Just a precaution," he says, his voice muffled. He sets three covered trays on Mother's sewing table as the door seals behind him, sanitizes his hands, and removes the hood.

"Broccoli cacciatore. Sybil says we're moving to printers in each compartment to decentralize meals, so this might be our last fresh produce for a bit."

Mother gnaws her lips. Her face is as white as the walls. "How's Ezekiel?"

Father shakes his head.

"It's contagious?"

"No one knows yet. Dr. Cha is with him."

"Why hasn't Sybil solved it?"

I am working on it, says Sybil.

"Work faster," says Mother.

Konstance and Father eat. Mother sits on her bunk, her food untouched. Again she asks Sybil to check their vital signs.

Pulse and respiration rates normal. Blood pressure shipshape.

Konstance climbs into her berth and Father stacks the trays by the door, then rests his chin on her mattress and pushes her curls out of her eyes.

"On Earth, when I was a boy, most everybody got sick. Rashes, funny little fevers. All the unmodified people got sick every now and then. It's part of being human. We think of viruses as evil but in reality few are. Life usually seeks to cooperate, not fight."

The diodes in the ceiling dim and Father presses a palm to her forehead and in a great dizzy uprush comes the sensation of standing inside the Atlas atop the Theodosian walls, all that white limestone crumbling under the sun. *For as long as we have been a species,* Mrs. Flowers said, *we humans have tried to defeat death. None of us ever has.*

The following morning Konstance stands in the Library at the second-tier railing with Jessi Ko and Omicron and Ramón waiting for Dr. Pori to arrive and commence the morning's lesson in precalculus. Jessi says, "Tayvon's late too," and Omicron says, "I don't see Mrs. Lee either, and she was the one with Zeke's chunder all over her," and the four children fall quiet.

Eventually Jessi Ko says she's heard that if you feel sick you're supposed to say, "Sybil, I'm not feeling well," and if Sybil detects something wrong with you, she sends Dr. Cha and Engineer Goldberg to your compartment wearing full biohazard containment suits, and Sybil will unlock the door so they can isolate you in the Infirmary. Ramón says, "That sounds awful," and Omicron whispers, "Look," because down on the main floor Mrs. Chen is leading all six members of the crew who have not yet turned ten across the atrium.

The children look tiny beneath the towering shelves. A few grown-ups send perfunctory *IT'S YOUR LIBRARY DAY* balloons up into the barrel vault and Ramón says, "They didn't even get pancakes."

Jessi Ko says, "What do you think it feels like, to be sick?" and Omicron says, "I hate polynomials, but I do wish Dr. Pori would show up," and below them the young children hold virtual hands and their bright voices fill the atrium,

> We move as one
> In everything we do.
> It takes everyone together,
> Everyone together,
> to get to—

and Sybil announces, *All non-medical personnel to their compartments, no exceptions, initiating Quarantine Level Two.*

Zeno

As the weather warms, Rex takes to gazing at the hills around Camp Five and chewing his lower lip as though contemplating some vision in the distance that Zeno cannot see. And one afternoon Rex waves him closer and, though there is not a soul for fifty feet in any direction, whispers, "What have you noticed, on Fridays, about the petrol drums?"

"They drive the empty ones to Pyongyang."

"And who loads them?"

"Bristol and Fortier."

Rex looks at him a moment longer, as though waiting to see how much can be transmitted between them without language.

"Have you ever noticed the two drums behind the kitchen sheds?"

After roll call Zeno examines them as he walks past, dread percolating through his gut. These drums, at one point used to store cooking oil, look identical to the gasoline drums, except that their lids can be removed. Each appears large enough for a man to crawl inside. But even if he and Rex managed to fold their bodies into them, as Rex seems to be suggesting, even if they convinced Bristol and Fortier to seal them inside, hoist them onto the fuel truck, and tuck them among the empty fuel barrels, they'd need to stay inside for who-knows-how-long while the truck drove the notoriously dangerous road to Pyongyang, without headlights, dodging overhead patrols of American bombers. Then—somehow—the two of them, night blind from vitamin deficiency, would need to climb out of the drums undetected and cross miles of mountains and villages in their disgusting clothes and ruined boots with their unshaven faces and nothing to eat.

Later, after dark, a new anxiety comes sliding into place: What if by some miracle they actually succeeded? What if they weren't killed by guards or villagers or a friendly B-26? If they made it all the way to the American lines? Then Rex would go back to London, to his students and friends, perhaps to another man, someone who has been waiting for him all these months, someone Rex has been too kind to mention, someone infinitely more sophisticated than Zeno, and more deserving of Rex's affection. Νόστος, *nostos*: the journey home, the safe return; the song sung around the feast table for the shipwrecked steersman who finally found his way back.

And where would Zeno go? Lakeport. Back to Mrs. Boydstun.

Escapes, he tries to tell Rex, are stories from movies, from some older, more courteous war. Besides, their ordeal is bound to end soon, isn't it? But seemingly every day, Rex spins up more and more detailed plans, stretching to make his joints more flexible, analyzing guard shift patterns, polishing a tin to make what he calls a "signaling mirror," speculating about how they might sew bits of food into the linings of their hats, where they might hide during the nightly count, how they might urinate while inside the drum without soaking themselves, whether they should approach Bristol and Fortier now or just hours before they do it. They'll use code names from Aristophanes's *The Birds*; Rex will be Peisetairos, which means Trustyfriend; Zeno will be Euelpides, Goodhope; they'll shout, *Herakles!* when the coast is clear. As though it will all be an amusing escapade, a first-class caper.

At night he can feel the activity of Rex's mind next to him like the glare of a spotlight—he worries the whole camp will see it. And each time Zeno contemplates wedging himself into an oil drum and being loaded onto a truck to be driven to Pyongyang, cords of panic draw tighter around his throat.

Three Fridays pass, white cranes migrating north over the camp in flocks, then yellow buntings, and Rex only whispers plans, and Zeno exhales. So long as it stays a rehearsal, so long as the rehearsal never turns into performance.

But one Thursday in May, the prisoners' kitchen full of low, silver light, Rex drifts past Zeno on his way to a re-education session and says, "We're going. Tonight."

Zeno scoops some soybeans into his bowl and sits. The thought of eating makes him queasy; he worries the others will hear his pulse thudding in his temples; he feels as if he should not move, as if, by speaking those three words, Rex has turned everything to glass.

Outside, seeds blow everywhere. Within the hour, the big Soviet flatbed truck, its hood pocked with bullet holes, its bed full of fuel drums, rumbles into camp.

By evening it's raining. Zeno gathers a last load of wood and manages to carry it to the kitchen. On his straw mat he curls up in his wet clothes as the light bleeds out of the day.

Men trickle in; rain rattles on the roof. Rex's mat stays empty. Could he really be out behind the kitchen sheds? Pale, determined, freckled Rex, folding his emaciated body into a rusted oil drum?

As night fills the barracks, Zeno tells himself to get up. Any minute now, Bristol and Fortier will load the truck. The truck will pull away, the guards will come and do the headcount, and Zeno's chance will have come and gone. His brain sends messages to his legs but his legs refuse to move. Or maybe it's his legs sending messages up the chain of command—*make me move*—and it's his brain that refuses.

A last few men come in and drop onto their mats and some whisper and some groan and some cough and Zeno sees himself rising, slipping out the door into the night. The time has come, or has already passed; Peisetairos is waiting inside his drum, but where is Euelpides?

Is that the growl of the truck engine starting?

He tells himself that Rex will never go through with it, that he will realize that his plan is unsound, suicidal even, but then Bristol and Fortier return and Rex is not with them. He studies their silhouettes for a clue but can read nothing. The rain lets up and the eaves drip and in the dark Zeno hears men snapping the bodies of lice with their fingernails. He sees Mrs. Boydstun's ceramic children, their rosy cheeks, their unblinking cobalt eyes, their accusatory red lips. Sheep Shagger, Wop, Swish. Fruit Punch. Zero.

Around midnight the guards roust them and shine battery-operated lights in everyone's eyes. They threaten interrogations, torture, death, but without much urgency. Rex does not reappear in the morning or the afternoon or the morning after that and over the next several days Zeno is interrogated five separate times. You are confidants, you are always together, we've heard that you two are always scratching code words in the dust. But the guards seem almost bored, as though they are participating in a show for an audience that has not arrived. Zeno waits to hear that Rex has been captured a few miles away, or relocated to another camp; he waits for his efficient little frame to come round a corner, push his glasses up his nose, and smile.

The other prisoners say nothing, at least not around Zeno; it's as though Rex never existed. Maybe they know Rex is dead and want to spare him the pain or maybe they think Rex is cooperating with propaganda officers and implicating them in lies or maybe they're too hungry and exhausted to care.

Eventually the Chinese stop asking questions and he is not sure whether this means Rex has escaped and they are embarrassed or Rex has been shot and buried and there are no more questions to which they seek answers.

Blewitt sits beside him in the yard. "Chin up, kid. Every hour we're aboveground is a good hour." But most hours Zeno does not feel like being aboveground anymore. Rex's pale arms, aswarm with freckles. The intricate flickering of the tendons in the backs of his hands while he scratched out words. He imagines Rex arriving safely back in London, five thousand miles away, bathing, shaving, dressing in civilian clothes, putting books under one arm, heading off to a grammar school made of bricks and ivy.

His longing is such that Rex's absence becomes something like a presence, a scalpel left behind in his gut. Dawn light glimmers on the surface of the Yalu and crawls up the hills; it sets the thorns on the brambles aglow; the men whisper, *Our forces are ten miles away, six miles away, just over that hill. They'll be here by morning.*

If Rex was killed, did he die alone? Did he murmur to Zeno in the night as the truck rumbled away, assuming that he was in the barrel next to his? Or did he expect Zeno to fail him all along?

In June, three weeks after Rex's disappearance, guards march Zeno and Blewitt and eighteen other of the youngest prisoners into the yard and an interpreter tells them they are being released. At a checkpoint two American MPs with shiny cheeks check Zeno's name on a roster; one hands him a manila card that reads *OK CHOW*. There's an ambulance ride across the demarcation line and then he's brought to a delousing tent where a sergeant sprays him head-to-toe with DDT.

The Red Cross gives him a safety razor, a tube of shaving cream, a glass of milk, and a hamburger. The bun is extraordinarily white. The meat glistens in a way that does not look real. It smells real, but Zeno is certain that it is a trick.

He returns to the United States on the same ship that took him to Korea two and a half years before. He is nineteen years old and weighs 109 pounds. On each of the eleven days he is on board he is interviewed.

"Give six examples of how you tried to sabotage the Chinese effort." "Who got better treatment than anyone else?" "Why was so-and-so given cigarettes?" "Did you ever feel any attraction to the communist ideology?" He hears that the Black soldiers have it worse.

At one point an army psychiatrist hands him a *Life* magazine opened to a photo of a woman in a bra and panties. "How does this make you feel?"

"Fine." He hands the magazine back. Fatigue rolls through him.

He approaches every debriefing officer he can about a British lance corporal named Rex Browning, last seen at Camp Five in May, but they say, we're not Royal Marines, we're the United States Army, we have enough men to keep track of. At the docks in New York there are no brass bands, no flashbulbs, no weeping families. On a bus outside of Buffalo, he begins to cry. Towns flash by, followed by long stretches of dark. Six floodlit signs, each twenty feet apart, wink past:

THE WOLF
IS SHAVED
SO NEAT AND TRIM
RED RIDING HOOD
IS CHASING HIM
BURMA-SHAVE

Seymour

Mr. Bates, the sixth-grade teacher, has a dyed mustache, a blazing, godlike temper, and zero interest in his students wearing ear defenders during class. Every morning, to start the day, he switches on his This-Is-Very-Expensive-So-You-Kids-Better-Not-Touch-It ViewSonic projector and shows videos of current events on the whiteboard. The class sits, uncombed and yawning, while at the front of the room landslides smash Kashmiri villages.

Every day Patti Goss-Simpson brings four fish sticks to school in her Titan Deep Freeze lunch box and every day at 11:52 a.m., because the cafeteria is being remodeled, Patti puts her terrible fish sticks in the terrible microwave at the back of Mr. Bates's room and presses the terrible beepy buttons and the smell that pours out feels to Seymour like he's being pressed face-first into a swamp.

He sits as far from Patti as he can, plugs his nose and ears, and tries to daydream Trustyfriend's forest back into existence: lichen hanging from branches, snow slipping from bough to bough, the teeming settlements of the NeedleMen. But one morning in late September, Patti Goss-Simpson tells Mr. Bates that Seymour's behavior toward her at lunch hurts her feelings, so Mr. Bates mandates that Seymour eat beside her at the center table, right beside the projector stand.

11:52 a.m. arrives. In go the fish sticks. Beep boop beep.

Even with his eyes closed Seymour can hear the fish sticks rotating, can hear Patti snap open the microwave door, can hear the fish flesh sizzling on her little plate as she sits back down. Mr. Bates sits behind his desk chomping baby carrots and watching mixed martial arts highlights on his smartphone. Seymour hunches over his lunch box trying to plug his nose and cover his ears at the same time. Not worth eating today.

He is counting to one hundred in his head, eyes closed, when Patti Goss-Simpson reaches and taps him with a fish stick on his left ear. He jerks backward; Patti grins; Mr. Bates misses the whole thing. Patti squints her left eye and points the fish stick at him like a gun.

"Pow," she says. "Pow. Pow."

Somewhere inside Seymour a final defense crumbles. The roar, which has chewed at the edges of every waking minute since he found Trustyfriend's wing, blitzkriegs the school. It swarms over the ridge above the football field, mashing everything in its path.

Mr. Bates dips a carrot into hummus. David Best belches; Wesley Ohman cracks up; the roar explodes across the parking lot. Locusts hornets chain saws grenades fighter jets screaming screeching fury rage. Patti bites off the barrel of her fish stick gun as the walls of the school splinter. The door of Mr. Bates's room flies away. Seymour puts both hands on the projector cart and pushes.

A radio in the waiting room says, *Nothing tastes better than a fresh-picked Idaho apple.* The crinkling of the paper on the examination table borders on the untenable.

The doctor taps a keyboard. Bunny is wearing her Aspen Leaf smock with the two pockets in front. Into her flip phone she whispers, "I'll work a double on Saturday, Suzette, I promise."

The doctor shines a penlight in each of Seymour's eyes. She says, "Your mother says you talked to an owl in the woods?"

A magazine on the wall says, *Be a Better You in Fifteen Minutes a Day.*

"What kinds of things would you tell the owl, Seymour?"

Don't answer. It's a trap.

The doctor says, "Why did you smash the classroom projector, Seymour?"

Not a word.

At checkout Bunny's arm spelunks in the cavern of her purse. "Is there any chance," she says, "you could just bill me?"

In a basket on the way out are coloring books with sailing ships in them. Seymour takes six. In his room he draws spirals around all the boats. Cornu spirals, logarithmic spirals, Fibonacci spirals: sixty different maelstroms swallow sixty different ships.

Night. He gazes out the sliding door, past the backyard, to where moonlight spills across the vacant lots of Eden's Gate. A single carpenter's lamp glows inside a half-finished townhome, illuminating an upstairs window. An apparition of Trustyfriend floats past.

Bunny lays a 1.69-ounce package of plain M&M's on the table. Beside that she sets an orange bottle with a white cap. "The doctor said they won't make you dumb. They'll just make things easier. Calmer."

Seymour grinds the heels of his hands into his eyes. The ghost of Trustyfriend hops to the sliding door. His tail feathers are gone; one wing is missing; his left eye is damaged. His beak is a dash of yellow in a radar dish of smoke-colored feathers. Into Seymour's head he says, *I thought we were doing this together. I thought we were a team.*

"One in the morning," Bunny says, "and one at night. Sometimes, kid, we all need a little help shoveling the shit."

Konstance

She is walking a street in Lagos, Nigeria, passing through a plaza near the waterfront, gleaming white hotels rising around her on all sides—a fountain caught mid-spray, forty coconut palms growing from black-and-white checkered planters—when she stops. She peers up, a faint prickling at the base of her neck: something not quite right.

In Farm 4 Father has a single coconut in a cold-storage drawer. All seeds, he said, are voyagers, but none more intrepid than the coconut. Dropped onto beaches where high tides can pick them up and carry them to sea, coconuts, he said, regularly crossed oceans, the embryo of a new tree safe inside its big fibrous husk, twelve months of fertilizer provisioned on board. He handed it to her, vapor rising from its shell, and showed her the three germination pores on the bottom: two eyes and a mouth, he said, the face of a little sailor whistling its way around the world.

To her left a sign says, *Welcome to the New Intercontinental.* She steps into the shade of the palms and continues squinting up when the trees ribbon away, her Vizer retracts from her eyes, and Father is there.

She feels the familiar lurch of motion sickness as she steps off her Perambulator. It's NoLight already. Mother sits on the edge of her bunk working sanitizing powder into the folds of her palms.

"I'm sorry," Konstance says, "if I was in there too long."

Father takes her hand. His white eyebrows bunch. "No, no, nothing like that." The only illumination comes from the lavatory light. In the shadows behind him she can see that Mother's usually orderly

260

stack of worksuits and patches has been upended, and her button bag is spilled everywhere—buttons under her bunk, under the sewing stool, in the curtain track around the commode.

When Konstance looks back up at her father, some part of her understands before he speaks what he will say, and she feels so acutely that they have left their planet and star behind, that they move at impossible speeds through a cold and silent void, that there is no turning around.

"Zeke Lee," he says, "is dead."

One day after Ezekiel's death, Dr. Pori dies, and Zeke's mother has reportedly lost consciousness. Twenty-one others—one quarter of the people on board—are experiencing symptoms. Dr. Cha spends her every hour tending to crew members; Engineer Goldberg works through NoLight in the Biology Lab trying to solve it.

How does a plague start inside a sealed disc that has had no contact with any other living thing for almost six and a half decades? Is it spreading via touch or spittle or food? Via the air? The water? Was deep-space radiation penetrating the shielding and damaging the nuclei of their cells, or was it something asleep in someone's genes, all these years, suddenly waking up? And why can't Sybil, who knows all things, solve it?

Though he has hardly used his Perambulator in Konstance's memory, her father now spends nearly every waking hour on it, Vizer locked over his eyes, studying documents at a Library table. Mother maps the minutes before quarantine. Did she pass Mrs. Lee in a corridor, did some microscopic fleck of Ezekiel's vomit land on her suit, could some of it have splashed into their mouths?

A week ago, it all seemed so secure. So settled. Everyone whispering down the corridors in their patched-up worksuits and socks. *You can be one, or you can be one hundred and two* . . . Fresh lettuce on Tuesdays, Farm 3 beans on Wednesdays, haircuts on Fridays, dentist in Compartment 6, seamstress in Compartment 17, precalc with Dr. Pori three mornings a week, the warm eye of Sybil keeping watch over them all. Yet, even then, in the deepest vaults of her subconscious, didn't Konstance sense the terrible precariousness of it all? The frozen immensity tugging, tugging, tugging at the outer walls?

She touches her Vizer and climbs the ladder to the second tier of the Library. Jessi Ko looks up from a book in which a thousand pale deer with oversized nostrils lie dead in snow.

"I'm reading about the saiga antelope. They had this bacteria in them that caused massive die-offs."

Omicron lies on his back, gazing up.

"Where's Ramón?" Konstance asks.

Below them images from long-ago pandemics flicker above grown-ups at tables. Soldiers in beds, doctors in hazmat suits. Unbidden into her head comes an image of Zeke's body being sent out the airlock, then Dr. Pori's a few hundred thousand kilometers later: a trail of corpses left through the void like breadcrumbs from some ghastly fairy tale.

"Says here that two hundred thousand of them died in twelve hours," Jessi says, "and no one ever figured out why." Far down the atrium, at the limit of her eyesight, Konstance sees her father at a table by himself, sheets of technical drawings sailing around him.

"I heard," says Omicron, staring up through the barrel vault, "that Quarantine Three lasts a year."

"I heard," whispers Jessi, "that Quarantine Four lasts forever."

Library hours are extended; Mother and Father hardly leave their Perambulators. More unusual still, inside Compartment 17, Father has taken down the bioplastic privacy curtain that enclosed the commode, snipped it into pieces, and is using Mother's sewing machine to make something with it—she hasn't dared to ask what. Sealed in Compartment 17, beneath the miasma of nutritional paste burping out of the food printer, Konstance can almost smell the collective fear as it moves through the ship: insidious, mephitic, seeping through walls.

Later, inside the Atlas, on the outskirts of Mumbai, she travels a jogging trail wound around the bases of huge, cream-colored towers, forty or fifty stories high. She slips past women in saris, women in jogging suits, men in shorts, everyone motionless. To her right, a wall of green mangroves runs alongside the trail for a half mile, something troubling her as she moves through the frozen joggers, some disquieting wrinkle in the texture of the software: in the people or the trees or the atmosphere. She picks up her pace, uneasy, passing through figures as though through ghosts: with every stride she can feel the fear pervading the *Argos*, about to lay its hand on the back of her neck.

By the time she climbs out of the Atlas, it's dark. Little sconces glow at the base of the Library columns and moonlit clouds scud over the barrel vault.

A few documents shuttle to and fro; a few figures hunch over tables. Mrs. Flowers's little white dog comes trotting to her and sits with its tail swishing back and forth, but Mrs. Flowers is nowhere to be seen.

"Sybil, what time is it?"

Four ten NoLight, Konstance.

She switches off her Vizer and steps off the Perambulator. Father is at Mother's sewing machine again, glasses low on his nose, working by the light of Mother's lamp. The hood of his containment suit sits in his lap like the severed head of some enormous insect. She worries that he will chide her for staying up too late again, but he is mumbling to himself, brooding on something, and she realizes that she would like to be chided for staying up too late.

Toilet, teeth, brush your hair. She's halfway up the ladder to her berth when her heart gives a frightened whump. Mother is not in her bed. Or in Father's. Or on the commode. Mother is not in Compartment 17 at all.

"Father?"

He flinches. Mother's blanket is rumpled. Mother always folds her blanket into a perfect rectangle when she gets out of bed.

"Where's Mother?"

"Hmm? She went to see someone." The sewing machine clatters back to life, the bobbin spinning, and she waits for it to stop.

"But how did she get out the door?"

Father holds up the edges of curtain to match them, places them under the needle, and the machine resumes drumming.

She repeats her question. Instead of answering he uses Mother's scissors to trim some thread, then says, "Tell me where you went this time, Zucchini. You must have walked for miles."

"Did Sybil really let Mother out?"

He rises and walks to her berth.

"Take these."

His voice is calm but his eyes scatter. In his palm are three of Mother's SleepDrops.

"Why?"

"They'll help you rest."

"Isn't three a lot?"

"Take them, Konstance, it's safe. I'll wrap you in your blanket like a pupa inside its chrysalis, remember? Like we used to? And you'll have answers in the morning, I promise."

The drops dissolve on her tongue. Father tucks her blanket around her legs and sits again at the sewing machine and the needle starts up again.

She glances over the railing at Mother's bunk. Her rumpled blanket.

"Father, I'm afraid."

"Want to hear some of Aethon's story?" The sewing machine rumbles and dies. "After Aethon escaped the miller, he walked all the way to the rim of the world, do you remember? The land ran down to an icy sea, and snow blew out of the sky, and there was only black sand and frozen seaweed, and not a scent of a rose for a thousand miles."

The lamp flickers. Konstance presses her back against the wall and strains to keep her eyes open. People are dying. The only way Sybil let Mother out of the compartment was if—

"But Aethon still hoped. There he was, trapped inside a body that wasn't his, far from home, at the very edge of the known world. He stared up at the moon as he paced the shore, and thought he could see a goddess spiraling down out of the night to assist him."

In the air above her berth Konstance sees moonlight shimmer on plates of ice, sees Aethon-the-donkey leaving hoof prints in cold sand. She tries to sit up but her neck is suddenly too weak to support the weight of her head. Snow is blowing across her blanket. She raises a hand to it, but her fingers fall away into the dark.

Two hours later Father leans over the rail in the NoLight and helps her out of bed. She's groggy and muddled from the SleepDrops, and he's shoving her legs and arms into what looks like a deflated person—a suit that he has fashioned from the bioplastic curtain. It's too large around her waist, and has no gloves, only sleeves sewn shut at the ends. As he zips her in, Konstance is so sleepy that she can hardly raise her chin.

"Father?"

Now he's fitting the oxygen hood over her head, pulling it down over her hair and sealing it to the collar of the suit with the same seal-tape he uses to seal drip-lines in the farm. He turns it on and she feels the suit inflate around her.

Oxygen at thirty percent, says a recorded voice inside the hood, directly into her ear, and the white beam of the headlamp switches on and ricochets across the contents of the compartment.

"Can you walk?"

"I'm boiling in here."

"I know, Zucchini, you're doing so well. Let me see you walk." Droplets of sweat on his forehead catch the light of the headlamp, and his pallor looks as white as his beard. Despite the fear and fatigue she manages to take a few steps, the strange, inflated sleeves crinkling. Father squats and picks up Konstance's Perambulator, and with his other hand also manages to pick up the aluminum stool from Mother's sewing table, and carries them to the door.

"Sybil," he says, "one of us is not feeling well."

Konstance leans against his hip, hot and frightened, and waits for Sybil to dispute, to argue, to say anything but what she does say.

Someone will be here in a moment.

Konstance can feel the gravity of the SleepDrops pulling at her eyelids, her blood, her thoughts. Father's wan face. Mother's unfolded blanket. Jessi Ko saying, *And if Sybil detects something wrong with you . . .*

Oxygen at twenty-nine percent, says the hood.

As the door opens, two figures in head-to-toe biohazard suits come clomping down the corridor through the NoLight. They have lights strapped to their wrists and their suits are inflated from within so that they look frighteningly large and their faces are lost behind bronze-mirrored face shields. Behind them trail long hoses wrapped in aluminum tape.

Father rushes them with Konstance's Perambulator still clutched to his chest and they stagger backward. "Don't come near. Please. She's not going to the Infirmary." He hurries her past them down the unlit corridor, following the quivering beam of her headlamp, her feet sliding in their bioplastic booties.

Things are shored up against the walls: food trays, blankets, what might be bandages. As they hurry past the Commissary, she glances in, but the Commissary is no longer the Commissary. Where tables and benches were arranged in three rows now stand about twenty white tents, tubes and wires running out of each, the lights of medical instruments flickering here and there. In the unzipped mouth of one she glimpses the bare sole of a foot sticking out of a blanket, and then they're around the corner.

Oxygen at twenty-six percent, says her hood.

Were those sick crew members? Was Mother in one of those tents?

They pass Lavatories 2 and 3, pass the sealed door of Farm 4— her pine sapling in there, six years old now and as tall as she is— curling down corridors toward the center of the *Argos*, Father breathing hard now as he urges her along, both of them slipping on the floor, the beam of her headlamp lurching. *Hydro-Access*, reads one door; *Compartment 8*, reads another, *Compartment 7*—she feels as though they're following a spiral toward the center of a vortex, as though she's being swept toward the hole at the heart of a whirlpool.

Finally they stop outside the door that reads *Vault One*. Pale, panting, his face shining with sweat, Father glances back over his shoulder, then presses his palm to the door. Wheels turn and the vestibule opens.

Sybil says, *Entering Decontamination Area.*

He ushers Konstance inside and sets her Perambulator beside her and braces the stool in the threshold against the door frame.

"Don't move."

She sits in the vestibule in the crinkling suit and wraps her arms over her knees and the hood says, *Oxygen at twenty-five percent,* and Sybil says, *Commencing decontamination process.* Konstance cries, "Father," through the mask of her hood, and the outer door closes in its track until it meets the stool.

The legs of the stool bend with a shriek and the door stops.

Please remove blockage in outer door.

Father returns carrying four sacks of Nourish powder, pitches them over the half-crushed stool into the vestibule, and rushes away again.

Next comes a recycling toilet, dry-wipes, a food printer still in its wrapper, an inflatable cot, a blanket sealed in containment film, more sacks of Nourish powder—back and forth Father hurries. *Please remove blockage in outer door,* repeats Sybil, and the stool crumples another centimeter under the pressure, and Konstance begins to hyperventilate.

Father pitches two more sacks of Nourish powder into the vestibule—why so many?—and steps through the gap in the door and slumps against the wall. Sybil says, *In order to begin decontamination you must remove the blockage in the outer door.*

Into Konstance's ear the hood says, *Oxygen at twenty-three percent.*

Father points to the printer. "You know how to operate that? Remember where the low-voltage line attaches?" He rests his hands on his knees, chest heaving, sweat dripping from his beard, and the stool shrieks against the pressure. She manages to nod.

"As soon as the outer door is closed, close your eyes, and Sybil will flush the air and sterilize everything. Then she'll open the inner door. Do you remember? When you go inside, bring everything else with you. All of it. Once you have everything inside and the inner door is sealed, count to one hundred, and it should be safe to take off the hood. Understood?"

Fear thrums through every cell in her body. Mother's empty bunk. The tents in the Commissary.

"No," she says.

Oxygen at twenty-two percent, says the hood. *Try to breathe more slowly.*

"When the inner door is sealed," repeats Father, "count to one hundred. Then you can take it off." He presses his weight against the edge of the door, and Sybil says, *The outer door is blocked, the blockage must be removed*, and Father glances out into the darkness of the corridor.

"I was twelve," he says, "when I applied to leave. All I could see, as a boy, was everything dying. And I had this dream, this vision, of what life could be. 'Why stay here when I could be there?' Remember?"

From the shadows crawl a thousand demons and she swings her headlamp toward them and the demons recede and her light swings away and the demons lunge right back into place. The stool shrieks again. The outer door closes another centimeter.

"I was a fool." His hand, as he runs it across his forehead, looks skeletal; the skin of his throat sags; the silver of his hair dims to gray. For the first time in her life, her father looks his age, or older, as though, breath by breath, his last years are being siphoned away. Into the mask of her hood she says, "You said that what's so beautiful about a fool is that a fool never knows when to give up."

He inclines his head toward her, blinking fast, as though a thought runs out in front of him, too quick to catch. "It was Grandmom," he murmurs, "who used to say that."

Oxygen at twenty percent, says the hood.

A bead of sweat clings to the tip of Father's nose, quivers, then drops.

"At home," he says, "in Scheria, an irrigation ditch ran behind the house. Even after it dried up, even on the hottest days, there was always a surprise if you knelt there long enough. An airborne seed, or a weevil, or a brave little starflower all by itself."

Wave after wave of drowsiness breaks over Konstance. What is Father doing? What is he trying to tell her? He rises and stumbles over the mangled stool and out of the vestibule.

"Father, please."

But his face passes out of sight. He braces one foot against the edge of the door, wrestles out the mangled stool, and the vestibule closes.

"No, don't—"

Outer door sealed, Sybil says. *Beginning decontamination.*

The noise of the fans builds. She feels cold jets against the bioplastic of her suit, shuts her eyes against the three pulses of light, and the inner door opens. Terrified, exhausted, biting back panic, Konstance drags the toilet inside, the sacks of Nourish powder, the cot, the food printer in its wrap.

The inner door seals. The only light is the glow of Sybil flickering inside her tower, now orange now rose now yellow.

Hello, Konstance.

Oxygen at eighteen percent, says the hood.

I adore visitors.

One two three four five.

Fifty-six fifty-seven fifty-eight.

Oxygen at seventeen percent.

Eighty-eight eighty-nine ninety. Mother's unfolded blanket. Father's hair damp with sweat. A bare foot sticking out of a tent. She reaches one hundred and disconnects the hood. Pulls it off her head. Lies on the floor as the SleepDrops drag her down.

TEN

THE GULL

Cloud Cuckoo Land by Antonius Diogenes, Folio K

. . . the goddess spiraled down from the night. She had a white body, gray wings, and a bright orange mouth like a beak, and although she was not as large as I expected a goddess to be, I became afraid. She landed on her yellow feet and took a few steps and began picking at a pile of seaweed.

"Exalted daughter of Zeus," I said, "I beg you, say the magic incantation to deliver me from this form into another, so that I might fly to the city in the clouds where all needs are met and no one suffers and every day shines like the very first days at the birth of the world."

"What in the world are you braying about?" asked the goddess, and the reek of her fish-breath nearly knocked me over. "I've flapped all over these parts, and found no place like that, in the clouds or anywhere else."

She was clearly a cold-blooded deity, playing tricks on me. I said, "Well, at least could you use your wings to fly somewhere bright and warm, and bring me back a rose, so that I might return to what I was before, and start my journey anew?"

The goddess pointed with one wing at a second pile of seaweed, frozen to the gravel, and said, "That's the rose of the northern sea and I've heard that if you eat enough of it, you'll feel funny. Though I can tell you right now, a jackass like you is never going to grow wings." Then she cried, *ah ah ah*, which sounded a lot more like laughter than magic words, but I put the slushy mess in my mouth and chewed.

Though it tasted like rotten turnips, indeed I did feel a transformation begin. My legs shrank, and so did my ears, and slits emerged behind my jaw. I felt scales sliding across my back, and a slime crept over my eyes . . .

THE LAKEPORT
PUBLIC LIBRARY

FEBRUARY 20, 2020

5:27 P.M.

Seymour

Crouched beside the upended shelf of audiobooks, peeking out a sliver of window, he watches two more police vehicles move into place, as though they are constructing a wall around the library. Bent figures hurry through the snow along Park Street, pinpoints of red traveling with them. Thermal scanners? Laser sights? Above the junipers, a trio of blue lights hover: some kind of remote-controlled drone. These, the creatures we have chosen to repopulate the earth.

Seymour crawls back to the dictionary stand and is trying to swallow the swirling panic in his throat when the phone atop the welcome desk rings. He clamps his hands around his ear defenders. Six rings seven eight and it stops. A moment later the phone in Marian's office—hardly more than a broom closet beneath the stairs—rings. Seven rings eight rings stop.

"You should answer," says the wounded man at the base of the stairs. The earmuffs keep his voice faraway. "They'll want to find a peaceful way to resolve this."

"Please be quiet," says Seymour.

Now the phone on the welcome desk rings again. The man at the base of the stairs has already made enough trouble, has in fact ruined everything. This would be a lot easier if he did not speak. Seymour made him take out his lime-green earbuds and throw them into Fiction, and still the man bleeds onto the dingy library carpet, confusing everything.

On all fours Seymour creeps to the welcome desk and rips the phone cord out of the wall jack. Then he crawls into Marian's broom-closet office, where the phone is ringing for a second time, and rips out that cord too.

"That was a mistake," calls the wounded man.

A sticker on Marian's door reads, *The Library: Where the shhh happens.* Images of her freckled face stream across his vision and he tries to blink them away.

Great grey owl. World's largest species of owl by length.

He sits in the doorway to her office with the pistol in his lap. The police lights send blurs of red and blue across the spines of young adult novels. He can feel the roar churning out there, just beyond the windowpanes. Are snipers tracking him right now? Do they have tools to see through walls? How long before they storm in here and shoot him dead?

From his left pocket he removes the phone with the three numbers written on the back. The first detonates bomb one, the second bomb two; he is supposed to dial the third if there's trouble.

Seymour dials the third number and removes one of the cups of his ear defenders. The connection rings multiple times, beeps, and he's disconnected.

Does that mean they've received the message? Is he supposed to say something after the tone?

"I need medical attention," says the man at the base of the stairs.

He dials again. It rings rings rings rings rings rings rings rings rings beeps.

Seymour says, "Hello?"

But the call has disconnected. Probably that means that help is coming. It means that they've received the message, that they'll be activating a support network. He will stall and wait. Stall, wait, and Bishop's people will call back or arrive to help, and everything will be sorted out.

"I'm thirsty," calls the wounded man, and from somewhere come the faint voices of children, and the whistle of howling wind, and the whisper of breaking waves. Deceits of the mind. Seymour replaces his ear defenders, takes a mug decorated with cartoon cats from

Marian's desk, crawls to the drinking fountain, fills it, and sets it within the man's reach.

The trash can beside the armchairs, collecting the leak, is three-quarters full. The boiler directly below him gives off a series of weary creaks. *We will all have to be strong*, Bishop said. *The coming events will test us in ways we cannot yet imagine.*

Zeno

Questions chase one another around the carousel of his mind. Who shot Sharif and how severe are his injuries? Why did Sharif wave him back? If the lights outside the library are law enforcement or paramedics, why aren't they rushing inside? Is it because the assailant is still here? Is there only one? Are parents being notified? What is he supposed to do?

Onstage Aethon-the-donkey is pacing along the frozen rim of the world. From Natalie's speaker comes the sound of ocean waves collapsing onto gravel. Olivia, wearing a big soft gull head and yellow tights, points with one of her homemade wings to a pile of green tissue paper on the stage. "I've heard," she says, "that if you eat enough of it, you'll feel funny. Though I can tell you right now, a jackass like you is never going to grow wings."

Alex-who-is-Aethon picks up some green tissue paper, jams it into his papier-mâché donkey mouth, and steps off the stage.

Olivia-the-gull turns to the chairs. "It's no use for an ass like that to chase after castles in the sky. Being sensible is called being 'down-to-earth' for a reason."

From offstage Alex calls, "Well, *some*thing's happening, I can feel it." Christopher converts the karaoke light from white to blue, and the towers of Cloud Cuckoo Land glimmer on the backdrop, and Natalie replaces the rumble of the waves with sunken bubbling and gurgling and trickling.

Alex steps onstage holding his papier-mâché fish head. Sweat has glued his bangs to his forehead. "Can we take a break, Mr. Ninis? Halftime?"

"He means intermission," says Rachel.

Zeno looks up from his trembling hands. "Yes, yes, of course, a nice quiet intermission. Good idea. You're doing so wonderfully, all of you."

Olivia lifts off her mask. "Mr. Ninis, do you really think I should say 'jackass'? Some people from church are coming tomorrow night."

Christopher heads for the light switch but Zeno says, "No, no, it's better in the dark. Tomorrow you'll be working backstage in low light. Come, let's sit backstage, behind the shelves Sharif set up, away from the audience, just the way it will be tomorrow night, and we can talk about it, Olivia."

He herds them behind the three bookcases, and Rachel gathers the pages of her script and sits in a folding chair and Olivia stows the crumpled green tissue paper in a bag and Alex crawls beneath the rack of costumes and sighs. Zeno stands at the center of them in his necktie and Velcro boots. At his feet the microwave-box-turned-sarcophagus transforms momentarily into an isolation box behind the headquarters at Camp Five—he half expects Rex to rise from it, emaciated and filthy, and adjust his broken glasses—and then it becomes a cardboard box once more.

"Do any of you," he whispers, "have a cell phone?"

Natalie and Rachel shake their heads. Alex says, "Grandma says not till sixth grade."

Christopher says, "Olivia has one."

Olivia says, "My mom took it away."

Natalie raises a hand. Onstage, on the other side of the book-shelves, the submarine gurgle still bubbles out of her speaker, disorienting him.

"Mr. Ninis, what's a jiff?"

"A what?"

"Miss Marian said she'd be back with the pizzas in a jiff."

"A jiff's like a fight," says Alex.

"That's a tiff," says Olivia.

"Jif is peanut butter," says Christopher.

"A jiff is a short time," says Zeno. "A little while." Somewhere out in Lakeport, sirens rise and dip.

"But hasn't it been more than a jiff, Mr. Ninis?"

"Are you hungry, Natalie?"

She nods.

"I'm thirsty," says Christopher.

"The pizzas were probably delayed because of the snow," Zeno says. "Marian will be back soon."

Alex sits up. "We could drink some of the Cloud Cuckoo Land root beer?"

"Those're for tomorrow night," says Olivia.

"I suppose it won't hurt," says Zeno, "if you each have a root beer. Can you get them quietly?"

Alex hops to his feet and Zeno rises to his tiptoes to watch over the tops of the shelves as the boy walks around the stage and ducks into the space between the painted backdrop and the wall.

"Why," asks Christopher, "does he have to do it quietly?" and Rachel reads her script with one index finger tracing the lines and Olivia says, "So about the swearing, Mr. Ninis?"

Is Sharif bleeding to death? Should Zeno be acting faster than this? Alex crawls out from the far end of the backdrop in his bathrobe and shorts carrying a case of twenty-four Mug root beers.

"Careful, Alex."

"Christopher," whispers Alex, as he rounds the apron of the plywood stage, all of his attention on fishing a can from the top of the case, "here's one for—" and he catches a toe on the riser and trips and a dozen cans of root beer take flight over the stage.

Seymour

He stares at the phone, thinks: Ring. Ring now. But it remains inert.

5:38 p.m.

Bunny will be done with her housekeeping shift by now. Footsore, back aching, she'll be waiting for him to pick her up and drive her to the Pig N' Pancake. Are police cruisers streaking past the window? Are her coworkers talking about something happening at the library?

He tries to imagine Bishop's warriors assembling somewhere nearby, using code words on radios, coordinating efforts to rescue him. Or—a new doubt slithers into place—maybe the police are somehow disrupting his ability to call out. Maybe Bishop's people didn't receive his calls. He thinks of the red lights moving out in the snow, the drone hovering over the hedges. Would the Lakeport Police Department have capabilities like that?

The wounded man is lying across the stairs with his right hand clamped against his bleeding shoulder. His eyes have closed, and the blood on the carpet beside him is drying, traveling past maroon toward black. Better not to look. Seymour diverts his attention instead into the long shadow of the middle aisle between Fiction and Nonfiction. What a shambles he's made of the whole thing.

Is he willing to die for this? To give voice to the innumerable creatures that humans have wiped off the earth? To stand up for the voiceless? Isn't that what a hero does? A hero fights for those who cannot fight for themselves.

Scared and confounded, body itching, armpits sweating, feet

cold, bladder brimming, Beretta in one pocket and cell phone in the other, Seymour removes the cups of his ear defenders and wipes his face with the sleeve of his windbreaker and looks down the aisle toward the restroom at the back of the library when he hears, coming from upstairs, a succession of booming thuds.

ELEVEN

IN THE BELLY OF THE WHALE

Cloud Cuckoo Land by Antonius Diogenes, Folio Λ

. . . I shadowed my scaly brothers through the endless deeps, fleeing the quick and terrible dolphins. Without warning, a leviathan came upon us, hugest of all living creatures, with a mouth as wide as the gates of Troy and teeth as tall as the pillars of Hercules, their points as sharp as the sword of Perseus.

His jaw gaped wide to swallow us, and I waited for death. I'd never make it to the city in the clouds. I'd never see the tortoise or taste a honeycake from the stack on his shell. I'd die in the cold sea, my fish bones lost in the belly of a beast. The whole school of us were swept into the cavern of its mouth, but the wickets of its enormous fangs proved too large to impale us, and we spilled past unharmed, down into its gullet.

Sloshing about inside the guts of the great monster, as though trapped inside a second sea, we zoomed over all of creation. Every time it opened its mouth, I rose to the surface and glimpsed something new: the crocodiles of Ethiopia, the palaces of Carthage, the snow thick upon the caves of the troglodytes along the girdle of the world.

Eventually I grew weary: I had traveled so far, yet was no closer to my destination than when I began. I was a fish inside a sea inside a bigger fish inside a bigger sea, and I wondered if the world itself swam also inside the belly of a much greater fish, all of us fish inside fish inside fish, and then, tired of so much wondering, I shut my scaly eyes and slept . . .

CONSTANTINOPLE

APRIL–MAY 1453

Omeir

For a mile in either direction, hammers ring, axes chop, camels bray, bark, and bleat. He passes camps of arrow makers, camps of harness makers, cobblers and blacksmiths; tailors are fabricating tents inside yet larger tents; boys scurry here and there with baskets of rice; fifty carpenters construct scaling ladders from debarked logs. Ditches have been cut to carry away human and animal waste; drinking water is stored in mountains of barrels; a great portable foundry has been constructed at the rear.

Men approach from every corner of the camp to ogle the cannon where it gleams, immense and bright, on its cart. The oxen, wary of the commotion, stick close together: Moonlight appears to sleep on his feet as he chews, unable to raise his head above his backline, and Tree finds a place beside him and lies on his side, twitching one ear. Omeir rubs a mixture of spit and crushed calendula leaves into his left hind leg, as Grandfather would have done, and worries.

At dusk the men who have brought the cannon from Edirne gather around steaming cauldrons. A captain climbs to a dais to announce that the sultan's gratitude is immense. As soon as the city is won, he says, they will each be able to choose which house will be theirs, and which garden, and which women will be their wives.

All night Omeir's sleep is broken by the noise of carpenters building a cradle to hold the cannon and a palisade to conceal it, and all the next day the teamsters and oxen work to hoist it into place. An occasional crossbow bolt comes whistling out from the crenelated parapet atop the city's outer wall and sticks into a board or into the mud. Maher shakes a fist at the walls. "We have something a little bigger than that to throw back at you," he calls, and everyone who hears him laughs.

That evening in the pasture where they feed the oxen Maher finds Omeir sitting atop a fallen block of limestone and squats beside him and picks at a scab on his knee. They gaze across the encampment to the moat and the chalk-white towers, striped red with brick. In the setting sun the jumble of rooftops on the far side of the walls seems to burn.

"Do you think by this time tomorrow, all of that will be ours?"

Omeir says nothing. He is ashamed to say that the size of the city terrifies him. How could men have built such a place?

Maher enthuses about the house he'll choose for himself, how it will have two stories and channels of water running through a garden with pear trees and jasmine, and how he'll have a dark-eyed wife, and five sons, and at least a dozen three-legged stools—Maher is always talking about three-legged stools. Omeir thinks of the stone cottage in the ravine, his mother making curds, Grandfather toasting pine nuts, and homesickness rolls through him.

Atop a low hill on their left, surrounded by shields, a series of ditches, and a curtain-wall of fabric, the sultan's compound of tents ruffles in the breeze. There are tents for his bodyguards, tents for his council and treasury, for his holy relics and his falconry, his astrologers and scholars and food-tasters; kitchen tents, toilet tents, contemplation tents. Beside an observation tower ripples the sultan's personal tent—red, gold, and as large as a grove of trees. Its interior is painted, Omeir has heard, the colors of paradise, and he aches to see it.

"Our prince, in his infinite wisdom," says Maher, following Omeir's gaze, "has discovered a weakness. A flaw. Do you see where the river enters the city? Where the walls dip beside that gate? Water has been running there since the days of the Prophet, peace be upon Him, collecting, seeping, chewing away. The foundations there are weak, and the mitering of the stones has begun to fail. It is there that we will smash through."

Up and down the city walls, sentry fires are being lit. Omeir tries to imagine swimming the moat, clambering over the scarp on the

far side, somehow scaling the outer wall, fighting across the battlements, then dropping into a no-man's-land before the huge bulwark
of the inner wall, its towers as tall as twelve men. You would need
wings; you would need to be a god.

"Tomorrow night," says Maher. "Tomorrow night two of those
houses will be ours."

The following morning ablutions are made and prayers recited. Then
flagbearers pick their way through the tents to the very front of the
lines and raise bright standards in the dawn light. Drums and tam-
bourines and castanets sound throughout the company, a racket
meant as much to frighten as to inspire. Omeir and Maher watch
the powder makers—many missing fingers, many with burns on
their throats and faces—prepare the huge gun. Their expressions are
strained from the constant fear of working with unstable explosives
and they reek of sulfur and they murmur to one another in their
strange dialect like necromancers, and Omeir prays that their eyes
will not meet his, that if something goes wrong they will not blame
the defect in his face.

Along the almost four miles of land wall, the cannons have been
organized into fourteen batteries, none larger than the great bombard Omeir and Maher have helped drag here. More familiar siege
weapons—trebuchets, slings, catapults—are loaded too, but all of
them seem primitive compared to the burnished guns and the dark
horses and carts and powder-stained tunics of the artillerymen.
Bright spring clouds cruise above them like vessels sailing to a parallel war, and the sun pushes above the city's rooftops, momentarily
blinding the armies outside the walls, and finally, at some signal from
the sultan, hidden by a shimmer of fabric atop his tower, the drums
and cymbals go quiet and the flagbearers drop their standards.

At more than sixty cannons, cannoneers set tapers to priming
powder. The whole army, from barefoot conscripted shepherds in the
vanguard with clubs and scythes to the imams and viziers—from the
attendants and grooms and cooks and arrowsmiths to the elite corps

of Janissaries in their spotless white headdresses—watches. People inside the city watch too, in sporadic lines along the outer and inner walls: archers, horsemen, counter-sappers, monks, the curious and the incautious. Omeir shuts his eyes and clamps his forearms over his ears and feels the pressure build, feels the huge cannon draw up its abominable energy, and for an instant prays that he is asleep, that when he opens his eyes he'll find himself at home, resting against the trunk of the half-hollow yew, waking from an immense dream.

One after another the bombards fire, white smoke ejecting forward from their barrels as the guns smash backward with the recoil, rocking the earth, and sixty-plus stone balls fly toward the city faster than eyes can track them.

Up and down the walls clouds of dust and pulverized stone rise. Fragments of brick and limestone rain onto men a quarter mile away, and a roar rolls through the assembled armies.

As the smoke drifts away, Omeir sees that a section of one tower in the outer wall has partially crumbled. Otherwise the walls appear unaffected. The gunners are pouring olive oil over the huge gun to cool it, and an officer prepares his crew to load a second thousand-pound ball, and Maher is blinking in disbelief, and it is a long time before the cheers subside enough for Omeir to hear the screaming.

Anna

She is chopping scavenged wood in the courtyard when the guns fire again, a dozen in succession, followed by the distant rumble of stonework falling to pieces. Days ago the thunder of the sultan's war engines could start half of the women in the workshop weeping. This morning they merely sign crosses in the air over their boiled eggs. A jug wobbles on a shelf and Chryse reaches up and settles it.

Anna drags the wood into the scullery and builds up the fire and the eight embroideresses who are left eat and shuffle back upstairs to work. It's cold and nobody sews with urgency. Kalaphates has fled with the gold, silver, and seed pearls, there's not much silk left, and what clergymen are buying embroidered vestments anyway? Everyone seems to agree that the world will end soon and the only essential task is to cleanse the besmirchment from one's soul before that day comes.

Widow Theodora stands at the workshop window, leaning on her stick. Maria holds her embroidery frame inches from her eyes as she glides her needle through the samite hood.

In the evenings, after she has settled Maria in their cell, Anna treks the mile to join other women and girls in the terrace between the inner and outer walls. They work in teams to fill barrels with turf, soil, and chunks of masonry. She sees nuns, still in their habits, helping to attach barrels to pulleys; she sees mothers taking turns with newborns so others can pitch in.

The barrels are hoisted by donkey-powered cranes to the battlements of the outer walls. After dark, impossibly brave soldiers, in full view of the Saracen armies, crawl over hastily built stockades, lower the barrels in, and pack the empty spaces around them with branches and straw. Anna sees whole bushes and saplings get lowered into the stockades—even carpets and tapestries. Anything to soften the blows of the terrible stone balls.

Out there, up against the outer wall, when the sultan's guns roar, she feels the detonations roll through her bones and shake her heart where it hangs inside its cage. Sometimes a ball overshoots its mark and goes screaming off into the city, and she hears it bury itself in an orchard or a ruin or a house. Other times the balls strike the stockades, and rather than shatter, they swallow the balls whole, and the defenders along the ramparts cheer.

The quiet moments frighten her more: when the work pauses and she can hear the songs of the Saracens out beyond the walls, the creaking of their siege machines, the nickering of their horses and bleats of their camels. When the wind is right, she can smell the food they're cooking. To be so close to men who want her dead. To know that only a partition of masonry prevents them from doing their will.

She works until she cannot see her hands in front of her face, then trudges home to the house of Kalaphates, takes a candle from the scullery, and climbs onto the pallet beside Maria, her fingernails broken, her hands veined with dirt, and pulls the blanket around them and opens the little brown goatskin codex.

The reading goes slowly. Some leaves are partially obscured by mold, and the scribe who copied the story did not separate the words with spaces, and the tallow candles give off a weak and sputtery light, and she is often so tired that the lines seem to ripple and dance in front of her eyes.

The shepherd in the story accidentally turns himself into an ass, then a fish, and now he swims through the innards of an enormous leviathan, touring the continents while dodging beasts who try to

eat him: it's silly, absurd; this cannot possibly be the sort of compendium of marvels the Italians sought, can it?

And yet. When the stream of the old Greek picks up, and she
climbs into the story, as though climbing the wall of the priory on
the rock—handhold here, foothold there—the damp chill of the
cell dissipates, and the bright, ridiculous world of Aethon takes its
place.

> Our sea monster battled with another, bigger and more
> monstrous even than he was, and the waters around us
> quaked, and ships with a hundred sailors on each sank
> in front of me, and whole uprooted islands were carried
> past. I closed my eyes in terror, and fixed my thoughts on
> the golden city in the clouds . . .

Turn a page, walk the lines of sentences: the singer steps out, and
conjures a world of color and noise in the space inside your head.

Not only, Chryse announces one night, has the sultan used his
Throat Cutter to strangle the city from the east, not only has he posi-
tioned his navy to blockade the sea from the west, not only has he
turned out a limitless army with terrifying artillery pieces—now he
has brought in crews of Serbian silver tunnelers, the best miners in
the world, to dig passages beneath the walls.

From the moment Maria hears this, a terror of these men seizes
her. She places bowls of water around their cell and crouches over
them, studying their surfaces for any evidence of subterranean activity. At night she wakes Anna to listen to the scraping of picks and
shovels beneath the floor.

"They're growing louder."

"I don't hear anything, Maria."

"Is the floor shifting?"

Anna wraps her arms around her. "Try to sleep, sister."

"I hear their voices. They are talking directly below us."

"It's only the wind in the chimney."

Yet, despite logic, Anna feels the fear slipping in. She imagines a platoon of men in caftans crouched in a hole just beneath their pallet, their faces black with soil, their eyes huge in the dark. She holds her breath; she hears the tips of their knives scratch against the undersides of the flagstones.

One evening at the end of the month, walking the eastern section of the city, scrounging for food, Anna is rounding the great weathered bulk of the Hagia Sophia when she stops. Between the houses, tucked against the harbor, the priory on the rock stands silhouetted against the sea and it is on fire. Flames flicker in crumbled windows, and a pillar of black smoke twists into the sky.

Bells ring—whether to urge people to fight the fire or for another purpose, she could not say. Perhaps they ring simply to exhort the people to carry on. An abbot, eyes closed, shuffles past carrying an icon, trailed by two monks, each with a smoking censer, and the smoke from the priory lingers in the dusk. She thinks of those dank, rotting halls, the moldering library beneath its broken arches. The codex back in her cell.

Day after day, the tall Italian said, *year after year, time wipes the old books from the world.*

A charwoman with scars on her face stops in front of her. "Get home, child. The bells are calling the monks to bury the dead, and this is no time to be out."

When she returns home, she finds Maria sitting rigid in their cell in complete darkness.

"Is that smoke? I smell smoke."

"It's only a candle."

"I feel faint."

"It's probably hunger, sister."

Anna sits and wraps the blanket around them and lifts the samite hood from her sister's lap, five of her twelve birds finished—the dove of the Holy Spirit, the peacock of the Resurrection, the crossbill who tried to pry the nails from Jesus's crucified hands. She rolls Maria's thimble and scissors inside it and retrieves the battered old codex from the corner and thumbs to the first leaf: *TO MY DEAREST NIECE WITH HOPE THAT THIS BRINGS YOU HEALTH AND LIGHT.*

"Maria," she says, "listen," and starts at the beginning.

Drunken, foolhardy Aethon mistakes a magical city in a play for a real place. He sets off for Thessaly, land of magic, and accidentally turns himself into a donkey. This time she is able to make quicker progress, and as she reads aloud, something curious happens: as long as she keeps a steady stream of words flowing past Maria's ears, her sister doesn't seem to suffer so much. Her muscles loosen; her head falls to Anna's shoulder. Aethon-the-donkey is kidnapped by bandits, gets lashed to a wheel by the miller's son, walks on his tired, cracking hooves to the place where nature comes to an end. Maria doesn't moan in pain or whisper about invisible subterranean miners scratching beneath the floor. She sits beside her, blinking into the candlelight, amusement playing over her face.

"Do you think it's really true, Anna? A fish so large it could swallow ships whole?"

A mouse scrabbles across the stone and rises onto its hind legs and stands twitching its nose at her with its head cocked as though awaiting her answer. Anna thinks of the last time she sat with Licinius. Μῦθος, he wrote, *mýthos*, a conversation, a tale, a legend from the darkness before the days of Christ.

"Some stories," she says, "can be both false and true at the same time."

Down the hall Widow Theodora touches the worn beads of her rosary in the moonlight. One cell away, Chryse the cook, half her teeth gone, drinks from a jug of wine and sets her cracked hands on her knees and dreams of a summer day outside the walls, walking beneath cherry trees, a sky full of crows. One mile east, in the belly of a carrack at anchor, the boy Himerius, drafted into the city's stop-gap naval defenses, sits with thirty other oarsmen, resting over the shaft of a great oar, his back throbbing, both palms bleeding, eight days left to live. In the underground cisterns beneath the church of the Hagia Sophia, three little boats float on the black mirror of the water, each packed with spring roses, while a priest intones a hymn into the echoing dark.

Omeir

The first time he comes north around the city walls and sees the estuary of the Golden Horn—a sheet of silver water a half mile wide, trundling slowly out to sea—it seems the most astonishing thing in the world. Gulls wheel overhead; wading birds as big as gods rise from reed brakes; two of the sultan's barges glide past as if by magic. Grandfather said that the ocean was large enough to contain every dream everyone had ever dreamed, but until now he had no comprehension of what that meant.

Up and down the western banks of the estuary, Ottoman landing stages swarm with activity. As the ox train descends toward the wharfs, Omeir makes out cranes and winches, stevedores unloading barrels and munitions, draft horses waiting with their carts, and is certain he will never see anything so resplendent again.

But as days turn to weeks, his initial wonder melts away. He and the bullocks are assigned to a team of eight hauling wagons of granite balls, quarried on the north shore of the Black Sea, from a landing stage along the Horn to the impromptu foundry outside the walls where stonecutters chisel and polish the balls to match the calibers of the bombards. The trip is four miles, uphill most of the way, and the guns' appetite for new projectiles is unappeasable. The ox trains work dusk to dawn, few of the animals have recovered from their long journey here, and all exhibit signs of distress.

Moonlight takes more of the load for his lame brother every day, and in the evenings, as soon as they are unyoked, Tree manages a few strides before he lies down. Omeir spends most of his nighttime hours bringing fodder and water to him. Chin on the ground, neck

bent, ribs rising falling rising falling: never in life would a healthy
bullock lie like that. Men eye him, sensing a meal.

Rain, then fog, then sun hot enough to raise billowing clouds of flies.
The sultan's infantry, working among whistling projectiles, fills sections of the moat along the Lycus River with felled trees, collapsed
siege engines, tent-cloth, anything and everything they can find, and
every few days, the commanders whip the men into a fever, then
send another wave across.

They die by the hundreds. Many risk everything to retrieve their
dead, and are killed while gathering the corpses, leaving yet more
dead to gather. Most mornings, as Omeir yokes his oxen, smoke
from funeral pyres lifts into the sky.

The road to the landing stages along the Horn bisects a Christian
graveyard which has been transformed into an open-air field hospital. Men lie injured and dying between the old headstones: Macedo-
nians, Albanians, Wallachians, Serbians, some in so much agony that
they seem reduced to something less than human, as though pain
were a leveling wave, a mortar troweled over everything that person once was. Healers move among the wounded carrying sheaves
of smoldering willow and medics lead donkeys carrying earthen
jars and from the jars they produce great handfuls of maggots to
clean wounds, and the men squirm or scream or faint and Omeir
imagines the dead buried just feet below the dying, their flesh rotted
green, their skeleton teeth champing, and he is wretched.

Donkey carts hurry past the oxen teams in both directions, the
faces of the carters crimped with impatience or fear or anger or all
three. Hatred, Omeir sees, is contagious, spreading through the
ranks like a disease. Already, three weeks into the siege, some of the
men fight no longer for God or the sultan or plunder but out of a
fearful rage. Kill them all. Get this over with. Sometimes the anger
flares inside Omeir too, and he wants nothing more than for God to
plunge a fiery fist through the sky and start crushing buildings one
after the next until all the Greeks are dead and he can go home.

On the first of May the sky knots with cloud. The Golden Horn turns slow and black and pocked with the circles of a hundred million raindrops. The wagon team waits as stevedores roll the huge granite balls, veined white with quartz, down the ramp and stack them in the wagon.

Far off, a trebuchet slings rocks that fly in wild arcs over the city walls and disappear. They are a half mile back up the road toward the foundry, deep in the ruts, the oxen drooling and panting, their tongues hanging, when Tree staggers. He manages to get back up, but a few strides later he staggers again. The entire train stops and men rush to brake the wagon as the traffic hurries past.

Omeir ducks in among the animals. When he touches Tree's hind leg, the bullock shudders. Mucus drains in twin streams from his nostrils and he licks the roof of his mouth with his enormous tongue over and over and his eyes vibrate gently back and forth in their sockets. Their surfaces look worn and foggy and carry the distant dreaminess of cataracts. As though the past five months have aged him ten years.

Goad in hand, in his ruined shoes, Omeir walks the line of heaving oxen and stands below the quartermaster who sits scowling in the wagon atop the load.

"The animals need rest."

The quartermaster gapes down half-bemused and half-disgusted and reaches for his bullwhip. Omeir feels his heart swing out over a black void. A memory rises: once, years before, Grandfather took him high on the mountain to watch the woodcutters bring down a huge, ancient silver fir, as tall as twenty-five men, a kingdom unto itself. They sang a low, determined song, driving their wedges into its trunk in rhythm as though hammering needles into the ankle of a giant, and Grandfather explained the names of the tools they used, caulks and punks and blocks and spars, but what Omeir remembers now, as the quartermaster rears back with his whip, is that when the tree tipped, its trunk exploding, the men shouting *hallo*, the air suddenly charged with the ripe, sharp aroma of cracking wood, what he felt was not joy but sorrow. All the timbermen seemed to exult in their collective power, watching branches that for generations knew only starlight and snow and ravens smash down through the undergrowth. But Omeir felt something close to despair, and sensed that, even at his age, his feelings would not be welcome, that he should hide them even from his own grandfather. Why mourn, Grandfather would say, what men can do? There's something wrong with a child who sympathizes more with other beings than he does with men.

The tip of the quartermaster's bullwhip cracks an inch from Omeir's ear.

A white-bearded teamster who has been with them since Edirne calls, "Leave the boy be. So he is kind to beasts. The Prophet Himself, peace be upon Him, once cut off a piece of his robe rather than wake a cat that was sleeping on it."

The quartermaster blinks down. "If we do not deliver this load," he says, "we'll all be lashed, myself included. And I'll see to it that you and that face of yours get the worst of it. Move your beasts, or we'll all be meat for the crows."

The men turn back to their animals, and Omeir climbs the rutted, ruined road, and crouches beside Tree and says his name and the bullock stands. He touches Moonlight on the withers with his goad and the bullocks lean into the yoke and begin to pull again.

TWELVE

THE WIZARD INSIDE THE WHALE

Cloud Cuckoo Land by Antonius Diogenes, Folio M

. . . the waters inside the monster calmed and I grew hungry. As I gazed up, a delicious morsel, a shiny little anchovy, landed on the surface, floated, then danced in the most enticing way. With a flick of my tail I swam straight for it, opened my jaws as wide as I could, and . . .

"Ouch, ouch," I cried, "my lip!" The fishermen had eyes like lamps and hands like fins and penises like trees and they lived on an island inside the whale with a mountain of bones at its center. "Unhook me," I said. "I'm hardly a meal for men as strong as you. Besides, I'm not even a fish at all!"

The fishermen looked at each other and one said, "Is that you talking or is that the fish?" They carried me to a cave high on the mountain where a disheveled castaway wizard had lived for four hundred years and taught himself how to speak fish. "Great wizard," I gasped. With every moment that passed it became harder to speak. "Transform me into a bird, please, a brave eagle, possibly, or a bright strong owl, so that I might fly to the city in the clouds where pain never visits and the west wind always blows."

The wizard laughed. "Even if you grew wings, foolish fish, you could not fly to a place that is not real."

"Wrong," I said, "it does exist. Even if you don't believe in it, I do. Otherwise what's it all been for?"

"All right," he said. "Show these fishermen where the big fish live, and I will give you wings." I flapped my gills in agreement and he mumbled magic words and tossed me into the air, high over the mountain, to the very rim of the leviathan's gums, where the gory pillars of his tusks sliced the moon . . .

THE ARGOS

MISSION YEAR 64

DAY 1–DAY 20 INSIDE VAULT ONE

Konstance

She wakes on the floor still wearing the bioplastic suit her father made. The machine flickers inside its tower.

Good afternoon, Konstance.

Scattered around her are the things Father pitched into the vestibule: Perambulator, inflatable cot, recycling toilet, dry-wipes, the sacks of Nourish powder, the food printer still in its wrapper. The oxygen hood lies beside her, its headlamp extinguished.

Drip by drip, horror trickles into her awareness. The two figures in the biohazard suits, the bronze mirror of their face shields reflecting back a warped version of the open doorway to Compartment 17. The tents in the Commissary. Father's haggard face, his pink-rimmed eyes. The way he flinched every time the beam of the headlamp passed over him.

Mother was not in her bed.

She feels exposed using the little recycling toilet. The bottom half of her worksuit is damp with sweat. "Sybil, how long was I asleep?"

You slept eighteen hours, Konstance.

Eighteen hours? She counts the sacks of Nourish powder: thirteen.

"Vital signs?"

Your temperature is ideal. Pulse and respiration rates perfect.

Konstance walks a lap of the vault, searching for the door.

"Sybil, please let me out."

I cannot.

"What do you mean you cannot?"

I cannot open the vault.

"Of course you can."

My primary directive is to tend to the well-being of the crew, and I have confidence that it is safer for you in here.

"Ask Father to come get me."

Yes, Konstance.

"Tell him I'd like to see him right now." The cot, the oxygen hood, the food sacks. Dread ticks through her. "Sybil, how many meals can a person print with thirteen sacks of Nourish powder?"

Assuming average caloric output, a Reconstituter could produce 6,526 fully nutritional meals. Are you hungry after your long rest? Would you like me to help you prepare a nutritious meal?

Father poring over technical drawings in the Library. The sewing stool screaming against the pressure of the outer door. *One of us is not feeling well.* Jessi Ko said the only way to get out of your compartment was to tell Sybil that you weren't feeling well. If Sybil detected something wrong with you, she'd send Dr. Cha and Engineer Goldberg to escort you to the Infirmary.

Father was not well. When he announced it, Sybil opened the door to Compartment 17 so he could be brought to wherever they were isolating sick crew members, but first he brought Konstance to Sybil's vault. With enough supplies to last her six and a half thousand meals.

Hands shaking, she touches the Vizer on the back of her head and the Perambulator on the floor whirs to life.

Off to the Library? asks Sybil. *Of course, Konstance. You can eat afterw—*

No one at the tables, no one on the ladders. No books fly through the air. Not a single person in sight. Above the aperture in the barrel vault, the sky radiates a pleasant blue. Konstance calls, "Hello?" and from beneath a desk trots Mrs. Flowers's dog, eyes shining, tail high.

No teachers leading classes. No teenagers sliding up and down the ladders to the Games Section.

"Sybil, where is everybody?"

Everyone is elsewhere, Konstance.

The numberless books wait in their places. The spotless rectangles of paper and pencils sit in their boxes. Days ago, at one of these tables, Mother read aloud: *The hardiest viruses can persist for months on surfaces: tabletops, door handles, lavatory fixtures.*

A cold weight drops through her. She takes a slip of paper, writes, *How many years would it take a person to eat 6,526 meals?*

The answer floats down: 5.9598

Six years?

"Sybil, please ask Father to meet me in the Library."

Yes, Konstance.

She sits on the marble floor and the little dog climbs into her lap. His fur feels real. The little pink pads on the bottom of his feet feel warm. High above her, a solitary silver cloud, like a child's drawing, crosses the sky.

"What did he say?"

He has not yet replied.

"What time is it?"

Six minutes past DayLight thirteen, Konstance.

"Is everyone at Third Meal?"

They are not at Third Meal, no. Would you like to play a game, Konstance? Do a puzzle? There's always the Atlas, I know you enjoy going in there.

The digital dog blinks its digital eyes. The digital cloud grinds silently through the digital dusk.

By the time she steps off her Perambulator, the walls of Vault One have dimmed. NoLight coming. She presses her forehead to the wall and shouts, "Hello?"

Louder: "Hello?"

Difficult to hear through walls on the *Argos* but not impossible: from her berth in Compartment 17 she has heard water trickling through pipes, the occasional argument between Mr. and Mrs. Marri in Compartment 16.

She smacks the walls with the heels of her hands, then picks up the inflatable cot, still wrapped and bound, and throws it. It makes a terrible clamor. Waits. Throws it again. Each heartbeat sends a new stroke of terror through her. Again she sees Father poring over schematics in the Library. Hears what Mrs. Chen said, years ago: *This vault has autonomous thermal, mechanical, and filtration processes, independent of the rest of . . .* Father must have been making sure of that. He put her in here on purpose to protect her. But why didn't he join her? Why not put others inside with her?

Because he was sick. Because they may have been carrying an infectious and lethal disease.

The room darkens to black.

"Sybil, how is my body temperature?"

Ideal.

"Not too hot?"

All signs are excellent.

"Will you open the door now, please?"

The vault will remain sealed, Konstance. This is the safest place for you to be. Best to make a healthy meal. Then you can assemble your cot. Would you like a bit of light?

"Ask my father if he'll change his mind. I'll put together the bed, I'll do whatever you say." She unstraps the cot, locks the aluminum legs into place, opens the valve. The room is very quiet. Sybil shimmers deep within her folds.

Maybe others are safe in the provision vaults, where the flour and new worksuits and spare parts are kept. Maybe those rooms also have their own thermal systems, their own water filtration. But then why aren't they in the Library? Maybe they don't have Perambulators? Maybe they're asleep? She climbs onto the cot and tears the blanket out of its wrapper and pulls it over her eyes. Counts to thirty.

"Did you ask him yet? Did he change his mind?"

Your father has not changed his mind.

· · ·

In the hours to come she checks her forehead for a fever twenty times. Is that the oncoming blur of a headache? The lilt of nausea? *Temperature good*, says Sybil. *Respiration and heart rate excellent.*

She paces the Library, shouts Jessi Ko's name down the galleries, plays Swords of Silverman, curls in a ball beneath a table and sobs while the little white dog licks her face. She sees no one.

Inside the vault the glimmering threads of Sybil tower above the cot. *Are you ready to resume your studies, Konstance? Our voyage continues, and it is paramount to maintain a daily—*

Are people dying thirty feet away in their compartments? Are the corpses of everyone she has ever known waiting to be jettisoned through the airlock?

"Let me out, Sybil."

I'm afraid the door remains sealed.

"But you can open it. You're the one controlling it."

Because I cannot say whether it is safe for you outside the vault, I am not capable of unsealing the door. My primary directive is to tend to the well-being—

"But you didn't. You didn't tend to the well-being of the crew, Sybil."

With every passing hour, I become more confident that you are safe where you are.

"What if," Konstance whispers, "I don't want to be safe anymore?"

Rage next. She unscrews one of the cot's aluminum legs and swings it at the walls, scratching and dimpling the metal. When that proves unsatisfying, she turns to the translucent tube that surrounds Sybil, beating it until the aluminum shears and her hands feel shattered.

Where has everyone gone and who is she to be the one who is still alive and for what reasons in the universe would Father ever leave his home and doom her to this wretched fate? The diodes in the ceiling are very bright. A drop of blood runs off a fingertip onto the floor. The tube protecting Sybil remains unscratched.

Do you feel better? asks Sybil. *It is natural to express anger from time to time.*

Why can't healing happen as quickly as wounding? You twist an ankle, break a bone—you can be hurt in a heartbeat. Hour by hour, week by week, year by year, the cells in your body labor to remake themselves the way they were the instant before your injury. But even then you're never the same: not quite.

Eight days alone, ten eleven thirteen: she loses track. The door doesn't open. No one bangs on the other side of the walls. No one enters the Library. The only incoming water line into Vault One is a single, slow-dripping tube that she alternately plugs into the food printer or the recycling toilet. It takes several minutes to fill her drinking cup; she is perpetually thirsty. Some hours she presses her hands against the walls and feels trapped like an embryo inside a seed coat, dormant, waiting to wake up. Other hours she dreams of the *Argos* settling onto a river delta on Beta Oph2, the walls opening, everyone walking out into clear, clean rain, falling in sheets from the alien sky, rain that tastes faintly of flowers. A breeze strikes their faces; flocks of strange birds rise and wheel; Father smears mud on his cheeks and looks at her with glee, while Mother stares up, mouth wide, drinking from the sky—to wake from a dream like that is the worst kind of loneliness.

DayLight NoLight DayLight NoLight: inside the Atlas she walks deserts, expressways, farm roads, Prague, Cairo, Muscat, Tokyo, searching for something she cannot name. A man in Kenya with a gun slung over his back stands holding a razor as the cameras pass. In Bangkok she finds an open shopfront where a girl hunches behind a desk; on the wall behind her hang at least one thousand clocks, clocks with cat faces, clocks with panda bears for numbers, wooden clocks with brass hands, all their pendulums stilled. Always the trees draw her, a rubber fig in India, mossy yews in England, an oak in Alberta, yet not one image in the Atlas—not even the ancient Bosnian pine in the mountains of Thessaly—possesses the meticulous, staggering complexity of a single lettuce leaf in Father's farm, or of her pine sapling in its little planter, its textures and surprises; the rich, living green of its long needles, tipped with yellow; the purple-blue of its cones; xylem trundling minerals and water up from the roots, phloem carrying sugars away from the needles to be stored, but just slowly enough that the eye cannot see it happen.

Finally she sits exhausted on the cot and shivers and the diodes in the ceiling dim. Mrs. Chen said Sybil was a book that contained the entire world: a thousand variations of recipes for macaroni and cheese, the record of four thousand years of temperatures of the Arctic Sea, Confucian literature and Beethoven's symphonies and the genomes of the trilobites—the heritage of all humanity, the citadel, the ark, the womb, everything we can imagine and everything we might ever need. Mrs. Flowers said it would be enough.

Every few hours the questions rise to her lips: Sybil, am I the only one left? Do you pilot a flying graveyard with one soul left on board? But she cannot bring herself to ask.

Her father is only waiting. He is waiting for everything to be safe. Then he will open the door.

LAKEPORT, IDAHO

1953–1970

Zeno

The bus drops him at the Texaco. Mrs. Boydstun stands outside smoking a cigarette and leaning against her Buick.

"So skinny. You get my letters?"

"You sent some?"

"First of the month, rain or shine."

"What'd they say?"

She shrugs. "New stoplight. Stibnite mine closed."

Her hair is neat and her eyes are bright but when she walks toward the diner he notices something off: one leg is a half second slower than it should be.

"It's nothing," she says. "My dad had the same. Look: your dog died. I gave her to Charlie Goss in New Meadows. He said she went easy."

Athena drowsing by the library fire. He's too exhausted to cry. "She was old."

"She was."

They sit in a booth and order eggs and Mrs. Boydstun lights a second cigarette. The waitress wears lunettes on a chain around her neck. Her apron is shockingly white. She says, "They brainwash you? They're saying some of you boys went and became turncoats."

Mrs. Boydstun taps her cigarette into the ashtray. "Just bring the coffee, Helen."

Knives of sunlight flash off the lake. Boats motor back and forth, unzipping the water. At the service station a shirtless man with a deep tan watches an attendant pump gas into his Cadillac. Impossible that such things have been going on all these months.

Mrs. Boydstun watches him. He understands that people will want to hear something, but not the truth: they'll want a story of perseverance and pluck, good overcoming evil, a homecoming song about a hero who brought light into dark places. Beside him the waitress is clearing a table: three of the plates still have food on them.

Mrs. Boydstun says, "You kill anybody over there?"

"No."

"Not a one?"

The eggs come sunny-side up. He pierces one with the tines of his fork and the yolk bleeds out, glistening obscenely.

"That's good," she says. "That's for the best."

The house is the same: the ceramic children, a Jesus suffering on every wall. The same mulberry curtains, the same junipers beneath which Athena crawled on the coldest nights. Mrs. Boydstun pours a drink.

"Cribbage, honey?"

"I think I'll lie down."

"Of course. You take your time."

In the dresser drawer the Playwood Plastic soldiers slumber in their tin box. Soldier 401 marches uphill with his rifle. Soldier 410 kneels behind his anti-tank gun. He gets into the same brass bed he slept in as a boy but the mattress is too soft and the day keeps getting brighter. Eventually he hears Mrs. Boydstun go out and he creeps down the stairs and unlatches every door in the house. He needs them unlocked at the least, open at best. Then he tiptoes into the kitchen, finds a loaf of bread, tears it in half, puts one half beneath his pillow, and divides the other between his pockets. Just in case.

He sleeps on the floor beside the bed. He is not quite twenty years old.

Pastor White gets him a job with the county highway department. In the golden days of fall, tamaracks blazing yellow on the mountain-sides, Zeno works with a road crew of older men pulling a motor grader with a Caterpillar RD6 crawler, filling in mud holes or graveling over washouts, improving the roads to the even smaller towns that lie even deeper in the mountains. When winter arrives, he requests the most solitary job on offer: driving an old hardtop army Autocar rotary snowplow. Its three big spiral blades send snow over the windshield in a kind of reverse avalanche—a skyward spout that, over the course of a night, illuminated by the glow of the headlights, tends to hypnotize him. It's a strange and lonely business: the wipers generally do little more than smear frost across the glass, and the heater works about twenty percent of the time, and the defroster is a caged fan mounted on the dashboard, and he has to drive with one hand on the wheel and the other holding a rag soaked in spirits, wiping the inside of the glass to keep it clear.

Every Sunday he sends a letter to a British veterans organization, seeking the whereabouts of a lance corporal named Rex Browning.

Time passes. The snow melts, falls again, a sawmill burns, is rebuilt again, the highway crew rocks over washouts, shores up bridges, and rain or rockfall washes them out, and they rebuild them again. Then it's winter and the rotary plow throws its mesmeric curtain of snow over the truck cab. Cars are always freezing up or going off the roads, sliding into the slush or mud, and he's always hauling them back up: chain, tackle, reverse.

Things occasionally go haywire with Mrs. Boydstun. Her moods seesaw. She forgets what she is supposed to buy at the store. She trips over nothing; she tries to put on lipstick but trails it back along one cheek. In the summer of 1955, Zeno drives her to Boise and a doctor diagnoses her with Huntington's chorea. The doctor tells him to watch for slips in her speech or for involuntary jerking movements. Mrs. Boydstun lights a cigarette and says, "You watch your mouth."

He writes to the British Commonwealth Forces Korea. He writes to a recovery unit at the British Commonwealth Occupation Force. He writes to every person named Rex Browning in England. What replies come back are conscientious but inconclusive. Prisoner of war, no known status, we regret we have no further information at this time. Rex's unit? He doesn't know. Commanding officer? He doesn't know. He has a name. He has East London. He wants to write: He fluttered his hand over his mouth when he yawned. He had a collarbone I wanted to put my teeth on. He told me that archaeologists have found the inscription ΚΑΛΟΣΟΠΑΙΣ scratched on thousands of ancient Greek pots, given as gifts by older men to boys they found attractive. ΚΑΛΟΣΟΠΑΙΣ, καλός ὁ παῖς, "the boy is beautiful."

How could a man with so much in his head, with so much energy and light, be erased?

A half-dozen times over the coming winters, he's leaning over a frozen engine out on the Long Valley Road, or unhooking a chain, when a man will brush his elbow, or fit a hand into the space between his bottom rib and the crest of his pelvis, and they'll go into a garage or climb into the cab of the Autocar in the foggy dark and grapple each other. One particular ranch hand contrives to make this happen several times, as though deliberately driving his car into a snowbank. But by spring the man is gone with no word, and Zeno never sees him again.

Amanda Corddry, the highway department dispatcher, asks him about various girls in town—how about Jessica from the Shell station? Lizzie at the diner?—and he cannot avoid a date. He wears a necktie; the women are unfailingly nice; some have been warned about the supposed perfidy of indoctrinated POWs in Korea; none understand his long silences. He tries to use his fork and knife in a masculine way, cross his legs in a masculine way; he talks about baseball and boat engines; still he suspects he does everything wrong.

One night, waves of confusion crashing over him, he almost tells Mrs. Boydstun. She's having a good day, her hair brushed and her eyes clear, two loaves of raisin bread in the oven, and it's a commercial break on the television, Quaker Instant Oatmeal, then Vanquish headache medicine, and Zeno clears his throat.

"You know, after Papa died, when I—"

She gets up and turns down the volume. Silence blares in the room as bright as a sun.

"I'm not—" he tries again, and she shuts her eyes, as though bracing for a blow. In front of him a jeep tears in half. Gun barrels flash. Blewitt swats flies and collects them in a tin. Men scrape carbonized corn from the bottom of a pot.

"Spit it out, Zeno."

"It's nothing. Your program is back on now."

The doctor suggests jigsaw puzzles to maintain Mrs. Boydstun's fine-motor skills, so he orders a new one every week from Lakeport Drug, and becomes accustomed to finding the little pieces all over the house: in the basins of sinks, stuck to the bottom of his shoe, in the dustpan when he sweeps the kitchen. A splotch of cloud, a segment of the *Titanic*'s smokestack, a section of a cowboy's bandanna. Inside a terror creeps: that things will be like this forever, that this will be all there ever is. Breakfast, work, supper, dishes, a half-completed jigsaw of the Hollywood sign on the dining table, forty of its pieces on the floor. Life. Then the cold dark.

Traffic increases on the road up from Boise, and most of the county plowing shifts to night. He pursues the beams of his headlights through the dark, beating back the snow, and some mornings, at the end of his shift, rather than go directly home, he parks in front of the library and lingers between the shelves.

There's a new librarian now, Mrs. Raney, who mostly lets him be. At first Zeno sticks to *National Geographic* magazines: macaws, Inuits, camel trains, the photographs stirring some latent restlessness inside. He inches his way into History: the Phoenicians, the Sumerians, the Jōmon period of Japan. He drifts past the little collection of Greeks and Romans—the *Iliad*, a few plays by Sophocles, no sign of a lemon-yellow copy of *The Odyssey*—but cannot bring himself to pull anything off the shelf.

Occasionally he gathers the courage to share tidbits of what he has read with Mrs. Boydstun: ostrich hunting in ancient Libya, tomb painting in Tarquinia. "The Mycenaeans revered spirals," he says one night. "They painted them on wine cups and masonry and gravestones, on the armored breastplates of their kings. But no one knows why."

From Mrs. Boydstun's nostrils gush twin columns of smoke. She sets down her glass of Old Forester and pokes through her puzzle pieces. "Why," she says, "would anyone ever want to know about that?"

Out the kitchen window curtains of snow blow through the dusk.

21 December, 1970

Dear Zeno,

What an absolute miracle to receive three letters from you all at once. The bureau must have misfiled them for years. I can't tell you how glad I am that you made it out. I searched for reports on the releases from the camp, but as you know, so much of that was buried, and I was working on reorienting myself to the living. I am elated that you found me.

I'm still mucking about with ancient texts—rummaging in the dusty bones of the dead languages like the old classics master I didn't want to become. It's even worse now, if you can believe it. I study lost books, books that no longer exist, examining papyri dug out of rubbish mounds at Oxyrhynchus. Even been to Egypt. Appalling sunburn.

Years pass in a blink now. Hillary and I will be hosting a bit of a function for my birthday in May. I know it's a terribly long way, but you could pay a visit if you're able? A holiday of sorts. We could scribble some Greek with paper and pen rather than stick and mud. Whatever you decide, I remain,

Your trusty friend,
Rex

LAKEPORT, IDAHO

2016–2018

Seymour

Eighth-grade world studies:

> *Write three things you learned about the Aztecs.*

In the library I learned that every 52 years Aztec priests
had to stop the world from ending. They put out every
torch in town and locked all the pregnant women
in stone grainerys so their babies didn't turn into
demons and kept all the kids awake so they wouldn't
turn into mice. Then they took a victim (had to be a
victim with zero sins) to the top of a sacred mountain
called Thorn Tree Place and when certain stars (one
book, NonFiction F1219.73, guessed maybe Vega, fifth
brightest in the sky) passed overhead, one priest split
open the prisoner's chest and ripped out her hot wet
heart while another started a fire with a drill where her
heart used to be. Then they carried the burning heart
fire down to the city in a bowl and lit torches with it
and people wanted to burn themselves with the torches
because to get burnt by the heart fire was lucky. Soon
thousands of torches were lit with that one fire and the
city glowed again and the world was saved for another
52 years.

Ninth-grade U.S. history:

> Not to hurt feelings but that chapter you assigned? That
> was all "Columbus is great," "The Indians sure loved
> Thanksgiving," "Let's brainwash everyone." I found way
> better stuff at the library, for example did you know
> before leaving England to pick up the tobacco the
> slaves grew, the Englishers filled their empty ships with
> mud so they didn't tip in storms? When they got to the
> New World (which was not new or called America, the
> America name came from a pickle seller guy who got
> famous because he lied about doing sex with natives) the
> Englishers dumped their mud on shore to make room for
> the tobacco. Guess what was in that mud? Earthworms.
> But earthworms had been extinct in America since
> the ice ages, like 10,000 years at least, so the English
> worms went EVERYwhere and changed the soils and
> the Englishers also brought other things this place had
> NEVER known such as: silkworms pigs dandelions
> grapevines goats rats measles pox and the belief that all
> animals and plants were put here for humans to kill and
> eat. There weren't honeybees in so-called America either,
> so the new bees had no competiters and spread fast. One
> book said when families in the native kingdoms saw
> honeybees they cried because they knew dying wasn't far
> behind.

Tenth-grade English:

> You said write something "fun" we did over summer
> to get our "grammer mussels flexing" again, so ok, Mrs
> Tweedy, this summer scientists announced that in the
> last 40 yrs humans have killed 60 percent of the wild
> mammals and fishes and birds on earth. Is that fun? Also
> in the past 30 yrs, we melted 95 percent of the oldest

thickest ice in the arctic. When we have melted all the
ice in Greenland, just the ice in Greenland, not the north
pole, not Alaska, just Greenland, Mrs Tweedy, know what
happens? The oceans rise 23 feet. That drowns Miami,
New York, London, and Shanghai, that's like hop on the
boat with your grandkids, Mrs Tweedy, and you're like,
do you want some snacks, and they're like, Grandma,
look underwater, there's the statute of liberty, there's Big
Ben, there's the dead people. Is that fun, are my grammer
mussels flexing?

A bumper sticker on Mrs. Tweedy's desk says, *The past, present, and future walked into a bar. It was tense.* Her hair looks soft enough to sleep on. Seymour is expecting a reprimand; instead she says that the Environmental Awareness Club at Lakeport High went defunct a couple of years ago and how would Seymour feel about reviving it?

Out the windows, September light bends over the football field. At fifteen he's old enough to understand that it's not only his state of fatherlessness or his thrift store jeans or that he has to swallow sixty milligrams of buspirone every morning to keep the roar at bay: his differences run deeper. Other tenth-grade boys hunt elk or shoplift Red Bulls from Jacksons or smoke weed at the ski hill or cooperate in online battle squads. Seymour studies the quantities of methane locked in melting Siberian permafrost. Reading about declining owl populations led him to deforestation which led to soil erosion which led to ocean pollution which led to coral bleaching, everything warming, melting, and dying faster than scientists predicted, every system on the planet connected by countless invisible threads to every other: cricket players in Delhi vomiting from Chinese air pollution, Indonesian peat fires pushing billions of tons of carbon into the atmosphere over California, million-acre bushfires in Australia turning what's left of New Zealand's glaciers pink. A warmer planet = more water vapor in the atmosphere = even warmer planet = more water vapor = warmer planet still = thawing permafrost =

more carbon and methane trapped in that permafrost releasing into the atmosphere = more heat = less permafrost = less polar ice to reflect the sun's energy, and all this evidence, all these studies are sitting there in the library for anybody to find, but as far as Seymour can tell, he's the only one looking.

Some nights, Eden's Gate glowing beyond his bedroom curtain, he can almost hear dozens of colossal feedback loops churning all over the planet, rasping and grinding like great invisible millwheels in the sky.

Mrs. Tweedy taps the eraser of her pencil against her desk. "Hello? Earth to Seymour?"

He draws a tsunami rearing over a city. Stick-people run from doorways, throw themselves from windows. He prints *ENVIRO-AWARENESS CLUB, TUESDAY, BREAK, ROOM 114* across the top and *TOO LATE TO WAKE UP, ASSHOLES?* across the bottom and Mrs. Tweedy tells him to erase *ASSHOLES* before she'll make copies on the faculty copier.

The following Tuesday, eight kids show up. Seymour stands in front of the desks and reads from a crumpled sheet of notebook paper. "Movies make you think civilization will end fast, like with aliens and explosions, but really it'll end slow. Ours is already ending, it's just ending too slow for people to notice. We've already killed most of the animals, and heated up the oceans, and brought carbon levels in the atmosphere to the highest point in eight hundred thousand years. Even if we stopped everything right now, like we all die today at lunch—no more cars, no more militaries, no more burgers—it'll keep getting hotter for centuries. By the time we're twenty-five? The amount of carbon in the air will have doubled again, which means hotter fires, bigger storms, worse floods. Corn, for example, won't grow as well ten years from now. Ninety-five percent of what cows and chickens eat is guess what? Corn. So meat will be more expensive. Also when there's more carbon in the air? Humans can't think as clearly. So when we're twenty-five, there will be way more hungry, scared, confused people stuck in traffic fleeing flooded or burning cities. Do you think we're gonna sit in our cars solving climate problems then? Or are we gonna fist-fight and rape and eat each other?"

A junior girl says, "Did you just say rape and eat each other?"

A senior boy holds up a sheet of paper that says *See-More Stool-Guy*. Ha ha hilarity everywhere.

From the back Mrs. Tweedy says, "Those are some alarming predictions, Seymour, but maybe we could discuss a few steps we could take toward living more sustainably? Some actionable items within reach of a high school club?"

A sophomore named Janet wonders if they couldn't ban plastic straws from the cafeteria and also give away reusable water bottles with the Lakeport Lion on them? They could also put, like, better posters over the recycling bins? Janet has frog patches sewn on her jean jacket and shiny black raven eyes and the ghost of a mustache on her upper lip and Seymour stands in front of the blackboard with his scrunched-up paper and the bell rings and Mrs. Tweedy says, "Next Tuesday, everybody, we'll brainstorm more ideas," and Seymour heads to biology.

He's walking home from school later that day when a green Audi pulls up beside him and Janet rolls down the window. Her braces are pink and her eyes are a mix of blue and black and she has been to Seattle, Sacramento, and Park City, Utah, which was wild, they went river rafting and rock climbing and saw a porcupine climb a tree, has Seymour ever seen a porcupine?

She offers to drive him home. Thirty-three units are in Eden's Gate now, lining both sides of Arcady Lane, zigzagging up the hillside behind the double-wide. Mostly people from Boise, Portland, and eastern Oregon use them as vacation homes: they park boat trailers in the cul-de-sacs and drive twenty-thousand-dollar UTVs to town and hang college football flags from their balconies and on weekend nights they stand around backyard firepits laughing and urinating into the huckleberries while their kids shoot Roman candles into the stars.

"Wow," says Janet, "you have a lot of weeds in your yard."

"The neighbors complain about it."

"I like it," says Janet. "Natural."

They sit on the front step and sip Shasta Twists and watch bumblebees drift between the thistles. Janet smells like fabric softener and cafeteria tacos and says fifty words for every one of Seymour's, talking about Key Club, summer camp, how she wants to go to college somewhere far from her parents but not too far, you know—as though her future were a pre-plotted exponential curve arcing ever higher—and a white-haired retiree who lives in the town house next door rolls his fifty-gallon trash bin to the end of his driveway and looks at them and Janet raises a hand in greeting and the man goes inside.

"He hates us. Everyone hopes my mom will sell so they can put in new houses."

"Seemed nice enough to me," says Janet, and responds to a warble from her smartphone.

Seymour looks at his shoes. "Did you know that every day internet data storage emits as much carbon as all the airplanes in the world combined?"

"You're weird," she says, but smiles when she says it. In the last breath before dark a black bear materializes from the twilight and Janet clutches his arm and takes a video as it sashays between the pools of streetlight. It moves between the half-dozen wheeled trash carts standing at the ends of the Eden's Gate driveways, sniffing sniffing. Eventually it finds a can it likes, raises one paw, and swats it to the ground. Carefully, with a single claw, the bear drags a plump white bag out of the can's mouth and scatters its contents across the asphalt.

THE ARGOS

MISSION YEAR 64

DAY 21–DAY 45 INSIDE VAULT ONE

Konstance

She touches her Vizer, steps on the Perambulator. Nothing.

"Sybil. Something's wrong with the Library."

Nothing is wrong, Konstance. I have restricted your access. It is time to return to your daily lessons. You need to bathe, eat a proper meal, and be ready in the atrium in thirty minutes. There is rinseless soap in the lavatory kit your father provided.

Konstance sits on the edge of the cot, head in her hands. If she keeps her eyes closed, maybe she can transform Vault One to Compartment 17. Here, in the space just below her, is Mother's bunk, her blanket neatly folded. Two paces away is Father's. Here's the sewing table, the stool, Mother's button bag. All time, Father once told her, is relative: because of the speed the *Argos* travels, the ship clock kept by Sybil runs faster than clocks back on Earth. The chronometers that run inside every human cell that tell us it's time to get drowsy, to make a baby, to grow old—all these clocks, Father said, can be altered by speed, software, or circumstance. Some dormant seeds, he said, like the ones in the drawers in Farm 4, can stop time for centuries, slowing their metabolisms to almost zero, sleeping away the seasons, until the right combination of moisture and temperature appears, and the right wavelength of sunlight penetrates the soil. Then, as though you spoke the magic words: they open.

Goobletook and dynacrack and jimjimsee.

"Fine," says Konstance. "I'll wash and eat. I'll continue my classes. But then you'll let me go into the Atlas."

She dumps powder into the printer, chokes down a bowl of

rainbow-colored paste, wipes her face, rakes at the snarls in her hair, sits at a table in the Library and does whatever lessons Sybil mandates. *What's the cosmological constant? Explain the etymology of the word* trivial. *Use addition formulas to simplify the following expression:*

$$\tfrac{1}{2}[\sin(A + B) + \sin(A - B)]$$

Then she summons the Atlas from its shelf, grief and anger coiled like springs inside her chest, and travels the roads of Earth. Office towers whisk past in late-winter light; a trash collection vehicle veined with filth sits at a stoplight; a mile farther on, she rounds a hill past a shining fenced compound with guards out front beyond which the Atlas cameras do not approach. She breaks into a run, as though chasing the notes of a faraway song just ahead, something she'll never catch.

One night, after nearly six weeks alone inside Vault One, Konstance dreams herself back into the Commissary. The tables and benches are gone, and rust-red sand swirls across the floor in thigh-deep drifts. She staggers out into the corridor, passing the closed doors of a half-dozen compartments, until she reaches the entrance to Farm 4.

Inside, the walls have given way to a sunbaked horizon of brown hills. Sand blows everywhere. The ceiling is a swirling red haze, and thousands of grow-racks, stretching for miles, stand half-buried in dunes. She finds Father kneeling at the base of one, his back to her, sand falling through his fingers. Just as she is about to touch his shoulder, he turns. His face is veined with salt; dust fills his eyelashes.

At home, he says, *in Scheria, an irrigation ditch ran behind the house. Even after it dried—*

She jerks awake. Scheria, scary-ah: it was just a word she heard him say when he talked about home. *In Scheria on the Backline Road.* She understood that it was the name of the farm where he grew up, but he always said life here was better than life there, so it never occurred to her to use the Atlas to find it.

She eats, tends to the cumulus of her hair, sits politely through her lessons, says please, Sybil, right away, Sybil.

Your behavior today, Konstance, has been delightful.

"Thank you, Sybil. May I go to the Library now?"

Of course.

Straight to a box of slips. She writes, *Where is Scheria?*

> *Scheria, Σχερία: Land of the Phaeacians, a mythical island of plenty in Homer's* Odyssey.

Confusing.

She takes a fresh slip, writes, *Show me all Library materials regarding my father.* A thin bundle of bound papers flies toward her from a third-tier shelf. A birth certificate, a grammar school transcript, a teacher's recommendation, a postbox address in southwest Australia. When she turns the fifth page, a foot-tall three-dimensional boy—a bit younger than Konstance is now—emerges and rambles across the table. *Howdy!* His head sports a helmet of red curls; he wears a homemade denim suit. *My name is Ethan, I'm from Nannup, Australia, and I love botany. C'mon, I'll show you my glasshouse.*

A structure appears beside him, wood-framed and sheathed in what looks like hundreds of multicolored plastic bottles that have been stretched, flattened, and sewn together. Inside, on aeroponic racks not unlike the racks in Farm 4, vegetables grow from dozens of trays.

> *Out here in Woop Woop, like Grandmom calls it, we've had heaps of troubles, only one green year in the past thirteen. Dieback killed the whole crop three summers ago, then the cattle tick infestation, probably you heard about that, and not one day of rain last year. I've grown every plant you see here with less than four hundred milliliters of water per day per rack, that's less than a person sweats in . . .*

When he smiles you can see his incisors. She knows that walk, that face, those eyebrows.

*. . . you're seeking volunteers of all ages from all over, so
why me? Well, Grandmom says my best quality is that I
always keep my chin up. I love new places, new things, and
mostly I love exploring the mysteries of plants and seeds. It
would be absolutely ace to be a part of a mission like this.
A new world! Give me the chance and I won't let you down.*

She grabs a slip of paper, summons the Atlas, and steps inside, a long needle of loneliness running through her. When Father would get excited, that boy still shone through. He had a love affair with photosynthesis. He could talk about moss for an hour. He said that plants carried wisdom humans would never be around long enough to understand.

"Nannup," she says into the void. "Australia."

The Earth flies toward her, inverts, the southern hemisphere pivoting as it rushes closer, and she drops from the sky onto a road lined with eucalyptus. Bronze hills bake in the distance; white fencing runs down both sides. A trio of faded banners, strung overhead, reads,

DO YOUR PART
DEFEAT DAY ZERO
YOU CAN DO WITH 10 LITRES A DAY

Corrugated sheds mottled with rust. A few windowless houses. Dead casuarinas baked black by sun. As she approaches what appears to be the center of town, she comes upon a quaint red-sided, white-roofed public hall, shaded by cabbage trees, and the grass turns viridescent, three shades greener than anything else she has passed. Bright begonias spill from flower boxes mounted on railings; everything looks freshly painted. Ten strange and magnificent trees with intensely bright gold-orange flowers shade a lawn in the center of which glimmers a circular pool.

A current of disturbance runs through Konstance again, something not quite right. Where are the people?

"Sybil, take me to a farm near here called Scheria."

I have no record of a landholding or cattle station nearby with that name.

"Backline Road then, please."

The road climbs past farms for miles. No cars, no bicycles, no tractors. She passes shadeless fields planted with what might once have been chickpeas, long since burned up by heat. Utility towers stand with the cables snapped and hanging. Bone-dry hedgerows; charred sections of forest; padlocked gates. The road is dusty and the pastures are camel brown. A sign says, *For Sale*, then another. Then a third.

In hours of searching Backline Road, the only figure she passes is a lone man wearing a coat and what looks like a filtration mask, his forearm braced over his eyes against dust or glare or both. She crouches in front of him. "Hello?" Talking to renderings, to pixels. "Did you know my father?" The man tilts forward as though he is held upright by a headwind. She reaches to steady him and her hands pass right through his chest.

After three days of searching the parched hills around Nannup, trekking up and down Backline Road, in a grove of dry eucalyptus she has already passed three or four times, Konstance finds it: a hand-painted sign wired to a gate.

Σχερία

Behind the gate runs a double row of desiccated gum trees, their trunks peeled white. Weeds rise in tufts on both sides of a single dirt track that leads to a yellow ranch house with honeysuckle on the railing, honeysuckle on the siding—all dead.

On either side of its windows hang black shutters. A solar panel skewed on the roof. To one side of the house, in the shade of the dead gum trees, stands the glasshouse from Father's video, half-built, a portion of its wooden frame covered with sheets of cloudy plastic. A pile of grimy plastic bottles lies beside it.

The dusty light, the dried-up field, the broken solar panel, a film of dust settled like beige snow onto everything, everything as quiet and still as a tomb.

We've had heaps of troubles.

Only one green year in the past thirteen.

Her father applied to join the crew when he was twelve, advanced through the application process for a year. At age thirteen—the same age Konstance is now—he would have received the call. Surely he understood that he would never live long enough to reach Beta Oph2? That he would spend the rest of his life inside a machine? Yet he left anyway.

She paddles her arms to enlarge the flexing, buckling digital representation in front of her, and the house degenerates into pixels. But as she presses against the limits of the Atlas's resolution, she notices that on the right end of the house, because of the circumstances of sunlight and angle, she is able to see through two panes of glass into a wedge of room.

She can make out a portion of a sun-bleached curtain with airplanes printed on it. Two homemade planets, one with rings around it, hang from the ceiling. The chipped headboard of a twin bed, a nightstand, a lamp. A boy's room.

It would be absolutely ace to be a part of a mission like this.

A new world!

Was he in that room when the cameras swept past? Is the ghost of the boy her father once was right there, just out of sight?

On the nightstand by the window a blue book with a worn spine rests faceup. On its cover birds swing around the tightly packed towers of a city. The city looks as if it stands on a bed of clouds.

She contorts her spine, leans as far as possible into the image, squints against the distorting pixels. At the bottom, below the city, the cover says *Antonius Diogenes*. Across the top: *Cloud Cuckoo Land*.

THIRTEEN

OUT OF THE WHALE
AND INTO THE STORM

Cloud Cuckoo Land by Antonius Diogenes, Folio N

. . . I was a bird, I had wings, I flew! An entire man-of-war was skewered on the fangs of the leviathan, and the sailors howled at me as I flapped by, and I was out! For a day and night I flapped over the infinitude of the ocean, and the sky above stayed blue and so did the waves below, and there were no continents and no ships, nowhere for me to set down and rest my wings. On the second day I grew tired, and the face of the sea darkened and the wind began to sing a frightening, phantom song. Silver fire flew in all directions, and thunderheads split the heavens, and my black feathers crackled white.

Hadn't I suffered enough? From the sea below rose a great spout of water, whirling and screaming, carrying islands and cows, boats, and houses, and when it caught my puny crow wings, it tore me from my flight, spinning me ever higher, until the white glow of the moon burned my beak as I spun past, so close I could see the moon-beasts charging along their ghostly plains and drinking milk from great white moon-lakes, as frightened by me looking down as I was of them looking up, and I dreamed again of the summer evenings in Arkadia when the clover grew deep upon the hills, and the happy bells of my ewes filled the air, and the shepherds sat with their pipes, and I wished I had never embarked upon this . . .

CONSTANTINOPLE

MAY 1453

Anna

I t is the fifth week of the siege, or maybe the sixth, each day bleeding into the last. Anna sits with Maria's head in her lap and her back against the wall and a fresh candle stuck to the floor among the melted stubs. Out in the lane something whumps and a horse whinnies and a man curses and the commotion is a long time fading.

"Anna?"

"I'm here."

Maria's world has gone entirely dark now. Her tongue does not cooperate when she tries to speak, and every few hours muscles in her back and neck seize. The eight embroideresses who still sleep inside the house of Kalaphates alternate between devotions and staring into space in nerve-shattered trances. Anna helps Chryse in the frost-stunted garden or scavenges what markets are still open for flour or fruit or beans. The rest of the time she sits with Maria.

She has grown quicker at deciphering the tidy, left-leaning script inside the old codex, and by now can lift lines off the page without trouble. Whenever she comes to a word she does not know, or lacunas where mold has obliterated the text, she invents replacements.

Aethon has managed to become a bird at last: not the resplendent owl he hoped, but a bedraggled crow. He flaps across a limitless sea, searching for the end of the earth, only to be swept up by a waterspout. So long as Anna keeps reading, Maria seems to be at peace, her face calm, as though she sits not in a damp cell in a besieged city listening to a silly tale, but in a garden in the hereafter listening to the hymns of the angels, and Anna remembers something Licinius said: that a story is a way of stretching time.

In the days, he said, when bards traveled from town to town carrying the old songs in their memories, performing them for anyone who would listen, they would delay the outcomes of their tales for as long as they could, improvising one last verse, one last obstacle for the heroes to overcome, because, Licinius said, if the singers could hold their listeners' attention for one more hour, they might be granted one more cup of wine, one more piece of bread, one more night out of the rain. Anna imagines Antonius Diogenes, whoever he was, setting knife to quill, quill to ink, ink to scroll, placing one more barricade in front of Aethon, stretching time for another purpose: to detain his niece in the living world for a little longer.

"He suffers so much," murmurs Maria. "But he keeps on."

Maybe Kalaphates was right: maybe dark magic does live inside the old books. Maybe as long as she still has more lines to read to her sister, as long as Aethon persists on his harebrained journey, flapping his way toward his dream in the clouds, then the city gates will hold; maybe death will stay outside their door for one more day.

On a bright, redolent May morning, when it feels as though the unseasonable cold has finally loosened its grip, the Hodegetria, the city's most venerated icon—a painting with the Virgin and Christ child on one side and the crucifixion on the other, purportedly made by the apostle Luke on a three-hundred-pound piece of slate and conveyed to the city from the Holy Lands by an empress a thousand years before Anna was born—is carried out of the church built to hold it.

If anything can save the city it is this: an object of immense power, the icon of icons, credited with safeguarding the city from numerous sieges in the past. Chryse picks up Maria and slings her over her back, and the embroideresses walk to the square to be a part of the procession, and when the icon comes out the church doors into the sunlight it blazes so brightly that it stamps Anna's vision with swimming designs of gold.

The six priests carrying the painting set it onto the shoulders of a hulking monk in crimson velvet with a thick embroidered band across his chest. Wobbling under his load, the icon-bearer processes barefoot through the city from church to church, going wherever the Hodegetria leads him. Two deacons follow his every step, propping a golden canopy over the icon, dignitaries with staves behind them, novices and nuns and citizens and slaves and soldiers in the back, many carrying candles and performing an eerie and beautiful chant. Children run alongside holding garlands of roses or little pieces of cotton that they hope to touch to the Virgin's likeness.

Anna and Chryse, with Maria draped over Chryse's back, march in the wake of the procession as the Hodegetria winds toward the Third Hill. All morning the city glows. Wildflowers carpet the ruins; a breeze scatters little white flower petals across the cobblestones; chestnut trees wave the ivory candles of their blooms. But as the parade climbs toward the huge crumbling fountain of the nymphaeum, the day darkens. The air turns chill, black clouds appear as if from nowhere, doves stop warbling, dogs start barking, and Anna glances up.

Not a single bird crosses the sky. Thunder rolls over the houses. A gust snuffs half the candles in the parade, and the chanting falters. In the stillness that follows, Anna can hear a drummer, out in the camps of the Saracens, pounding his drum.

"Sister?" asks Maria, her cheek pressed to Chryse's spine. "What is happening?"

"A storm."

Forks of lightning lash the domes of the Hagia Sophia. Trees thrash, shutters bang, sheets of hail assault the rooftops, and the procession scatters. At its head, the wind rips the gold canopy sheltering the icon from its standards and carries it off between houses.

Chryse scrambles for cover, but Anna waits a moment longer, watching the monk at the front of the train try to keep carrying the Hodegetria up the hill. Wind drives him back, whipping debris past his feet. Still he pushes higher. He nearly crests the hill. Then he staggers, and slips, and the thirteen-hundred-year-old painting falls crucifixion-side-down onto the rain-soaked street.

• • •

Agata rocks at the table with her head in her hands; Widow Theodora mumbles into the cold hearth; Chryse curses over the wreckage of her vegetable garden. The hallowed Hodegetria has failed; the
Mother of God has forsaken them; the beast of the apocalypse rises
from the sea. The Antichrist scratches at the gate. Time is a circle,
Licinius used to say, and every circle eventually must close.

As darkness falls, Anna crawls onto the horsehair pallet and sits
with Maria's head in her lap, the old manuscript open in front of
them. The storm propels Aethon-the-crow past the moon and tumbles him into the blackness between the stars. There is not much left
to go.

Omeir

That same afternoon the ox train is rumbling toward the Golden Horn to collect yet another load of stone cannonballs, a hundred yards from the landing stage, the air rinsed clean by the morning's storm, the estuary blue-green and aglitter with sunlight, when Moonlight—not Tree—stops in his tracks, tucks his forelegs under his body, lowers himself to the ground, and dies.

He is dragged forward a body length and the train stops.

Tree stands in his harness, his three good legs splayed, the yoke cocked against the weight of his brother. Red spume leaks from Moonlight's nostrils; a little white petal, carried on the breeze, sticks to his open eye. Omeir leans into the harness, tries to lend his little strength to the bullock's great one, but the animal's heart no longer beats.

The other teamsters, accustomed to seeing animals fail in the yoke, squat or sit on the edge of the road. The quartermaster shouts toward the quay and four porters start up from the docks.

Tree bends to make it easier for Omeir to remove the yoke. The porters and four teamsters, two on each leg, drag Moonlight to the edge of the road, and the oldest among them gives thanks to God, draws his knife, and opens the animal's throat.

Halter and rope in one hand, Omeir leads Tree down a cattle trail into the rushes at the edge of the Bosporus. Through the dazzle of sunlight swim memories of Moonlight as a little calf. He liked to scratch his ribs against one particular pine tree beside the byre. He loved to wade into the creek up to his belly and call to his brother in delight. He wasn't very good at hide-and-seek. He was frightened of bees.

Tree's hide shivers up and down his back and a mantle of flies takes off and settles again. From here the city and its girdle of walls look small, a pale stone beneath the sky.

A few hundred paces away, two porters build a fire while the two others disassemble Moonlight, carving off his head, cutting away the tongue, spitting the heart, liver, and each of the kidneys. They wrap the thigh muscles in fat and secure them to pikes, and lean the pikes over the fire, and bargemen and stevedores and teamsters walk up the road in groups and squat on their heels as the meat cooks. At Omeir's feet hundreds of little blue butterflies sip minerals from a patch of tidal mud.

Moonlight: his ropy tail, his shaggy cloven hooves. God knits him together in the womb of Beauty beside his brother and he lives for three winters and dies hundreds of miles from home and for what? Tree lies down in the reeds and fouls the air around him and Omeir wonders what the animal understands and what will happen to Moonlight's two beautiful horns and every breath sends another crack through his heart.

That evening the guns fire seemingly nonstop, battering the towers and walls, and the men are ordered to light as many torches, candles, and cookfires as possible. Omeir helps two teamsters fell olive trees and drag them to a great bonfire. The sultan's ulema move between the fires delivering encouragement. "The Christians," they say, "are devious and arrogant. They worship bones and die for mummies. They cannot sleep unless it's on feather beds and cannot go an hour without wine. They think the city is theirs, but it already belongs to us."

Night becomes like day. Moonlight's flesh travels the intestines of fifty men. Grandfather, Omeir thinks, would have known what to do. He would have recognized the early signals of lameness, would have taken better care of Moonlight's hooves, would have known some remedy involving herbs and ointment and beeswax. Grandfather, who could see signs of game birds where Omeir saw nothing, who could steer Leaf and Needle with a click of his tongue.

He shuts his eyes against the smoke and remembers a story a teamster told in the fields outside Edirne about a man in hell. The devils there, the teamster said, would cut the man every morning, many thousands of times, but the cuts were just small enough that they would not kill him. All day the wounds would dry, and scab over, and the next morning, just as the cuts began to heal, they were opened up again.

After morning prayer he goes to find Tree in the pasture where he has staked him and the ox cannot get up. He lies on his side, one horn pointing to the sky. The world has swallowed his brother and Tree is ready to join him. Omeir kneels and runs his hands over the bullock's flank and watches the reflection of the sky quake in the bullock's trembling eye.

Does Grandfather look up this morning at this same cloud, and Nida, and their mother, and he and Tree, all five of them looking up at this same drifting white shape as it passes over them all?

Anna

Church bells no longer keep the hours. She drifts through the scullery, the hunger in her gut a snake uncoiling, then stands in the open doorway looking at the sky above the courtyard. Himerius used to say that as long as the moon was getting larger, the world could never end. But now it wanes.

"First," Widow Theodora whispers into the hearth, "wars rage among the peoples of the earth. Then the false prophets rise. Soon the planets will fall from the sky, followed by the sun, and everyone will become ash."

Maria's legs are discolored now, and she has to be carried to the toilet. They are in the last parts of the codex, and some leaves are so deteriorated that Anna can make out only one line of text for every three. Still she keeps Aethon's journey going for her sister. The crow flaps through the void, tumbling through the Zodiac.

> From these Icarian heights, my feathers powdered with the
> dust of the stars, I saw the earth far below as it really was, a
> little mud-heap in a great vastness, its kingdoms only cobwebs,
> its armies only crumbs. Storm-broken and singed, worn out
> and wind-plucked, half my feathers lost, I drifted among the
> constellations at the end of hope, when I glimpsed a distant
> glow, a golden filigree of towers, the puff of clouds—

The text peters out, the lines dissolved beneath a water stain, but for her sister Anna conjures it: a city made of silver and bronze towers, windows glowing, banners flapping from rooftops, birds of every size and color wheeling round. The weary crow spirals down out of the stars.

Cannonballs thud in the distance. The flame of the candle bows.

"He never stops believing," whispers Maria. "Even when he is so tired."

Anna blows out the candle and closes the codex. She thinks of Ulysses washing onto the island of the Phaeacians. "He could smell jasmine among the stars," she says, "and violets, and laurel, and roses, grapes and pears, apples upon apples, figs on figs."

"I smell them, Anna."

Beside the icon of Saint Koralia sits the little snuffbox she took from the abandoned workshop of the Italians, its cracked lid painted with a miniature of a turreted palace. There are men in Urbino, the scribes said, who make lenses that let you see thirty miles. Men who can draw a lion so real it looks as though it will walk off the page and eat you.

Our master dreams of constructing a library to surpass the pope's, they said, a library to contain every text ever written. To last until the end of time.

Maria dies on the twenty-seventh of May, the women of the household praying around her. Anna sets a palm on her sister's forehead and feels the heat leave her. "When you see her again," Widow Theodora says, "she'll be clothed in light." Chryse lifts Maria's body as easily as she might lift a piece of linen dried stiff in the sun, and carries her across the courtyard to the gates of Saint Theophano.

Anna rolls up the samite hood—five finished birds entwined by blooming vines. In some other universe, perhaps, a great bright community weeps: their mother and father, aunts and cousins, a little chapel packed with spring roses, a thousand organ pipes resounding with song, Maria's soul afloat among cherubs, grapevines, and peacocks—like a design from one of her embroideries.

In the *katholikon* at Saint Theophano nuns keep a nonstop vigil of prayer rising toward the throne of God. One points to where Chryse should set the body, and another covers Maria with a shroud, and Anna sits on the stones beside her sister while a priest is fetched.

Omeir

After the death of his oxen, time disintegrates. He is sent to work behind the latrines with conscripted Christian boys and Indian slaves, burning the feces of the army. They dump the slop into pits, then throw hot pitch on top, and he and a few of the older boys use poles to stir the vile, smoking mess, the poles burning down from the tips, so that they grow ever shorter. The smell saturates his clothes, his hair, his skin, and soon Omeir has more than his face to make men scowl.

Birds of prey wheel overhead; big, merciless flies besiege them; outside the tents, as May tips toward June, there is no shade. The great cannon they worked so hard to bring here finally cracks, and the defenders of the city give up trying to repair their battered stockades, and everyone can sense the fate of the conflict tilting on a fulcrum. Either the starving city will capitulate, or the Ottomans will retreat before disease and hopelessness sweep through their camps.

The boys in Omeir's company say that the sultan, may God bless and keep his kingdom, believes the decisive moment has come. The walls have been weakened at multiple spots, the defenders are exhausted, and a final assault will tip the balance. The best fighters, they say, will be held at the back while the least-equipped and least-trained among them are sent first across the fosse to soften the city's defenses. We'll be caught, one boy whispers, between a hailstorm of stones from the ramparts above and the whips of the sultan's Chavushes behind. But another boy says that God will see them through, and that if they die their rewards in the next life will extend beyond number.

Omeir shuts his eyes. How grand it all felt when the curious would stop and gape at the size of Tree and Moonlight; when men came by the thousands with the hope of setting a finger to the gleaming cannon. *A way for a small thing to destroy a much larger thing.* But what is it that they have destroyed?

Maher sits beside him and unsheathes his knife and picks at rust along its blade with a fingernail. "I hear that we will be sent tomorrow. At sundown." Both of Maher's oxen have long since died too, and deep hollows haunt his eyes. "It will be wonderful," he says, though he sounds unconvinced. "We will strike terror into their hearts."

Around them the sons of farmers sit holding shields, clubs, javelins, axes, horseman's hammers—even stones. Omeir is so tired. It will be a relief to die. He thinks of the Christians sitting up on the walls, and the people praying inside the houses and churches of the city, and he wonders at the mystery of how one god can manage the thoughts and terrors of so many.

Anna

At night she rejoins the crews of women and girls in the terrace between the inner and outer walls, hauling stones to the parapets so that they can be dropped onto the heads of the Saracens when they come. Everyone is hungry and under-rested; no one sings hymns or murmurs encouragements anymore. Just before midnight, monks haul a hydraulic organ up to the top of the outer wall and play an awful, screeching caterwaul, like the moans of a great beast dying in the night.

How do men convince themselves that others must die so they might live? She thinks of Maria, who owned so little and who left so quietly, and of Licinius telling her about the Greeks camped outside the walls of Troy for ten years, and of the Trojan women trapped inside, weaving and worrying, wondering whether they would ever walk the fields or swim in the sea again, or whether the gates would fall, and they would have to watch their babies be tossed over the ramparts to die.

She works until dawn and when she returns, Chryse tells her to wait in the courtyard, then reappears from the scullery with a wooden chair in one hand and Widow Theodora's bone-handled scissors in the other. Anna sits and Chryse pulls back her hair and opens the blades and for a moment Anna worries the old cook is about to cut her throat.

"Tonight or tomorrow," Chryse says, "the city will fall."

Anna hears the blades rasp, feels her hair falling onto her feet.

"You're sure?"

"I have dreamed it, child. And when it does, the soldiers will take everything they can get their hands on. Food, silver, silk. But the most valuable thing will be girls."

Anna has a vision of the young sultan somewhere among the tents of his men, seated on a carpet with a model of the city in his lap, probing it with one finger, searching each tower, each crenellation, each battered section of the walls for a way in.

"They'll strip you to the skin and either keep you for themselves or bring you to a market and sell you. Our side or theirs, it is always the same in war. Do you know how I know this?"

The blades flash so near to her eyes that Anna is afraid to turn her head.

"Because that is what happened with me."

Her hair newly shorn, Anna eats six green apricots and lies down with a stomachache and tumbles into sleep. In a nightmare she walks the floor of a vast atrium with a vaulted ceiling so high it seems to hold up the sky. On tiers of shelves running down either side are stacked hundreds upon hundreds of texts, like a library of the gods, but each time she opens a book, she finds it full of words in languages she does not know, incomprehensible word after incomprehensible word in book after book on shelf after shelf. She walks and walks, and it's always the same, the library indecipherable and infinite, the sound of her footsteps tiny in all that immensity.

Dusk descends on the fifty-fifth evening of the siege. In the imperial palace of the Blachernae, tucked against the Golden Horn, the emperor gathers his captains around him in prayer. Up and down the outer walls, sentries count arrows, stoke fires beneath great pitchers of tar. Just beyond the fosse, inside the private tent of the sultan, a servant lights seven tapers, one for each of the heavens, and withdraws, and the young sovereign kneels to pray.

On the Fourth Hill of the city, above the once-great embroidery house of Kalaphates, a flock of gulls, soaring high over the roof, catches the last glow of the sun. Anna rises from her pallet, surprised to see that she has slept away the daylight.

In the scullery the embroideresses who are left, none younger than fifty, step away from the hearth so that Chryse can shove the pieces of a sewing table into the fire.

Widow Theodora comes inside with an armful of what looks to Anna like deadly nightshade. She strips away the leaves, drops the shiny black berries into a basin, and puts the roots into a mortar. As she crushes the roots, Widow Theodora tells them that their bodies are just dust, that all their lives their souls have yearned toward a more distant place. Now that they're close, Widow Theodora says, their souls quiver with joy at the prospect of leaving the shells of their bodies behind to come home to God.

The last blue light of day is sucked away into night. In the firelight the faces of the women take on ancient suffering that is almost sublime: as though they suspected all along that things would end like this and are resigned to it. Chryse calls Anna into the storeroom and lights a candle. She hands her a few strips of salted sturgeon and a loaf of dark bread wrapped in cloth.

"If any child ever born," Chryse whispers, "can outsmart them, outlast them, or outrun them, it is you. There is still life to be had. Go tonight, and I will send prayers at your heels."

She can hear Widow Theodora, out in the scullery, say, "We leave our bodies behind in this world so that we may take flight into the next."

Omeir

As darkness falls, boys all around him, still strangers to their own bodies, pray, worry, sharpen knives, sleep. Boys brought here by rage or curiosity or myth or faith or greed or force, some dreaming of glories in this life or in lives to come, some aching simply to wreak violence, to act against those who they believe have caused them pain. Men dream too: of earning honor in the eyes of God, of deserving the love of their fellow soldiers, of returning home to a familiar field. A bath, a lover, a drink from a jug of clean, cool water.

From where he sits outside the tents of the cannoneers Omeir can just see moonlight sifting across the cascading domes of the Hagia Sophia: as close as he'll ever come. Watchfires burn in towers; a plume of white rises from the easternmost part of the city. Behind him the evening star brightens. In memories he hears Grandfather speak slowly about the merits of animals, about the weather, about the qualities of the grass, Grandfather's patience like that of the trees. It has been a little more than half a year and yet the distance between those evenings and this one feels immense.

As he sits, his mother glides between the tents and places a hand on his cheek and leaves it there. *What do I care*, she whispers, *for cities and princes and histories?*

He is only a boy, Grandfather told the traveler and his servant.

You think that now but his true nature will show in time.

Maybe the servant was right; maybe Omeir does harbor a demon inside. Or a ghoul or a mage. Something formidable. He feels it stir and wake. It uncurls, rubs its eyes, gives a yawn.

Get up, it says. *Go home.*

He coils Moonlight's rope and halter over one shoulder and rises. Steps over Maher where he sleeps on the bare ground. Picks his way through the company of frightened young men.

Come back to us, whispers his mother, and around her head swims a cloud of bees.

He skirts a company of drummers carrying oxhide bull-roarers as they make their way forward through the ranks, moving toward the front of the lines. Past the camp of the smiths with their anvils and aprons. Past the arrow fletchers and bow stringers. It is as if Omeir has been yoked and harnessed to a wagon full of stone balls, and now, with each step away from the city, the stone balls are rolling out behind him.

Shapes of horses and wagons and broken siege engines loom up out of the dark. Look at no one. You are good at hiding your face.

He trips over a tent rope, gets back to his feet, weaves to stay out of firelight. Any moment, he thinks, someone will ask me my errand, which unit I belong to, why I'm walking in the wrong direction. Any moment one of the sultan's military police with their long curved blades will pull up his horse beside me and call me a deserter. But men sleep or pray or murmur or brood over the coming assault, and no one seems to notice him. Perhaps they assume he's on his way to the pens to check on an animal. Perhaps, he thinks, I am already dead.

He keeps the road to Edirne off to his right. At the edge of the encampment the spring grasses have grown chest-high, the broom tall and yellow, and it is easy to duck below their crowns as he walks. Behind him, the drummers reach the front of the lines, spin double-headed drumsticks above their heads in figure eights, and begin pounding their drums so quickly that they seem less a pulse of drumbeats than a sustained roar.

From soldiers all through the Ottoman camps rise the clash of weapons against shields. Omeir waits for God to send a streak of light through a rift in the clouds and reveal him for what he is: traitor, coward, apostate. Boy with the ghoul's face and the demon's heart. Boy who killed his own father. Who, on the night he was to be left exposed on the mountain to die, bewitched his own grandfather into bringing him back. Everything the villagers intuited about him coming true.

In the dark he draws no notice. The clamor of drums and cymbals and voices builds at his back. Any moment now the first wave will be sent across the moat.

Anna

Even a mile away, inside the house of Kalaphates, the noise of the drums penetrates: a weapon in itself, the forefinger of the sultan probing the alleys, searching, searching. Anna glances back toward the scullery, where Widow Theodora holds the mortar full of crushed nightshade. In the shadows she sees Kalaphates drag Maria by her hair down the corridor past her feet, sees Licinius's mottled quires go up in flames.

One bad-tempered abbot, the tall scribe said, *one clumsy friar, one invading barbarian, an overturned candle, a hungry worm—and all those centuries are undone.* You can cling to this world for a thousand years and still be plucked out of it in a breath.

She wraps the old goatskin codex and the snuffbox in Maria's silk hood and puts them in the bottom of Himerius's sack. Then she sets the bread and salt fish on top and ties the bag shut. All she owns in the world.

Out in the streets, the pounding of the drums mixes with distant shouts: the final assault has begun. She hurries toward the harbor. In many houses there are no signs of life, while in others multiple lamps burn as though the occupants have decided to use up every last thing they own and leave nothing for the invaders. Details leap out bright and sharp: the centuries-old grooves of chariot wheels in the paving stones in front of the Philadelphion. Green paint flaking off a door to a carpenter's workshop. The breeze lifting petals from a flowering cherry and tumbling them through the moonlight. Each a sight she may be seeing for the last time.

A single arrow covered with pitch bounces off a roof and clatters onto the stones and smokes. A child, no older than six, emerges from a doorway, picks it up, and holds it like something he is considering eating.

The sultan's cannons fire, three five seven, and a distant clamor rises. Is this the moment? Are they breaching the gates? The tower of Belisarius, at the base of which she used to meet Himerius, is dark, and the little fisherman's gate is unmanned, all the sentries sent to shore up weak points in the land walls.

She clutches the sack. West, she thinks, this is all she knows, west where the sun goes down, west across the Propontis, and her mind sends up visions of the blessed island of Scheria, and of the bright oil and soft bread of Urbino, and of Aethon's city in the clouds, each paradise blurring into the last. *It does exist,* Aethon-the-fish told the wizard inside the whale. *Otherwise what's it all been for?*

She finds Himerius's skiff in its customary spot above the tideline on the cobbled beach, the least seaworthy craft in the world. A moment of terror: What if the oars are not there? But they are stowed beneath the boat where he always kept them.

The noise of the hull scraping over stones on the way to the waterline is perilously loud. In the shallows float shapes the size of corpses: don't look. She sets the skiff afloat, climbs in, and kneels with the sack on the thwart in front of her, and pulls the starboard oar, then the port one, making little diagonal stitches toward the breakwater. The night stays blessedly dark.

Three gulls bobbing in the black water watch her glide past. Three a lucky number, Chryse always said: Father, Son, Holy Spirit. Birth, life, death. Past, present, future.

She cannot seem to keep the skiff going in a straight line, and the knocking of the oars against the oarlocks is far too loud; she never appreciated Himerius's skill until now. But with each heartbeat the shore appears to retreat, and she keeps rowing with the sea at her back and the city walls before her, the rower facing what she has already passed.

As she nears the breakwater, she pauses to bail the skiff with the earthenware jug, as Himerius used to do. Somewhere inside the city walls, a glow rises: a sunrise in the wrong place and time. Strange how suffering can look beautiful if you get far enough away.

She clings to the words of Himerius: *When the tide is wrong, a current comes here that would sweep us straight out to sea.* Now she needs the wrong tide to be right.

Just off the bow, in the swells beyond the breakwater, she glimpses a long, dark shape. A ship. Is it Saracen or Greek? Does its captain call to his rowers, do gunners ready their guns? She crouches as low as she can, flattens herself down into the hull, the sack on her chest, cold water seeping around her back, and it is here that Anna's courage finally wanes. Fear comes slipping in from a thousand fissures: tentacles rise from the gloom on either side of the boat, and Kalaphates's vulture eyes blink down from the starless sky.

Girls don't go to tutors.

It was you? All along?

The current catches the little skiff and carries it. She thinks of how Aethon must have felt, trapped inside all those different bodies, unable to speak his own language, mistreated, derided—it was a horrible fate and she was cruel to laugh.

No one shouts and no arrows whistle past. The skiff turns, wobbles, and slips beyond the breakwater into the dark.

FOURTEEN

THE GATES OF
CLOUD CUCKOO LAND

Cloud Cuckoo Land by Antonius Diogenes, Folio Ξ

Folios from the second half of the Diogenes codex are considerably more deteriorated than the first, and the gaps in the manuscript present significant challenges for both translator and reader. Folio Ξ has been at least sixty percent effaced. Illegible portions are indicated by ellipses and conjectural representations are delivered inside brackets. Translation by Zeno Ninis.

. . . In the Pleiades I saw a nation of swans eating bright fruits, and on the far shores of the Sun I drank from {a river of steaming wine}, though it singed my beak. I visited a thousand strange lands but never did I find one where tortoises carried honeycakes on their backs and war was unknown and suffering unheard of.

. . . from these Icarian heights, my feathers powdered with the dust of the stars, I saw the earth far below as it really was, a little mud-heap in a great vastness, its kingdoms only cobwebs, its armies only crumbs.

. . . I {glimpsed?} a distant glow, a golden filigree of towers, the puff of clouds, just as I envisioned that day in the square in Arkadia . . .

. . . except that it was grander, more ravishing, more heavenly . . .

. . . ringed by falcons, redshanks, quails, moorhens, and cuckoos . . .

. . . hyacinth and laurel, phlox and apple, gardenia and sweet alyssum . . .

. . . delirious with joy, weary as the world, I dropped . . .

THE ARGOS

MISSION YEAR 64

DAY 45–DAY 46 INSIDE VAULT ONE

Konstance

She stands in the Library alone. From the nearest desk she takes a slip of paper, writes *Cloud Cuckoo Land by Antonius Diogenes*, and drops it into the slot. Documents volley toward her from multiple sections and arrange themselves in a dozen stacks. Many are academic papers in German, Chinese, French, Japanese. Nearly all seem to have been written during the second decade of the twenty-first century. She opens the first book at hand in English: *Selected Ancient Greek Novels.*

> The 2019 discovery of the late Greek prose tale *Cloud Cuckoo Land* inside a badly corrupted codex in the Vatican Library briefly set the world of Greco-Roman scholarship aflame. Alas, what archivists were able to salvage of the text left plenty to be desired: twenty-four mangled folios, each damaged to some degree. Chronology confuses and lacunae abound.

From the next volume, foot-high projections of two men emerge and walk to opposing podiums. *This was a text*, says the first, a bow-tied man with a silver beard, *intended for a single reader, a young girl on her deathbed, and therefore it's a narrative about death-anxiety . . .*

Wrong, says the other speaker, also with a silver beard, also wearing a bow tie. *Diogenes clearly wanted to play with notions of pseudo-documentarianism, placing fiction on one side and nonfiction on the other, claiming the story was a true transcription discovered in a tomb, while constructing a contract with the reader that the tale was of course invented.*

She shuts the book and the men disappear. The next title appears to spend three hundred pages exploring the provenance and tonality of the ink used inside the codex. Another speculates about tree sap found on some of the pages. Another is a numbing account of various attempts to arrange the salvaged folios in their original order.

Konstance rests her forehead in her hands. The English translations of the folios that she can find among the stacks mostly bewilder: either they're boring and spangled with footnotes, or they're too fragmented to make much sense of. In them she can see the contours of Father's stories—Aethon kneels at the door of a witch's bedroom, Aethon becomes a donkey, the donkey is kidnapped by bandits who rob the inn—but where are the silly magic words and the beasts drinking moon-milk and the boiling river of wine on the sun? Where's the squawk Father would make when Aethon mistakes a gull for a goddess, and the growl he'd use for the wizard inside the whale?

The hope she'd felt minutes before flags. All these books, all this knowledge, but what's any of it for? None of it will help her understand why her father would leave his home. None of it will help her understand why she has been consigned to this fate.

She takes a slip from a box, and writes, *Show me the blue copy with the drawing of a city in the clouds on the cover.*

A scrap of paper comes fluttering down. *The Library contains no records of such a volume.*

Konstance gazes down the unending rows of shelves. "But I thought you contained everything."

Another NoLight, another printed First Meal, more lessons from Sybil. Then she climbs back into the Atlas, drops into the sunbaked hills outside Nannup, and walks Backline Road to her father's house. Σχερία, says the hand-painted sign.

She crouches, twists, presses as close to the house as she can, the view through the bedroom window degrading into a quivering field of color. The book on the nightstand is royal blue. The cloud city in the center of the cover looks faded by sun. She goes to her tiptoes and squints. Beneath Diogenes's name run four words in smaller type that she missed the first time.

Translation by Zeno Ninis.

Into the sky, out of the Atlas, back to the atrium. She takes a slip from the nearest desk. Writes: *Who was Zeno Ninis?*

LONDON

1971

Zeno

London! May! Rex! Alive! A hundred times he examines Rex's stationery, inhales its smell. He knows that handwriting, squashed at the tops of the letters as though someone has stepped on the lines: how many times did he see it scratched into the frost and dirt of Korea?

What an absolute miracle to receive three letters from you all at once.

You could pay a visit if you're able?

Every few minutes a fresh gust of lightness sweeps through Zeno. There was that name, Hillary, but what of it? If Rex has found a Hillary, bless him. He made it out. He is alive. He has invited Zeno to "a bit of a function."

He imagines Rex in a wool suit in a tranquil garden, sitting down to write the letter. Pigeons coo; hedges rustle; clocktowers soar past oaks into a wet sky. Elegant, matronly Hillary comes out with a porcelain tea service.

No, it's better without Hillary.

I can't tell you how glad I am that you made it out.

A holiday of sorts.

He waits until Mrs. Boydstun goes out for groceries, then calls a travel agency in Boise, whispering questions into the telephone as though perpetrating crimes. When he tells Amanda Corddry at the highway department that he'll be taking his vacation time in May, her eyes double in size.

"Well, Zeno Ninis, I'll be shoveled sideways. If I didn't know better, I'd guess you were in love."

With Mrs. Boydstun, things are trickier. Every few days he slips it into an exchange as though spooning sugar into her coffee. London, May, a friend from the war. And every few days Mrs. Boydstun finds a way to spill food on the floor, or get a headache, or locate a new tremor in her left leg, and end the conversation.

Rex writes back, *Delighted. Sounds like you arrive during school hours, Hillary will meet you,* and March passes, and April. Zeno lays out his one suit, his green-striped tie. Mrs. Boydstun trembles at the bottom of the stairway in her robe. "You're not really going to leave a sick woman by herself? What kind of man are you?"

Out his bedroom window a blue helmet of sky is fixed above the pines. He shuts his eyes. *Years pass in a blink now,* Rex wrote. How much more is written in the spaces between the lines? Go now or forever hold your tongue.

"It's eight days in all." Zeno buckles his suitcase. "I've loaded the cupboards. Got extra cigarettes too. Trish has promised to look in on you every day."

He burns so much adrenaline during the flights that by the time he gets off in Heathrow, he is practically hallucinating. Outside passport control he looks for an Englishwoman; instead a six-foot-six man with prematurely silver hair and apricot-colored pants that flare at the calf seizes his forearm.

"Oh, you are a little box of cocoa," says the giant, and air-kisses both of Zeno's cheeks. "I'm Hillary."

Zeno clutches his suitcase, trying to comprehend. "How did you know I was me?"

Hillary shows his canines. "Lucky guess."

He plucks Zeno's suitcase from his grasp and marshals him through the crowds. Beneath a blue vest, Hillary wears what looks like a peasant's blouse with sequins randomly applied to the sleeves. Are his fingernails painted green? Is a man allowed to dress like this here? Yet, as Hillary's boots clip-clop across the terminal, as they weave into a crush of buses and taxis, no one pays much mind. They clamber into a pocket-sized wine-colored two-door, something called an Austin 1100, Hillary insisting on holding the door for Zeno, then walking around the rear of the little car and folding his long body behind the right-hand drive, knees practically in his teeth as he works the pedals, his hair brushing the roof, and Zeno tries not to hyperventilate.

London is smoke-gray and endless. Hillary chatters: "Brentford on your right, old dunghead boyfriend lived right over there, big, disobedient nipper. Rex finishes school in one hour, so we'll surprise him at home. That's Gunnersbury Park there, see?"

Parking meters, creeping traffic, soot-stained facades. Wrigley's Spearmint Gold Leaf One of the Great Cigarettes Ales Spirits and Wines. They park outside a sun-deprived brick house in Camden. No gardens, no hedges, no warbling greenfinches, no matronly wife with teacups. A leaflet glued by rain to the sidewalk reads, *The easy way to pay.* "We go up," Hillary says and bends through the doorway like a mobile tree. He carries Zeno's suitcase up four flights, his long strides skipping every other stair.

Inside, the flat appears bisected in two. On one side run tidy bookshelves while on the other tapestries, bicycle frames, candles, ashtrays, brass elephants, thickly frosted abstract paintings, and dead houseplants all seem to have been thrown into piles by a cyclone. "Make yourself at home, I'll just wet some leaves," Hillary says. He lights a cigarette from a stove burner and emits a titanic sigh. His forehead is unlined, his cheeks smooth-shaven; when Zeno and Rex were in Korea, Hillary could not have been more than five years old.

From the turntable exuberant voices sing, "Love Grows Where My Rosemary Goes" and the realization hits: Rex and Hillary live together. In a one-bedroom apartment.

"Sit, sit."

Zeno sits at the table while the record plays, gusts of confusion and exhaustion blasting over him. Hillary ducks light fixtures as he flips the record, then taps ashes into a houseplant.

"It's such fun to have one of Rex's friends visit. Rex never has friends visit. Sometimes I think he had none before I met him."

Keys jingle at the door, and Hillary raises his eyebrows at Zeno, and a man comes into the apartment in a raincoat and galoshes and his face is the color of cheese curd and he has a little paunch sticking out over his belt and a concave chest and his eyeglasses are fogged and his freckles are faded but still exuberant in their quantity and it is Rex.

Zeno puts out a hand, but Rex embraces him.

Emotion rises unbidden to Zeno's eyes. "Jet lag," he says, and wipes his cheeks.

"Of course."

A mile above them Hillary brings a cracked green fingernail to his own eye and scoops away a tear. He fills two cups with black tea, sets out a plate of biscuits, switches off the record player, wraps himself in a big purple raincoat, and says, "Right, I'll leave you two old muckers to it then." Zeno listens to him scuttle down the stairs like a giant multicolored spider.

Rex takes off his coat and shoes. "So, plowing snow?" The apartment seems to be teetering on the edge of a cliff. "And me, I'm still reading Iron Age poems to boys who don't want to hear them."

Zeno nibbles a biscuit. He wants to ask Rex if he ever wishes he were back at Camp Five, if he ever longs for the hours the two of them sat in the shadows of the kitchen shed, slatted with sunlight, and drew characters in the dust—a perverse kind of homesickness. But wishing you were back in a prison camp is raving mad, and Rex is talking about his trips to northern Egypt combing through the rubbish dumps of the ancients. All these years, all those miles, so much hope and dread, and now he has Rex all to himself and in the first five minutes he has already lost his way.

"You're writing a book?"

"Already wrote one." From one of the shelves Rex slides a tan hardcover with plain blue capitals on the front. *Compendium of Lost Books.* "We've sold, I think, forty-two copies, about sixteen of those to Hillary." He laughs. "Turns out no one wants to read a book about books that no longer exist."

Zeno runs a finger over Rex's name where it is printed on the jacket. Books have always seemed to him like clouds or trees, things that were just there, on the shelves at the Lakeport Public Library. But to know someone who made one? "Take the tragedies alone," Rex is saying. "We know that at least one thousand of them were written and performed in Greek theaters in the fifth century B.C. You know how many we have left? Thirty-two. Seven of Aeschylus's eighty-one. Seven of Sophocles's one hundred and twenty-three. Aristophanes wrote forty comedies that we know of—we have eleven, not all of them complete."

As Zeno turns pages, he sees entries for Agathon, Aristarchus, Callimachus, Menander, Diogenes, Chaeremon of Alexandria. "When all you have is a shard of papyrus with a few words on it," Rex says, "or a single line quoted in somebody else's text, the potential of what's lost haunts you. It's like the boys who died in Korea. We grieve them the most because we never saw the men they would become." Zeno thinks of his father: how much easier it was to be a hero when you no longer walked the earth.

But now the fatigue is like a second force of gravity, threatening to tip him out of his chair. Rex puts the book back on the shelf and smiles. "You're exhausted. Come, Hillary made up a bed for you."

He wakes on the sleeper sofa in the bottom of the night with the acute awareness that two men share a bed through a closed door seven feet away. When he next wakes, spine aching from jet lag or some darker heartbreak, it is afternoon, and Rex left for school hours before. Hillary is standing at an ironing board, wearing what looks like a silk kimono, hunched over a book that appears to be in Chinese. Without raising his nose from the page, he holds out a cup of tea. Zeno takes it and stands in his rumpled travel clothes and looks out the window at a meshwork of brick and fire escapes.

He takes a lukewarm shower, standing in the bath and holding the nozzle over his head, and when he comes out of the bathroom Rex is standing in the tidy half of the apartment examining his thinning hair with a hand mirror. He smiles at Zeno and yawns.

"Shagging so many handsome lads tires the old man out," whispers Hillary, and winks, and Zeno feels a shock of horror before he realizes Hillary is joking.

They see a dinosaur skeleton, ride a double-decker bus, and Hillary visits a makeup counter at a department store and returns with matching swirls of blue paint around his eyes, and Rex teaches Zeno about different brands of gin, and Hillary is always with them, rolling tight little cigarettes, dressing in platform shoes, in blazers, in an epic, monstrous prom dress. Soon it's the fourth night of his visit, and they're eating meat pies in a cellar after midnight, Hillary asking Zeno if he has reached the part in Rex's book yet where he writes about how every lost book, before it vanished forever, got down to one final copy somewhere, and how it made Hillary think about seeing a white rhinoceros in a zoo in Czechoslovakia once, how the sign said the rhino was one of the last twenty northern white rhinos in the world, the only one left in Europe, and how the beast just stared out through the bars of his cage, making a moaning sound, while flies swarmed his eyes. Then Hillary looks over at Rex and wipes his eyes and says that every time he reads that part, he thinks about the rhino and cries, and Rex pats his arm.

On Saturday Hillary heads off to "the gallery," though Zeno does not know what to imagine—art gallery? shooting gallery?—and he and Rex sit at a café table surrounded by women with prams, Rex in a black tweed vest still dusted with blackboard chalk from the previous days' classes, which makes Zeno's heart race. A tiny waiter who makes no sound as he moves brings them a teapot painted all over with raspberries.

Zeno is hoping the conversation might come around to the night, in Camp Five, when Bristol and Fortier loaded Rex onto the flatbed truck, hidden inside a fuel drum, that he might hear the story of Rex's escape, and whether Rex forgives him for staying behind, but Rex is enthusing about a trip he took to the Vatican Library in Rome where he combed through heaps of ancient papyrus salvaged from the dumps of Oxyrhynchus, little pieces of Greek texts buried in sand for two thousand years. "Ninety-nine percent of it is dull, of course, certificates, farm receipts, tax records, but to find one sentence, Zeno—even a few words—of a literary work that was previously unknown? To rescue one phrase from oblivion? It's the most exciting thing, I can't tell you: it's like digging up one end of a buried wire and realizing that it's connected to someone eighteen centuries dead. It feels like *nostos*, do you remember?" He's waving his nimble hands and blinking his eyes, the same gentleness in his face he carried all those years ago in Korea, and Zeno wants to leap across the table and put his mouth on Rex's throat.

"One of these days we're going to piece together something really significant, a tragedy by Euripides or a lost political history, or better still, some old comedy, some impossible fool's journey to the ends of the earth and back. Those are my favorites, do you know what I mean?" He raises his eyes and flames flare inside Zeno. For an instant he spins out a possible future, an afternoon argument between Rex and Hillary: Hillary pouts, Rex asks Hillary to leave, Zeno helps clean out all of Hillary's detritus, carries boxes, unpacks his own suitcase into Rex's bedroom, sits on the edge of Rex's bed; they take walks, travel to Egypt, read in silence across a teapot from one another. For a moment Zeno feels that he might be able to speak it into existence: if he says exactly the right words, right now, like a magic spell, it will happen. I think of you all the time, the veins in your throat, the fuzz on your arms, your eyes, your mouth, I loved you then, I love you now.

Rex says, "I'm boring you."

"No, no." Everything tilts. "The opposite. It's just—" He sees the valley road, the plow blade, the swirling ghosts of snow. A thousand dark trees whisk past. "It's all new for me, understand, late nights, gin and tonics, the Underground, your—Hillary. He's reading Chinese, you're digging up lost Greek scrolls. It's intimidating."

"Ah." Rex waves a hand. "Hillary is full of projects that go nowhere. Never finishes a one. And I'm a teacher at a middling boys' school. In Rome I get sunburned walking from the hotel to the taxi."

The café bustles, a baby fusses, the waiter pads noiselessly back and forth. Rain trickles down the awning. Zeno feels the moment slipping.

"But isn't that," Rex says, "what love is?" He rubs his temple, and drinks his tea, and glances at his wristwatch, and Zeno feels as though he has walked to the center of the frozen lake and fallen through the ice.

The birthday party falls on Zeno's last day. They take a black cab to a club called The Crash. Rex leans on Hillary's arm and says, "Let's try to keep it tame tonight, shall we?" and Hillary bats his lashes, and they descend into a series of connected rooms that get sequentially stranger and more dungeon-like, each stuffed with boys and men in silver boots or zebra leggings or top hats. Many of the men seem to know Rex, clasping him on the arm or kissing his cheeks or blowing party noisemakers at him, and several try to engage Zeno in conversation but the music is too loud, so he mostly nods and sweats in his polyester suit.

In a final room at the very bottom of the club Hillary appears carrying three glasses of gin, wobbling above the crowd in his high boots and emerald topcoat like a walking tree-god and the gin sends heat roaring through the corridors of Zeno's body. He tries to get Rex's attention, but the music doubles in volume, and as if by some signal, every man in the room begins to sing, "Hey hey hey hey hey," as strobe lights in the walls switch on, transforming the room into a flip book, limbs ratcheting here and there, mouths leering, knees and elbows flashing, and Hillary tosses his drink in the air and wraps his tree limbs around Rex, everybody doing a version of the same dance, launching first one, then the other arm toward the ceiling, as though shaping semaphores to one another, the air aflame with noise, and rather than let go, rather than join, Zeno feels so miserable, so deficient, so overwhelmed by his own naïveté—his cardboard suitcase, his all-wrong suit, his lumberjack boots, his Idaho manners, his misconceived hope that Rex invited him here because he wanted something romantic from him—*we could scribble some Greek with paper and pen rather than stick and mud*. He is, he sees now, so much of a yokel that he's basically a barbarian. Amid the pulsing music and flickering bodies, he is surprised to find himself yearning for the monochromatic predictability of Lakeport: Mrs. Boydstun's afternoon whiskey, the unblinking porcelain children, the air striped with woodsmoke, and the silence over the lake.

He fights his way back up through the various rooms to the street and wanders frightened and ashamed through Vauxhall for two hours without any sense of where he is. When he finally gathers the nerve to wave down a cab and ask if he can be taken to a brick house in Camden beside a Gold Leaf cigarette sign, the cabbie nods and drives him directly to Rex's building. Zeno climbs the four flights and finds the door unlocked. A cup of tea has been left on the table. When, a few hours later, Hillary wakes him so that he does not miss his flight, he touches him on the forehead with a gesture so tender that Zeno has to turn away.

Outside Departures Rex parks the Austin, lifts a wrapped box from the backseat, and sets it on Zeno's lap.

Inside is a copy of Rex's *Compendium* and a bigger, thicker volume. "Liddell and Scott, a Greek-English lexicon. Indispensable. In case you wanted to take a crack at translating again."

Outside the car a rush of passengers spurts past and for a moment the ground beneath Zeno's seat opens and he is swallowed and then he's back in the seat once more.

"You had a knack for it, you know. More than a knack."

Zeno shakes his head.

Horns honk and Rex glances behind them. "Don't be so quick to dismiss yourself," he says. "Sometimes the things we think are lost are only hidden, waiting to be rediscovered."

Zeno gets out of the car, suitcase in his right hand, books under his left arm, something inside him (regret) thrusting to and fro like a spearman, pulverizing bone, destroying vital tissue. Rex leans over and puts out his right hand and Zeno squeezes it with his left, as awkward a handshake as there's ever been. Then the little car is swallowed by traffic.

LAKEPORT, IDAHO

FEBRUARY–MAY 2019

Seymour

In February he and Janet huddle shoulder-to-shoulder over her smartphone in a corner of the cafeteria. "Gotta warn you," she says, "he's kinda scary." On-screen a little man in black denim and a goat mask paces back and forth across an auditorium stage. He goes by the name of "Bishop"; an assault rifle is slung over his back. *Start*, he says,

> with the Book of Genesis. *"Be fruitful,"* it begins, *"and multiply, and replenish the earth, and subdue it, and have dominion over the fish of the sea, and over the fowl of the air, and over every living thing that moveth upon the earth."*

The video cuts to a restless mash of faces. *For 2,600 years*, the man continues,

> *those of us in the Western tradition have been assured that the role of humanity is to subdue the earth. That all creation was created for us to harvest. And for 2,600 years we pretty much got away with it. Temperatures remained constant, seasons stayed predictable, and we cut down forests and fished out oceans and elevated one god above all others: Growth. Expand your property, increase your wealth, enlarge your walls. And when each new treasure you drag inside your walls doesn't relieve your pain? Go get some more. But now? Now the human species is beginning to reap what it has—*

The bell sounds and Janet taps the screen and Bishop freezes mid-sentence, arms outstretched. A link flashes at the bottom of the screen: Join Us.

"Seymour, give me my phone. I need to get to Spanish."

At the new Ilium terminal in the library, he puts on headphones and hunts down more videos. Bishop wears a Donald Duck mask, a raccoon mask, a Kwakiutl Nation beaver mask; he's in a clear-cut in Oregon, a village in Mozambique.

> *When Flora got married, she was fourteen. Now she has three kids and the village wells are dry and the nearest reliable water source is a two-hour walk from her home. Here in the Funhalouro District adolescent moms like Flora spend about six hours a day searching for and transporting water. Yesterday she walked three hours to harvest water lilies from a lake so her kids would have something to eat. And what do our most enlightened leaders suggest we do? Switch to e-billing. Buy three LED bulbs and get a free tote bag. Earth has eight billion people to feed and the extinction rate is a thousand times higher than it was at pre-human levels. This is not something we fix with tote bags.*

Bishop is recruiting warriors, he says, to dismantle the global industrial economy before it's too late. They will, he says, rebuild societies around new thought systems, where resources will be shared; they will reclaim the old wisdom, seek answers to the questions commerce cannot answer, meet the needs money cannot meet.

The faces Seymour can make out in Bishop's audiences glow with purpose; he remembers how it felt, his whole body taut, when he sprung the lid off the crate of Pawpaw's old grenades for the first time. All that latent power. Never before has someone articulated his own anger and confusion like this.

*"Wait," they said. "Be patient," they said. "Technology
will solve the carbon crisis." In Kyoto, in Copenhagen, in
Doha, in Paris, they said, "We'll cut emissions, we'll wean
ourselves off hydrocarbons," and they rolled back to the
airport in armor-plated limos and flew home on jumbo
jets and ate sushi thirty thousand feet in the air while
poor people choked on the air in their own neighborhoods.
Waiting is over. Patience is over. We must rise up now,
before the whole world is on fire. We must—*

When Marian fans a hand in front of his eyes, for a few breaths
Seymour cannot remember where he is.

"Anyone home?"

The link flashes Join Us Join Us Join Us. He takes off the headphones.

Marian swings her car keys around one finger. "Closing time,
kiddo. Can you turn off the *Open* sign for me, please? And, listen,
Seymour, are you free Saturday? At noon?"

He nods, collects his book bag. Outside rain is falling on the old
snow and the streets are full of slush.

"Saturday," Marian calls after him. "Noon. Don't forget. I have a
surprise for you."

At home Bunny is at the kitchen table frowning over the check-
book. She looks up, her attention returning from a long way off.

"How was your day? Did you walk all the way home in the rain?
Did you sit with Janet at lunch?"

He opens the fridge. Mustard. Shasta Twists. Half a bottle of
ranch dressing. Nothing.

"Seymour? Can you look at me, please?"

In the glare of the kitchen bulb, her cheeks look made of chalk.
Her throat sags; her roots show; her upper spine has begun to hunch.
How many hotel toilets did she scrub today? How many beds did she
strip? Watching the years take Bunny's youth has been like watching
the forest behind the house go down all over again.

"Listen, honey, the Aspen Leaf is shutting down. Geoff said they can't compete with the chains anymore. He's letting me go."

Envelopes litter the table. V-1 Propane, Intermountain Gas, Blue River Bank, Lakeport Utilities. His medication alone, he knows, costs $119 a week.

"I don't want you to worry, honey. We'll figure something out. We always do."

He skips math, crouches in the parking lot with Janet's phone.

> *In a world warmer by two degrees centigrade, 150 million more people—most of them poor—will die from air pollution alone. Not violence, not floods, just inferior air. That's 150 times more fatalities than the American Civil War. Fifteen Holocausts. Two World War Twos. In our actions, in our attempts to throw some wrenches into the market economy, we hope that no one will die. But if there are a few deaths, isn't it still worth it? To stop fifteen Holocausts?*

A tap on his shoulder. Janet shivers on the curb. "This is getting annoying, Seymour. I have to ask for my phone back five times a day."

Friday he comes home from school to find Bunny drinking wine from a plastic cup on the love seat. She beams, takes his backpack off his shoulder, and curtsies. She has, she announces, taken out a payday loan to see them through until she finds a new job. And on the way home, she was passing by the Computer Shack beside the lumber yard, and had to stop.

From behind the cushion she produces a brand-new Ilium tablet computer, still in its box. "Voilà!"

She grins. The burgundy she has been drinking makes her teeth look as though she has been eating ink.

"And remember Dodds Hayden? At the store? He threw this

in for free!" Next from behind the cushion she produces an Ilium smart speaker. "It tells the weather and plays trivia and remembers shopping lists. You can order pizza just by talking to it!"

"Mom."

"I'm happy to see you doing so well, Possum, spending time with Janet, and I know it's hard to be the kid without the new tech stuff, and I thought, well, you deserve it. We deserve it. Don't we?"

"Mom."

Out the sliding door the lights of Eden's Gate shimmer as though borne along by an underwater current.

"Mom, you need Wi-Fi to use these."

"Huh?" She sips her wine. Her shoulders deflate. "Wi-Fi?"

Saturday he walks to the ice rink, sits on a bench high above the swirling skaters, switches on the new tablet, and logs on to the wireless network. It takes a half hour to download all the updates. Then he watches a dozen videos of Bishop, everything he can find, and by the time he remembers Marian's invitation, it's after 3 p.m. He scurries up the block: at the corner of Lake and Park, bolted to the concrete, is a brand-new book drop box painted to look like an owl.

It's a fat cylinder, painted gray, brown, and white, and looks as if it has wings pressed to its sides and talons on its feet. Big yellow eyes glow in the center of its face and it wears a little bow tie: a great grey.

Across the door it says, *PLEASE RETURN BOOKS HERE.* On its breast:

LAKEPORT PUBLIC LIBRARY
"OWL" YOU NEED ARE BOOKS!

The front door of the library opens and Marian bustles out with her bag and keys wearing a cherry-red parka and her buttons are done up wrong and her expression is hurt or angry or annoyed or all three.

"You missed the dedication. I asked everybody to wait."

"I—"

"I reminded you twice, Seymour." The painted owl seems to fix accusatory eyes on him as Marian tugs up her collar. "You know," she says, "you're not the only person in the world," and gets in her Subaru and drives away.

April is warmer than it should be. He stops going to the library, skips Environmental Awareness Club meetings, dodges Mrs. Tweedy in the halls. After school he sits on a low wall behind the ice rink, in Wi-Fi range, and chases Bishop's videos into ever shadier corners of the internet. *Humans are best understood as exterminators,* he says. *Every habitat we enter, we decimate, and now we have overrun the earth. The next thing we exterminate will be ourselves.*

One for the toilet, one for the sink—Seymour stops taking the buspirone. For several days his body crashes. Then it wakes up. Sensations roar back; his mind feels as if it becomes the huge, curved mirror of a radar telescope, gathering light from the farthest corners of the universe. Every time he steps outside, he can hear the clouds grinding through the sky.

"How come," Janet asks one day as she drives him home, "you never want to meet my parents?"

A dump truck rumbles past. Out there Bishop's warriors are gathering. Seymour feels as though he is preparing for a metamorphosis; he can almost feel himself breaking down at the molecular level, building himself into an entirely new thing.

Janet pulls up in front of the double-wide. He balls his hands into fists.

"I'm talking," she says, "but you're not listening. What's going on with you?"

"Nothing's going on with me."

"Just get out of the car, Seymour."

• • •

*They call us militants and terrorists. They argue that change
takes time. But there is no time. We can no longer live in a
world culture where the rich are allowed to believe that their
way of life has no consequences, that they can use whatever
they want and throw away whatever they want, that they are
immune to catastrophe. I know that it's not easy to have your
eyes opened. It's not fun. We will all have to be strong. The
coming events will test us in ways we cannot yet imagine.*

The link flashes Join Us Join Us Join Us.

He studies the Eden's Gate townhomes closest to the double-wide,
looking for the ones with no signs of life, whose owners are clearly
somewhere else, and on the fifteenth of May, while Bunny is working a dinner shift at the Pig N' Pancake, he crosses the backyard past
the egg-shaped boulder and hops the ranch-rail fence and scurries
through the shadows trying various windows. When he finds one that
is unlocked, he climbs through the blinds and stands in the dimness.

The oven clock sends a soft green glow through the kitchen.

The modem is in the hall closet. The network name and password
are taped to the wall. For a few breaths he stands in someone else's
life: a magnet on the refrigerator reads *Beer: The Reason I Wake Up
Every Afternoon*; a framed family photo on the sideboard; the linger-
ing odors of coffee and last weekend's Crock-Pot; an empty dog bowl
by the pantry. Four ski helmets hang on hooks by the front door.

In the grocery store, people push carts full of brightly packaged
food, none of them realizing they stand beneath the towering wall of
a dam about to give way. A boxed cake studded with blue and yellow
frosting-stars that says *Congratulations, Sue* is seventy-five percent
off. He keeps his ear defenders on in the checkout line.

When Bunny gets home she pulls off her shoes and says, "What's
this?"

Seymour sets two pieces of cake on plates and carries over the
blue Ilium smart speaker. Bunny looks at him. "I thought—"

"Try it."

She leans over the capsule. "Hello?"

A little green light draws a circle around the rim. *Hello*. It sounds vaguely British. *I'm Maxwell. What's your name?*

Bunny claps her hands to her cheeks. "I'm Bunny."

Lovely to meet you, Bunny. Happy birthday. What may I do for you this evening?

She looks at Seymour, mouth open.

"Maxwell, I would like to order a pizza."

Absolutely, Bunny. What size?

"Large. With mushrooms. And sausage."

One moment, says the capsule and the green dot trundles and she grins her beautiful doomed smile and Seymour feels the world around him crumble a little bit more.

A week later Janet parks the Audi downtown and they buy ice cream and Janet tells the girl behind the counter that she should use compostable spoons instead of plastic ones and the girl says, "You want sprinkles or not?"

They sit on boulders overlooking the lake and eat their ice cream and Janet takes out her phone. To their left, in the marina parking lot, idles a thirty-two-foot RV with slide-outs on either side and two air-conditioning condenser units on the roof. A man gets out, sets down a little leashed poodle, and walks it around the bend.

"When everything falls apart," Seymour says, "guys like him will be the first to go."

Janet pokes the screen of her phone. Seymour fidgets. The roar is close today; he can hear it crackling like a wildfire. From where they sit he can see into the core of downtown to the newly remodeled Eden's Gate Realty office beside the library.

The RV has Montana plates. Hydraulic jacks. A satellite TV dish.

"He went to walk his dog," he says, "but left the engine running."

Beside him Janet takes a photo of herself, then deletes it. Over the lake the eyes of Trustyfriend open, two yellow moons.

In the grass at the edge of the marina lot Seymour spies a round piece of granite as big as a baby's head. He walks to it. It's heavier than it looks.

Janet is still looking at her phone. *A warrior*, Bishop says, *truly engaged, does not experience guilt, fear, or remorse. A warrior, truly engaged, becomes something more than human.*

Seymour remembers the weight of the grenade in his pocket as he carried it through the vacant lots of Eden's Gate. Remembers putting his finger through the safety ring. Pull the pin. Pull it pull it pull it.

He lugs the stone over to the motor home. Through the buzz of the roar in his head, he hears Janet call, "Seymour?"

No guilt no fear no remorse. The difference between us and them is action.

"What are you doing?"

He raises the rock above his head.

"Seymour, if you do that, I will never—"

He glances at her. Back at the motor home. *Patience*, Bishop says, *is over.*

THE ARGOS

MISSION YEAR 64

DAY 46–DAY 276 INSIDE VAULT ONE

Konstance

Records flutter down from the shelves and stack themselves on the desk in chronological order. An Oregon birth certificate. A bleached piece of paper called a Western Union telegram.

WUX Washington AP 20 551 PM
ALMA BOYDSTUN
431 FOREST ST LAKEPORT

DEEPLY REGRET TO INFORM YOU THAT YOUR WARD PRIVATE
ZENO NINIS US ARMY IS MISSING IN ACTION SINCE 1 APRIL
1951 IN THE KOREAN AREA DURING THE PERFORMANCE OF
HIS DUTY DETAILS NOT AVAILABLE

Next come transcripts of prisoner-of-war release interviews dated July and August 1953. A passport with one arrival stamp: London. A deed for a house in Idaho. A commendation for four decades of service to the Valley County Highway Department. The bulk of the stack consists of obituaries and articles detailing how, at the age of eighty-six, on the twentieth of February in the year 2020, Zeno Ninis died protecting five children who were trapped in a rural library by a terrorist.

COURAGEOUS KOREA VET SAVES KIDS AND LIBRARY, reads one headline. *IDAHO HERO MOURNED*, reads another.

She finds nothing connected to the fragments of an ancient comedy titled *Cloud Cuckoo Land*. No listed publications, no indications that Zeno Ninis translated, adapted, or published anything.

A prisoner of war, a county employee in Idaho, an elderly man who thwarted a planned bombing of a small-town library. Why was a book with this man's name on it on Father's nightstand in Nannup? She writes, *Was there another Zeno Ninis?* and drops the question through the slot. A moment later the reply flutters down: *The Library contains no records of any other individuals by that name.*

At NoLight she lies on the cot and watches Sybil flicker inside her tower. How many times, as a little girl, was she assured that Sybil contained everything she could ever imagine, everything she would ever need? The memoirs of kings; ten thousand symphonies; ten million television shows; whole baseball seasons; 3-D scans of the Lascaux caves; a complete record of the Great Collaboration that produced the *Argos*: propulsion, hydration, gravity, oxygenation—all right here, the collected cultural and scientific output of human civilization nested inside the strange filaments of Sybil at the heart of the ship. The premier achievement of human history, they said, the triumph of memory over the obliterating forces of destruction and erasure. And when she first stood in the atrium on her Library Day, gazing down the seemingly infinite rows of shelves, hadn't she believed it?

But it wasn't true. Sybil couldn't stop a contagion from spreading through the crew. She couldn't save Zeke or Dr. Pori or Mrs. Lee or anybody else, it seems. Sybil still doesn't know if it's safe for Konstance outside of Vault One.

There are things that Sybil doesn't know. Sybil doesn't know what it meant to be held by your father inside the leafy green twilight of Farm 4, or how it felt to sift through your mother's button bag and wonder about the provenance of each button. The Library has no records of a royal blue copy of *Cloud Cuckoo Land* translated by Zeno Ninis, yet Konstance has seen one inside the Atlas, faceup on Father's nightstand.

Konstance sits up. Into her mind swims a vision of another library, a less presuming place, hidden inside the walls of her own skull, a library of just a few dozen shelves, a library of secrets: the library of things Konstance knows but Sybil does not.

• • •

She feeds herself, scrubs the rinseless soap into her hair, does what-ever sit-ups and lunges and precalculus Sybil prescribes. Then she goes to work. She rips apart the one Nourish powder sack that she has already emptied and tears the scraps into rectangles: paper. She takes a replacement nylon tube out of the food printer's repair pack and chews it into a nib: pen.

Her early attempts at ink—synthetic gravy, synthetic grape juice, synthetic coffee bean paste—are pitiful: too runny, too feathery, too slow to dry.

Konstance, what are you doing?

"I'm playing, Sybil. Let me be."

But after a few dozen experiments, she's able to write her name without smearing it. In the Library she tells herself, read, reread, take a snapshot of it in your mind. Then she touches her Vizer, steps off the Perambulator, and writes it out.

Courageous Korea Vet Saves Kids and Library

With the makeshift pen, those seven words take her ten minutes to write. But after a few more days of practice, she's quicker, memo-rizing whole sentences from texts in the Library, stepping off her Perambulator, and scrawling them onto a scrap. One reads,

Proteomic analysis of the Diogenes codex turned up
traces of tree sap, lead, charcoal, and gum tragacanth,
a thickening agent commonly used in ink in medieval
Constantinople.

Another:

But if it is probable that the manuscript survived
the Middle Ages, like so many other ancient Greek
texts, in a monastic library of Constantinople, how it

traveled out of the city and to Urbino must be left to the
imagination.

A current of red light ripples through Sybil. *Are you playing a
game, Konstance?*

"Just making notes, Sybil."

*Why not write your notes in the Library? Far more efficient and
you could use whatever colors you would like.*

Konstance drags the back of her hand across her face, smearing
ink across one cheek. "This suits me fine, thank you."

Weeks pass. *Happy birthday, Konstance,* Sybil says one morning. *You
are fourteen years old today. Would you like me to help you print a cake?*

Konstance peers over the edge of her cot. On the floor around
her flutter almost eighty scraps of sacking material. One reads, *Who
Was Zeno Ninis?* Another: Σχερία.

"No, thank you. You could let me out. Why not let me out for my
birthday?"

I cannot.

"How many days have I been in here, Sybil?"

*You have been safe inside Vault One for two hundred and seventy-
six days.*

From the floor she picks up a scrap on which she has written,

Out here in Woop Woop, like Grandmom calls it, we've
had heaps of troubles.

She blinks and sees Father lead her into Farm 4 and pull open a
seed drawer. Vapor spills out and flows along the floor; she reaches
into the rows, selects a foil envelope.

Sybil says, *There are several recipes for birthday cake we could try.*

"Sybil, you know what I would like for my birthday?"

Tell me, Konstance.

"I would like you to leave me alone."

Inside the Atlas she floats miles above the rotating Earth, questions whispering through the black. Why did her father have a copy of Zeno Ninis's translation of Aethon's story on his nightstand in Nannup? What does it mean?

I had this dream, this vision, of what life could be, Father said in the last minute she spent with him. *"Why stay here when I could be there?"* The same words Aethon said before he left home.

"Take me," she says, "to Lakeport, Idaho."

She plummets through clouds to a mountain town bunched at the south end of a glacial lake. She walks past a marina, two hotels, a boat ramp. An electric tourist tram runs to the top of a nearby peak. Traffic clogs the main road: trucks pull boats on trailers; faceless figures pedal bicycles.

The public library is a steel-and-glass cube a mile south of downtown in a weedy field. A platoon of heat pumps gleams to one side. No plaques, no memorial garden, no mention of any Zeno Ninis.

She returns to Vault One and paces in her ragged socks, the scraps at her feet stirring lightly. She collects four, sets them in a row, and crouches over them.

Courageous Korea Vet Saves Kids and Library

Translation by Zeno Ninis

The Library contains no records of such a volume.

February 20, 2020.

What is she missing? She remembers Mrs. Flowers standing beneath the crumbling Theodosian Walls in Istanbul: *Depending on when this imaging was done, this is the city as it looked six or seven decades ago, before the* Argos *left Earth.*

Again she touches her Vizer, climbs onto the Perambulator, takes a slip of paper from a Library table. *Show me*, she writes, *what the Lakeport Public Library looked like on February 20, 2020.*

Old-fashioned two-dimensional photographs descend onto the table. The library in these images is entirely different from the steel-and-glass cube inside the Atlas: it's a high-gabled light-blue house partially concealed behind overgrown bushes at the corner of Lake and Park. Shingles are missing; the chimney is crooked; dandelions grow from cracks in the front walk. A box painted to look like an owl stands on the corner.

Atlas, writes Konstance and the big book lumbers off its shelf.

She finds her way to the corner of Lake and Park and stops. On the southeast corner, where the ramshackle library in the photographs once stood, now rises a three-story hotel full of balconies. Four faceless teenagers in tank tops and swim trunks are stopped mid-stride on the corner.

An awning, an ice cream shop, a pizza restaurant, a parking garage. The lake is dotted with boats and kayaks. Traffic is stopped in a line up and down the road. No sign that a public library inside a rickety old blue house was ever here.

She turns in a half circle and stands beside the teenagers, a wave of hopelessness rearing behind her. Her notes on the floor of the vault, her trips along Backline Road, her discovery of Scheria, the book on her Father's night table—all this investigation was supposed to lead her somewhere. It felt like a puzzle she was supposed to solve. But she's no closer to understanding her father than she was when he locked her in the vault.

She's about to leave when she notices, on the southwest corner of the intersection, a squat cylindrical box that has been painted to look like an owl with its wings pressed to its sides. *PLEASE RETURN BOOKS HERE*, it says on the door. On the owl's breast:

LAKEPORT PUBLIC LIBRARY
"OWL" YOU NEED ARE BOOKS!

Its two big amber eyes seem almost to track her as she approaches. They tore down the old library, built a new one at the edge of town, but left a box behind where people could return books? For decades?

From a certain angle, one of the kids on the corner seems to be walking right into the box, as though it was not there when the kids were imaged. Strange.

The owl's feathers are exquisitely detailed. Its eyes look wet and alive.

. . . and her eyes, they grew three times as large and turned the color of liquid honey . . .

The book drop box, she realizes, like the coconut palms that stopped her in Nigeria, or the emerald lawn and blooming trees in front of the public hall in Nannup, looks more vibrant than the building behind it—more vivid than the ice cream parlor or the pizza place or the four kids caught by the Atlas cameras. The owl's feathers almost quiver as Konstance reaches for them. Her fingertips strike something solid and her heart thumps.

The handle of the door feels like metal: cold, firm. Real. She grabs it and pulls. It starts to snow.

FIFTEEN

THE GUARDIANS AT THE GATES

Cloud Cuckoo Land by Antonius Diogenes, Folio O

... through the gateposts I could glimpse twinkling jewels in the pavements, and what appeared to be a steaming river of broth. Round the towers above, birds flew in rainbow-colored flocks, bright green, purple, crimson. Was I dreaming? Had I really arrived? After so many miles, after so much {believing?} still my heart doubted what my eyes saw.

"Halt, little crow," said an owl. He rose above me, five times my size, and carried a golden spear in each talon. "For you to pass through the gates, we must make sure you are actually a bird, a noble creature of the air, older than Kronos, than Time itself."

"Not one of those foul, treacherous humans, made of dust and dirt, wearing a disguise," said a second owl, even larger than the first.

Behind them, just inside the gates, beneath the hanging plums, almost within reach, a tortoise plodded slowly past with a pillar of honeycakes piled on his back. I leaned forward but the owls bristled their feathers. After crossing half the Milky Way, would the Fates really have me torn to pieces by magnificent beasts such as these?

... stood as tall as I could and ruffled my wings. "I am just a humble crow," I said, "and I have traveled far."

"Solve our riddle, little crow," said the first guardian. "And you can come right in."

"Though it will seem simple at first," said the second, "it's actually ..."

THE LAKEPORT
PUBLIC LIBRARY

FEBRUARY 20, 2020

5:41 P.M.

Seymour

Ear defenders around his neck, he listens. A radiator clangs some-where in Nonfiction; the wounded man breathes at the base of the stairs; a police radio crackles out in the snow. Blood ticks through his ears. Nothing else.

But he heard thuds upstairs, didn't he? He remembers the police SUV rolling onto the curb, Marian dropping the pizza boxes into the snow. Why was she bringing a stack of pizzas to the library just before closing time?

Someone else is here.

Beretta in his right hand, Seymour creeps toward the stairwell where the wounded man lies on his side, eyes closed, sleeping or worse-than-sleeping. The glitter in his arm hair glints. It occurs to Seymour that maybe he placed his body there as a barricade.

He holds his breath, steps over the thickening lagoon of blood, over the man, and goes up. Fifteen steps, the edge of each lined with nonslip adhesive. Blocking the entrance to the Children's Section is something unexpected: a plywood wall painted gold, the gold almost green in the glow of an *EXIT* sign. In the center is a little arched door, and above the arched door runs a single line of words written in an alphabet he does not recognize.

Ὦ ξένε, ὅστις εἶ, ἄνοιξον, ἵνα μάθῃς ἃ θαυμάζεις

Seymour sets his palm on the little door and pushes.

Zeno

He crouches among the children behind the L-shaped barrier of shelves and looks at each in turn: Rachel, Alex, Olivia, Christopher, Natalie. Shh shh shh. In the gloom their faces become the faces of a half-dozen little Korean deer that he and Rex came upon one day while gathering wood in the snow near Camp Five: their antlers and noses looming up out of the white, their black eyes blinking, their big ears twitching.

Together they listen to the little door in the plywood wall creak shut. Footfalls move through the folding chairs. Zeno keeps his index finger pressed to his lips.

A floorboard squeaks; underwater bubbles gurgle from Natalie's portable speaker. Is it only one person? It sounds like only one.

Be a police officer. Be Marian. Be Sharif.

Alex holds a can of root beer with two hands as though it were full of nitroglycerin. Rachel huddles over her script. Natalie shuts her eyes. Olivia's eyes fix on Zeno's. Christopher opens his mouth—for a moment Zeno believes the boy is going to cry out, that they are going to be discovered, murdered where they sit.

The footsteps stop. Christopher closes his mouth without making a sound. Zeno tries to remember what he and the children have left scattered among the chairs for someone to see. The dropped case of root beer, multiple cans rolled beneath the chairs. Backpacks. Pages of scripts. Natalie's laptop. Olivia's gull wings. The gold-painted encyclopedia on its lectern. The karaoke light, thankfully, is off.

Footfalls on the stage now. The rustle of a nylon jacket. Icy bands are compressing his chest and Zeno grimaces against the pressure. θεοὶ is the gods, ἐπεκλώσαντο means they spun, ὄλεθρον is death, plague, destruction. Ruin.

That's what the gods do, they spin threads of ruin through the fabric of our lives, all to make a song for generations to come. Not now, gods. Not tonight. Let these children stay children for another night.

Seymour

The smell of fresh paint on the little stage is very strong; it catches at the back of his throat. Shelves block the windows and the lights are off and those strange underwater sound effects—coming from where?—unsettle him. Here's a kid's parka, here a pair of snow boots, here a soda can. Cartoon clouds hang above him. Against the backdrop, a thick book sits open on a lectern. What is this?

Beside his foot lies a spill of photocopied legal pages covered in handwriting. He picks up one, holds it close to his eyes:

> GUARDIAN #2: Though it will seem simple at first, it's actually quite complicated.
>
> GUARDIAN #1: No, no, it will seem complicated at first, but it's actually quite simple.
>
> GUARDIAN #2: Ready, little crow? Here's our riddle. "He that knows all that Learning ever writ, knows only this."

Pistol in one hand, page in the other, Seymour stands on the stage and gazes at the painting on the drop curtain. The towers floating on clouds, trees winding up through the center—it seems like an image from a dream he had long ago. The hand-printed sign on the library door comes back to him:

TOMORROW
ONE NITE ONLY
CLOUD CUCKOO LAND

410

The world: it's all he ever loved. The forest behind Arcady Lane, the busy meanderings of ants, the zip and swerve of dragonflies, the rustling of the aspens, the tart sweetness of the first huckleberries of July, the sentinels of the ponderosas, older and more patient than any beings he would ever know, and Trustyfriend the owl on his branch overseeing it all.

Are bombs going off in other cities, other nations right now? Are Bishop's warriors mobilizing? And is Seymour the only one who has failed?

He steps off the stage and is moving toward the corner, where three bookcases have been arranged to create an alcove, when the wounded man calls from the bottom of the stairs.

"Hey, kid! I have your backpack. If you don't come downstairs right now, I am going to carry it outside and give it to the police."

SIXTEEN

THE RIDDLE OF THE OWLS

Cloud Cuckoo Land by Antonius Diogenes, Folio Π

Though there have been many guesses, the riddle of the owls guarding the gates has been lost to time. The solution here has been inserted by the translator and was not part of the original text. Translation by Zeno Ninis.

. . . I thought, "Simple but actually complicated. Or was it complicated but actually simple? {He that knows all that Learning ever writ. Could the answer be water? An egg? A horse?"}

. . . Though the tortoise with his honeycakes had plodded out of sight, I could still smell them. I {paced?} on my crow feet, my talons sinking into the soft pillow of the clouds. The rich scents of cinnamon and honey and roasting pork flowed over me from the far side of the gates, and I flapped through the caverns of my mind, traveling from one end to the other, but I found nothing there.

The other shepherds were right to call me a dimwit and an airhead, a muttonheaded lamebrain. I turned to the two enormous owls with their golden spears and said, "I know {nothing}."

The two owls {stood straight up and the first guardian said, "That is correct, little crow. The answer is nothing," and the second guardian said, " 'He that knows all that Learning ever writ, knows only this—that he knows nothing yet.' "}

. . . they stepped aside and {as though I'd said the magic words} the golden gates swung wide . . .

FOUR MILES WEST OF CONSTANTINOPLE

MAY 1453

Anna

From the top of the occasional swell, she can glimpse the now-distant shape of the city to the northeast, glowing faintly. In all other directions lies nothing but heaving blackness. Wet, exhausted, and seasick, the sack clamped to her chest, Anna ships the oars and gives up bailing. The sea is too large and the boat is too small. Maria, you were always the better sister, the wiser sister, moving on to the next world just as this one broke in half. *An angel in one child*, Widow Theodora used to say, *and a wolf in the other*.

In something deeper than a dream she hurries again across the tiled floor of a vast atrium lined on both sides with tiers of books. She breaks into a run, but no matter how far she seems to travel, the hall does not end, and the light dims, and her fear and desolation deepen with every stride. Finally she approaches a light ahead where a lone girl huddles beside a candle with a single book on a table. The girl raises the book she's holding, and Anna is trying to read the title when Himerius's skiff grinds onto a rock and turns broadside to the waves.

She has just enough time to gather the sack against her dress before she is dumped overboard.

She thrashes, inhales seawater. A swell sucks her out, throws her forward, and her knee strikes a submerged stone: the water is only waist deep. She sputters to the surface and drives her body toward shore, the sack soaked through but still clutched to her chest.

Anna crawls onto a stony beach and huddles over her throbbing knee and opens the neck of the sack. The silk, the book, the bread:

417

all drenched. Out among the dark seething waves Himerius's skiff is nowhere.

The beach draws an arc in the predawn light: no cover here. She climbs through a storm-driven barrier of driftwood at the tideline into a land of devastation: burned houses, every tree in an olive grove hacked down, the earth rutted as though God has raked away soil with his hands.

At first light she ascends a gentle hillside terraced with grapevines. The rumble of the waves recedes. She takes off her dress and wrings it dry and puts it back on and chews a piece of sturgeon and runs a hand over her cropped hair as dawn traces a pink line over the horizon.

She hoped that over the course of the night she would be swept to a new land, Genoa or Venice or Scheria, the kingdom of brave Alcinous, where a goddess might conceal her in magical mist and escort her to a palace. But she has been carried only a few miles up the coast. The city is still visible in the distance, a saw's blade of rooftops capped by the clustered domes of the Hagia Sophia. A few spires of smoke lift into the sky. Are armed men pouring through the neighborhoods, breaking into houses, herding everyone into the streets? Unbidden, an image rises of Widow Theodora and Agata and Thekla and Eudokia dead in the scullery, tea of nightshade in the center of the table, and she forces it away.

Birdsong rises from the vines. She glimpses a group of soldiers on horseback, maybe a half mile away, moving in the direction of the city, silhouetted against the sky, and she lies as flat as she can against the ground with the damp sack beside her as a fog of gnats clusters around her head.

When the men are out of sight, she creeps to the bottom of the vineyard and wades a stream and hurries up a second rise away from the sea. Atop the next hill, a stand of hazel trees huddle around a well as though frightened. A single cart track leads in and out. She crawls beneath the low-slung boughs and waits in the leaf litter as the silence of the morning beats down upon the fields.

In the quiet she can almost hear the bells of Saint Theophano, the clatter of the streets, broom and pan, needle and thread. The sound of Widow Theodora climbing the stairs to the workroom, opening the shutters, unlocking the thread cabinet. Blessed One, protect us from idleness. For we have committed sins without number.

She lays out the book and samite hood to dry in the early sun and devours the rest of the salt fish as cicadas sing in the branches above her. The leaves of the codex are saturated, but at least the ink has not bled. All through the brightest hours of the day she sits with her knees against her chest, sleeping and waking and sleeping again.

Thirst twists through her as shadows pool in the grove of trees. She has seen no one come to the well and she wonders if it has been poisoned against the invaders so she does not risk a drink. It's dusk when she reassembles her sack and climbs back through the boughs and moves through the coastal scrub, keeping the sea to her left. A waning quarter-moon holds pace with her as she scrambles over one boundary wall, then another, and she wishes the night were darker.

Every few hundred yards her passage is stymied by water: inlets she must circumnavigate, a brook tumbling through brambles that she drinks from before crashing through. Twice she skirts villages that appear abandoned: no figures moving, no smoke rising. Maybe a few last families hide there, crouched in cellars, but no one calls to her.

Behind her lies slavery and terror and worse. Ahead lies what? Saracens, mountain ranges, ferries where extortionists demand payment for river crossings. The moon sinks away and the thick band of stars that Chryse calls the Way of the Birds stretches wide and gold overhead. Step step step: there comes a point where the pressure of relentless fear perforates rationality and the body moves independently of the mind. It's like climbing the wall of the priory: foothold, handhold, up you go.

Before dawn she is pushing her way through a spindly forest, rounding the edge of what looks like a large body of water, when she sees firelight twinkling between trunks. She is about to skirt it when the air brings the odor of roasting meat.

The smell is a hook through the gut. A few paces closer: just to see.

A little fire in the woods, flames no higher than her shins. She picks her way through the trees, her slippers crunching leaves. At the fire's edge she can make out what looks like a single headless bird spitted beside the flames.

She tries not to breathe. No figures move; no horses nicker. For a hundred heartbeats she watches the flames burn down. No movement, no shadows: no one tends the meal. Just the bird: a partridge, she thinks. Is it a hallucination?

She can hear the fat sizzling. If it cooks much longer without being turned, the side facing the embers will burn. Maybe somebody was scared off. Maybe whoever made the fire heard news about the capture of the city and took his horse and left his meal.

For a breath she becomes Aethon-the-crow, bone-weary and disheveled, peering through the golden gates, watching a tortoise trudge past with a tower of cakes balanced on his shell.

Though it will seem simple at first, it's actually quite complicated.

No, no, it will seem complicated at first, but it's actually quite simple.

Logic deserts her. If she could just lift the bird from the coals. Her mind is already concocting the experience of tasting it, its flesh beneath her teeth, its juices spurting into her mouth. She tucks her sack behind a trunk, dashes, and uproots the spit. She has the bird in her left hand, one fraction of her consciousness registering a halter, rope, and oxhide cape at the edge of the firelight, the rest of her wholly bent on eating, when she hears an inhalation behind her.

Such is her hunger that her arm continues to bring the bird to her mouth even as a stroke of lightning cracks from the back of her head to the front, a long, branching fracture of white, as though the vault of the sky has splintered, and the world goes dark.

SEVENTEEN

THE WONDERS OF
CLOUD CUCKOO LAND

Cloud Cuckoo Land by Antonius Diogenes, Folio P

. . . mild, fragrant . . .
   . . . a river of cream . . .
   . . . sloping glens and {orchards?} . . .
   . . . met by a bright hoopoe, who bowed his feathery crown and said, "I am the vice-undersecretary to the viceroy of Provisions and Accommodations," and he draped a garland of ivy round my neck. Every bird swerved overhead in welcome, and sang its most tuneful . . .
   . . . unchanging, everlasting, no months, no years, every hour like spring on the clearest, most gold-green morning, the dew like {diamonds?}, the towers like honeycombs, and the western zephyr was the only breeze . . .
   . . . plumpest raisins, finest custards, salmon and sardines . . .
   . . . came the tortoise, the honeycakes, poppies and squills, and the {next?} . . .
   . . . I ate until I could {burst?}, then ate more . . .

LAKEPORT, IDAHO

1972–1995

Zeno

Supper is boiled beef. Across the table looms Mrs. Boydstun's face, haloed by smoke. On the television beside her, a brush strokes the upper eyelashes of an enormous eye.

"Mouse poops in the pantry."

"I'll set some traps tomorrow."

"Get the Victors. Not the garbage ones you bought last time."

Now an actor in a suit testifies to the miraculous sound of his Sylvania color television. Mrs. Boydstun drops her fork trying to bring it to her mouth and Zeno retrieves it from beneath the table.

"I'm done," she announces. He wheels her into her bedroom, lifts her onto the bed, measures out her medication, pushes the TV cart and its extension cord into her room. Beyond the windows, out toward the lake, the last daylight evacuates the sky. Sometimes, at moments like this, as he scrapes the plates, the sensation of his flight home from London comes back: how it seemed as though the planet would never stop unspooling below—water then fields then mountains then cities lit like neural networks—it seemed to him that between Korea and London he'd had enough adventure for a lifetime.

For months he sits at the desk beside the little brass bed with the first verses of Homer's *Iliad* on his left and the Liddell and Scott lexicon Rex gave him on the right. He hoped that vestiges of the Greek he learned at Camp Five might still be embedded in his memory, but nothing comes easily.

Μῆνιν, the poem begins, ἄειδε θεὰ Πηληϊάδεω Ἀχιλῆος, five words, the last the name Achilles, the second-to-last identifying that Achilles's father was Peleus (though also suggesting Achilles is godlike), yet somehow, with only three words in play, *mênin* and *aeide* and *theá*, the line bristles with landmines.

Pope: *Achilles's wrath, to Greece the direful spring.*

Chapman: *Achilles's bane full wrath resound, O Goddesse.*

Bateman: *Goddess, sing the destroying wrath of Achilles, Peleus's son.*

But does *aeide* fully suggest "to sing," because it's also the word for *poet*? And *mênin*, how best to translate that? Fury? Outrage? Vexation? To select one word was to commit to a single path when the maze contains thousands.

Tell us, Goddess, about the wild temper of Achilles, son of Peleus.

Not good enough.

Speak, Calliope, about the outrage of Peleus's boy.

Worse.

Tell the people, Muses, why Peleus's kid Achilles was so fucking furious.

In the year following his return, Zeno sends a dozen letters to Rex, adhering strictly to questions regarding translation—imperative or infinitive? accusative or genitive?—ceding all romantic ground to Hillary. He sneaks the letters out of the house inside his shirt and mails them before work, cheeks burning as he slips them into the box. Then he waits for weeks, but Rex's replies do not come quickly or regularly, and Zeno loses whatever bravery he began with. The gods on Olympus, sipping from their cups of horn, peer through the roof of the house and watch him struggle at his desk, mockery on their faces.

The vanity of assuming that Rex might have wanted him in that way. An orphan, a coward, a snowplow driver with a cardboard suitcase and a polyester suit: Who was Zeno to expect anything?

He learns of Rex's death from Hillary in an airmail letter written in purple cursive. Rex, Hillary reports, was in Egypt, working with his beloved papyrus, trying to claw back one more sentence from oblivion, when he had a heart attack.

You were, Hillary writes, *very dear to him*. His huge, loopy signature takes up half the page.

Seasons tick past. Zeno wakes in the afternoons, dresses in the cramped upstairs room, creaks downstairs, rouses Mrs. Boydstun from her nap. Puts her in her chair, brushes her hair, feeds her dinner, wheels her to her puzzle, pours her two fingers of Old Forester. Turns on the television. Takes the note from the counter: *Beef, onions, lipstick, buy the right red this time*. Before he leaves for work, he carries her to her bed.

Tantrums, doctor's appointments, therapies, a dozen drives to and from the specialist's office in Boise—he sits with her through it all. Still he sleeps upstairs in the little brass bed, Rex's *Compendium of Lost Books* and the Liddell and Scott entombed in a cardboard box beneath his desk. Some mornings, on the way home from work, he eases his plow to the side of the road and watches light seep into the valley, and it's all he can do to get himself to drive the final mile home. In the last weeks of her life, Mrs. Boydstun's coughs go submarine, as though she carries lakewater in her chest. He wonders if she'll share any last words, any memories of his father, any insight into their relationship, if she'll call him son or say she's grateful for his years of care, grateful that she became his guardian, or show any sign that she understands his predicaments, but at the end she's hardly there: just morphine and glassy eyes and an odor that carries him back to Korea.

On the day she dies he steps outside while the hospice nurse makes the necessary calls and hears a trickling and purring: roof draining, trees waking, swallows swooping, the mountains stirring, mumbling, buzzing, shifting. The melting world full of noise.

He removes every curtain in the house. Tugs the antimacassars off the chairs, dumps the potpourri, pours out the bourbon. Takes every rosy-cheeked porcelain child off every shelf, inters them in boxes, and deposits the boxes at the thrift shop.

He adopts a silver-muzzled sixty-five-pound brindle dog named Luther, walks him through the front door of the house, dumps a can of beef and barley stew into a bowl, and watches Luther engulf it. Then the dog sniffs around his surroundings as though in disbelief at his reversal of fortune.

Finally he yanks the discolored lace runner off the dining room table, retrieves the cardboard box from upstairs, and arranges his books across the old ring-stained walnut. He pours a cup of coffee and unwraps a new legal pad from Lakeport Drug and Luther curls up on top of his feet and lets off a ten-second sigh.

Of all the mad things we humans do, Rex once told him, there might be nothing more humbling, or more noble, than trying to translate the dead languages. We don't know how the old Greeks sounded when they spoke; we can scarcely map their words onto ours; from the very start, we're doomed to fail. But in the attempt, Rex said, in trying to drag something across the river from the murk of history into our time, into our language: that was, he said, the best kind of fool's errand.

Zeno sharpens his pencil and tries again.

THE ARGOS

MISSION YEAR 64

DAY 276 INSIDE VAULT ONE

Konstance

Behind her the line of traffic remains backed up for all eternity along the lakefront. The faceless kids in tank tops remain frozen mid-stride on the corner. But in front of her, things inside the Atlas are moving: the sky above the owl-shaped book drop box becomes a seething, swirling mat of silver, and snowflakes are tumbling out of it.

She takes a step forward. Unruly juniper hedges rise on either side of a snow-covered walk, and at the far end, a dilapidated, light-blue two-story gingerbread Victorian house shimmers into place. The porch leans, the chimney looks crooked; a blue *OPEN* sign flickers to life in a front window.

"Sybil, what is this?"

Sybil does not answer. A sign, partially buried in snow, reads:

Public Library

Everything behind her in Lakeport remains the same: static, summery, locked in place, the way the Atlas always is. But here, at the corner of Lake and Park, beyond the book drop box, it's winter.

Snow collects on the junipers; snowflakes blow into her eyes; the wind carries the taste of steel. As she heads up the walk, she hears her feet crunch in the snow; she leaves footprints behind her. She climbs five granite steps to the porch. In the glass in the top half of the front door is a sign in child's handwriting:

TOMORROW
ONE NITE ONLY
CLOUD CUCKOO LAND

The door creaks as it opens. Straight ahead is a desk with pink paper hearts taped to it. A day calendar reads *February 20, 2020*. A framed needlepoint says: *Questions Answered Here*. One arrow points left to Fiction, another points right to Nonfiction.

"Sybil, is this a game?"

No reply.

On three antediluvian computer monitors, green-blue spirals drill ever-deeper. A leak, seeping through a stained ceiling tile, falls into a plastic trash can half full of water. Plip. Plop. Plip.

"Sybil?"

Nothing. On the *Argos* Sybil is everywhere; she can hear you in every compartment at every hour; never in Konstance's life has she called to Sybil and not received a reply. Is it possible that Sybil does not know where she is? That Sybil does not know this exists inside the Atlas?

The spines of the shelved books give off an odor of yellowing paper. She opens a hand beneath the dripping leak and feels the drops strike her palm.

Halfway down the center aisle a sign says, *CHILDREN'S SEC-TION*, with an arrow pointing up. Legs trembling, Konstance climbs the stairs. The landing at the top is blocked by a golden wall. Written across it in what Konstance thinks might be classical Greek are the words:

Ὦ ξένε, ὅστις εἶ, ἄνοιξον, ἵνα μάθῃς ἃ θαυμάζεις

Below the writing waits a little arched door. The air smells of lilacs, mint, and roses: a smell like Farm 4 on its best, most fragrant day.

She steps through the door. On the other side paper clouds on strings glitter above thirty folding chairs, and the entire far wall is covered by a painted backdrop of a cloud city, birds swinging around its towers. From all around her comes the babble of falling water, of creaking trees, of chirping songbirds. At the center of a small stage, illuminated in a shaft of light angling through the clouds, a book rests atop a plinth.

She drifts transfixed through the folding chairs and climbs onto the stage. The book is a gilded duplicate of the blue book on Father's nightstand in Scheria: the cloud city, the many-windowed towers, the whirling birds. Above the city it says, *Cloud Cuckoo Land*. Below it: *By Antonius Diogenes. Translation by Zeno Ninis.*

LAKEPORT, IDAHO

1995–2019

Zeno

He translates one book of the *Iliad*, two of the *Odyssey*, plus an admirable slice of Plato's *Republic*. Five lines on an average day, ten on a good one, scribbled onto yellow legal pads in his crimped pencil-writing and stuffed into boxes beneath the dining table. Sometimes he believes his translations are adequate. Usually he decides they're terrible. He shows them to no one.

The county gives him a plaque and a pension, Luther the big brindle dog dies a peaceful death, and Zeno adopts a terrier and names him Nestor the king of Pylos. Every morning he wakes in the little brass bed upstairs, does fifty push-ups, pulls on two pairs of Utah Woolen Mills socks, buttons up one of his two dress shirts, ties one of his four ties. Green today, blue tomorrow, the duck tie on Wednesdays, penguin tie on Thursdays. Black coffee, plain oatmeal. Then he walks to the library.

Marian, the library director, finds online videos of a seven-foot-tall professor from a Midwestern university teaching intermediate ancient Greek, and most mornings Zeno starts his day at a table beside the large-print romances—what Marian calls the Bosoms and Bottoms section—with big headphones on and the volume turned up.

Past tense literally causes him back pain, the way it flings all the verbs into the dark. Then there's the aorist tense, a tense unbound by time, that can make him want to crawl into a closet and huddle in the darkness. But at the best moments, working through the old texts, for an hour or two, the words fall away and images rise to him through the centuries—warriors in armor packed into boats; sunlight spangling on the sea; the voices of gods carried on the wind—and it's almost as though he's six years old again, in front of the fireplace with the Cunningham twins, and simultaneously adrift with Ulysses in the waves off the coast of Scheria, hearing the tide roar against the rocks.

One bright afternoon in May of 2019, Zeno is hunched over his legal pads when Marian's new hire, a children's librarian named Sharif, calls him to the welcome desk. On Sharif's computer screen floats a headline: *New Technologies Uncover Ancient Greek Tale Inside Previously Unreadable Book.*

According to the article, a crate of severely damaged medieval manuscripts, stored for centuries at the ducal library in Urbino, then moved to the Vatican Library, had long been considered illegible. A little nine-hundred-year-old goat leather codex in particular piqued the interest of scholars from time to time, but water damage, mold, and age had collaborated to fuse its pages into a solid, illegible mass.

Sharif enlarges the accompanying photo: a puckered black brick of parchment, no longer even rectangular. "Looks like a paperback soaked in a toilet for a thousand years," he says.

"Then left in a driveway for another thousand," Zeno adds.

Over the past year, the article continues, a team of conservators using multispectral scanning technology has managed to image bits of the original text. At first, speculation among scholars surged. What if the manuscript contained a lost play of Aeschylus or a scientific tract by Archimedes or an early Christian gospel? What if it were the lost comedy attributed to Homer called *The Margites*?

But today the team is announcing that they have recovered enough of the text to conclude that it is a first-century work of prose fiction titled Νεφελοκοκκυγία by the little-known writer Antonius Diogenes.

Νεφέλη, cloud; κόκκῡξ, cuckoo; Zeno knows that title. He hurries back to his table, pushes aside drifts of paper, excavates his copy of Rex's *Compendium*. Page 29. Entry 51.

> The lost Greek tale *Cloud Cuckoo Land*, by the writer
> Antonius Diogenes, relating a shepherd's journey to a

city in the sky, was probably written around the end of
the first century C.E. We know from a ninth-century
Byzantine summary of the novel that it opened with a
short prologue in which Diogenes addressed an ailing
niece and declared that he had not invented the comical
story which followed but instead discovered it in a tomb
in the ancient city of Tyre, written on twenty-four cypress
wood tablets. Part fairy tale, part fool's errand, part
science-fiction, part utopian satire, Photios's epitome
suggests it could have been one of the more fascinating of
the ancient novels.

Zeno's breath catches. He sees Athena run through the snow; he
sees Rex, angular and bent from malnutrition, scratch verses with
charcoal onto a board. θεοὶ is the gods, ἐπεκλώσαντο means they
spun, ὄλεθρον is ruin.

Better still, Rex said that day in the café, *some old comedy, some
impossible fool's journey to the ends of the earth and back. Those are
my favorites, do you know what I mean?*

Marian stands in the doorway of her office cradling a mug with
cartoon cats all over it.

Sharif says, "Is he okay?"

"I think," says Marian, "that he's happy."

He asks Sharif to print every article about the manuscript he can
find. The ink used in the codex has been traced to tenth-century
Constantinople; the Vatican Library has promised that every folio
that contains anything legible will be digitized and uploaded into
the public domain. A professor in Stuttgart predicts that Diogenes
may have been the Borges of the ancient world, preoccupied with
questions of truth and intertextuality, that the scans will reveal a new
masterpiece, a forerunner of *Don Quixote* and *Gulliver's Travels.* But
a classicist in Japan says the text is likely to be inconsequential, that
none of the surviving Greek novels, if they can even be called nov-

els, approach the literary value of classical poetry and drama. Just because something is old, she writes, doesn't guarantee that it's any good.

The first scan, labeled Folio A, is uploaded on the first Friday of June. Sharif prints it on the newly donated Ilium printer, magnified to eleven inches by seventeen, and carries it to Zeno at his table in Nonfiction. "You're going to make sense of *that*?"

It's dirty and wormholed, colonized with mold, as though fungal hyphae, time, and water have collaborated to make an erasure poem. But to Zeno it looks magical, the Greek characters seeming to glow somewhere deep beneath the page, white on black, not so much handwriting as the specter of it. He remembers when Rex's letter arrived, how at first he could not allow himself to believe that Rex had survived. Sometimes the things we think are lost are only hidden, waiting to be rediscovered.

During the first weeks of summer, as the scanned folios trickle onto the internet and out of Sharif's printer, Zeno is euphoric. Bright June light flows through the library windows and illuminates the printouts; the opening passages of Aethon's story strike him as sweet and silly and translatable; he feels he's found his project, the one thing he needs to do before he dies. In daydreams he publishes a translation, dedicates it to Rex's memory, hosts a party; Hillary travels from London with an entourage of sophisticated companions; everyone in Lakeport sees that he is more than Slow-Motion Zeno, the retired snowplow driver with the barky dog and the threadbare neckties.

But day by day his enthusiasm dims. Many of the folios remain so damaged that sentences dissolve into illegibility before they become comprehensible. Worse, the conservators report that at some point over its long history the codex must have been disbound and rebound in the wrong order, so that the intended sequence of events in Aethon's tale is no longer obvious. By July he begins to feel as if he's trying to solve one of Mrs. Boydstun's jigsaw puzzles, a third of the pieces kicked under the stove, another third missing altogether. He's too inexperienced, too undereducated, too old; his mind is not up to it.

Sheep Shagger, Fruit Punch, Pansy, Zero. Why is it so hard to transcend the identities assigned to us when we were young?

In August the library's air conditioner gives out. Zeno spends an afternoon sweating through his shirt as he agonizes over a particularly problematic folio from which at least sixty percent of the words have been effaced. Something about a hoopoe leading Aethon-the-crow to a river of cream. Something about a prick of doubt—disquietude? restlessness?—beneath his wings.

That's as far as he gets.

At closing time he gathers his books and legal pads as Sharif pushes in the chairs and Marian shuts off the lights. Outside, the air smells of wildfire smoke.

"There are professionals out there working on this," Zeno says as Sharif locks the door. "Proper translators. People with fancy degrees who actually know what they're doing."

"Could be," says Marian. "But none of them are you."

On the lake a surf boat roars past, its speakers thumping bass. A hot, silvery pressure hangs in the atmosphere. The three of them pause beside Sharif's Isuzu and Zeno feels the ghost of something moving through the heat, invisible, elusive. Over the ski mountain on the far side of the lake, a thundercloud flares blue.

"In the hospital," Sharif says, as he lights a cigarette, "before she died, my mother used to say, 'Hope is the pillar that holds up the world.'"

"Who said that?"

He shrugs. "Some days she said Aristotle, some days John Wayne. Maybe she made it up."

EIGHTEEN

IT WAS ALL SO MAGNIFICENT, YET . . .

Cloud Cuckoo Land by Antonius Diogenes, Folio Σ

. . . my feathers grew shiny and full and I flapped about eating whatever I pleased, sweets, meats, fishes—even fowls! There was no pain, no hunger, my {wings?} never throbbed, my talons never {stung?}.

. . . the nightingales gave {evening?} concerts, the warblers sang love songs in the gardens {and} no one called me dull-witted or muttonheaded or lamebrained, or spoke a cruel word at all . . .

I had flown so far, I had proven everyone wrong. Yet as I perched on my balcony and peered past the happy flocking birds, over the gates, over the ruffled edges of the clouds, down at the patchwork mud-heap of earth far below, where the cities teemed and the herds, wild and tame, drifted like dust across the plains, I wondered about my friends, and my little bed, and the ewes I'd left behind in the field. I had traveled so far, and it was all so magnificent, yet . . .

. . . still a needle of doubt pricked beneath my wing. A dark restlessness flickered within . . .

THE ARGOS

MISSION YEAR 65

DAY 325 INSIDE VAULT ONE

Konstance

Weeks have passed since Konstance discovered the little ramshackle library hidden inside the Atlas. She has painstakingly copied three-quarters of Zeno Ninis's translations—Folios Alpha through Sigma—from the golden book on the pedestal in the Children's Section onto scraps of sackcloth in the vault. More than one hundred and twenty scraps, covered with her handwriting, now blanket the floor around Sybil's tower, each alive with connections to the nights she spent in Farm 4, listening to the voice of her father.

> . . . I rubbed myself head to toe with the ointment
> Palaestra chose, took three pinches of frankincense . . .

> . . . Even if you grew wings, foolish fish, you could not fly
> to a place that is not real . . .

> . . . he that knows all that Learning ever writ, knows only
> this—that he knows nothing yet.

Tonight she sits on the edge of the cot, ink-stained and weary, as the light turns leaden. These are the hardest hours, as DayLight bleeds into NoLight. Each time she's struck anew by the silence beyond the vault, where she fears no living person has stirred for more than ten months, and the silence beyond that, beyond the walls of the *Argos*, that stretches for distances beyond human ability to comprehend them. She curls onto her side and pulls her blanket to her chin.

447

Going to sleep already, Konstance? But you have not eaten since this morning.

"I'll eat if you open the door."

As you know, I have not yet been able to determine if the contagion persists outside this vault. Since we have established that you are safe in here, I must keep the door closed.

"It seems dangerous enough in here. I'll eat if you open the door. If you don't, I'll starve myself."

It hurts me to hear you talk like this.

"You can't be hurt, Sybil. You're just a bunch of fibers inside a tube."

Your body requires nourishment, Konstance. Picture one of your favorite—

Konstance plugs her ears. Everything we have on board, the grown-ups said, is everything we will ever need. Anything we cannot solve for ourselves, Sybil will solve for us. But this was just a story they told to comfort themselves. Sybil knows everything, and yet she knows nothing. Konstance picks up the drawing she made of the city on the clouds and runs a fingertip over the dried ink. Why did she think re-creating this old book would unlock anything for her? For what reader is she making it? After she dies, won't it sit unread in this vault for eons?

I'm falling apart, she thinks, I'm ungluing. I'm a fool on a tread-mill, stumbling through the specter of a planet ten trillion kilometers behind me, searching for answers that don't exist.

From beneath the millstone of her mind, Father stands, plucks a dried leaf out of his beard, and smiles. *But what's so beautiful about a fool*, he says, *is that a fool never knows when to give up. It was Grandmom who used to say that.*

She scrambles back onto her Perambulator, touches her Vizer, hurries to a Library table. *On February 20, 2020*, she writes on a slip, *who were the five children in the Lakeport Public Library saved by Zeno Ninis?*

LAKEPORT, IDAHO

AUGUST 2019

Zeno

In late August, twin forest fires in Oregon burn a million acres each, and smoke gushes into Lakeport. The sky turns the color of putty, and anyone who steps outdoors returns smelling like a campfire. Restaurant patios close; weddings move inside; youth sports are canceled; the air is deemed too dangerous for children to play outside.

As soon as school lets out for the day, the library floods with kids with nowhere else to be. Zeno sits at his table behind his haystack of legal pads and sticky notes struggling through his translation. On the floor beside him, a redheaded girl in shorts and Wellington boots pops her chewing gum as she pages through gardening books. A few feet beyond that, a thick-chested kid with a lion's mane of blond hair is pressing the bar of the water fountain with his knee and using both hands to scoop water over his head.

Zeno shuts his eyes: a headache simmering. When he opens them, Marian is there.

"One," she says, "these fires have turned my workplace into a juvenile jamboree. Two, the window air conditioner upstairs sounds like someone force-fed it a metal sandwich. Three, Sharif went to Bergesen Hardware to buy a new one, so I've got to deal with about twenty sugar-frenzied fiends upstairs." As though on cue, a little boy rides a tattered bean bag down the stairs behind her and lands on his knees and looks up at her and grins.

"Four, as far as I can tell, you've spent the whole week trying to decide whether to call your drunken shepherd 'illiterate,' 'humble,' or 'clueless.' Some fifth graders are here for the next couple of hours, Zeno. Five of them. Would you help me?"

" 'Humble' and 'clueless' are actually quite different—"

"Show them what you're up to. Or do a magic trick, something. Please."

Before he can concoct an excuse, Marian drags the sopping child from the drinking fountain to his table.

"Alex Hess, meet Mr. Zeno Ninis. Mr. Ninis is going to show you something cool."

The boy lifts one of the big facsimile printouts from the table and a dozen of Zeno's legal pages tumble to the carpet like injured birds.

"What is this? Alien writing?"

"Looks Russian," says the redhead in the boots, standing at the table now too.

"It's Greek," says Marian, as she nudges another boy and two more girls toward Zeno's table. "A very old story. It has wizards inside whales and guard-owls that ask riddles and a city in the clouds where every wish comes true and even"—Marian lowers her voice and glances dramatically over one shoulder—"fishermen who have tree-penises."

Two of the girls giggle. Alex Hess smirks. Drops of water fall from his hair and strike the page.

Twenty minutes later five kids sit in a ring around Zeno's table, each studying a facsimile of a different folio. A girl with a bob that looks as if it was cut by a weed-whacker raises her hand, then immediately starts talking. "So okay from what you're saying, this Ethan guy has all these insane adventures—"

"Aethon."

"Should be Ethan," says Alex Hess. "Easier."

"—and his story gets written down a zillion years ago on twenty-four wooden tablet-thingys, which are buried with his body when he's dead? Which are then discovered, centuries later, in a graveyard by Dyed-Jeans? And he recopies the whole story onto like hundreds of pieces of paper—"

"Papyrus."

"—and mails it to his niece who's like dying?"

"Right," says Zeno, bewildered and excited and enervated all at once. "Though you should remember there wasn't really mail, not as we understand it. If there was a niece at all, Diogenes probably gave his scrolls to a trusted friend, who—"

"Then that copy somehow got copied in Constant-a-wherever, and *that* copy got lost for like another zillion years, only it just got re-found in Italy, but it's still a big mess because a ton of words are missing?"

"You've got it exactly."

A slight boy named Christopher squirms in his chair. "So switching all this old writing into English is really hard, and you only have pieces of the story, and you don't even know what order they go in?"

Rachel the redhead turns her facsimile this way and that. "And the pieces you do have look like somebody smeared Nutella all over them."

"Right."

"So like," asks Christopher, "why?"

All the children look at him: Alex; Rachel; little Christopher; Olivia, the girl with the weed-whacker bob; and a quiet girl with brown eyes, brown skin, brown clothes, and jet-black hair named Natalie.

Zeno says, "You ever see a superhero movie? Where the hero keeps getting beat up and it always seems like he—"

"Or she," says Olivia.

"—or she will never make it? That's what these fragments are: superheroes. Try to imagine the epic battles they survived over the last two thousand years: floods, fires, earthquakes, failed governments, thieves, barbarians, zealots, who knows what else? We know that somehow a copy of this text made it to a scribe in Constantinople nine or ten centuries after it was first written, and all we know about him—"

"Or her," says Olivia.

"—is this tidy handwriting, leaning slightly to the left. But now the few people who can make sense of that old writing have a chance to breathe life back into these superheroes so that maybe they can do battle for a few more decades. Erasure is always stalking us, you know? So to hold in your hands something that has evaded it for so long—"

He wipes his eyes, embarrassed.

Rachel runs her fingers over the faint lines of text in front of her. "It's like Ethan."

"Aethon," says Olivia.

"The fool you were telling us about. In the story? Even though he keeps going the wrong way, keeps getting turned into the wrong thing, he never gives up. He survives."

Zeno looks at her, some new understanding seeping into his consciousness.

"Tell us some more," says Alex, "about the fishermen with the tree-penises."

That night, at his dining table, with Nestor the king of Pylos curled at his feet, Zeno lays out his legal pads. Everywhere he looks he sees the inadequacies of his early attempts. He was too concerned about recognizing clever allusions, steering clear of syntactical reefs, getting every word right. But whatever this strange old comedy was, it wasn't proper or elevated or concerned with getting things right. It was a story intended to bring comfort to a dying girl. All those academic commentaries he forced himself to read—*was Diogenes writing lowbrow comedy or elaborate metafiction?*—in the face of five fifth graders, smelling of chewing gum, sweaty socks, and wildfire smoke, those debates flew out the window. Diogenes, whoever he was, was primarily trying to make a machine that captured attention, something to slip the trap.

A great weight slides away. He brews coffee, unwraps a new legal pad, sets Folio β in front of him. *Word gap wordwordword gap*

gap word—they're just marks on the skin of a long-dead goat. But beneath them, something crystallizes.

> I am Aethon, a simple shepherd from Arkadia, and
> the tale I have to tell is so ludicrous, so incredible, that
> you'll never believe a word of it—and yet, it's true. For
> I, the one they called birdbrain and nincompoop—yes,
> I, dull-witted muttonheaded lamebrained Aethon—
> once traveled all the way to the edge of the earth and
> beyond . . .

THE ARGOS

MISSION YEAR 65

DAY 325–DAY 340 INSIDE VAULT ONE

Konstance

The slip of paper settles onto the table.

Christopher Dee
Olivia Ott
Alex Hess
Natalie Hernandez
Rachel Wilson

One of the children held hostage in the Lakeport Public Library on February 20, 2020, was Rachel Wilson. Her great-grandmother. That's why the book of Zeno's translations was on Father's night table. His grandmother was in the play.

If Zeno Ninis doesn't save Rachel Wilson's life on February 20, 2020, then her father is never born. He never signs up for the *Argos*. Konstance doesn't exist.

I had traveled so far, and it was all so magnificent, yet . . .

Who was Rachel Wilson and how many years did she live and how did she feel every time she looked at that book, translated by Zeno Ninis? Did she ever sit in the windswept evenings in Nannup with Konstance's father and read to him from Aethon's story? Konstance stands, walks laps around the table in the atrium, certain now that she is missing something else. Something hidden right in front of her eyes. Some other thing that Sybil does not know. She summons the Atlas off its shelf. First to Lagos, to the downtown plaza near the gulf, where brilliant white hotels soar above her on three sides, and forty coconut palms grow from black-and-white checkered planters. *Welcome*, says the sign, *to the New Intercontinental.*

Around and around Konstance paces through the unchanging

Nigerian sunlight. Again the sensation descends on her, gnawing the edges of her consciousness: something is not right. The scars on the trunks of the palms, the old dry leaf sheaths still stuck to the bases of the fronds, the coconuts high above her and the ones tumbled down in the planters: none of the coconuts, she realizes, have the three germination pores Father showed her. Two eyes and a mouth, the face of a little sailor whistling its way around the world—it's not there.

The trees are computer-generated. They weren't originally there.

She remembers Mrs. Flowers standing at the base of the Theodosian Walls in Constantinople. *Wander around in here long enough, dear,* she said, *and you'll discover a secret or two.*

Twenty paces away, a vendor's bicycle with a white barrow mounted in front of the handlebars leans against one of the planters. On the barrow cartoon owls hold ice cream cones. Inside its open receptacle, a dozen canned drinks shine in a bed of ice. The ice glimmers; the cartoon owls seem to almost blink. Like the book drop box in Lakeport, it's more vibrant than everything else around it.

She reaches for one of the drinks and, rather than pass through it, her fingertips strike something solid, cold, and wet. When she lifts the drink out of the ice, a thousand windows shatter silently in the hotels around her. The tiles of the plaza strip away; the false palm trees evaporate.

All around her figures appear, people sitting or standing or lying not in a shady city plaza but on broken and begrimed concrete: some without shirts, more without shoes, living skeletons, some tucked so deeply within homemade tents of blue tarpaulins that she can see only their calves and mud-caked feet.

Old tires. Trash. Sludge. Several men sit on plastic jugs that once contained a drink called SunShineSix; a woman waves an empty rice sack; a dozen emaciated children crouch over a patch of dust. Nothing moves the way things moved after she touched the book drop box outside the old library in Lakeport; the people are only static images and her hands pass through them as if through shadows.

She bends, tries to see into the blurry patches of the children's faces. What is happening to them? Why were they hidden?

Next she returns to the jogging trail on the outskirts of Mumbai she found a year ago, the heavy green of the mangroves running alongside her like an ominous wall. Up and down the railing she trots, a half mile up, a half mile down, until she finds it: a little owl painted on the sidewalk. She touches the owl and the mangroves tear away and a wall of red-brown water, full of debris and garbage, gushes into place. It obliterates the people, submerges the path, rides up the sides of the apartment towers. Boats are tethered to second-floor balconies; someone is frozen atop the roof of a submerged car, her arms raised for help, her scream blurred off her face.

Queasy, quaking, Konstance whispers, "Nannup." She rises; the Earth pivots, inverts, and she drops. A once-quaint little Australian cattle town. The faded banners strung across the roadway read,

DO YOUR PART
DEFEAT DAY ZERO
YOU CAN DO WITH 10 LITRES A DAY

In front of the public hall, shaded by cabbage trees, the begonias stand sprightly in their boxes. The grass looks as green as ever: five shades greener than anything for thirty miles. The fountain sparkles; the bright-blooming trees stand proud. But as with the plaza in Lagos, as with the jogging trail outside Mumbai, something feels altered.

Three times Konstance laps the block, and eventually, on a side door of the public hall, she finds it: a graffiti owl with a gold chain around its neck and a crown cocked on its head.

She touches it. The grass bakes brown, the trees fly apart, the paint on the public hall flakes off, and the water in the fountain evaporates. A tractor trailer with a six-thousand-gallon water tank shimmers into place, a ring of armed men around it, and beyond that a line of dusty vehicles stretches into the distance.

Hundreds of people holding empty jugs and cans press against a chainlink barricade. The Atlas cameras have caught a man with a machete leaping from the top of the barrier, his mouth open; a soldier is in the process of firing his weapon; several people sprawl on the ground.

At the spigot on the water truck, two men tug at the same plastic jug, every tendon in their arms standing out. She sees, among the bodies against the chainlink, mothers and grandmothers carrying babies.

This. This is why Father left.

By the time she climbs off the Perambulator, it's DayLight in the vault. She limps through her scraps of sackcloth and disconnects the water line from the food printer and puts it in her mouth. Her hands shake. Her socks have finally disintegrated, all holes becoming one, and two of her toes are bleeding.

You just walked seven miles, Konstance, says Sybil. *If you don't sleep and eat a proper meal, I will restrict your Library access.*

"I will, I'll eat, I'll rest. I promise." She remembers Father working among his plants one day, adjusting a mister, then letting the water spray the back of his hand. "Hunger," he said, and she had the sense that he was speaking not to her but to the plants, "after a little while you can forget about hunger. But thirst? The worse it gets, the more you think about it."

She sits on the floor and examines a bleeding toe and remembers Mother's stories about Crazy Elliot Fischenbacher, the boy who wandered the Atlas until his feet cracked and then his sanity too. Crazy Elliot Fischenbacher, who tried to hack through the skin of the *Argos*, imperiling everyone and everything. Who saved enough SleepDrops to take his own life.

She eats, cleans her face, brushes a mat out of her hair, does her grammar and physics, whatever Sybil asks. The Library atrium looks bright and serene. The marble floor gleams as though it has been polished overnight.

When she has finished her studies she sits at a table and Mrs. Flowers's little dog curls at her feet. With trembling fingers Konstance writes: *How was the Argos constructed?*

From the flocks of books, registers, and charts that come wheeling around the table, she weeds out all the documents that were sponsored by the Ilium Corporation: glossy schematics on nuclear pulse propulsion technology; materials analyses; artificial gravity; compartment designs; spreadsheets exploring carrying capacity; plans for water treatment systems; diagrams of food printers; images of the ship's modules being prepared for assembly in low Earth orbit; hundreds of booklets detailing how the crew would be handpicked, transported, quarantined, trained for six months, and sedated for launch.

Hour by hour, the multitude of documents dwindles. Konstance can find no independent reports evaluating the feasibility of constructing an interstellar ark in space and propelling it at sufficient speed to reach Beta Oph2 in 592 years. Each time a writer begins to question whether the technologies are ready, if the thermal systems will be adequate, how a human crew might be shielded from prolonged deep-space radiation, how gravity would be simulated, whether the costs can be managed or the laws of physics can support a mission like this, the documents go blank. Academic papers cut off mid-sentence. Chapter numbers jump from two to six or four to nine, nothing in between.

For the first time since her Library Day, Konstance summons the catalogue of known exoplanets off its shelf. Page after page, row after row of the known worlds beyond Earth, their little images rotating on the pages: pink, maroon, brown, blue. She runs her finger down the line to Beta Oph2 where it slowly rotates in place. Green. Black. Green. Black.

4.0113×10^{13} kilometers. 4.24 light-years.

Konstance gazes out into the echoing atrium, feeling as though millions of thread-thin cracks radiate invisibly through it. She takes a slip of paper. Writes: *Where was the crew of the Argos gathered before launch?*

A single slip of paper drops from the sky:

Qaanaaq

Inside the Atlas she descends slowly over the north coast of Greenland: three thousand meters, two thousand. Qaanaaq is a treeless harbor village trapped between the sea and hundreds of square miles of moraine sediment. Picturesque little houses—many slumped from being built on thawing permafrost—have been painted green, bright blue, mustard yellow, with white window frames. Along the coastline, among the rocks, lies a marina, some docks, a few boats, and a tumult of construction equipment.

It takes her days to solve it. She eats, sleeps, submits to Sybil's lessons, searches, searches again, roaming outward in circles from Qaanaaq, skimming the sea. Finally, in a region of Baffin Bay eight miles from the town, on a bare island, all rock and lichen, a place that was probably covered by ice only a decade before, she finds it: a lone red house that looks like a child's drawing of a barn with a white flagpole out front. At the base of the flagpole stands a little wooden owl no taller than her thigh, looking as if it were sleeping.

Konstance walks up, touches it, and its eyes flip open.

Long concrete piers reach into the sea. A fifteen-foot fence, topped with razor wire, grows out of the ground behind the little red house, and wraps itself around the entire circumference of the island.

No Trespassing, read signs in four languages. *Property of Ilium Corporation. Keep Out.*

Behind the fence stretches a vast industrial complex: cranes, trailers, trucks, mountains of construction materials piled among rocks. She walks as much of the fence line as the software will permit, then rises and hovers above it. She sees cement trucks, figures in hard hats, a boat shelter, a rock road: in the center of the complex is a huge white circular half-finished structure with no windows.

Handpicked, transported, quarantined, trained for six months, sedated for launch.

They are constructing the thing that will become the *Argos*. But there are no rockets; there is no launchpad. The ship wasn't assembled in modules in space: it never went to space at all. It's on Earth.

She is looking at the past, images taken seven decades before, then redacted from the Atlas by the Ilium Corporation. But she is also looking at herself. Her home. All these years. She touches her Vizer, steps off the Perambulator, a whirlwind turning inside her.

Sybil says, *Did you have a nice walk, Konstance?*

NINETEEN

AETHON MEANS BLAZING

Cloud Cuckoo Land by Antonius Diogenes, Folio T

. . . I said, "Why do the others {seem?} content to fly about, singing and eating, day after day, bathed by the warm zephyrs, soaring round the towers, yet inside me this {sickness?} . . ."

. . . the hoopoe, vice-undersecretary to the viceroy of Provisions and Accommodations, swallowed his beakful of sardines and flared his feathered crown.

He said, "You sound an awful lot like a human right now."

I said, "I'm not human, sir, dear me, don't be ridiculous. I'm a humble crow. Why just look at me."

"Well," he said, "here's an idea, to rid yourself of this {restless mortal affliction?}, travel to the palace at {the center?} . . .

". . . a garden there, brighter and greener than every other, and inside the goddess keeps a book containing {all the knowledge of the gods}. Inside you just might find what you . . ."

LAKEPORT, IDAHO

AUGUST 2019–FEBRUARY 2020

Seymour

The instructions say to use a Tor browser to download a secure messaging platform called Pryva-C. He has to load several updates to get it to work. Days pass before he receives a response.

MATHILDA: thank u 4 reaching out sry for delay just needed
SEEMORE6: ur with bishop? at his camp?
MATHILDA: to verify
MATHILDA: ur not with authorities
SEEMORE6: not I swear
SEEMORE6: want 2 help want 2 join fight
MATHILDA: i have been assigned to u
SEEMORE6: want 2 break machine

At the end of the summer, a hurricane shatters two Caribbean islands, drought squeezes Somalia, the global monthly average temperature breaks another record, an intergovernmental report announces that ocean temperatures have risen four times faster than anyone expected, and the smoke from two separate megafires in Oregon rides eastward currents into Lakeport, where it collects in shapes that look to Seymour, in the satellite images on his tablet, very much like whirlpools.

He has not seen Janet since he smashed the big side window of the RV at the marina and ran. As far as he knows, she didn't call the police; if the police somehow found her, he doesn't think she told them about him. All summer he avoids the library, avoids the lakefront, works at the ice rink cleaning locker rooms and stocking sodas with the drawstring of his hoodie pulled tight. Other than that he stays in his bedroom.

> MATHILDA: they say eighty dead in the flooding what they don't count is how many depressed, how many PTSD, how many have no $ to relocate, how many will die from mold, how many
> SEEMORE6: wait which floods
> MATHILDA: will die of broken hearts
> SEEMORE6: the smoke here is v bad today
> MATHILDA: in the future they will look back and marvel at how we lived
> SEEMORE6: not us tho? not you & me?
> MATHILDA: our complacency
> SEEMORE6: not the warriors?

In September collection agencies ring Bunny's phone three times a day. The poor air quality keeps Labor Day tourists away; the marina is practically deserted, the restaurants empty; tips at the Pig N' Pancake are nonexistent, and Bunny can't find hours to replace the ones she lost when the Aspen Leaf closed.

Some swivel in Seymour has locked: he can no longer see the planet as anything but dying, and everyone around him complicit in the killing. The people in the Eden's Gate houses fill their trash cans and pilot SUVs between their two homes and play music on Bluetooth speakers in their backyards and tell themselves they're good people, conducting honorable, decent lives, living the so-called dream—as though America were an Eden where God's warm benevolence fell equally across every soul. When in truth they're participating in a pyramid scheme that's chewing up everybody at the bottom, people like his mother. And they're all congratulating themselves for it.

MATHILDA: sorry im late we only use terminals at night when chores are done

SEEMORE6: what chores

MATHILDA: planting pruning cutting hauling harvesting preparing pickling

SEEMORE6: vegetables?

MATHILDA: ya super fresh

SEEMORE6: don't rly love vegetables

MATHILDA: tonight all the trees are standing up big and straight around camp so beautiful

MATHILDA: sky purple like eggplant

SEEMORE6: another vegetable

MATHILDA: ha u r funny

SEEMORE6: where do u sleep? tents

MATHILDA: tents ya also cabins barracks

MATHILDA: . . .

SEEMORE6: u still there

MATHILDA: they just said I could have ten xtra minutes

MATHILDA: because u are special u are important u have promise

SEEMORE6: me?

MATHILDA: ya not just to them to me

MATHILDA: to every1

SEEMORE6: . . .

MATHILDA: night birds flying over greenhouse creek trickling full tummy good feeling

SEEMORE6: wish I was there

MATHILDA: u will love it even the veggies ha ha

MATHILDA: we have showerhouse rec room armory plus beds are comfy too

SEEMORE6: real beds or sleeping bags

MATHILDA: both

SEEMORE6: is it like boys in one place girls in other?

MATHILDA: its whatever we want we don't follow the old ways

MATHILDA: u will see
MATHILDA: soon as u do your task

During classes his eyes cloud with visions of Bishop's camp. White
tents beneath dark trees, machine-gun nests atop stockades, gardens
and greenhouses, solar panels, men and women in fatigues singing
songs, telling tales, mysterious brewmasters brewing healthy elixirs
from forest herbs. Always the imagination rotates back to Mathilda:
her wrists, her hair, the intersection of her thighs. She comes down a
path carrying two pails of berries; she is blond, she is Japanese, Serbian, a Fijian skin diver with ammunition belts crisscrossing over
her breasts.

MATHILDA: u will feel so much better after you act
SEEMORE6: all the girls here are clueless
SEEMORE6: none of them get me
MATHILDA: u will feel so much power
SEEMORE6: none of them r like u

He looks it up: *Maht* means might, *Hild* means battle, *Mathilda*
means might in battle, and after that Mathilda becomes an eight-
foot-tall huntress moving silently through a forest. He leans back in
bed, the edge of the tablet warm on his lap; Mathilda stoops through
his doorway, props her bow against the door. Bougainvillea for a
belt, roses in her hair, she blocks out the ceiling light and wraps one
leafy hand around his groin.

Zeno

By mid-September Alex, Rachel, Olivia, Natalie, and Christopher want to transform the *Cloud Cuckoo Land* fragments into a play, dress up in costumes, and perform it. Rain falls, the smoke clears, the air quality improves, and still the children walk to the library on Tuesdays and Thursdays after school and gather around his table. These are the kids, he realizes, without club volleyball or math tutors or boat slips at the marina. Olivia's parents run a church; Alex's dad is searching for a job in Boise; Natalie's parents work days and nights in a restaurant; Christopher is one of six kids; and Rachel is visiting the U.S. for a year while her Australian father does something involving fire mitigation at the local office of the Idaho Department of Lands.

Every minute he's with them, Zeno learns. Earlier in the summer, all he could focus on was what he didn't know, how much of Diogenes's text wasn't there. But now he sees that he doesn't have to research every known detail about ancient Greek sheepherding or master every idiom of the Second Sophistic. He just needs the suggestions of story offered by what remains on the folios, and the children's imaginations will do the rest.

For the first time in decades, maybe for the first time since the days with Rex in Camp Five, sitting knee-to-knee beside the fire in the kitchen shed, he feels fully awake, as though the curtains have been ripped off the windows of his mind: what he wants to do is here, right in front of him.

• • •

One Tuesday in October, all five fifth graders sit around his little library table. Christopher and Alex engulf donut holes from a carton that Marian has produced from somewhere; Rachel, rail-thin, in her boots and jeans, leans over a legal pad, scribbling, erasing, scribbling again. By now Natalie, who barely spoke for the first three weeks, talks practically nonstop. "So after this whole journey," she says, "Aethon answers the riddle, gets through the gates, drinks from the rivers of wine and cream, eats apples and peaches, even honeycakes, whatever those are, and the weather is always great, and no one is mean to him, and he's still unhappy?"

Alex chews another donut hole. "Yeah, that sounds crazy."

"You know what?" says Christopher. "In my Cloud Cuckoo Land? Instead of rivers of wine, there'd be root beer. And all that fruit would be candy."

"So much candy," says Alex.

"Infinity Starburst," says Christopher.

"Infinity Kit Kats."

Natalie says, "In my Cloud Cuckoo Land? Animals would be treated the same as people."

"Also no homework," says Alex. "And no strep throat."

"But," says Christopher, "the Super Magical Extra Powerful Book of Everything in the garden at the center? That would still be in my Cloud Cuckoo Land. That way you could just read, like, one book for five minutes and know everything."

Zeno leans over the mound of papers on the desk. "Have I told you kids what Aethon means?"

They shake their heads; he writes αἴθων across an entire sheet of paper. "Blazing," he says. "Burning, fiery. Some say it can mean hungry too."

Olivia sits down. Alex puts a fresh donut hole in his mouth.

"Maybe that's it," says Natalie. "Why he never gives up. Why he can't settle down. He's always burning inside."

Rachel looks off over the table, her eyes faraway. "In my Cloud Cuckoo Land," she says, "there'd be no droughts. Rain would fall every night. Green trees for as far as you could see. Big cold creeks."

They spend a Tuesday in December at the thrift store hunting for costumes, a Thursday making a donkey head, a fish head, and a hoopoe head from papier-mâché. Marian orders black and gray feathers so they can construct wings; everybody cuts out clouds from cardboard. Natalie collects sound effects on her laptop; Zeno hires a carpenter to construct a plywood stage and wall, offsite and in pieces, so he can surprise them. Soon there are only two Thursdays left and there's still so much to do, an ending to write, scripts to make, folding chairs to rent; he remembers how Athena the dog, when she sensed they were going down to the water, would vibrate with excitement: it was like lightning was ripping through her body. This is how it feels every night as he tries to sleep, his thoughts ranging across mountains and oceans, weaving through stars, his brain a lantern inside his skull, blazing.

At 6 a.m. on the twentieth of February, Zeno does his push-ups, pulls on two pairs of Utah Woolen Mills socks, ties his penguin tie, drinks a cup of coffee, and walks to Lakeport Drug, where he makes five photocopies of the latest version of the script and buys a case of root beer. He crosses Lake Street, scripts in one hand, soda in the other. A silver-blue sky is braced over the snow-mantled lake, and the high ridges are lost in clouds—storm coming.

Marian's Subaru is already in the library parking lot and a single upstairs window is illuminated. Zeno climbs the five granite steps to the porch and stops to catch his breath. For a split second he's six years old, shivering and lonely, and two librarians open the door.

Why, you don't look warm at all.

Where is your mother?

The front door is unlocked. He climbs the stairs to the second floor and pauses outside the golden plywood wall. Stranger, whoever you are, open this to learn what will amaze you.

When he opens the little door, light spills through the arched doorway. Atop the stage, Marian stands on a step stool, touching a brush to the gold and silver towers of her backdrop. He watches her climb off the stool to examine her work, then climb back on, dip her brush, and add three more birds swinging around a tower. The smell of fresh paint is strong. Everything is quiet.

To be eighty-six years old and feel this.

Seymour

Just as the first snows stick to the ridges above town, Idaho Power shuts off the electricity to the double-wide. The propane tank in the front yard is still one-third full, so Bunny heats the house by turning on the oven and leaving its door open. Seymour charges his tablet at the ice rink, and gives his mother most of the money he makes.

> MATHILDA: cold tonite been thinking of u
> SEEMORE6: cold here 2
> MATHILDA: when its dark like this I want to take off clothes run outside feel air on my skin
> MATHILDA: then get back in bed all cozy
> SEEMORE6: rly?
> MATHILDA: u have 2 hurry have 2 get here i can hardly stand it
> MATHILDA: have 2 come up with ur task

On Christmas morning Bunny sits him at the kitchen table. "I'm giving in, Possum. I'm going to sell. Find a place to rent. After next year, you'll be off, and I don't need a whole acre to myself."

Behind her the gas whooshes blue inside the open oven.

"I know this place has been important to you, maybe more important than I realize. But it's time now. They're hiring a housekeeper at the Sachse Inn, a longer drive, I know, but it's a job. If I'm lucky, between the job and the house sale, I can pay off all this debt and have enough left over to get my teeth fixed. Maybe even help with college."

Out the sliding door the lights of the townhomes flicker behind an icy fog. A terrible sensitivity has been building inside Seymour: a hundred voices in the basement of his head speaking all at once. Eat this, wear this, you're inadequate, you don't belong, your pain will go away if you purchase this right now. See-More Stool-Guy, ha ha. Out there, in the ground beneath the toolshed, waits Pawpaw's old Beretta and his crate of hand grenades, nestled in their five-by-five grids. If he holds his breath, he can hear the grenades rattling lightly in their places.

Bunny sets her palms flat on the table. "You're going to do something special with your life, Seymour. I know it."

He stands in the night in his windbreaker at the corner of Lake and Park. Christmas lights dot the gutters of the Eden's Gate showroom at perfectly spaced intervals. Black cameras have been mounted under the eaves, and stickers shaped like badges gleam in the bottom corners of windows, and complicated-looking locks protect the front and rear gates.

Security systems. Alarms. Getting in there and leaving something behind without being noticed is not feasible. But the west side of the realty office and the east side of the library, he observes, are less than four feet apart. In the space between, there's hardly room for a gas meter and a frozen stripe of snow. Smuggling an explosive into the realty office might be impossible. But the library?

SEEMORE6: I came up with a spot
MATHILDA: a target?
SEEMORE6: a task, my way 2 disrupt machine 2 help wake people
    up begin real change
MATHILDA: what have you
SEEMORE6: 2 earn my way 2 the camp

MATHILDA: come up with?

SEEMORE6: 2 u

The PDF Mathilda sends via Pryva-C is full of typos and klutzy diagrams. But the concept is plain: fuses, pressure cookers, prepaid phones, everything duplicated in case the first bomb fails. He buys one pressure cooker at Lakeport Drug and a second at Ridley's and two padlock hasps at Bergesen Hardware and mounts these to the inside of his bedroom door and to the door of the toolshed.

Unscrewing the grenades is easier than he imagined. The explosive filler inside looks harmless, like little blond flakes of quartz. He uses an old letter scale of Pawpaw's: twenty ounces into each cooker.

He keeps going to school. Keeps mopping floors at the rink. All his life a prologue and now it's finally going to begin.

In early February he is charging three prepaid Alcatel Tracfones behind the skate-rental counter when he looks up to see Janet in her denim jacket.

"Hi."

New frog patches line her sleeves. Her hat is the kind of wool that looks so soft that you never want to take it off, the kind he has never had. She has the tanned cheekbones of a skier and looking at her he feels as if he has matured a decade since tenth grade, as if the Janet Infatuation was an era humans lived through a thousand years ago.

She says, "I haven't seen you."

Act normal. Everything is normal.

"I never told anyone what you did. If you're wondering."

He glances at the soda machine, the skates in their cubbies. Better not to say anything.

"Eighteen kids showed up last week to EAC, Seymour. I thought you might want to know. We got the cafeteria to reduce food waste, and it's all bamboo napkins, now, bamboo is like regrowable, or what's the word?"

"Sustainable."

Out on the ice teenagers in sweatshirts laugh as they glide past the safety glass. Fun: all anyone cares about.

"Yeah, sustainable. We're driving to Boise for a sit-in on the fifteenth. You could come, Seymour. People are starting to pay attention." She smiles a lopsided smile and her blue-black eyes are on him but she has no power over him anymore.

SEEMORE6: i made 2 from the instructions u sent

MATHILDA: 2 pies

SEEMORE6: ha yeah 2 pies

MATHILDA: these pies how do they get cooked

SEEMORE6: prepaid phones, pie cooks on the fifth ring just like on the PDF

MATHILDA: 2 different numbers? one for each?

SEEMORE6: 2 pies 2 phones 2 different numbers like the instructions

SEEMORE6: though as soon as first pie gets cooked the other will also

MATHILDA: when?

SEEMORE6: soon

SEEMORE6: maybe thursday, storm in forecast, was thinking less people would be out

MATHILDA: . . .

SEEMORE6: u still there?

MATHILDA: message me the 2 numbers

On Wednesday he comes home from school to find Bunny packing boxes in the living room by flashlight. She looks up at him, tipsy, nervous.

"Sold. We sold it."

Seymour thinks of the cookers, packed with Composition B, under the bench in the toolshed and eels go swimming through his guts.

"Did they—?"

"Bought it after seeing pictures online. All cash, as is. Gonna tear down the house. They just want the lot. Imagine having enough money to buy a house on your computer."

She drops her flashlight and he picks it up and hands it back and he wonders what truths are imparted unspoken between a mother and son and what truths are not.

"Can I use the car tomorrow, Mom? I'll drive you to work in the morning."

"Sure, Seymour, that'll be fine." She shines the light into a box. "Twenty-twenty," she calls as he heads down the hall. "Gonna be our year."

SEEMORE6: after pies r cooked how will I know where 2 go

MATHILDA: head north

MATHILDA: call number we gave

SEEMORE6: north

MATHILDA: yes

SEEMORE6: canada?

MATHILDA: drive north we will give instructions after

SEEMORE6: but border?

MATHILDA: u will be tremendous so brave a warrior

SEEMORE6: what if theres trouble

MATHILDA: there won't be

SEEMORE6: but in case

MATHILDA: call the number

SEEMORE6: and someone will come

MATHILDA: every1 here

SEEMORE6: nervous

MATHILDA: will be proud

MATHILDA: overjoyed

TWENTY

THE GARDEN OF THE GODDESS

Cloud Cuckoo Land by Antonius Diogenes, Folio Y

. . . I sipped from the river of wine, once for valor, twice for pluck, and flapped toward the palace at the center of the city. Its towers pierced the Zodiac, and {inside?} clear {bright?} streams ran through fragrant orchards.

. . . stood the goddess, one thousand feet tall, tending the gardens in {her kaleidoscope dress}, picking up whole plots of trees and setting them down again. Her head was circled by flocks of owls, and more owls roosted on her arms and her shoulders, and they studied their reflections in the glimmering shield strapped across her back.

. . . ahead, at her foot, surrounded by white {butterflies?} on a pedestal so ornate it must have been fashioned by the smith-god himself, I saw it: the book the hoopoe said held the {solution?} to my gnawing predicament. I fluttered above it, {prepared to read, when the goddess bent. Her great pupils loomed over me, each as big as a house. With one flick of one finger she could smite me out of the sky.}

"I see," she said, fifteen trees in each hand, "what you are, little crow. You are a pretender, a creature of clay, not a bird at all. In your heart you are still a feeble human, hammered from earth, with {the blaze of hunger inside} . . ."

". . . only wanted to {peek?} . . ."

"Read from the book all you wish," she said, "but if you read to the end you will become like us, free of desire . . .

". . . never will you be able to return to your prior form. Go on, child," said the flickering goddess. "Decide . . ."

EIGHT MILES WEST OF CONSTANTINOPLE

MAY–JUNE 1453

Omeir

A girl. A Greek girl. This fact is so startling, so unexpected, that he almost cannot recover his wits. He who wept at the castrations of Moonlight and Tree, who winced at the killing of trout and hens, has broken a branch over the head of a crop-headed fair-skinned Christian girl younger than his sister.

She lies in the leaf litter unmoving, the spitted partridge still in her hand. Her dress is filthy, her slippers hardly slippers anymore. In the starlight the blood running down her cheek looks black.

Smoke rises from the coals, frogs rasp in the dark, some clockwork inside the night advances one notch, and the girl moans. He binds her wrists with Moonlight's old halter. She moans again, then thrashes. Blood runs into her right eye; she scrambles to her knees and brings her bound wrists to her teeth; when she sees him, she screams.

Omeir glances back through the trees, frightened.

"Quiet. Please."

Is she calling to someone nearby? He was stupid to make a fire: too much of a risk. As he smothers the embers the girl howls a torrent of language he cannot understand. He tries to clap a hand over her mouth but comes away bitten.

She gets to her feet, takes several dizzy steps into the dark, then falls. Maybe she is drunk: the Greeks are always drunk, isn't that what everyone says? Half-beasts permanently inebriated on their own somatic pleasure.

Yet she is so young.

Probably it is a trick, a witch's disguise.

He tries to simultaneously listen for anyone approaching and

examine the wound on the edge of his hand. Then he takes a bite
of the partridge, the skin charred, the center raw, and the girl lies
panting in the leaves, blood still flowing down her face, and a new
thought rises: Does she guess why he is alone? Does she sense what
he has done? Why he isn't rushing into the city with the other victors
to claim his rewards?

She squirms away from him. Maybe this creature, too, is alone.
Maybe she also has abandoned some post. When he notices that
she is crawling toward an object at the base of a tree, he steps in and
takes up her sack and she riots. Inside is a little ornamental box and
a bundle wrapped in what might be silk—impossible to tell in the
dark. She rolls again to her knees, screeching curses in her language,
then emits a scream so high and plaintive that it seems more lamb
than human.

Terror rockets up his spine. "Please be quiet." He imagines her
scream traveling out through the trees in every direction: across
the dark body of water ahead, down the roads leading to the city,
directly into the ear of the sultan.

He pushes the sack closer to her and she grabs it with her bound
wrists, then staggers again. She is weak. It was hunger that drew her.

Omeir places what's left of the still-warm bird on the ground
near her and she picks it up with her teeth and eats like a dog and
in the quiet he tries to gather his thoughts. They are far too close to
the city. Any moment men, either beaten or triumphant, will come
through here on horses. She will be taken as a slave and he will be
hanged for desertion. But, he considers, if they find the two of them
together, maybe the girl can serve as a kind of shield: a prize he has
won. Maybe, traveling with her, he will draw less suspicion than if
he were alone.

Her eyes stay fixed on him as she sucks the partridge bones and
a breeze rises and the still-new leaves tremble in the darkness. As
he tears a strip from his linen shirt a memory ambushes him: of
standing with Grandfather in morning light, their trousers wet to
the knees with dew, fitting Moonlight and Tree to their first yoke.

The girl remains still and does not scream as he ties the linen over the wound on her head. Then he hitches Moonlight's lead to the halter binding her hands. "Come," he whispers. "We must go."

He puts her sack over his shoulder and pulls her by the lead as though she were a recalcitrant donkey. They pick their way around the rushes fringing a broad wetland, the girl stumbling now and then as the sun rises behind them. In the early light he finds a patch of brown-capped hog mushrooms and squats in their midst eating the caps.

He holds some out to her and she watches him for a bit, then eats as well. The bandage seems to have staunched the bleeding and the blood on her neck and throat has dried to the color of rusted iron. In the noon light they give wide berth to a burned village. A pack of five or six skeletal dogs rushes them and draws dangerously close before Omeir drives them off with stones.

By evening they traverse a landscape pocked with ruins—orchards raided, dovecotes emptied, vineyards burned. When he kneels beside creeks to drink, she does too. Just before nightfall they discover peas in a half-trampled garden and eat, and well after midnight, he finds a little hollow inside a hedgerow beside an unplanted field and secures her lead around the trunk of a cypress. She looks at him, her eyelids slipping, and he watches sleep overcome her terror.

In the moonlight he drags the sack away from her and removes the snuffbox. It's empty, smells of spice. A scene Omeir cannot quite make out is painted on the lid. A tall house beneath a sky. Perhaps it is her home?

The bundle is wrapped in dark silk, embroidered with blossoms and birds, and inside is a stack of animal skin stripped of hair, beaten flat, trimmed into rectangles, and bound along one edge. A book. Its leaves are damp and smell like fungus and their surfaces are covered with glyphs in neat lines and upon seeing them he is afraid.

He remembers a tale Grandfather once told about a book left behind by the old gods when they fled the earth. The book, Grandfather said, was locked inside a golden box, which was in turn locked inside a bronze box, then inside an iron box, inside a wooden chest, and the gods placed the chest at the bottom of a lake, and set water-dragons a hundred feet long swimming around it that not even the bravest men could kill. But if you ever could retrieve the book, Grandfather said, and read it, you would understand the languages of the birds in the sky and of the crawling things beneath the ground and if you were a spirit you would resume again the shape you had on earth.

Omeir rewraps the parcel with trembling hands and re-stores it inside the sack and studies the sleeping girl in the moon shadow. The bite mark on his hand throbs. Could she be a ghost made flesh again? Could the book she carries contain the magic of the old gods? But if her witchcraft were so powerful, why would she be alone, desperate enough to steal his partridge from his fire? Couldn't she have simply turned him into a meal and eaten him? Turned all the sultan's soldiers into beetles, for that matter, and stomped them dead?

Besides, he tries to reassure himself, Grandfather's stories were just stories.

The night wanes and he longs to be home. In another hour the sun will rise over the mountain, and his mother will pick her way through the mossy boulders to fill the kettle at the creek. Grandfather will restart the fire, and the sun will send shadows quivering through the ravine, and Nida will sigh beneath her blanket, chasing one last dream. Omeir imagines climbing into the warmth beside his sister and twining his limbs with hers as they did when they were little, and when he wakes it is late morning and the girl has untied herself and she is holding her sack and standing over him, studying the gap in his upper lip.

After that he does not bother to bind her wrists. They move north-west along undulating plains, hurrying across open fields from copse to copse, the road to Edirne occasionally coming into view far to the northeast. The wound on the girl's head no longer weeps and she seems to never tire, while Omeir has to rest every hour or so, fatigue sunk into his marrow, and sometimes as he walks he hears the creak of the wagons and the bellowing of animals, and senses Moonlight and Tree beside him, huge and docile beneath the beam of their yoke.

By their fourth morning together, they grow dangerously hungry. Even the girl stumbles every few steps and he knows they cannot go much farther without food. At midday he spies dust rising behind them and they crouch off the road in a little brake of thorns and wait.

First come two banner men, blades knocking against their saddles, the very image of conquerors returning. Then drivers with pack camels loaded with plunder: rolled carpets, bulging sacks, a torn Greek ensign. Behind the camels in loose double-file through the dust march twenty bound women and girls. One howls with grief while the others shuffle in silence, their hair uncovered, and their faces betray a wretchedness that makes Omeir look away.

Behind the women a rawboned ox pulls a wagon crowded with marble statuary: the torsos of angels; a robed and curly headed philosopher with his nose flaked off; a single enormous foot, bone white in the June light. Finally in the rear rides an archer with a shield slung across his back and a bow across his saddle, murmuring a song to himself or to his horse, looking off into the fields as they pass. Across the rump of his horse a little slain goat is tied, and seeing it, hunger vaults inside Omeir. He rises and is about to step out of the brake to call to them when he feels the girl's hand on his arm.

She sits holding her sack, arms scratched, head shorn, desperation written into every line of her face. Little brown birds rustle in the thorns above his head. She taps her chest with two fingers and stares at him, and his heart pounds, and he sits, and in another minute the wagons are past.

That afternoon rain falls. The girl clasps her bundle as she walks, trying everything she can to keep it dry. They make their way through a muddy field and find an abandoned house blackened by fire and sit starving beneath the thatch, and an oceanic fatigue enters him. He shuts his eyes and hears Grandfather pluck and dress two pheasants, stuff them with leeks and coriander, and set them to roast over a fire. He smells the cooking meat, hears the rain hiss and spit in the coals, but when he opens his eyes there is no fire and no pheasants, only the girl shivering at his side in the growing darkness, bent over her sack, and rain slashing onto the fields.

In the morning, they enter a vast forest. Great dripping pendulums of catkins hang from the trees and they move through them as if passing through thousands of curtains. The girl coughs; rooks screech; something clatters high in the branches above: then silence and the hugeness of the world.

Whenever he stands, the trees bleed away in long streaks and take several heartbeats to right themselves. He aches to see the shape of the mountain on the horizon but it does not appear. Once in a while the girl mutters words, prayers or curses, he cannot say. If only, he thinks, they had Moonlight with them. Moonlight would know the way. He had heard it said that God made men above beasts, but how many times had they lost a dog high on the mountain only to find it covered with burrs back home? Was it by smell or the angle of the sun in the sky or some deeper, hidden faculty, possessed by animals but lost to men?

In the long June dusk, he sits on the forest floor, too weak to go on, and peels bark from the branches of a wayfarer shrub. He chews the bark until it is a paste, and with his last remaining energy, smears as many branches as he can with the sticky lime, as Grandfather used to do.

The girl helps him gather firewood, and the sun drops, and three times he gets up to check his traps, and each time they are empty. All night he drifts in and out. When he wakes he sees the girl tending the little fire, her face pale and dirty, the hem of her dress torn, her eyes as big as fists. He sees a shadow separate from his body and fly off into the forest, over the river, over the house of his family, herds of deer running through trees high on the mountain, and wolves slipping through the shadows behind, until he reaches the place in the far north where sea dragons slither between mountains of ice and a race of blue giants holds up the stars. When he comes back into his body, shafts of moonlight are falling through the leaves and touching the forest floor in bright shifting patches. Beside him the girl has the sack in her lap and she is running fingers along the lines of the book and murmuring words in her strange language. He listens, and when she stops—as though she has summoned it with her magical book—a flock of stone-curlews comes flowing through the underbrush, clicking and nattering, and Omeir hears the panicked flutter of one caught in a snare, then more, and still more, and the night fills with their shrieks, and she looks at him, and he looks at the book.

The hummocks become foothills and the foothills mountains. They are close to home now, he can sense it. The varieties of trees, the texture of the air, a smell of wild mint halfway up a climb, the bright round pebbles in a streambed: all these are memories, or run parallel to memories. Like oxen, pulling through the rainy dark, maybe there is something in him too, some magnet pulling him homeward.

By the time they come over a ridge and descend a trail to the river road, news of the fall of the city has reached the villages. He keeps the girl bound at the wrists with the rope attached and to each person they pass he tells the same story: victory was glorious; all honor to the sultan, may God keep him; he has sent me home with my rewards. Despite his face, no one seems to begrudge him, and though many eye the dirty bundle and sack he carries, no one asks to see what's inside. A few carters even congratulate him and wish him well, and one gives him cheese, and another a basket of cucumbers.

Soon they near the tall black gorge where the road pinches and the log-bridge extends over the narrows. A few carts come and go; two women drive a gaggle of geese across, on their way to market.

Omeir listens to the river cut deeper through the gorge and then they're across.

In the dusk they pass the village where he was born. A half mile from home, he leads her off the road and to a bluff above the river and they stop beneath the spread boughs of the half-hollow yew.

"The children," he says, "say that this tree is as old as the first men, and that on the darkest nights their ghosts dance in its shade." The tree waves its thousand branches in the moonlight. She watches him, eyes alert. He points into its crown, then at the sack she keeps clutched to her chest.

He takes off his oxhide cape and lays it down. "What you carry will be safe here. It will be out of the weather and no one will come near."

She looks at him and the moon-shadow plays across her face and just when he decides she understands none of what he is saying, she passes him the sack. He wraps it in his cape, swings himself into the branches, squeezes inside the hollow tree, and presses the bundle deep inside.

"It will be safe."

She stares up.

He draws a circle in the air. "We will come back."

When they reach the road again she volunteers her wrists and he ties her. The river is loud and in the starlight the needles on the pines seem to glow. He knows each step of the road now, knows the timbre and tone of the water. When they reach the track leading up to the ravine he glances back at her: slight, filthy, scratched, shuffling inside her torn dress. All my life, he thinks, my best companions cannot speak the same language as me.

TWENTY-ONE

THE SUPER MAGICAL
EXTRA POWERFUL
BOOK OF EVERYTHING

Cloud Cuckoo Land by Antonius Diogenes, Folio Φ

. . . Looking into the {book,} I felt as though I'd hung my head over the lip of a magical well. Across its surface spread the heavens and the earth, all its lands scattered, all its beasts, and in the {center?} . . .

. . . I saw cities full of lanterns and gardens, could hear faint music and singing. I saw a wedding in one city with girls in bright robes, and boys with golden swords . . .

. . . dancing . . .

. . . and my {heart was glad?}. But when I turned {to the next page?} I saw dark, flaming cities in which men burned alive in their fields, and were enslaved in chains, hounds eating corpses, and newborns pitched over walls onto pikes, and when I bent my ear low, I could hear the wailing. And as I looked, turning the leaf over and back . . .

. . . beauty and ugliness . . .

. . . dancing and death . . .

. . . {was too much?} . . .

. . . grew afraid . . .

THE LAKEPORT
PUBLIC LIBRARY

FEBRUARY 20, 2020

6:39 P.M.

Zeno

Behind the bookshelves the children sit with their scripts in their laps: Christopher Dee with his squinty blue eyes and that charming way of talking out of the corner of his mouth; Alex Hess, the thick-chested lion-headed boy who wears gym shorts no matter how cold the weather, who seems impervious to any discomfort save hunger, who has that surprisingly high, silken voice; Natalie, her pink headphones around her neck, who has a real feel for the old Greek; Olivia Ott with her short bob, frighteningly smart, wearing the kaleidoscope dress she worked so hard to make; and red-headed rail-thin Rachel, on her stomach on the carpet, surrounded by props, following the lines of the play with the tip of her pencil as the actors read them.

"On one side is dancing, and the other is death," whispers Alex, and pretends to turn pages in the air. "Page after page after page."

The children know. They know someone is downstairs; they know they are in danger. They are being brave, incredibly brave, completing a read-through of the play behind the shelves at a whisper, trying to use the story to slip the trap. But it's long past time for them to go home. It seems an eternity since they heard Sharif call upstairs that he was going to take the backpack to the police. They haven't heard a sound since; Marian hasn't come upstairs with pizza; nobody has called on a bullhorn to tell them it's over.

Pain shudders through Zeno's hip as he rises.

"Just read to the end of the book, little crow," whispers Olivia-the-goddess, "and you'll learn the secrets of the gods. You can become an eagle, or a bright strong owl, free from desire and death."

He should have told Rex he loved him. He should have told him at Camp Five; he should have told him in London; he should have told Hillary, and Mrs. Boydstun, and every Valley County woman he went on a miserable date with. He should have risked more. It has taken him his whole life to accept himself, and he is surprised to understand that now that he can, he does not long for one more year, one more month: eighty-six years has been enough. In a life you accumulate so many memories, your brain constantly winnowing through them, weighing consequence, burying pain, but somehow by the time you're this age you still end up dragging a monumental sack of memories behind you, a burden as heavy as a continent, and eventually it becomes time to take them out of the world.

Rachel flaps her hand, whispers, "Stop," and fans the pages of her script. "Mr. Ninis? The two really messed-up folios, the one with the wild onions, and the dancing? I think we have them in the wrong place. Those don't happen in Cloud Cuckoo Land—they happen back in Arkadia."

"What," says Alex, "are you talking about?"

"Quietly," whispers Zeno. "Please."

"It's the niece," whispers Rachel. "We're forgetting about the niece. If what really matters, like Mr. Ninis said, is that the story gets passed on—that it was sent in pieces to a dying girl far away—why would Aethon choose to stay up in the stars and live forever?"

Olivia-the-goddess crouches beside Rachel in her sequined dress. "Aethon doesn't read to the end of the book?"

"That's how he writes his story on the tablets," says Rachel. "How they get buried in the tomb with him. Because he doesn't stay in Cloud Cuckoo Land. He chooses . . . What's the word, Mr. Ninis?"

The beating of hearts, the blinking of eyes. Zeno sees himself walk out onto the frozen lake. He sees Rex in the rainy light of the tea room, one hand trembling over his saucer. The children gaze down at their scripts.

"You mean," says Alex, "Aethon goes home."

Seymour

He sits with his back against the dictionaries and the Beretta in his lap. A white glare bends through the front windows and sends eerie shadows across the ceiling: the police have installed floodlights.

His phone refuses to ring. He watches the wounded man breathe at the bottom of the stairs. He didn't find the backpack; he hasn't moved. It's the dinner hour, and Bunny will be carrying plates between tables at the Pig N' Pancake, her eleventh hour of work. She will have had to beg a ride there from the Sachse Inn because he didn't pick her up. By now she'll have heard that something is happening at the public library. A dozen police vehicles will have streaked past; they'll be talking about it at all of her tables, and in the kitchen too. Somebody holed up in the library, somebody with a bomb.

Tomorrow, he tells himself, he'll be at Bishop's camp, far to the north, where the warriors live with purpose and meaning, where he and Mathilda will walk through the layers of sun and shadow in the forest. But does he believe that anymore?

Footfalls on the staircase. Seymour raises a cup of his ear defenders. He recognizes Slow-Motion Zeno as he comes down the last steps: a slight old man who always wears a necktie and occupies the same table near the large-print romances, lost behind a molehill of papers, touching them lightly one by one, like a priest seated before a pile of artifacts that hold meaning only for him.

Zeno

Sharif's shirt is not sitting right on his body, and it looks as though someone has thrown a bucket of ink on him, but Zeno has seen worse. Sharif shakes his head no; Zeno merely bends, touches him on the forehead, and steps over his friend and into the aisle between Nonfiction and Fiction.

The boy is so motionless he might be dead, a handgun resting on his knee. A green backpack sits on the carpet beside him, a mobile phone beside that. What looks like rifle-range ear defenders are cocked on his head, one muff on, one off.

Down through the centuries tumble the words of Diogenes: *I had traveled so far, and it was all so magnificent, yet—*

"So young," says Zeno.

—still a needle of doubt pricked beneath my wing. A dark restlessness flickered—

The boy doesn't move.

"What's inside the bag?"

"Bombs."

"How many?"

"Two."

"How are they triggered?"

"Tracfones, taped to the top."

"How do the bombs go off?"

"If I call either of the phones. On the fifth ring."

"But you're not going to call them. Are you?"

The boy brings his left hand to his earmuffs as though hoping to blot out any further questions. Zeno remembers lying on the straw mat in Camp Five, knowing Rex was folding his body into one of the empty oil drums. Waiting to hear Zeno climb into the other drum. For Bristol and Fortier to lift them onto the truck.

He shuffles forward and lifts the backpack and pins it gently against his necktie as the boy steers the barrel of the pistol toward him. Zeno's breath is strangely steady.

"Does anyone besides you have the numbers?"

The boy shakes his head. Then his forehead wrinkles, as though realizing something. "Yes. Someone does have them."

"Who?"

He shrugs.

"What you mean is, someone besides you can detonate the bombs?"

The trace of a nod.

Sharif watches from the base of the stairs, every inch of him alert. Zeno wraps his arms through the backpack straps. "My friend there, the children's librarian? His name is Sharif. He requires medical attention right away. I'm going to use the telephone to call an ambulance now. In all likelihood, there's one right outside."

The boy grimaces, as though someone has resumed playing loud, screeching music that only he can hear. "I'm waiting for help," he says, but without conviction.

Zeno walks backward to the welcome desk and lifts the receiver of the telephone. No dial tone. "I'll need to use your phone," he says. "Just for the ambulance. That's all I'll do, I promise, and I'll give it right back. And then we'll wait for your help to arrive."

The gun remains pointed at Zeno's chest. The boy's finger remains on the trigger. The cell phone stays on the floor. "We will live lives of clarity and meaning," the boy says, and rubs his eyes. "We will exist entirely outside of the machine even as we work to destroy it."

Zeno takes his left hand off the backpack. "I'm going to reach down with one hand and pick up your phone. Okay?"

Sharif is rigid at the base of the stairwell. The children remain silent upstairs. Zeno bends. The gun barrel is inches from his head. His hand has almost reached the phone when, inside the backpack in his arms, one of the Tracfones taped to one of the bombs rings.

THE ARGOS

MISSION YEAR 65

DAY 341–DAY 370 INSIDE VAULT ONE

Konstance

"Sybil, where are we?"

We are en route to Beta Oph2.

"What speed are we traveling?"

7,734,958 kilometers per hour. You would remember our velocity from your Library Day.

"You're sure, Sybil?"

It is fact.

She gazes a moment into the trillion resplendent tributaries of the machine.

Konstance, are you feeling well? Your heart rate is rather high.

"I feel fine, thank you. I'm going back to the Library for a bit."

She studies the same schematics that her father studied during Quarantine Two. Engineering, storage, fluid recycling, waste treatment, oxygen plant. The farms, the Commissary, the kitchens. Five lavatories with showers, forty-two living compartments, Sybil at the center. No windows, no stairs, no way in, no way out, the whole structure a self-sustaining tomb. Sixty-six years ago the original eighty-five volunteers were told they were embarking on an interstellar journey that would outlast them by centuries. They traveled to Qaanaaq, trained for six months, boarded a boat, and were sedated and sealed inside the *Argos* while Sybil prepared the launch.

Except there was no launch. It was just an exercise. A pilot study, a trial run, an intergenerational feasibility experiment that may have ended long ago or may be ongoing still.

Konstance stands in the Library atrium touching the place on her worksuit where Mother stitched a pine seedling four years before. Mrs. Flowers's little dog stares up at her and wags his tail. He is not real. The desk beneath her fingertips feels like wood, sounds like wood, smells like wood; the slips in the box look like paper, feel like paper, smell like paper.

None of it is real. She stands on a circular Perambulator in a circular room at the center of a circular white structure on a mostly circular island eight miles across Baffin Bay from a remote village called Qaanaaq. How does a contagion suddenly present itself on a ship streaking through interstellar space? Why couldn't Sybil solve it? Because none of them, Sybil included, knew where they actually were.

She writes a series of questions on slips of paper and tucks them one by one into the slot. Above the atrium, clouds stream through a yellow sky. The little dog licks his upper lip. Down from the stacks fly books.

Inside Vault One she unscrews all four legs off the cot, and uses the frame to pound one end of one of the legs flat.

Why, Sybil asks, *are you dismantling your bed?*

Don't answer. Konstance spends hours discreetly sharpening the edge of the cot leg. She inserts the sharpened leg into a slot on a second leg that will serve as a handle, secures it with a screw, makes cord from the lining of her blanket, and lashes the sharpened cot leg fast: a homemade axe. Then she takes several scoops of Nourish powder, runs them through the food printer, and the machine fills the bowl past the rim.

I am glad, says Sybil, *that you are preparing a meal, Konstance. And such a large one too.*

"I'll have another after this one, Sybil. Is there a recipe you might recommend?"

How about pineapple fried rice? Doesn't that sound nice?

Konstance swallows, fills her mouth again. "It does, yes. It sounds wonderful."

Once she is full, she crawls around the floor gathering her transcriptions of Zeno Ninis's translations. *Aethon Has a Vision. The Bandits' Hideout. The Garden of the Goddess.* She gathers all the scraps into a stack, Folio A to Folio Ω, sets her drawing of a cloud city on top, and, using one of the aluminum screws from the cot legs, bores a row of holes through the left edge. Then she unravels more blanket lining, braids the fibers together to make twine, lines up the holes, and sews the scraps of food sacks together along one edge to bind them.

An hour left before NoLight, she cleans her food bowl and fills it with water. By running her fingers along her scalp, she collects a little nest of hair and wedges it into the bottom of her empty drinking cup.

Then she sits on the floor and waits and watches Sybil gleam inside her tower. She can almost feel Father bundling her in her blanket, sitting with her against the wall of Farm 4, the space around them crammed with racks of lettuce and watercress and parsley, the seeds sleeping in their drawers.

Will you tell some more of the story, Father?

When NoLight comes, she takes the bioplastic suit her father sewed for her twelve months before and pulls it on. Leaving her arms free, she zips it to her chest, the fit more snug now that she has grown, and tucks her handmade book deep inside her worksuit. Then she balances one end of the legless cot, its mattress still inflated, on the food printer and the other on the toilet to form a kind of canopy.

Konstance, says Sybil, *what are you doing to your bed?*

She crawls beneath the elevated cot. From the back of the printer she unplugs the low-voltage power connection, strips away the thermoplastic sheath, and attaches the wires inside the cable to the two remaining cot legs. Positive to one, negative to the other. These she sticks into the water in her food bowl.

She holds her drinking cup, her hair wadded inside, upside down over the positive electrode and waits as oxygen rises from the water and collects in the inverted cup.

Konstance, what are you up to under there?

She counts to ten, takes the wires off the cot legs, and rubs their ends together. The ensuing spark, rising into the pure oxygen, ignites the hair.

I insist that you reply. What are you doing beneath your bed?

As she turns over the cup, smoke rises, and with it the odor of burning hair. Konstance sets a crumpled square of dry-wipe on it, then another. According to the schematics, extinguishers are embedded into the ceiling of every room on the *Argos*. If this is not true in Vault One—if the schematics were wrong, and there are extinguishers in the walls, or in the floor, this will never work. But if they are only in the ceiling, it might.

Konstance, I sense heat. Please answer me, what are you doing under there?

Little nozzles extend from the ceiling and begin to spray a chemical mist onto the cot above her head; she can feel it pattering onto the legs of her suit as she feeds the flames beneath the cot.

The fire fades as she nearly smothers it with more dry-wipes, then surges back to life. Threads of black curl around the edges of the upside-down cot, and into the mist raining down from the ceiling. She blows on the flames, layers on more wipes, then feeds it scoops of Nourish powder. If this does not work, she will not have enough material to burn a second time.

Soon the underside of her mattress catches fire and she has to crawl out from beneath the cot. She pitches in the last of the dry-wipes. Green flames rise from the mattress's edge and an acrid, burnt-chemical smell fills the vault. Konstance slides across the room beneath the spray of the extinguishers, puts her hands into the suit's sleeves, pulls on the oxygen hood, and seals it to the suit's collar.

She feels it catch, feels the suit inflate.

Oxygen at ten percent, says the hood.

Konstance, this is outrageously irresponsible behavior. You are jeopardizing everything.

The underside of the cot glows brighter as the mattress burns. The beam of the headlamp flickers through the smoke.

"Sybil, your prime directive is to protect the crew, isn't it? Above all else?"

Sybil raises the lights in the ceiling to full brightness and Konstance squints into the glare. Her hands are lost in sleeves; her feet slide on the floor.

"It's mutualism, right?" Konstance says. "The crew needs you and you need a crew."

Please remove the cot frame so the fire beneath it can be extinguished.

"But without a crew—without me—you have no purpose, Sybil. This room is already so full of smoke that it is not possible for me to breathe. In a few minutes the hood I'm wearing will run out of oxygen. Then I will asphyxiate."

Sybil's voice deepens. *Remove the cot immediately.*

The falling droplets cloud the lens of her hood, and each time she tries to wipe it clean, she only smudges it further. Konstance shifts the book zipped inside her worksuit and picks up her hatchet.

Oxygen at nine percent, says the hood.

Green and orange flames are licking around the top of the cot now, and Sybil is mostly obscured behind smoke.

Please, Konstance. Her voice changes, softens, becomes a mimicry of Mother's. *You must not do this.*

Konstance backs against the wall. The voice changes again, flows to a new gender. *Listen, Zucchini, can you flip over the cot?*

Hairs rise on the back of Konstance's neck.

We must put out the fire immediately. Everything is in danger.

She can hear a hissing, something melting or boiling inside the mattress, and through the billowing smoke she can just glimpse the tower that is Sybil, sixteen feet tall, rippling with crimson light, and from her memory whispers Mrs. Chen: *Every map ever drawn, every census ever taken, every book ever published* . . .

For an instant, she hesitates. The images on the Atlas are

decades old. What waits out there now, beyond the walls of the *Argos*? What if Sybil is the only other intelligence left? What is she risking?

Oxygen at eight percent, says the hood. *Try to breathe more slowly.*

She turns away from Sybil and holds her breath. In front of her, where a moment before there was only wall, the door to Vault One slides open.

TWENTY-TWO

WHAT YOU ALREADY HAVE
IS BETTER THAN WHAT YOU
SO DESPERATELY SEEK

Cloud Cuckoo Land by Antonius Diogenes, Folio X

Folio X is severely degraded. What happens next in Aethon's tale has been long debated and need not be belabored here. Many argue this section belongs earlier in the tale, and points to a different conclusion, and that it's not the translator's job to speculate. Translation by Zeno Ninis.

the ewes lambing and the rain falling and the hills greening and the lambs being weaned and the ewes growing old and curmudgeonly and trusting only me. Why {did I leave?}? Why this compulsion to be {elsewhere?}, to constantly seek something new? Was hope a curse, {the last evil left in Pandora's jar}?

You fly all the way to the end of the stars, and all you want {to do is go home . . .}

. . . creaking knees . . .

. . . mud and all . . .

My flock, some cheap wine, a bath, {that's} as much magic as any foolish shepherd needs. I opened {my beak and croaked, "In much wisdom is much sorrow, and in ignorance is much wisdom."}

The goddess straightened, {her head bumped a star, brought down a colossal hand, and afloat in the center of her lake-sized palm, there rested a single white rose.}

IDAHO STATE CORRECTIONAL INSTITUTION

2021–2030

Seymour

It's medium security, a campus of low beige buildings wrapped in a double layer of chainlink that could pass for a run-down community college. There's a woodshop, a gym, a chapel, and a library populated with legal textbooks, dictionaries, and fantasy novels. The food is third-rate.

He spends every hour he can inside the computer lab. He has learned Excel, AutoCAD, Java, C++, and Python, taking comfort in the clear logic of code, input and output, instruction and command. Four times a day electronic chimes sound and he goes outside for a "movement" where he can peer through the fencing to a rising plain of cheatgrass and skeleton weed. The Owyhee Mountains shimmer in the distance. The only trees he sees are sixteen underwatered honey locusts huddled in the visitors' parking lot, none taller than twelve feet.

His coveralls are denim; all the cells are singles. On the wall opposite his little window is a rectangle of painted cinderblock where men are allowed to post family snapshots, postcards, or art. Seymour's is empty.

For the first several years, before she gets sick, Bunny visits when she can, riding the Greyhound three hours from Lakeport, then taking a cab to the prison, wearing a surgical mask, her eyes blinking at him across the table in the fluorescent lights.

Possum, are you listening?

Can you look at me?

Once a week she deposits five dollars into his prisoner account, and he spends it on 1.69-ounce packages of plain M&M's from the vending machine.

Sometimes, when he closes his eyes, he's back in the courtroom, the gazes of the children's families like propane torches aimed at the back of his head. He could not look at Marian. Who made the PDF we found on your tablet? Why assume Bishop's camp was real? Why assume the recruiter you messaged with was female, why assume she was your age, why assume she was human? Each question a needle into an overneedled heart.

Kidnapping, use of a weapon of mass destruction, attempted murder—he pled guilty to it all. The children's librarian, Sharif, survived his wound, which helped. A buzz-cut prosecutor with a high-pitched voice argued for the death penalty; Seymour got forty to life instead.

One morning when he's twenty-two, the chimes sound for the 10:31 movement, but the computer room supervisor asks Seymour and two other good behavior guys to stay put. Officers wheel in three free-standing terminals with trackballs mounted in front, and the assistant warden escorts in a severe-looking woman in a blazer and V-neck.

"As you likely know," she says, speaking with zero inflection, "Ilium has been scanning the world's surface with ever-advancing fidelity for years, assembling the most comprehensive map ever constructed, forty petabytes of data and counting."

The supervisor plugs in the terminals and the Ilium logo spins on the screens as the terminals boot.

"You have been selected for a pilot program to review potentially undesirable items inside the raw image sets. Our algorithms flag hundreds of thousands of images per day and we don't have the manpower to scan them all. Your task will be to verify whether or not these images are objectionable, and in the process enhance the machine learning. Either keep the flag up or take it down and move on."

"Basically," the assistant warden says, "a fancy steakhouse doesn't want you to jump on Ilium Earth and find a homeless guy peeing in their doorway. If you see something on there that you wouldn't want Grandma to see, leave the flag up, draw a circle around it, and the software will eliminate it. Got it?"

"These are skills," says the supervisor. "This is a job."

Seymour nods. On the screen in front of him, the Earth spins. The view sinks through digital clouds over a swath of South America— Brazil maybe—and touches down on a rural highway as straight as a ruler. Red dirt runs down both sides; what might be sugarcane grows beyond that. He nudges the trackball forward: the flag ahead gradually enlarges as he draws closer.

Beneath it, a little blue sedan has struck a cow head-on, and the car is crumpled, and there is blood on the road, and a man in jeans is standing beside the cow with his hands behind his head, either watching it die or trying to figure out if it is going to die.

Seymour confirms the flag, circles the image, and in an instant the cow, car, and man are concealed with a section of computer-generated roadway. Before he has time to process any of it, the software whisks him to the next flag.

A faceless little boy in front of a roadside *churrascaria* shows the camera his middle finger. Someone has painted a penis on the sign of a little Honda dealership. He checks forty flags around Sorriso, Brazil; the computer launches him back into the troposphere, the planet spins, and he drops into northern Michigan.

Sometimes he has to poke around a bit to understand why a flag has been placed. A woman who might be a prostitute leans into a car window. Beneath a church marquee that says *GOD LISTENS*, someone has spray-painted *TO SLAYER*. Sometimes the software misinterprets a pattern of ivy for something obscene, or flags a kid walking to school for reasons Seymour cannot guess. He rejects or verifies the flag, draws an outline around the offending image with his cursor, and it's gone, hidden behind a high-resolution bush or erased by a smear of counterfeit sidewalk.

The movement chime sounds; the other two men trundle off to lunch; Seymour stays put. By roll call, he has not moved for nine hours; the supervisor is gone; an old man sweeps beneath the teaching terminals; the windows are dark.

They pay him sixty-one cents an hour, which is eight more cents than the guys make in the furniture shop. He's good at it. Pixel by pixel, boulevard by boulevard, city by city, he helps Ilium sanitize the planet. He effaces military sites, homeless encampments, queues outside medical clinics, labor strikes, demonstrators and dissidents, picketers and pickpockets. Sometimes he comes upon scenes that engulf him with emotion: a mother and son, bundled in parkas, holding hands beside an ambulance in Lithuania. A woman in a surgical mask kneeling on a Tokyo expressway in the middle of traffic. In Houston several hundred protesters hold banners in front of an oil refinery; he half expects to recognize Janet among them, twenty new frog patches sewn on her jean jacket. But all the faces are blurred, and he confirms the flag, and the software replaces the protesters with thirty digital sweetgum saplings.

Seymour Stuhlman's stamina, the Ilium supervisors report, is remarkable. Most days he triples his quotas. By the time he is twenty-four, he is a legend in the Ilium Earth offices, the most efficient cleaner in the entire prison program. They send him an upgraded terminal, give him his own corner of the computer room, and raise his pay to seventy cents an hour. For a while, he manages to convince himself that he's doing something good, removing toxicity and ugliness from the world, rinsing the earth of human iniquity and replacing it with vegetation.

But as the months tick past, especially after dark, in the isolation of his cell, he sees the old man in the dark of the library, wobbling in his penguin tie, holding the green backpack to his chest, and doubts worm their way in.

He's twenty-six when Ilium develops its first treadmill prototype. Now rather than sit at a terminal and twitch through spaces with a scroll wheel, he's walking through them on his own two feet, helping the AI cleanse the map of the ugly and the inconvenient. He averages fifteen miles a day.

One afternoon when Seymour is twenty-seven, he puts on his wireless headset, saturated with the smell of his own sweat, mounts the treadmill, hangs over the Earth, and a dark blue lake in the rough shape of a G comes flying toward him.

Lakeport.

The town has metastasized over the past decade, condos grown like carbuncles around the southern shore of the lake, housing developments unfurling beyond that. The software drops him in front of a liquor store where someone has shattered a front window; he fixes it. Then to a pickup truck driving along Wilson Road, its bed jammed with teenagers. A banner streaming behind them reads: *You'll die of old age, we'll die of climate change.* He traces an oval around them, and the truck evaporates.

The icon he's supposed to touch to send him to his next flag flashes; instead Seymour begins walking home. A quarter mile down Cross Road, the aspens are turning gold. An automated voice crackles in his headset, *Moderator 45, you are traveling in the wrong direction. Please head to your next flag.*

The Eden's Gate sign is still there on the side of Arcady Lane. The double-wide is gone, the acre of weeds replaced by three townhomes with overwatered lawns, so seamlessly integrated into the other homes on Arcady Lane that it looks as though software has placed them there instead of carpenters.

Moderator 45, you are off course. In sixty seconds you will be sent to your next flag.

He breaks into a run, heading east down Spring Street, the treadmill bouncing beneath his feet. Downtown, at the corner of Lake and Park, the library is gone. There's a new hotel in its place, three stories with what looks like a rooftop bar. Two teenaged valets in bow ties stand out front.

Junipers gone, book drop box gone, front steps gone, library gone. Into his mind flickers a vision of the old man, Zeno Ninis, sitting at a little table in Fiction, hunched behind stacks of books and legal pads, his eyes damp and cloudy, blinking as though watching words flow invisibly in rivers around him.

Moderator 45, you have five seconds . . .

Seymour stands on the corner, breathing hard, feeling as though he could live a thousand more years and never make sense of the world.

Redirecting you now.

He is yanked straight up into the air, Lakeport shrinking to a dot, the mountains swiveling away, southern Canada unfurling far below, but something has gone wrong inside him; everything is spinning; Seymour falls off the treadmill and breaks his wrist.

May 31, 2030

Dear Marian,

    I know that I will never understand all the consequences of what I have done or apprehend all the pain I caused. I think of the things you did for me when I was young and you should not have to do any more. But I was wondering. During the trial I learned that Mr. Ninis worked on translations and that he was working on a play with the children before he died. Do you know what became of his papers?

                                Yours,
                                Seymour

Nine weeks later, he is called to the prison library. An officer wheels in a dolly stacked with three cardboard boxes marked with his name and red *Scanned* stickers.

"What's all this?"

"They just told me to bring it here."

Inside the first carton is a letter.

July 22, 2030

Dear Seymour,

I was happy to hear from you. Here is everything I could gather from the trial, from Mr. Ninis's house, and that we recovered at the library. The police might have more, I'm not sure. Nobody ever did anything with all this, so I'm trusting you with it. Access is part of the librarian's creed, after all.

If you can make any sense of it, I think one of the children Zeno worked with would be interested: Natalie Hernandez. Last I heard from her, she's taking classes at Idaho State in Latin and Greek.

At one time you were a thoughtful and sensitive boy and it is my hope that you have become a thoughtful and sensitive man.

Marian

The cartons are crammed with legal pads covered with crimped pencil-writing. Sticky notes blanket every other page. Down the sides of each box someone has stuffed plastic sleeves containing eleven-by-seventeen-inch facsimiles of battered manuscript pages with half the text missing. There are books too, a five-pound Greek-English lexicon, and a compendium on lost texts by someone named Rex Browning. Seymour shuts his eyes, sees the golden wall at the top of the stairs, the strange lettering, cardboard clouds twisting over empty chairs.

The prison librarian lets him keep the boxes in a corner, and every evening, Seymour, tired from walking the earth, sits on the floor and sifts through them. At the bottom of one, inside a folder stamped *EVIDENCE*, he finds five photocopied scripts the police recovered the night he was arrested, the night of the children's dress rehearsal. On the last pages of one copy are multiple edits, not in Zeno's hand, but in bright cursive.

While he was downstairs with his bombs, the children upstairs were rewriting their ending.

The underground tomb, the donkey, the sea bass, a crow flapping through the cosmos: it's a ridiculous tale. But in the version rendered by Zeno and the kids, it's beautiful too. Sometimes as he works, Greek words come flashing up from the depths of the facsimiles— ὄρνις, *ornis*, it means both bird and omen—and Seymour feels like he used to when he was caught in the gaze of Trustyfriend, as though he's being allowed to glimpse an older and undiluted world, when every barn swallow, every sunset, every storm, pulsed with meaning. By age seventeen he'd convinced himself that every human he saw was a parasite, captive to the dictates of consumption. But as he reconstructs Zeno's translation, he realizes that the truth is infinitely more complicated, that we are all beautiful even as we are all part of the problem, and that to be a part of the problem is to be human.

He cries at the end. Aethon steals into the garden in the center of the cloud city, talks to the gigantic goddess, and opens the Super Magical Extra Powerful Book of Everything. The academic articles among Zeno's papers suggest that translators arrange the folios in such a way that leaves Aethon in the garden, inducted into the secrets of the gods, finally freed of his mortal desires. But evidently the children have decided at the last moment that the old shepherd will look away and not read to the end of the book. He eats the rose proffered by the goddess and returns home, to the mud and grass of the Arkadian hills.

In a child's cursive, beneath the crossed-out lines, Aethon's new line is handwritten in the margin, "The world as it is is enough."

TWENTY-THREE

THE GREEN BEAUTY
OF THE BROKEN WORLD

Cloud Cuckoo Land by Antonius Diogenes, Folio Ψ

Debate continues over the intended location of Folio Ψ in Diogenes's tale. By the time it was imaged, deterioration had progressed so far across the leaf that over eighty-five percent of the text was affected. Translation by Zeno Ninis.

. . . I woke . . .
   . . . {found myself?} . . .
   . . . down from that high place . . .
   . . . crawled in the grass, the trees . . .
   . . . fingers, toes, a tongue to speak!
   . . . the smell of wild onions . . .
   . . . dew, the {lines?} of the hills,
   . . . sweetness of light, moon overhead . . .
   . . . the green beauty of the {broken?} world.
   . . . would wish to be like them . . . a god . . .
   . . . {hungry?}
   . . . only a mouse quivering in the grass, in the {mist?}
   . . . the mild sunshine . . .
   . . . falling.

NINE MILES FROM A WOODCUTTERS' VILLAGE IN THE RHODOPE MOUNTAINS OF BULGARIA

1453–1494

Anna

They live in the cottage the boy's grandfather built: stone walls, stone hearth, a peeled log for a ridge beam, thatch roof full of mice. Fourteen years of dung and straw and bits of food have compacted the dirt floor into something resembling concrete. No images hang inside, and only the simplest of ornaments adorn the bodies of his mother and sister: an iron ring, an agate strung on a piece of cord. Their crockery is heavy and plain, their leather untanned. The purpose of everything, from pots to people, seems to be to survive as long as possible, and anything that is not durable is not valued.

A few days after Anna and Omeir arrive, the boy's mother walks along the creek and digs up a pouch of coins and the boy heads alone down the river road and returns four days later with a castrated bull and a donkey on its last legs. With the bull he manages to plow an overgrown series of terraces above the cottage and plant some August barley.

The boy's mother and sister regard her with as much interest as they might a broken jar. And indeed, during those first months, what use is she? She can't understand the simplest directives, can't get the goat to stand still for milking, doesn't know how to care for fowls or make curds or harvest honey or bundle hay or irrigate the terraces above the cottage. Most days she feels like a thirteen-year-old infant, incapable of all but the very simplest tasks.

But the boy! He shares his food with her, murmurs to her in his strange language; he seems, as Chryse the cook might have said, as patient as Job and as gentle as a fawn. He teaches her how to check the barley for aphids, how to clean trout for smoking, how to fill the kettle at the creek without getting sediment in the water. Sometimes she finds him alone in the wooden byre, touching old bird snares and spring-nets, or standing on a terrace above the river, three big white stones at his feet, with a stricken look on his face.

If she is his possession, he does not treat her as such. He teaches her the words for milk, water, fire, and dog; in the dark he sleeps beside her but does not touch her. On her feet she wears an outsize pair of wooden clogs that belonged to the boy's grandfather, and his mother helps her make a new dress from homespun wool, and the leaves turn yellow, and the moon waxes and wanes again.

One morning, frost sparkling in the trees, his sister and mother load the donkey with jars of honey, wrap themselves in cloaks, and head upriver. As soon as they round the bend, the boy calls Anna into the byre. He wraps pieces of honeycomb in a cheesecloth and sets it to boil. When the wax is rendered, he lifts out the cakes and mashes them into a paste. Then he unrolls a piece of oxhide across the crude table, and together they work the still-warm beeswax into the leather. When all the wax has been worked in, he rolls the hide and tucks it under his arm and beckons her up a faint trail at the head of the ravine to the old half-hollow yew on the bluff.

In daylight, the tree is magnificent: its trunk swirls with ten thousand intertwined gnarls; dozens of low branches, decked with bright red berries, eddy toward the ground like snakes. The boy clambers up through the limbs, squeezes himself into the hollow part of the trunk, and emerges holding Himerius's sack.

Together they examine the silk hood and snuffbox and book to make sure they're still dry. Then he unrolls the newly waxed oxhide across the ground, wraps the box and book with the silk inside the hide, and ties the whole thing shut. He stows it back inside the tree, and Anna understands that this will be their secret, that the manuscript, like the boy's face, will be feared and mistrusted, and she remembers the flaring pits of Kalaphates's eyes, his rage and exultation as he held Maria's unconscious face to the hearth and burned Licinius's quires to ash.

• • •

She learns the words for home, cold, pine, kettle, bowl, and hand. Mole, mouse, otter, horse, hare, hunger. By the time for spring planting, she is grasping nuance. To brag is to "pretend to be two and a half." To get into trouble is to "wade into the onions." The boy has multiple expressions for the various feelings one experiences in the rain: most convey wretchedness, but several do not. One is the same sound as joy.

In early spring she is hauling water up from the creek when she passes him and he pats the stone on which he sits. She sets down the pole and its two pots and sits beside him. "Sometimes," he says, "when I feel like working, I just sit and wait for the feeling to pass," and his eyes catch Anna's and she realizes that she understands the joke, and they laugh.

The snow retreats, the elderflowers bloom, the ewes lamb, a pair of wood pigeons nests in the thatch of the roof, and Nida and her mother sell honey and melons and pine nuts in the village market, and by late summer they have enough silver to buy a second bullock to pair with the first. Soon Omeir is using an old dray to cart felled trees down from the high forests, and sell them to mills downriver, and in the fall Nida is wed to a woodcutter in a village twenty miles away. During Anna's second winter in the ravine, the boy's mother, in her loneliness, begins to talk to her, slowly at first, then in torrents, about the secrets of cultivating bees, about Omeir's father and grandfather, and finally about her life in the little stony village nine miles downriver before Omeir was born.

As the days warm they sit beside the creek and watch Omeir work his spindly, uncooperative oxen, using the solicitous voice he reserves only for cattle, and his mother says that his gentleness is like a flame that he carries inside him, and in good weather Anna and Omeir walk together beneath trees, and he tells her stories of funny things that his grandfather used to say: that the breath of deer can kill snakes, or that the gall of an eagle, mixed with honey, can restore a person's eyesight, and she comes to see that the little ravine beneath the broad-shouldered mountain is not as foreboding and steep and barbaric as it first seemed—that indeed in every season, at some unexpected moment, it will reveal a beauty that makes her eyes water and her heart thump in her chest, and she comes to believe that perhaps she has indeed journeyed to that better place she always imagined might lie beyond the city walls.

In time she ceases to notice the defect in Omeir's face: it becomes part of the world, no different than the mud of spring, the mosquitoes of summer, or the snows of winter. She gives birth to six sons and loses three, and Omeir buries the lost sons in the clearing above the river, where his grandfather and sisters are buried, and marks each grave with a white stone he carries down from a high place known only to him. The cottage grows crowded, and Anna manages to construct clothes for the boys, sometimes adding a clumsy vine or a lopsided bloom with thread, smiling when she thinks of how crude Maria would find her needlework, and Omeir takes his mother on the donkey to live with Nida, and then it is only the five of them in the ravine by the mouth of the cavern.

Sometimes in dreams she is back in the embroidery house, where Maria and the others remain bent over their tables, plying their needles, faint, phantasmal, and when she reaches to touch them, her fingers pass right through. Sometimes pains flash through the back of her head, and Anna wonders if the affliction that took Maria will come for her too. But in other moments those thoughts are far away, and she can no longer remember the faces of the women who raised her, and it seems that her life with Omeir is the only life she has ever known.

One morning in Anna's twenty-fifth winter, on a night cold enough to freeze the water across the top of the kettle, her youngest son descends into fever. His eyes smolder in their sockets, and he soaks his clothes with sweat. She sits on the stack of rugs where they sleep, puts the sick boy's head in her lap, and strokes his hair, and Omeir paces, clenching and unclenching his fists. Finally he fills the lamp, lights it, and goes out, and returns covered with snow. From his coat he produces the bundle wrapped in waxed oxhide and hands it to her with great solemnity and she understands that he believes the book can save their son as he believes it saved them on their journey here more than a decade before.

Outside, the pines roar. The wind throws snow down the chimney, blowing ash around the room, and the two older boys crowd her on the carpets, dazzled by the glow of the lamp and by this strange new package their father has produced as though from nowhere. The donkey and goat stand close around them, and the whole world outside their door seems to bellow and seethe.

The oxhide has done its work: the contents are dry. One boy examines the snuffbox while the other runs his fingers over the samite hood, tracing the birds both finished and half-finished, and Omeir holds the lamp for Anna as she opens the book.

It has been years since she last tried to read the old Greek. But memory is a strange thing, and whether it's fear for one son or the excitement of the other two, when she peers into the even, steady script with its leftward cant, the meanings of the letters return.

A is alpha is ἄλφα. Β is beta is βῆτα. Ω is omega is ὦ μέγα; Ἄστεα are cities; νόον is mind; ἔγνω is learned. Slowly, in the language of her second life, translating one word at a time, she begins.

> ". . . the one they called birdbrain and nincompoop—
> yes, I, dull-witted muttonheaded lamebrained Aethon—
> once traveled all the way to the edge of the earth and
> beyond . . ."

She works as much from memory as from the manuscript, and inside the little stone cottage, something happens: the sick child in her lap, his forehead sheened with sweat, opens his eyes. When Aethon is accidentally transformed into an ass and the other boys burst into laughter, he smiles. When Aethon reaches the frozen rim of the world, he bites his fingernails. And when Aethon finally sees the gates of the city in the clouds, tears spring to his eyes.

The lamp spits, the oil drawing low, and all three boys beg her to go on.

"Please," they say, and their eyes glitter in the light. "Tell us what he found inside the goddess's magical book."

"When Aethon peered into it," she says, "he saw the heavens and the earth and all its lands scattered around the ocean, and all the animals and birds upon it. The cities were full of lanterns and gardens, and he could faintly hear music and singing, and he saw a wedding in one city with girls in bright linen robes, and boys with gold swords on silver belts, jumping through rings, doing handsprings and leaping and dancing in time. But on the next page he saw dark, flaming cities in which men were slaughtered in their fields, their wives enslaved in chains, and their children pitched over the walls onto pikes. He saw hounds eating corpses, and when he bent his ear low to the pages, he could hear the wailing. And as he looked, turning the leaf over and back, Aethon saw that the cities on both sides of the page, the dark ones and the bright ones, were one and the same, that there is no peace without war, no life without death, and he was afraid."

The lamp sputters out; the chimney moans; the children draw closer around her. Omeir rewraps the book, and Anna holds their youngest son against her breast, and dreams of bright clean light falling across the pale walls of the city, and when they wake, late into the morning, the boy's fever is gone.

In years to come, if the children catch a rheum or simply get too insistent—always after dark, always when there is no one else for miles—Omeir will look at her and an understanding will pass between them. He'll light the oil lamp, disappear outside, and return with the bundle. She'll open the book and the boys will gather around her on the carpets.

"Tell again, Mama," they say, "about the magician who lives inside the whale."

"And about the nation of swans that lives among the stars."

"And about the mile-high goddess and the book that contained all things."

They act out parts; they beg to know what tortoises are, and honeycakes, and they seem to instinctively sense that the book wrapped in silk and again in waxed oxhide is an object of strange value, a secret that both enriches and endangers them. Each time she opens it, more text has been lost to illegibility, and she remembers the tall Italian standing in the candlelit workshop.

Time: the most violent war engine of all.

The oldest ox dies and Omeir brings home a new calf, and Anna's sons grow taller than she is and go to work on the mountain, bringing logs from the high forests and carting them down the river road to sell at the mills outside Edirne. She loses track of the winters, loses memories. At unexpected moments, when she's carrying water, or stitching a wound on Omeir's leg, or picking lice from his hair, time folds over itself and she sees Himerius's hands on the oars, or feels the vertiginous pull of gravity as she lowers herself down the wall of the priory. Toward the end of her life these memories intermingle with memories of the stories she has loved: homesick Ulysses abandoning his raft in the storm and swimming toward the island of the Phaeacians, Aethon-the-donkey wrapping his soft lips around a stinging nettle, all times and all stories being one and the same in the end.

She dies in May, on the finest day of the year, at the age of fifty-four, leaning against a stump beside the byre, with her three sons around her, the sky such a deep blue above the shoulder of the mountain that it hurts her teeth to look at it. Her husband buries her in the clearing above the river, between his grandfather and the sons they lost, with her sister's silk hood across her breast and a white stone to mark her place.

THAT SAME RAVINE

1505

Omeir

He sleeps beneath the same smoke-stained roof beam that he slept beneath as a child. His left elbow occasionally locks up, his inner ear throbs before storms, and he has had to pull out two of his own molars. His primary companions are three laying hens, a large black dog who frightens people but at heart is harmless, and Clover, a twenty-year-old donkey with breath like a graveyard and chronic gas but a sweet temperament.

Two of his sons have moved into forests farther to the north and the third lives with a woman in the village nine miles away. When Omeir visits with Clover, the children still shy from his face, and some openly burst into tears, but his youngest granddaughter does not, and if he sits very still, she'll climb into his lap and touch his upper lip with her fingers.

Memories fail him now. Banners and bombards, the screaming of wounded men, the reek of sulfur, the deaths of Moonlight and Tree—sometimes his recollections of the siege on the city seem no more than the residue of bad dreams, lifting into consciousness for a moment before dissipating. Forgetting, he is learning, is how the world heals itself.

He has heard that the new sultan (bless and keep him forever) takes his trees from forests even farther away, and that the Christians have sailed ships to new lands at the farthest edge of the ocean where there are entire cities made of gold, but he has little use for such stories anymore. Sometimes as he stares into his fire, the tale Anna used to tell comes back to him, of a man transformed into a donkey, then a fish, then a crow, journeying across earth, ocean, and stars to find a land without suffering, only to choose to return home in the end, and live a last few years among his animals.

One day in early spring, long after he has lost all track of his age, a series of storms sweeps over the mountain. The river turns brown, and mudslides block the road, and the rumble of falling rocks echoes through the gorges. The worst night finds Omeir huddled atop his table with the dog beside him listening to a sloshing fill the cottage: not the usual dripping and trickling, but a flood.

Water flows beneath the door in sheets and streams trickle down the walls and Clover stands blinking up to her hocks in the rising water. At dawn he wades through dung and bark and debris and checks on the hens and leads Clover up to the highest terrace to nibble what grasses she can find and finally he looks up at the limestone bluff overlooking the ravine and panic lurches through him.

The old half-hollow yew has fallen in the night. He claws his way up the trail, sliding in mud. Moss-decked branches splay everywhere and the huge root network lies unearthed like a second tree ripped out of the earth. The smell is of sap and shattered wood and things long buried lifted into the light.

It takes him a long time to locate Anna's bundle in the wreckage. The oxhide is soaked. Little jangles of alarm ride through him as he carries the sodden bundle down to the cottage. He shovels mud out of the hearth and manages to start a smoky fire and hangs his sleeping rugs in the byre to dry and finally unwraps the book.

It is wringing wet. Leaves separate from the binding as he teases them apart, and the dense strings of symbols upon them—all those little sooty bird-tracks crammed together—seem more faded than he remembers.

He can still hear Anna's shriek when he first touched the sack. The way the book protected them as they left the city; the way it summoned a flock of stone-curlews to his snares; the way it brought their son back from fever. The quick humor in Anna's eyes as she bent over the lines, translating as she went.

He banks up the fire and strings webs of cording around the cottage and hangs bifolios over the lines to dry as if he were smoking game birds, and all this time his heart races, as though the codex were a living thing left to his trust and he has endangered it—as though he were charged with a single, simple responsibility, to keep this one thing alive, and has bungled it.

When the leaves are dry, he reassembles the book, uncertain that he is putting the folios back in the correct order, and wraps it in a new square of waxed leather. He waits for the first migrating storks to come over the ravine, a lopsided chevron of them following their ancient directive, leaving whatever distant place in the south where they have spent the winter and heading to whatever distant place in the north where they will spend the summer. Then he takes his best blanket, two skins of water, several dozen pots of honey, the book, and Anna's snuffbox, and pulls shut the door of the cottage. He calls to Clover and she comes trotting, ears up, and the dog rises from the splash of sunlight where it drowses beside the byre.

First to the house of his son, where he gives his daughter-in-law the three hens and half his silver and tries to give away the dog too, though the dog will have none of it. His granddaughter loops a wreath of spring roses around Clover's neck, and he starts northwest around the mountain, Omeir on foot and Clover, half-blind, climbing steadily beside, the dog at their heels.

He avoids inns, markets, crowds. When he passes through hamlets he generally keeps the dog close and his face hidden beneath the drooping brim of his hat. He sleeps outdoors, and chews the blue starflowers Grandfather used to chew to soothe aches in his back, and takes heart from Clover and her levelheaded gait. The few people they pass are charmed, and ask him where he found such a bright and pretty little donkey, and he feels blessed.

Now and then he gathers enough courage to show travelers the little enameled painting on the lid of the snuffbox. A few speculate that it might depict a fortress in Kosovo and others a palazzo in the

Republic of Florence. But one day, as he draws near the Sava River, two merchants on horseback with two servants each stop him. One asks his business in Anna's language, and the other says, "He's a wandering Mohammedan with one foot in the grave, he can't understand a word you say," and Omeir removes his hat and says, "Good afternoon, sirs, I understand you well enough."

They laugh, and offer him water and dates, and when he passes over the snuffbox, one holds it to the sun, turning it this way and that, and says, "Ah, Urbino," and hands it to his companion.

"Fair Urbino," says the second, "in the mountains of the Marche."

"It's a long journey," says the first, and gestures vaguely to the west. He looks at Omeir and Clover. "Particularly for one so gray in the beard. That donkey is no filly either."

"Surely to live so long with a face like that must have taken some ingenuity," says the second.

He wakes creaking and stiff, his feet swollen, and checks Clover's hooves for cracks, and some days it's noon before he can shake feeling into his fingers. As they turn south through the Veneto, the countryside grows hilly again, and the roads steepen, little castles sitting atop crags, peasants in fields, olive groves around tiny churches, flowering weeds rolling down to tangled creeks. He runs out of silver, trades his last pot of honey. At night, dreams and memories mix: he sees a city, shimmering in the distance, and hears the voices of his sons when they were small.

Tell again, Mama, about the shepherd whose name means blazing. And about the lakes of milk on the moon.

The eyes of his youngest blink. *Tell us,* he says, *what the fool does next.*

He approaches Urbino under an autumn sky, silver sheafs of light dropping through rifts in the clouds onto the twisting road ahead.

The city emerges atop a hill, built from limestone and adorned with bell towers, the brickwork looking as though it has grown out of the bedrock.

As he winds upward, the huge double-turreted facade of the palazzo with its tiers of balconies looms against the sky, the painting on the snuffbox made real: it's like a construction from a dream, if not one of his own, perhaps one of Anna's, as though now, in his last years, he moves along the paths of her dreams rather than his.

Clover brays; swallows cut overhead. The light, the violet-colored hills in the distance, the little cyclamens glowing like embers on either side of the road—Omeir feels like Aethon-the-crow spiraling down out of the stars, weary and wind-plucked, half his feathers gone. How many last barriers lie between him and Grandfather and his mother and Anna and the great rest to come?

He worries that gatekeepers will turn him away because of his face, but the town gates are open and people come and go freely, and as he and the donkey and the dog scale the maze of streets toward the palazzo, no one pays him much mind—there are many people about, and their faces are many colors, and if anything, it's Clover who draws looks for her long eyelashes and her pretty way of walking.

In the courtyard in front of the palace, he tells a crossbowman that he has a gift for the learned men of this place. The man, uncomprehending, gestures for him to wait and Omeir stands with Clover and puts an arm around her neck and the dog lies down and immediately goes to sleep. They wait perhaps an hour, Omeir drowsing on his feet, dreaming of Anna standing beside the fire, hands on her hips, laughing at something one of their sons said, and when he wakes he checks for the leather bundle with the book inside and looks up at the high walls of the palazzo, and through the windows he can see servants moving from room to room lighting tapers.

Eventually an interpreter appears and asks his business. Omeir unwraps the bundle and the man glances at the book, chews his lip, and disappears again. A second man, dressed in dark velvet, comes down with him, out of breath, and sets a lantern in the gravel and blows his nose into a handkerchief, then takes the codex and leafs through it. "I have heard," Omeir says, "that this is a place that protects books."

The man glances up and back at the book again and says something to the interpreter.

"He would like to know how you came to possess this."

"It was a gift," Omeir says, and he thinks of Anna surrounded by their sons, the hearth glowing, lightning flashing outside, shaping the story with her hands. The second man is busy examining the stitching and binding in the lantern light.

"I assume you would like to be paid?" asks the interpreter. "It is in very bad shape."

"A meal will suffice. And oats for my donkey."

The man frowns, as though the stupidity of the world's imbeciles never ceases to amaze, and even without translation, the man in velvet nods, delicately closes the codex with both hands, bows, and takes the book inside without another word. Omeir is directed to a stable beneath the palace where a groomsman with a tidy mustache leads Clover to a stall by the light of his candle.

Omeir sits on a milking stool against the wall as night drapes itself across the Apennines, feeling as though he has accomplished some final task, and prays that another life exists beyond this one where Anna waits for him beneath the wing of God. He dreams he is walking to a well, and peers into it with Tree and Moonlight at his side, all three of them looking down into the cool, emerald-colored water, and Moonlight startles when a little bird flies up out of the well and rises into the sky, and when he wakes a servant in a brown coat is setting a platter of flatbreads, stuffed with sheep's cheese, beside him. Beside that a second servant sets a roll of rabbit meat seasoned with sage and roasted fennel seeds, and a flagon of wine, enough food and drink for four men, and one servant fixes a lit torch in a bracket on the wall, and the other sets a great clay bowl of oats beneath it, and they back away.

The three of them, dog, donkey, and man, eat their fill. And when they are done the dog curls up in the corner, and Clover sighs an immense sigh, and Omeir sits with his back against the stall, his legs stretched out in the good clean straw, and they sleep, and out in the dark it begins to rain.

TWENTY-FOUR

NOSTOS

Cloud Cuckoo Land by Antonius Diogenes, Folio Ω

The quality of Folio Ω deteriorates substantially farther down the page. The final five lines are severely lacunose and only isolated words could be recovered. Translation by Zeno Ninis.

. . . they brought down the jars and the singers gathered . . .
    . . . {young men?} danced, the shepherds {piped?} . . .
    . . . {platters} were passed, bearing hard bread . . .
    . . . rind of pork. I rejoiced to see the {meager?} feast . . .
    . . . four lambs, each bawling for its mother . . .
    . . . {rain?} and mud . . .
    . . . the women came . . .
    . . . old spindly {crone} took {my hand?} . . .
    . . . the lamps . . .
    . . . still dancing, {spinning?} . . .
    . . . {breathless?} . . .
    . . . everyone dancing . . .
    . . . dancing . . .

BOISE, IDAHO

2057–2064

Seymour

His work-release apartment has a kitchenette that overlooks a sun-hammered hillside of rabbitbrush. It's August and the sky is beige with smoke and everything wavers with heat blurs.

Six mornings a week he rides a self-driving bus to an office park where he crosses an acre of broiling asphalt to a sprawling stucco Ilium-owned low-rise. In the lobby a polyurethane raised-relief Earth, twelve feet in diameter, turns on a pedestal, dust gathered in the clefts of the mountains. A faded placard on the wall says, *Capturing the Earth.* He works twelve hours a day with teams of engineers testing next-generation iterations of the Atlas treadmill and headset. He's a ropy and pallid man who prefers to eat prepackaged sandwiches at his desk rather than visit the cafeteria, and who finds peace only in work, in accumulating mile after mile on the treadmill like some Dark Age pilgrim walking off a great penance.

Occasionally he orders a new pair of shoes, identical to the pair he has worn out. Besides food, he buys little else. He messages Natalie Hernandez once a week, on Saturdays, and most of the time she messages back. She teaches Latin and Greek to reluctant high schoolers, has two sons, a self-driving minivan, and a dachshund named Dash.

Sometimes he removes his headset, steps off his treadmill, and blinks out over the heads of the other engineers, and lines from Zeno's translation come winging back: . . . *Across its surface spread the heavens and the earth, all its lands scattered, all its beasts, and in the center . . .*

He turns fifty-seven, fifty-eight; the insurgent inside him lives still. Every night when he gets home, he boots his terminal, disables its connectivity, and gets to work. Simmering on servers all over the world, the harvest of raw, high-density Atlas images remains: columns of migrants fleeing Chennai, families packed onto tiny boats outside Rangoon, a tank on fire in Bangladesh, police behind Plexiglas shields in Cairo, a Louisiana town filled with mud—the calamities he spent years expunging from the Atlas are all still there.

Over the course of months, he constructs little blades of code so sharp and refined that when he slips them into the Atlas object code, the system cannot detect them. Inside the Atlas, all over the world, he hides them as little owls: owl graffiti, an owl-shaped drinking fountain, a bicyclist in a tuxedo with an owl mask. Find one, touch it, and you peel back the sanitized, polished imagery to reveal the original truth beneath.

In Miami, six potted ferns stand outside a restaurant, a little owl sticker stuck to planter number three. Touch the owl and the ferns evaporate; a smoldering car materializes; four women lay crumpled on the pavement.

Whether users discover his little owls, he does not risk finding out. The Atlas is fading from the company's priorities anyway; whole regions of the Boise complex are being devoted to perfecting and miniaturizing the treadmill and headset for other projects, in other departments. But Seymour keeps constructing his owls, night after night, smuggling them into the object code, unweaving some of the lies he has spent the day weaving, and for the first time since finding the severed wing of Trustyfriend on the side of the road, he feels better. Calmer. Less frightened. Less like he has something to outrun.

Three days at a new resort on the lake in Lakeport. Airfare, all meals included, any water sports they want—all on him, for as long as his savings hold out. Families welcome. He relies on Natalie to handle the communication. At first she says that she does not think all five will come, but they do: Alex Hess and two sons travel from Cleveland; Olivia Ott flies in from San Francisco; Christopher Dee drives up from Caldwell; Rachel Wilson comes all the way from southwest Australia with her four-year-old grandson.

Seymour doesn't drive up the canyon from Boise until their last night: no need to upset anyone by showing his face too soon. At dawn he swallows an extra antianxiety drop and stands on the balcony wearing a suit and tie. Out beyond the hotel docks, the lake sparkles in the sunlight. He waits to see if an osprey might come overhead but none do.

Notes in his left pocket, room key in his right. Recall things you know. Owls have three eyelids. Humans are complicated. For many of the things you love, it's too late. But not for all.

He meets the two Ilium technicians in a hexagonal lakeside room used primarily for wedding receptions, and supervises as they carry in five brand-new state-of-the-art multidirectional treadmills that they are calling Perambulators. The technicians pair them with five headsets and depart.

Natalie meets him there early. Her kids, she says, are finishing lunch. It's brave of him, she says, to do this.

"Braver of you," says Seymour. Every time he inhales he fears his skin might unbuckle and his bones will fall out.

At 1 p.m., the families arrive. Olivia Ott has a chin-length bob and linen capri pants and her eyes look as though she has been crying. Alex Hess is flanked by two gigantic and sullen teens, the hair of all three bright yellow. Christopher Dee appears with a small woman; they sit in the corner, removed from the others, and hold hands. Rachel enters last, wearing jeans and boots; her face has the deep-grained wrinkles of someone who works long days under the sun. A cheerful-looking flame-haired grandson trundles in behind her and sits and swings his feet in his chair.

"He doesn't look like a murderer," says one of Alex's sons.

"Be polite," says Alex.

"He just looks old. Is he rich?"

Seymour avoids looking at their faces—faces will derail the whole thing. Keep your eyes down. Read from your notes. "That day," he says, "all those years ago, I took something precious from each of you. I know I can never fully atone for what I did. But because I, too, know what it's like to lose a place you cared about when you were young—to have it taken from you—I thought it might mean something to you if I tried to give yours back."

From his bag he takes five hardcover books with royal blue jackets and hands one to each. On the cover birds swing around the towers of a cloud city. Olivia gasps.

"I had these made from the translations of Mr. Ninis. With a lot of help from Natalie, I should add. She wrote all of the translator's notes."

Next he distributes the headsets. "The five of you can go first. Then everybody else, if they'd like. Do you remember the book drop box?"

Nods all around. Christopher says, "'Owl' you need are books."

"Pull the handle on the box. You'll know what to do from there."

The adults stand. Seymour helps them fit the headsets over their heads and the five Perambulators hum to life.

Once they're settled atop their treadmills, he walks to the window and looks out at the lake. *There are at least twenty places like that north of here your owl could fly to*, she said. *Bigger forests, better forests*. She was trying to save him.

The Perambulators whir and spin; the grown-up children walk. Natalie says, "Oh my God."

Alex says, "It's exactly how I remember."

Seymour recalls the silence of the trees behind the double-wide as they filled with snow. Trustyfriend on his limb, ten feet up in the big dead tree: he would twitch at the crunch of tires across gravel a quarter mile away. He could hear the heart of a vole beating beneath six feet of snowpack.

Pneumatic motors raise the fronts of the Perambulators. They are climbing the granite steps to the porch. "Look," says Christopher. "It's the sign I made."

In the chair next to Rachel's vacant one, Rachel's grandson reaches over, picks up the blue book, sets it in his lap, and turns pages.

With her right hand, Olivia Ott reaches into space and opens the door. One by one the children enter the library.

THE ARGOS

MISSION YEAR 65

Konstance

Oxygen at seven percent, says the voice inside the hood.

Turn left out of the vestibule. Past Compartments 8, 9, 10, all the doors sealed. Does the contagion swirl even now through the air in the corridor, waking from its long sleep? Do bodies almost four-hundred-days-dead molder in the shadows? Or are crew members stirring all around her beneath the hiss of the extinguishers: friends, children, teachers, Mrs. Chen, Mrs. Flowers, Mother, Father?

Little nozzles in the corridor ceiling rain their mist down on her. Homemade book stuffed inside her worksuit, homemade axe in her left hand, she spirals outward from the center of the *Argos*, the booties over her feet sliding through the chemicals on the floor.

Scattered along the corridor are rumpled blankets, discarded masks, a pillow, the pieces of a shattered meal tray.

A sock.

A humped shape furred with gray mold.

Eyes up. Keep moving. Here the dark entrance to the classroom, then more closed compartment doors, past what looks like a glove from one of the biohazard suits that Dr. Cha and Engineer Goldberg wore. Ahead someone's Perambulator rests upside down in the center of the hall.

Oxygen at six percent, says the hood.

On her right is the entrance to Farm 4. Konstance pauses on the threshold and paws chemicals off her face shield: on every level of the haphazard racks, the plants are dead. Her little Bosnian pine still stands, four feet tall: around its base lies a halo of desiccated needles.

Alarms sound. Her headlamp flickers as she hurries to the far wall: no time to think. She chooses the handle four from the left and pulls open a seed drawer. Cold vapor spills over her feet: inside wait hundreds of ice-cold foil envelopes in rows. She scoops up as many as she can with her mitts, spilling a number, and clasps them and the axe to her chest.

Somewhere nearby is the ghost of Father or the corpse of him or both. Keep going. You have no time.

Not much farther down the corridor, between Lavatories 2 and 3, is the titanium patch where Mother said Elliot Fischenbacher spent multiple nights attacking the wall. The patch has been secured with perhaps three hundred rivets, far more than she remembered. Her heart sinks.

Oxygen at five percent.

She drops her haul of seed packets and raises the hatchet with both hands. From her memory whisper the warnings she has been hearing since before she can remember. Cosmic radiation, zero gravity, 2.73 Kelvin.

She swings and the blade dents the patch but bounces off. She swings harder. This time the blade sticks through and she has to put all her weight into it to pry it free.

A third. A fourth. She'll never get through in time. Sweat builds up inside the suit and fogs her hood. The alarms increase in volume; the extinguishers rain down around her. Twenty paces to her right is the entrance to the Commissary, full of tents.

All hands, says Sybil. *The integrity of the ship is in jeopardy.*

Oxygen at four percent, says the hood.

With each strike, the gash in the patch grows.

In three seconds outside the walls, your hands and feet will double in size. You'll suffocate. You'll freeze solid.

The gap widens, and through the vapor on her face shield Konstance can see into the interior, where Elliot has pushed aside conduits of wires wrapped in aluminum tape and cut through several layers of insulation. On the far side is another layer of metal: what she hopes is the exterior wall.

She pries the axe free, inhales, rears back, swings again.

Child, Sybil booms, and her voice is terrible. *Stop what you are doing at once.*

An atavistic fear flows through Konstance. She reaches back and with all the strength of months of anger, isolation, and grief, she swings and the blade severs wires and bites through the outer sheet. She wiggles the handle back and forth.

When she pulls it free, there is a puncture in the outer wall, a slice of darkness.

Konstance, Sybil booms. *You are making a grave mistake.*

She was wrong. It's the nothingness, the vacuum of deep space—she is a hundred trillion kilometers from Earth; she will asphyxiate and that will be it. The hatchet falls from her grasp; space wrinkles around her; time folds up. Her father tears open an envelope and onto his palm slides a little seed clasped by a pale brown wing.

Hold your breath.

"Not yet."

The seed trembles.

"Now."

Beyond the breach in the outermost layer, the darkness stays put. She is not sucked out, her eyes don't freeze solid: it is only night.

Oxygen at three percent.

Night! She picks up the axe, swings again and again; fragments of metal tumble into the dark. Out beyond the steadily enlarging hole, thousands upon thousands of tiny silver flecks, illuminated in the dying beam of the headlamp, are falling through the black. She pushes one arm through and her sleeve comes back wet.

Rain. It is raining out there.

Oxygen at two percent.

Konstance keeps swinging until her shoulders burn and the bones in her hands feel as if they have broken. The puncture gets more jagged as it grows; she can fit her head through, a shoulder. Her face shield is hopelessly fogged, and she's tearing the bioplastic of her suit, but it's worth the risk, and with another blow the hole is almost large enough to wriggle her torso through.

The smell of wild onions.

The dew, the lines of the hills.

Sweetness of light, moon overhead.

Oxygen at one percent.

The raindrops are falling much farther below the gap than she expected, but there is no time. She pitches armfuls of seed envelopes out into the dark, then the axe, and drives her body through the rift after them.

Miss Konstan—roars Sybil but Konstance's head and shoulders are outside the *Argos* now. She wriggles, catches one thigh on a dagger of metal.

Oxygen depleted, says the hood.

Her legs still inside the structure of the wall, her waist stuck, Konstance takes one last breath, then rips off the hood, tearing away the sealing tape, and lets it go. It bounces, rolls, and comes to rest maybe fifteen feet below, among what look like wet stones and long blades of tundra grass, its headlamp shining straight up, into the rain.

The only way out is to drop. Still holding her breath, she braces her arms against the outside of the ship, pushes, and falls.

An ankle twists, her elbow strikes a rock, but she is able to sit up and breathe—she is not dead, not suffocated, not frozen solid.

The air! Rich wet salty alive: if viruses lurk inside this air, if they spill from the perforation she has made in the side of the *Argos* above her, if they are replicating inside her nostrils right now, if all the atmosphere of the Earth is poison, so be it. May she live five more minutes, breathing it, smelling it.

Rain pelts her sweat-soaked hair, her cheeks, her forehead. She kneels in the grasses and listens to it strike her suit, feels it land on her eyelids. It seems so incredibly, dangerously, promiscuously wasteful: water, given from the sky, in such quantities.

The headlamp dies, and only a glimmer emits from the gash she has chopped in the side of the *Argos*. But the darkness of this place is nothing like NoLight. The sky, webbed with cloud, appears to glow, and the wet grass blades catch the light and send it back, tens of thousands of droplets gleaming, and she peels Father's suit down to her waist, and kneels in the tundra grass, and remembers what Aethon said: *A bath, that's as much magic as any foolish shepherd needs.*

She finds her axe, strips off the rest of the bioplastic, gathers as many seed envelopes as she can find, and zips them into her work-suit alongside her homemade book. Then she limps her way through the grass and rocks to the perimeter fence. The *Argos* looms huge and pale behind her.

The fence is topped with razor wire and too high to climb but with the blade of her hatchet, working against one of the posts, she manages to chop through a dozen links, bend them back, and squirm through.

On the other side lie thousands more shining wet stones. On each grows lichen in crusts, lichen in scales—she could spend a year studying any one of them. Beyond the stones a roar rises, the roar of something perpetually in motion, seething, changing, moving—the sea.

Dawn takes an hour and she tries not to blink for any of it. First comes a slow spread of purples, then blues, a diversity of hues infinitely more complex and rich than any simulation inside the Library. She stands barefoot in the water, up to her ankles, the low, flat surf moving ceaselessly in a thousand different vectors, and for the first time in her life, the thrum of the *Argos*, of trickling pipes, of humming conduits, of the creeping tendrils of Sybil—the machine that has whirred all around her, all her life, since before she was conceived—is gone.

"Sybil?"

Nothing.

Far to her right she can just make out the gray outbuilding she uncovered on the Atlas, the boat shelter, a rocky pier. Over her shoulder, the *Argos* looks smaller: a white bolus beneath the sky.

In front of her, out on the horizon, the blue rim of dawn is turning pink, raising its fingers to push back the night.

EPILOGUE

THE LAKEPORT PUBLIC LIBRARY

FEBRUARY 20, 2020

7:02 P.M.

Zeno

The boy lowers his gun. The phone inside the backpack rings a second time. There, past the welcome desk blocking the door, beyond the porch, waits the next world. Does he have the strength?

He crosses the space to the entry and leans into the desk; power flows into his legs as though sent by Athena herself. The desk slides away; he clutches the backpack, pulls open the door, and charges into the glare of the police lights.

The phone rings a third time.

Down the five granite steps, down the walk, into the untracked snow, into a web of sirens, into the sights of a dozen rifles, one voice calling, "Hold fire, hold fire!" another—perhaps his own—yelling something beyond language.

So much snow pours from the sky that the air seems more snow than air. Down through the tunnel of junipers Zeno runs, moving as well as an eighty-six-year-old man with a bad hip can run in Velcro boots and two pairs of wool socks, the backpack pressed against his penguin necktie. He runs the bombs past the yellow owl eyes on the book drop box, past a van that reads *Explosives Ordnance Disposal*, past men in body armor; he is Aethon turning his back on immortality, happy to be a fool once more, the shepherds are dancing in the rain, playing their pipes and plucking their lyres, the lambs are bleating, the world is wet and muddy and green.

From the backpack comes the fourth ring. One ring left to live. For a quarter second, he glimpses Marian crouched behind a police car, sweet Marian in her cherry-red coat with her almond eyes and paint-flecked jeans; she watches him with a hand over her mouth, Marian the Librarian, whose face, every summer, becomes a sandstorm of freckles.

Down Park Street, away from the police vehicles, library at his back. *Imagine,* says Rex, *how it felt to hear the old songs about heroes returning home.* A quarter mile away is Mrs. Boydstun's old house, no curtains on the windows, translations all over the dining table, five Playwood Plastic soldiers in a tin box upstairs beside the little brass bed, and Nestor the king of Pylos drowsing on the kitchen mat. Someone will need to let him out.

Ahead is the lake, frozen and white.

"Why," says one librarian, "you don't look warm at all."

"Where," says the other, "is your mother?"

He runs through the snow, and for the fifth time the phone rin

QAANAAQ

2146

Konstance

There are forty-nine of them in the village. She lives in a little one-story pastel-blue house built from wood and scrap metal with a greenhouse attached. She has a son: three years old, busy, hot, eager to test everything, learn everything, put everything in his mouth. Inside her grows a second child, not much more than a flicker, a little intelligence unfurling.

It's August, the sun has not set since mid-April, and tonight most everyone else is out gathering bunchberries. In the distance, at the bottom of the town, past the docks, the ocean glimmers. On the very clearest days, at the farthest edge of the horizon, she can see a low lump that is the rocky island eight miles away where the *Argos* rusts beneath the weather.

She works in her container garden behind the house while the boy sits among the stones. In his lap is a misshapen book made from the scraps of empty Nourish powder sacks. He pages through it back to front, past *Aethon Means Blazing*, past *The Wizard Inside the Whale*, his mouth moving silently as he goes.

The summer twilight is warm and the leaves of the lettuces in her containers flutter and the sky turns lavender—as close to dark as it will get—as she moves back and forth with a watering can. Broccoli. Kale. Zucchini. A Bosnian pine as tall as her thigh.

Παράδεισο, parádeisos, paradise: it means garden.

When she is done she sits in a weather-faded nylon chair and the boy brings the book over and pulls her pant leg. His eyelids grow heavy and he fights to hold them up. He says, "You tell the story?"

She looks at him, his round cheeks, his eyelashes, his damp hair. Does the boy sense, already, the precarity of all this?

She hauls him into her lap. "Go to the first page and do it properly." She waits for him to turn the book right side up. He sucks his lower lip, then pulls back the cover. She runs her finger under the lines.

"I," she says, "am Aethon, a simple shepherd from Arkadia, and—"

"No, no," says the boy. He bats the page with his hand. "The voice, with the voice."

She blinks; the planet rotates another degree; beyond her little garden, below the town, a wind hazes the tops of the swells. The boy raises an index finger and pokes the page. Konstance clears her throat.

"And the tale I have to tell is so ludicrous, so incredible, that you'll never believe a word of it, and yet"—she taps the end of his nose—"it's true."

Author's Note

This book, intended as a paean to books, is built upon the foundations of many other books. The list runs too long to include them all, but here are a few of the brightest lights. Apuleius's *The Golden Ass* and "Lucius the Ass" (an epitome possibly by Lucian of Samosata) retell the doofus-turns-into-a-donkey story with far more zest and skill than I do. The metaphor of Constantinople serving as a Noah's ark for ancient texts comes from *The Archimedes Codex* by Reviel Netz and William Noel. I discovered Zeno's solution to Aethon's riddle in *Voyages to the Moon* by Marjorie Hope Nicolson. Many of the details of Zeno's experiences in Korea were found in *Remembered Prisoners of a Forgotten War* by Lewis H. Carlson, and I was introduced to early Renaissance book culture by Stephen Greenblatt's *The Swerve*.

This novel owes its greatest debt to an eighteen-hundred-plus-year-old novel that no longer exists: *The Wonders Beyond Thule* by Antonius Diogenes. Only a few papyrus fragments of that text remain, but a ninth-century plot summary written by the Byzantine patriarch Photios suggests that *The Wonders* was a big globetrotting tale, full of interlocking subnarratives and divided into twenty-four books. It apparently borrowed from sources both scholarly and fanciful, mashed up existing genres, played around with fictionality, and may have included the first literary voyage to outer space.

According to Photios, Diogenes claimed in a preface that *The Wonders* was actually a copy of a copy of a text discovered centuries before by a soldier in the armies of Alexander the Great. The soldier, Diogenes said, had been exploring the catacombs beneath the city of Tyre when he discovered a small cypress chest. On top of the chest were the words *Stranger, whoever you are, open this to find what will amaze you*, and when he opened it he found, engraved onto twenty-four cypress-wood tablets, the story of a journey around the world.

Acknowledgments

Profound thanks are due to three extraordinary women: to Binky Urban, whose enthusiasm for early drafts saw me through many months of doubt; to Nan Graham, who edited and improved more versions of this manuscript than I or she could count; and most of all, to Shauna Doerr, who spent much of our pandemic year hunched over pages of this book, who kept me from throwing it away on five separate occasions, and who fills my soul with music and my heart with hope.

Big thanks, too, to our sons Owen and Henry, who helped me dream up the Ilium Corporation and the dropped root beers of Alex Hess, and who make me laugh every day. I love you guys.

Thanks to my brother Mark for his abiding optimism; to my brother Chris who came up with the idea of Konstance using electrolysis to ignite her own hair; to my father, Dick, for cheering me up and on; and to my mother, Marilyn, for growing the libraries and gardens of my youth.

Thanks to Catherine "Perambulator" Knepper, whose encouragement helped me through an arduous series of revisions; to Umair Kazi for believing in Omeir; to the American Academy in Rome—and especially to John Ochsendorf—for once again granting me access to their brilliant community; and to Professor Denis Robichaud for repairing my neophytic Greek.

Thanks to Jacque and Hal Eastman for encouraging, to Jess Walter for understanding, and to Shirley O'Neil and Suzette Lamb for listening. Thanks to every librarian who helped me find a text I needed or didn't yet know I needed. Thanks to Cort Conley for sending me interesting stuff. Thanks to Betsy Burton for being a champion. Thanks to Katy Sewall for helping me research Seymour's incarceration.

Thanks to all the wonderful people at Scribner, especially Roz Lippel, Kara Watson, Brianna Yamashita, Brian Belfiglio, Jaya Miceli, Erich Hobbing, Amanda Mulholland, Zoey Cole, Ash Gilliam, Stu Smith, Annie

Craig, and Sabrina Pyun. Thanks to Laura Wise and Stephanie Evans for upgrading my sentences. Thanks to Jon Karp and Chris Lynch for their amazing support.

Thanks to Karen Kenyon, Sam Fox, and Rory Walsh at ICM, and to Karolina Sutton, Charlie Tooke, Daisy Meyrick, and Andrea Joyce at Curtis Brown.

Mega–super thanks to Kate Lloyd, who gets it.

A novel is a human document, made by a single (particularly fallible) human, so despite my efforts and the efforts of the fantastic Meg Storey, I'm sure that errors remain. All inaccuracies, insensitivities, and historical liberties taken-too-far are my fault.

Enduring thanks to Dr. Wendell Mayo, who I like to think would have enjoyed this book, and to Carolyn Reidy, who passed away one day before we were going to send her the manuscript.

To my friends: thank you.

Finally, thanks most of all to you, dear reader. Without you I'd be all alone, adrift atop a dark sea, with no home to return to.

CLOUD CUCKOO LAND

READING GUIDE

1. Consider Sybil, the omnipresent, teacherly AI system aboard the *Argos*, to whom we are introduced in the prologue. Sybil's core objective is to keep the crew safe. As the novel progresses, Sybil's objective remains the same, but her role in Konstance's story grows more and more complicated. How does your opinion of Sybil change as the novel progresses? In your opinion, is she a sinister character, a benevolent one, or neither?

2. Early on in the novel, Anna is enchanted by an ancient fresco in an archer's turret; each time she looks at it, "something stirs inside her, some inarticulable sense of the pull of distant places, of the immensity of the world and her own smallness inside it" (page 32). How does Anna's response to the image of Cloud Cuckoo Land compare to Aethon's when he envisions a city in the clouds in Folio β? What does Cloud Cuckoo Land represent for each character?

3. Libraries play a central role throughout the novel, both as sanctuaries for children and as storehouses of knowledge. Compare the library in Lakeport and the one aboard the *Argos*. How does the virtual library of Konstance's time differ from the library in modern-day Idaho? Imagine a library in the year 2200 AD. What does your futuristic library look like?

4. In the immediate lead-up to the siege of Constantinople, Anna and Omeir suffer personal tragedies on opposite sides of the city walls. How does the loss of Maria, Moonlight, and Tree affect these characters? What do you think would have happened to them had they not encountered one another in the forest outside Constantinople?

5. After the death of Trustyfriend, Seymour falls into deeper and deeper mourning for his beloved forests and their inhabitants. As a teenager, he becomes enraptured with a militant environmental justice group, led by a mysterious figurehead known only as Bishop. In what ways does Seymour's ideology initially match that of Bishop's group? How does Seymour's ideology in his adolescence compare to his thinking later in life?

6. Throughout the novel, Konstance wonders what drove her father to join the crew of the *Argos*. Name a few plausible motivations. If you were in his position, would you be willing to accept a spot on the *Argos* and leave the Earth forever? Why, or why not?

7. Consider Zeno's epiphany—that "Diogenes, whoever he was, was primarily trying to make a machine that captured attention, something to slip the trap" (page 454). Why is this realization so important to Zeno? What is an example of a story that was meaningful to you during your childhood, and what impact has it had on your life?

8. To gain entry to Cloud Cuckoo Land, Aethon must correctly answer a riddle. "He that knows all that Learning ever writ, knows only this." The correct answer is "nothing." Recall that this section of the original Greek manuscript was too eroded to read. Why do you think Zeno chose to complete the riddle in this way?

9. On page 494, Omeir thinks, "All my life . . . my best companions cannot speak the same language as me." What does he mean?

What role does Omeir's empathy for all creatures, regardless of their ability to communicate verbally, play in the story?

10. Ilium employs Seymour to help overwrite "potentially undesirable items inside the raw image sets" (page 518). Over the years, Seymour begins to rebel, hiding bits of code in Ilium's system that, if touched, reveal the gritty reality beneath the corporation's glossy alterations. Why does Seymour decide to stop cooperating with Ilium? Do you agree with Seymour, that it is important to remember the past in its entirety, sadness, ugliness, and all?

11. Consider the two possible endings to Aethon's story. Based on Zeno's translation up to Folio X, which path do you think Antonius Diogenes intended Aethon to take? Why do the children at the Lakeport library prefer the version in which Aethon returns home, and how would your perception of Diogenes's tale be different if Aethon had remained in Cloud Cuckoo Land? How would it have changed your perception of Doerr's novel as a whole?

12. Consider the many examples of *nostos*, or "homecoming," in the novel: Konstance breaks free from the *Argos* and embarks on a life on Earth; Zeno returns home after the war to his quiet life in Lakeport; Omeir returns home from war, to his beloved valley in the Bulgarian mountains; Seymour finds himself drawn to the virtual version of the hometown he left behind; Anna, always so restless, finds a peaceful life of love and intellectual freedom with Omeir. Which story did you connect with the most, and why? In your opinion, what does the novel have to say about the value of "home"?

13. Konstance's narrative bookends the novel. Why do you think the author chose to start and finish *Cloud Cuckoo Land* with her story?